About the Authors

With a background of working in medical laboratories and a love of the romance genre it's no surprise that **Sue Mackay** writes medical romance stories. She wrote her first story at age eight and hasn't stopped since. She lives in New Zealand's Marlborough Sounds where she indulges her passions for cycling, walking and kayaking. When she isn't writing she also loves cooking and entertaining guests with sumptuous meals that include locally caught fish.

S̶ ̶ ̶ ̶ ̶ ̶ ̶n wrote her first story aged eight and has ̶ ̶ ̶ ̶ ̶ ̶ned. She's worked in the health service for ̶ ̶ ̶ ̶ ̶ars, trained as a nurse and a health visitor. Sca̶ ̶ ̶ now works in public health and lives on the Wes̶ ̶ ̶ast of Scotland with her fiancé and their two sons. Writ̶ng medical romances and contemporary romances is a dream come true for her.

Married to the man she met at eighteen, **Susanne Hampton** is the mother of two adult daughters, Orianthi and Tina. Her varied career titles have included dental nurse, personal assistant, contract manager and now Medical Romance author. The family also extends to a Maltese shih-tzu, a poodle, three ducks and four hens. Susanne has always read romance novels and says, 'I love a happy ever after so writing for Mills & Boon is a dream come true.'

D1493907

Midwives on Call

Midwives on Call: Her Baby Surprise

SUE MacKAY

SCARLET WILSON

SUSANNE HAMPTON

MILLS & BOON

First Published in Great Britain 2020
By Mills & Boon, an imprint of HarperCollins*Publishers*
1 London Bridge Street, London, SE1 9GF

MIDWIVES ON CALL: HER BABY SURPRISE © 2020
Harlequin Books S.A.

Midwife... to Mum! © 2015 Harlequin Books S.A
It Started with a Pregnancy © 2011 Scarlet Wilson
Midwife's Baby Bump © 2015 Harlequin Books S.A.

Special thanks and acknowledgement are given to Sue MacKay and Susanne Hampton for their contribution to the *Midwives On-Call* series.

ISBN 978-0-263-28104-0

Printed and bound in Spain
by CPI, Barcelona

MIDWIFE...TO MUM!

SUE MacKAY

CHAPTER ONE

ALYSSA PARKER DROPPED her bags in the middle of the lounge and stared around what would be her next temporary living quarters. She could pretty much see it all from where she stood. Dusting and vacuuming weren't going to take up her spare time, like it had at the last place. She'd have to find something else to keep her busy after work. Take up knitting? Or hire a dog to walk every day?

Her phone rang. Tugging it from her jacket pocket, she read the name on the screen and punched the 'talk' button. 'Hey, boss, I've arrived on Phillip Island.' The bus trip down from Melbourne city had been interminable as she'd kept dozing off. It had taken the ferry crossing and lots of fresh air to clear her head.

'How's the head?' Lucas Elliot, her senior midwife, asked.

'It's good now. Who have you been talking to?' She and some of the crew from the Melbourne Midwifery Unit had gone out for drinks, which had extended to a meal and more drinks.

'My lips are sealed,' Lucas quipped. 'So, Phillip Island—another place for you to tick off on the map.'

'Yep.' Her life was all about new destinations and experiences. Certainly not the regular nine to five in the same place, year in, year out, that most people preferred.

'How's the flat?'

'About the size of a dog kennel.' Stepping sideways, Ally peered into what looked like an overgrown cupboard. 'It's an exaggeration to call this a kitchen. But, hey, that's part of the adventure.' Like she needed a kitchen when she favoured takeout food anyway.

'Ally, I forgot to tell you where the key to the flat would be, but it seems you've taken up breaking and entering on the side.'

She was Ally to everyone except the taxman and her lawyer. And the social welfare system. 'It was under the pot plant on the top step.' The first place she'd looked.

'Why do people do that? It's so obvious.' Lucas sounded genuinely perplexed.

Still looking around, she muttered, 'I doubt there's much worth stealing in here.' Kat, the midwife she was replacing temporarily, certainly didn't spend her pay packet on home comforts.

'Are you happy with the arrangements? I know you enjoy everywhere we send you, but this should be the best yet as far as location goes. All those beaches to play on.'

'It's winter, or haven't you noticed?' Ally shook her head. 'But so far the island's looking beautiful.'

His chuckle was infectious. 'I'll leave you to unpack and find your way around. You're expected at the medical centre at eight thirty tomorrow. Dr Reynolds wants to run through a few details with you before you get started with the Monday morning antenatal list.'

'Same as any locum job I do, then?' She couldn't help the jibe. She'd been doing this relief work for two years now. It suited her roving lifestyle perfectly and was the only reason she remained with the Melbourne Midwifery Unit. They'd offered her fixed positions time and again. She'd turned them all down. Fixed meant working continuously at the midwifery unit, which in turn meant getting too close to those people she'd work with every day.

The days when she set herself up to get dumped by anyone—friends, colleagues or lovers—were long over. Had been from the monumental day she'd turned sixteen and taken control of her life. She'd walked out of the social welfare building for the very last time. It hadn't mattered that she'd had little money or knowledge on how to survive. She'd known a sense of wonder at being in charge of herself. Since then no one had screwed up her expectations because she'd been in charge of her own destiny. Because she hadn't allowed herself to hope for family or love again.

'I'm being pedantic.' Lucas was still on the other end of the line. 'I wanted to make sure everything's okay.'

Why wouldn't it be? She didn't need him fussing about her. She didn't like it. It spoke of care and concern. But Lucas did care about the people he worked with, which, despite trying not to let it, had always warmed her and given her a sense of belonging to the unit. Since she didn't do belonging, it showed how good Lucas was with his staff.

She told him, 'I'll take a walk to get my bearings and suss out where the medical centre is as soon as I've unpacked.' Tomorrow she'd collect the car provided for the job.

'Even your map-reading skills might just about manage that.' He laughed at his own joke. 'I'll leave you to get settled. Catch you in four weeks, unless there's a problem.'

Stuffing the phone back in her pocket, she headed into the bedroom and dumped a bag on the bed. At least it was a double. Not that she had any man to share the other half with. Not yet. *Who knows? There might be a hot guy at the surf beach who'd like a short fling, no strings.* Her mouth watered at the thought of all those muscles surfers must have. Winter wouldn't stop those dudes getting on their boards. There were such things as wetsuits.

After dropping her second, smaller bag full of books and DVDs out of the way in the corner of the lounge, she slapped her hands on her hips and stared around. Four o'clock in the afternoon and nothing to do. Once she started on the job she'd be fine, but these first hours when she arrived in a new place and moved into someone else's home always made her feel antsy. It wasn't her space, didn't hold her favourite possessions.

Except... Unzipping the bag, she placed two small silver statues on the only shelf. 'Hey, guys, welcome to Cowes.' Her finger traced the outlines of her pets. If she ever got to own a pet it would be a springer spaniel like these. Make that two spaniels. One on its own would be lonely.

She hadn't forgiven the Bartlett family who'd given her these on the day they'd broken her heart, along with their promise they'd love her for ever. She'd wrapped the statues in an empty chocolate box and tied it with a yellow ribbon, before burying them in the Bartletts' garden. The gift had been a consolation prize for abandoning her, but one dark day when she'd felt unable to carry on, she'd remembered the dogs *she'd* abandoned and had sneaked back to retrieve them. They'd gone everywhere with her ever since, a talisman to her stronger self.

Having the statues in place didn't make the flat hers, though. Again Ally stared around. She could do a lap of the cupboards and shelves, learning where everything was kept. By then it'd be five past four and she'd still not know what to do with herself.

This moment was the only time she ever allowed that her life wasn't normal. *Define normal.* Doing what other people did.

Standing in the middle of a home she'd never been in before, didn't know the owner of, always brought up the question of what would it be like to settle down for ever in her own place.

As if she'd ever do that.

What if it was with a man who loved me regardless?

The answer never changed. That person didn't exist.

She followed her established routine for first days in new towns. First, off came her new and amazing knee-high black boots, then she pulled on her top-of-the-line walking shoes.

Sliding on her sunglasses, she snatched up the house key and stuffed it and her wallet into her pocket and headed out. There had to be a decent coffee shop some-where. Might as well check out the options for takeout dinners, too. Then she'd head to the nearest beach to do some exploring.

The coffee turned out to be better than good. Ally drained the paper mug of every last drop and tossed it into the next rubbish bin she came across. The beach stretched ahead as she kicked up sand and watched the sea relentlessly rolling in. Kids chased balls and each other, couples strolled hand in hand, one grown-up idiot raced into the freezing water and straight back out, shout-ing his head off in shock.

Ally pulled out her phone and called the midwifery centre back in the city, sighing happily when Darcie answered. 'Hey, how's the head?'

'Nothing wrong with mine, but, then, I was on orange juice all night.'

'You shouldn't be so quick to put your hand up for call.'

Darcie grumped, 'Says the woman who works more hours than the rest of us.' Then she cheered Ally up with, 'You can move into my spare room when you get back to town. As of this morning it's empty, my flatmate having found her own place.'

'Great, that's cool.' Darcie was fast becoming a good friend, which did bother her when she thought about it. But right this moment it felt good to have a friend onside when she was feeling more unsettled than usual at the start of a new assignment. Today she sensed she might be missing out on the bigger picture. This was the loneliness she'd learned to cope with whenever she'd been shuffled off to yet another foster home full of well-meaning people who'd always eventually packed her bags and sent her away.

'You still there?' Darcie asked.

'Did you get called in today?'

'I've just finished an urgent caesarean, and I'm about to get something to eat.'

'I'll leave you to it, then. Thanks for the bed. I'll definitely take you up on that.' After saying goodbye, she shoved her hands deep into her jacket pockets and began striding to the farthest end of the beach, feeling better already. Being alone wasn't so bad when there were people at the end of a phone. At least this way she got to choose which side of the bed she slept on, what she had for dinner, and when to move on to the next stop.

A ball came straight for her and she lined it up, kicked it back hard, aiming for the boys running after it. One of them swung a foot at it and missed, much to his mates' mirth at a girl kicking it better.

'Girls can do anything better.' She grinned and continued walking a few metres above the water's edge, feeling happier by the minute. How could she remain gloomy out here? The beach was beautiful, the air fresh, and she had a new job in the morning. What else could she possibly need?

The sun began dropping fast and Ally stopped to watch the amazing reds and yellows spreading, blending the sky and water into one molten colour block, like a young child's painting. Her throat ached with the beauty of it.

Thud. Something solid slammed into her. For a moment, as she teetered on her feet, she thought she'd keep her balance. But another shove and she toppled into an ungainly heap on the sand with the heavy weight on top of her. A moving, panting, licking heavy weight. A dog of no mean proportions with gross doggy breath sprawled across her.

'Hey, get off me.' She squirmed between paws and tried to push upright onto her backside.

One paw shoved her back down, and the dark, furry head blocked out all vision of the sunset. The rear end of the animal was wriggling back and forth as its tail whipped through the air.

'Sheba, come here.' A male voice came from somewhere above them. 'Get off now.'

Sheba—if that was the name of her assailant—gave Ally's chin a final lick and leapt sideways, avoiding an outstretched hand that must've been aiming for her collar.

'Phew.'

Her relief was premature. The dog lay down beside her as close as possible, and farthest away from the man trying to catch her. One paw banged down on her stomach, forcing all the air out of her lungs.

Somewhere behind her a young child started laughing. 'Sheba, you're funny.'

The sweet childish sound of pure enjoyment had Ally carefully pushing the paw aside and sitting up to look round for the source. A cute little boy was leaping up and down, giggling fit to bust.

'Sheba. Sit now.' The man wasn't nearly as thrilled about his dog's behaviour.

Ally stared up at the guy looming above her. 'It's all right. I'm fine, really.' She even smiled to prove her point.

'I'm very sorry Sheba bowled you over. She doesn't understand her own strength.' As he glanced across at the child his annoyance was quickly replaced by something soft she couldn't read. 'Adam, don't encourage her.'

'But it's funny, Dad.' The boy folded in half, still giggling.

Ally clambered to her feet, dusting sand off her jeans, and grinned. 'What is it about kids and giggling? They don't seem to know how to stop.' Just watching the boy made her happy—especially now that the dog had loped across to bunt him in the bottom, which only made the giggles louder. Laughter threatened to bubble up from deep inside her stomach.

The guy was shaking his head, looking bemused. 'Beats me how he keeps going so long.'

Ally winced. Slapping the sand off her left hip just made it sore. Sheba must've bruised her.

'Are you all right?' the man asked, worry darkening his expression. 'Look, I apologise again. I hope you haven't been hurt.'

'Look,' she used his word back at him. 'I'm fine. Seriously. Sheba was being playful and if I hadn't been staring at the sunset I'd have seen her coming.' She stuck her hand out. 'I'm Ally. That's Sheba, and your boy's called Adam. You are?'

'Flynn. We've been visiting friends all day and needed some fresh air before settling down for the night.' He looked at her properly, finally letting go the need to watch his boy and dog. 'What about you?'

'Much the same. The beach is hard to resist when the weather's so balmy.' He didn't need to know she'd only just arrived. Running her hands over the sleeves of her jacket, she smoothed off the remaining sand, trying to refrain from staring at him. But it was impossible to look away.

Despite the sadness in his eyes, or because of it, she was taking more notice of him than a casual meeting on the beach usually entailed. The stubble darkening his chin was downright sexy, while that tousled hair brought heat to her cold cheeks. If she played her cards right, could this be the man she had her next fling with?

She glanced downward, taking in his athletic build, his fitted jeans that defined many of his muscles. The sun glinted off something on the guy's hand and she had her answer. A band of gold. Said it all, really.

'Can I call you Ally?' Adam bounced up in front of her.

Blink, blink. Refocus on the younger version now that the older one was out of bounds. 'Of course you can.' As if they were going to see each other again. Though they might, she realised, if Flynn brought his son to the beach often. She'd be walking along here most days that she wasn't caught up with delivering babies and talking to pregnant mums.

Hopefully, if they ran into each other again, Flynn would have his wife with him. A wife would certainly dampen the flare of attraction that had snagged her, and which should've evaporated the moment she'd seen that ring. Flings were the way to go, but never, ever with a man already involved with someone else. She didn't do hurting for the sake of it, or for any reason at all, come to think of it.

Guess she'd have to keep looking for someone to warm the other half of that bed. *Whoa, Ally, you haven't been here more than an hour. What's the hurry?*

The thing was, if she was playing bed games there wouldn't be long, empty nights that had her dreaming of the impossible. She could shove the overpowering sense of unworthiness aside as she and a man made each other happy for a short while, and then bury her face in the pillow while he left. Every parting, even as casual as her relationships were, was touched with a longing for the life she craved, had never known, and was too afraid to try for.

Flynn Reynolds dragged his gaze away from the most attractive woman he'd met in a long while and focused on his son. Except Adam stood directly in front of her, talking nonstop, and Flynn's gaze easily moved across the tiny gap to a stunning pair of legs clad in skin-tight jeans. His breathing hitched in his throat. Oh, wow. Gorgeous.

The woman—*Ally, she has a name*—laughed at something Adam said, a deep, pure laugh that spoke of enjoyment with no hidden agenda. Very refreshing, considering most women he met these days seemed intent on luring him into their clutches with false concern about him and Adam. He hated it that many women believed the way to attract him was by being overfriendly to his son. What they didn't get was that Adam saw through them almost as quickly as he did.

What they also didn't get was that Flynn wasn't interested. Not at all. So why was his gaze cruising over the length of this curvy woman with a smile that had him smiling back immediately, even when it wasn't directed at him? Especially since he apparently didn't do smiling very much these days.

He looked directly at his son. 'Time we made tracks for home. The sun's nearly gone and it will be cold soon.' Any excuse to cut this short and put some space between him and Ally before his brain started thinking along the lines of wanting to get to know her better. He wasn't ready for another woman in his life. Certainly wouldn't have time for years to come, either.

'Do we have to?'

'Yes, I'm afraid so.'

What I'm really afraid of is staying to talk to Ally too long and ending up inviting her home to share dinner with us. If she's free and available. As if a woman as attractive as her would be seriously single. The absence of rings on her fingers didn't mean a thing.

He looked around and groaned. 'Sheba,' he yelled. 'Come here.'

Too late. The mutt was belly deep in the sea, leaping and splashing without any concern for how cold the water had to be.

Adam ran down to the water's edge and stood with his hands on his skinny hips. 'Sheba, Dad says we're going home. You want your dinner?'

Beside Flynn, Ally chuckled. 'Good luck with that.'

Glancing at her, he drew a deep breath. Her cheeks had flushed deep pink when the mutt had dumped her on the sand, and the colour still remained, becoming rosier every time she laughed. Which was often.

He noticed her rubbing her hip. 'You did hurt yourself.'

She jammed her hand in her pocket. 'Just a hard landing, nothing to worry about.'

'You're sure?' He'd hate it if Sheba had caused some damage.

'Absolutely.'

Adam and Sheba romped up to him. Then the dog did what wet dogs did—shook herself hard, sending salty spray over everyone. Now Ally would complain and walk away. But no. Her laughter filled the air and warmed the permanent chill in his soul. It would be unbelievably easy to get entangled with someone like her. Make that with this woman in particular.

He sighed his disappointment. There was no room in his life for a woman, no matter how beautiful. Not even for a short time. Adam and work demanded all his attention. Besides, how did a guy go about dating? He hadn't been in that market for so long he wouldn't know where to start. Was there a dating book for dummies? *I don't need one. It's not happening.* He gave himself a mental slap. All these questions and doubts because of a woman he'd met five minutes ago. He was in need of a break. That was his real problem. Solo parenting and work gobbled up all his time and energy.

'Let's go.' He grabbed Sheba's collar and turned in the direction of their street. 'Nice meeting you.' He nodded abruptly at the woman who'd been the first one to catch his interest since Anna had died two years ago. It had to be a fleeting interest; one that would've disappeared by the time he reached home and became immersed in preparing dinner, folding washing and getting ready for work tomorrow. Damn it all. It could've been fun getting to know her.

'Bye, Ally,' Adam called, as they started walking up the beach.

She stood watching them, both hands in her jacket pockets. 'See you around.' Was that a hint of wistfulness in her voice?

'Okay,' Adam answered, apparently reluctant to leave her. 'Tomorrow?'

'Adam,' Flynn growled. 'Come on.' He aimed for the road, deliberately stamping down on the urge to invite the woman home to share dinner. He did not need anyone else's problems. He did not need anyone else, full stop.

Anyway, she probably wouldn't like baked beans on toast.

Baked beans. He only had to close his eyes to hear Anna saying how unhealthy they were. They'd eaten lots of vegetables for lunch so he could relax the rules tonight. Beans once in a while wouldn't hurt Adam, and would save *him* some time. Who knew? He might get to watch the late news. Life was really looking up.

CHAPTER TWO

PLASTERING ON HER best smiley face the next morning, Ally stepped inside the medical centre, unzipping her jacket as she crossed to the reception desk. 'Hi, I'm Alyssa Parker.' Lucas always wrote her full name on her credentials when sending them to medical centres. It was a technicality he adhered to, and she hated it. 'Ally for short. I'm covering for Kat while she's away.'

A man straightened from the file he was reading and she gasped as the piercing blue eyes that had followed her into sleep last night now scanned her. Her smile widened. 'Flynn.' The buzz she'd felt standing by this man yesterday returned in full force, fizzing through her veins, heating her in places she definitely didn't need warmed by a married man. He was still as sexy, despite the stubble having been shaved off. *Stop it.* But she'd have to be six feet under not to react to him.

'Ally. Or do you prefer Alyssa?'

'Definitely Ally. Never Alyssa. So you're Dr Reynolds?' They hadn't swapped surnames the previous day. Hardly been any point when the chances of meeting again had seemed remote. Neither had she learned his first name when she was told about this job. She became aware of the receptionist glancing from her to Flynn, eyebrows high and a calculating look in her eyes.

Fortunately Flynn must've seen her, too. 'Megan's our office lady and general everything girl. She'll help you find files and stock lists and anything else you want.'

'You two know each other?' Megan asked her burning question.

Ally left that to Flynn to deal with and took a quick look around the office, but listened in as Flynn told the receptionist, 'We met briefly yesterday. Can you tell the others as they arrive that we're in the tearoom and can they come along to meet Ally?' Then he joined her on the other side of the counter. 'I'll show you around. You've got a busy clinic this morning. Three near full-term mums and four who are in their second trimester.'

'Three close to full term? Was there a party on the island eight months back that everyone went to?' She grinned.

'You'd be surprised how many pregnant ladies we see. Phillip Island's population isn't as small as people think. One of the women, Marie Canton, is Adam's daytime caregiver when he's not at preschool.'

So Adam's mum worked, too. Ally wondered what she did. A doctor, like her husband? 'Will Marie be bringing Adam with her?'

'I'm not sure.'

'What time's my first appointment?' she asked, suddenly needing to stay on track and be professional.

But Flynn smiled, and instantly ramped up that heat circulating her body, defying her professionalism. 'Nine. Was it explained to you that Kat also does high school visits to talk to the teenagers about contraception?' Flynn stood back and indicated with a wave of his hand for her to precede him into a kitchen-cum-meeting-room. 'You've got one on Thursday afternoon.'

'I didn't know, but not a problem.' What was that

aftershave? She sniffed a second time, savouring the tangy scent that reminded her of the outdoors and sun and...? And hot male. She tripped over her size sevens and grabbed the back of a chair to regain her balance. 'I'm still breaking these boots in,' she explained quickly, hoping Flynn wouldn't notice the sudden glow in her cheeks. He mustn't think she was clumsy but, worse, he mustn't guess what had nearly sent her crashing face first onto the floor.

But when she glanced at him she relaxed. His gaze was firmly fixed on the boots she'd blamed. Her awesome new boots that had cost nearly a week's pay. His eyes widened, then cruised slowly, too slowly, up her thighs to her hips, up, up, up, until he finally locked gazes with her. So much for relaxing. Now she felt as though she was in a sauna and there was no way out. The heat just kept getting steamier. Her tongue felt too big for her mouth. Her eyes must look like bug's eyes; they certainly felt as though they were out on stalks.

Flynn was one sexy unit. The air between them sparked like electricity. His hair was as tousled as it had been yesterday and just as tempting. Her fingers curled into her palms, her false nails digging deep into her skin as she fought not to reach out and finger-comb those thick waves.

'You must be the midwife.' A woman in her midforties suddenly appeared before her. 'Faye Bellamy, part-time GP for my sins.'

Ally took a step back to put space between her and Flynn, and reached for Faye's proffered hand. 'That's me. Ally Parker. Pleased to meet you.'

'Pleasure's all ours. Darned nuisance Kat wanting time off, but I've read your résumé and it seems you'll be a perfect fit for her job.' Bang, mugs hit the benchtop. 'Coffee, everyone?'

Kat wasn't meant to take holidays? Or just this one? 'Yes, thanks. Where's Kat gone?'

Flynn was quick to answer. 'To Holland for her great-grandmother's ninetieth birthday. She's been saving her leave for this trip.' He flicked a glance at Faye's back, then looked at Ally. 'She could've taken two months and still not used up what she's owed,' he added.

'Europe's a long way to go for any less time.' Not that it had anything to do with her, except she would have been signed on here for longer and that meant more weeks—okay, hours—in Flynn's company. Already that looked like being a problem. His marital status wasn't having any effect on curtailing the reaction her body had to him.

She took the mug being handed to her and was surprised to see her hand shaking. She searched her head for something ordinary to focus on, and came back to Kat. 'Bet the trip's another reason why there isn't much furniture or clutter in the flat.' A girl after her own heart, though for a different reason.

'Morning, everyone.' A man strolled in. 'Coffee smells good.' Then he saw Ally. 'Hi, I'm Jerome, GP extraordinaire, working with this motley lot.'

Amidst laughter and banter Ally sat back and listened as the nurses joined them and began discussing patients and the two emergencies that had happened over the weekend. She felt right at home. This was the same Monday-morning scenario she'd sat through in most of the clinics she'd worked at ever since qualifying. Same cases, different names. Same egos, different names. Soon her gaze wandered to the man sitting opposite her, and she felt that hitch in her breathing again.

Flynn was watching her from under hooded eyes, his chin low, his arms folded across his chest as he leaned as far back in his chair as possible without spilling over backwards.

Ally's breathing became shallow and fast, like it did after a particularly hard run. The man had no right to make her feel like this. Who did he think he was? The sooner this meeting was finished the better. She could go and play with patients and hide from him until all her body parts returned to their normal functions. At the rate she was going, that'd be some time around midnight.

The sound of scraping chairs on the floor dragged her attention back to the other people in the room and gave her the escape she desperately needed.

But fifteen minutes after the meeting ended, Flynn was entering her room with a frightened young girl in tow. 'Ally, I'd like you to meet Chrissie Gordon.' He ushered the girl, dressed in school uniform, to a chair.

'Hi, Chrissie. Love your nail colour. It's like hot pink and fiery red all mixed up.' It would have lit up a dark room.

'It's called Monster Red.' Chrissie shrugged at her, as if to say, Who gives a rat's tail? Something serious was definitely on this young lady's mind.

Given that Flynn had brought Chrissie to see *her*, they must be about to talk about protection during sex or STDs. Or pregnancy. The girl looked stumped, as if her worst possible nightmare had just become real. Ally wanted to scoop her up into her arms and ward off whatever was about to be revealed. Instead, she looked at Flynn and raised an eyebrow.

'Chrissie's done several dip-stick tests for pregnancy and they all showed positive.' Flynn's face held nothing but sympathy for his patient's predicament. 'I'd like you to take a blood sample for an HCG test to confirm that, and then we'll also know how far along she is if the result's positive.'

It wasn't going to be negative with all those stick tests showing otherwise. 'No problem.'

Ally took the lab form he handed her and glancing down saw requests for WR and VDRL to check for STDs, antibodies and a blood group. She noted the girl's date of birth. Chrissie was fifteen. Too young to be dealing with this. Ally's heart went out to the frightened child as she thought back to when she'd been that age. She'd barely been coping with her own life, let alone be able to manage looking after a baby. Face it, she doubted her ability to do that *now*. Locking eyes with Flynn, she said, 'Leave it to me.'

His nod was sharp. 'Right, Chrissie, I'll call you on your cell when the lab results come back.'

'Thanks, Dr Reynolds,' Chrissie whispered, as her fingers picked at the edge of her jersey, beginning to unravel a thread. 'You won't tell Mum, will you?'

'Of course not. You know even if I wanted to—which I don't—I'm not allowed to disclose your confidential information. It's up to you to decide when to talk to your mother, but let's wait until we get these tests done and you can come and see me again first, if that'll make it easier for you.' Flynn drew a breath and added, 'You won't be able to hide the pregnancy for ever.'

'I know. But not yet, okay?' The girl's head bowed over her almost flat chest. 'I'm afraid. It hurts to have a baby, doesn't it?'

Ally placed a hand over Chrissie's and squeezed gently. 'You're getting way ahead of yourself. Let's do those tests and find out how far along you are. After I've taken your blood I'll explain a few things about early-stage pregnancy if you like.'

'Yes, please. I think.' Fat tears oozed out of Chrissie's eyes and slid down her cheeks to drip onto her jersey. 'Mum's going to kill me.'

'No, she won't,' Flynn said. About to leave the room, he turned back to hunker down in front of Chrissie and said emphatically, 'Angela will be very supportive of you. You're her daughter. That's what mothers do.'

Yeah, right, you don't know a thing, buster, if that's what you believe. Did you grow up in la-la land? Ally clamped her lips shut for fear of spilling the truth. *Some mothers couldn't care two drops of nothing about their daughters. Some dump their babies on strangers' doorsteps.*

But when she glanced at Flynn, he shook his head and mouthed, 'It's true of Angela.'

Had he known what she'd been thinking? The tension that had been tightening her shoulders left off as she conceded silently that if he was right then Chrissie was luckier than some. A big positive in what must feel like a very negative morning for the girl. 'Good,' she acknowledged with a nod at Flynn. As for his mind-reading, did that mean he'd known exactly what she'd been thinking about him back there in the staffroom?

'Have you had a blood test before?' she asked Chrissie. She'd wasted enough time thinking about Dr Reynolds.

Flynn disappeared quietly, closing the door behind him.

'Yeah, three times. I hate them. I fainted every time.'

'You can lie on the bed, then. No way do I want to be picking you off the floor, now, do I?'

She was rewarded with a glimmer of a smile. 'I don't weigh too much. You'd manage.'

It was the first time anyone had suggested she looked tough and strong. 'I might manage, but me and weight-lifting don't get along. How heavy are you anyway?'

'Forty-eight k. I'm lucky, I can eat and eat and I stay thin. My mum's jealous.' At the mention of her mum her face fell and her mouth puckered. 'I can't tell her. She'll be really angry. She had me when she was seventeen. All my life she's told me not to play around with boys. She wants me to go to university and be educated, unlike her. She missed out because she had me.'

Handing Chrissie a cup of cold water and a box of tissues, Ally sat down to talk. Her first booked appointment would have to wait. 'I won't deny your mother's going to be disappointed, even upset, but she'll come round because she loves you.' Flynn had better have got that right because she didn't believe in giving false hope. It just hurt more in the long run.

'You think? You don't even know her.'

'True. But I see a young woman who someone's been making sure had everything that's important in life. You look healthy, which means she's fed you well and kept you warm and clothed. Your uniform's in good condition, not an op-shop one. You're obviously up to speed with your education.' She daren't ask about her father. It didn't sound like he factored into Chrissie's current situation so maybe he didn't exist, or wasn't close enough for it to matter. 'I'm new here. Where do you live?'

'Round in San Remo. It's nice there. Granddad was a fisherman and had a house so Mum and I stayed with him. He's gone now and there's just us. I miss him. He always had a hug and a smile for me.'

'Then you've been very lucky. Not everyone gets those as they're growing up.' She sure as heck hadn't. 'Let's get those blood samples done.'

Chrissie paled but climbed onto the bed and tugged one arm free of her jersey and shirt. Lying down, she found a small scared smile. 'Be nice to me.'

Ally smiled. 'If I have to.' She could get to really like this girl. Pointless when she'd be gone in a month. Despite Chrissie's fear of what the future had in store for her, she managed to be friendly and not sulky, as most teens she'd met in this situation had been.

Ally found the needle and tubes for the blood in the top drawer of the cabinet beside the bed. 'Do you play any sport at school?' She swabbed the skin where she would insert the needle.

'I'm in the school rep basketball team and play soccer at the club. I get knocked about a bit in basketball because I'm so light, but my elbows are sharp.' The needle slid in and the tube began to fill. 'I'm fast on my feet. Learnt how to get out of the way when I was a kid and played rough games with the boys next door.'

Ally swapped the full tube for another one, this time for haematology tests. Flynn was checking Chrissie's haemoglobin in case she had anaemia. 'I see one of the beaches is popular for surfing. You ever given that a try?' All done.

'Everyone surfs around here. Sort of, anyway. Like belly-surfing and stuff.'

'You can sit up now.' Ally began labelling the tubes.

'What? Have you finished? I didn't feel a thing.'

'Of course you didn't.' She smiled at the girl, stopped when she saw the moment Chrissie's thoughts returned to why she was there, saw the tears building up again. 'You're doing fine.'

'I'm not going to play sport for a while, am I?'

'Maybe not competitively, but keeping fit is good for you and your baby.'

Chrissie blew hard into a handful of tissues. 'You haven't told me I'm stupid for getting caught out. Or asked who the father is, or anything like that.'

'That's irrelevant. I'm more concerned about making sure you do the right things to stay healthy and have an easy pregnancy. Have you got any questions for me?'

Chrissie swung her legs over the side of the bed and stared at the floor. 'Lots, but not yet. But can I come see you later? After school? You'll have the tests back by then, right?'

'The important one, anyway. But won't you want to see Dr Reynolds about that?' She was more than happy to tell Chrissie the result, but she had no idea how Flynn might feel if she did.

'He's going to phone me, but I might need to see someone and I don't want to talk to a man. It would be embarrassing. I'd prefer it's you.'

'That's okay.' Ally scribbled her cell number on a scrap of paper. 'Here, call me. Leave a message if I don't answer and I'll get back to you as soon as I'm free. Okay?'

'Thanks.' Sniff. 'I didn't sleep all night, hoping Dr Reynolds would tell me I'd got it wrong, that I wasn't having a baby. But I used up all my pocket money on testing kits and every one of them gave me the same answer so I was just being dumb.'

'Chrissie, listen to me. You are not dumb. Many women I've been midwife to have told me the same thing. Some of them because they couldn't believe their luck, others because, just like you, they were crossing their fingers and toes they'd got it wrong.' Ally drew a long breath. 'Chrissie, I have to ask, have you considered an abortion? Or adoption?'

The girl's head shot up, defiance spitting out of her eyes. 'No. Never.' Her hands went to her belly. 'This is my baby. No one else's. I might be young and dependent on Mum, but I am keeping it.'

In that moment Ally loved Chrissie. She reached over

to hug her. 'Attagirl. You're awesome.' It would be the hardest thing Chrissie ever did, and right now she had no idea what she'd let herself in for, but that baby would love her for it.

'Have you ever had a baby?' Chrissie pulled back, flushing pink. 'Sorry, I guess I'm not supposed to want to know.'

'Of course it's all right to ask. The answer's no, I haven't.'

An image of a blue-eyed youngster bent over double and giggling like his life depended on it flicked up in her mind. *Go away, Adam. You've got a mother, and anyway I'd be a bad substitute.*

'So while I will tell you lots of things over the weeks I'm here, I only know them from working with other mums-to-be and not from any first-hand experience.' She would never have that accreditation on her CV. She would not raise a child on her own, and she wouldn't be trusting any man to hang around long enough to see a baby grow to adulthood with her.

Flynn appeared in the doorway so fast after Chrissie left that she wondered if he'd been lurking. She said, 'She's only fifteen and is terrified, and yet she's coping amazingly well, given the shock of it all.'

'You must've cheered her up a little at least. I got the glimmer of a smile when she came out of here.' He leaned one shoulder against the doorframe. 'I meant what I said about her mother. Angela is going to be gutted, but she'll stand by Chrissie all the way. From what I've been told, Angela's always been strong, and refused to marry Chrissie's dad just because people thought it was the done thing. Her father supported them all the way.'

Another baby with only one parent. But one decent parent was a hundred percent better than none. 'Aren't you jumping the gun? Chrissie didn't mention the father of her baby, but that could be because she's protecting him. They might want to stick together.'

'They might.' Flynn nodded, his eyes fixed on her. Again.

When he did that, her stomach tightened in a very needy way. Heat sizzled along her veins, warming every cell of her body. *Damn him. Why does he have to be married?*

'Right, I'd better see my first patient. First booked-in one, that is. I told Chrissie I'll talk to her later today. Is that all right with you?'

'Go for it. As long as she's talking with someone, I'm happy. You did well with her.' There was something like admiration in his voice.

She didn't know whether to be pleased, or annoyed that he might be surprised. 'Just doing my job.'

'Sure.'

The way he enunciated that one word had her wondering if he had issues with Kat and her work. But that didn't make sense after he'd been fighting the other woman's corner about using her holiday time. 'Being a filler-in person, I don't have the luxury of knowing the patients I see. Neither do I have a lot of time with them so I work hard to put them at ease with me as quickly as possible.'

'So why aren't you employed at a medical practice on a permanent basis? Wouldn't you prefer getting to know your mums, rather than moving on all the time?'

If he hadn't sounded so genuinely interested she'd have made a joke about being a wandering witch in a previous life and ignored the real question. But for some inexplicable reason she couldn't go past that sincerity. 'I get offers all the time from my bosses to base myself back at the midwifery unit, but I don't do settled in one spot very well. Yes, I miss out on seeing mothers going the distance. I'm only ever there for the beginning of some babies and the arrival of others, but I like it that way. Keeps me on my toes.'

'Fly in, do the job and fly out.' Was that a dash of hope in his eyes? Did he think she might be footloose and fancy-free enough to have a quick fling with him and then move on? Because she'd seen the same sizzle in his eyes that buzzed along her veins.

Then reality hit. Cold water being tipped over her wouldn't have chilled her as much. *Sorry, buster, but you're married and, worse, you're not even ashamed to show it.*

She spun around to stare at the screen in front of her. What was the name of her next patient?

'Ally, I've upset you.'

Of course he had. He only had to look at her to upset her—her hormones anyway. Flicking him a brief smile, she continued staring at the computer. 'Holly Sargent, thirty-five weeks. Anything I need to know about her that's not on here?'

When Flynn didn't answer, she had to lift her head and seek him out. That steady blue gaze was firmly fixed on her. It held far too many questions, and she didn't answer other people's enquiries about anything personal. 'Flynn? Holly Sargent?'

'Third pregnancy, the last two were straightforward. She's had the usual colds and flu, a broken wrist and stitches in her brow from when she walked through a closed glass slider. Full-time mum.'

Ally looked at her patient list. 'Brenda Lewis?'

'First pregnancy, took six months to conceive, family history of hypertension but so far she's shown no signs of it, twenty-five years old, runs a local day care centre for under-fives.'

Her anger deflated and laughter bubbled up to spill between them as she stared at this man who had her all in a dither with very little effort. 'That's amazing. Do you know all your patients as thoroughly?'

'How long have you got?' He grinned. 'Makes for scintillating conversations.'

Deliberately rolling her eyes at him, she said, 'Remind me not to get stuck with you at the workplace Friday night drinkies.'

'Shucks, and I was about to ask you on a date,' he quipped, in a tone that said he meant no such thing.

So he was as confused as she was. That didn't stop a quick shiver running down her spine. She'd love to go out with this man. *But hello. If that isn't a wedding ring, then what is it? He's obviously a flagrant playboy.* 'Sorry, doing my hair that night.'

'Me, too,' he muttered, and left her to stare at his retreating back view.

A very delectable view at that. Those butt muscles moved smoothly under his trousers as he strode down the hall, those shoulders filled the top of his shirt to perfection. A sigh trickled over her bottom lip. He would've been the perfect candidate for her next affair. *Flynn might be the one you can't easily walk away from.*

'Get a grip, man,' Flynn growled under his breath. How? Ally was hot. Certain parts of his anatomy might've been in hibernation for the past couple of years, but they weren't dead. How did any sane, red-blooded male ignore Ally without going bonkers?

'Flynn.' Megan beckoned from the office. 'Can you explain to this caller why she should have a flu jab?'

'Can't Toby do that?' The practice nurse was more than capable of handling it.

'Busy with a patient and...' Megan put her hand over the phone's mouthpiece '...this one won't go away.'

'Put her through.' He spun around to head to his consulting room. *See? You're at work, not on the beach with nothing more important to think about than getting laid.* Forget all things Alyssa. *Alyssa.* Such a pretty name, but it had been blatantly obvious no one was allowed to use it when talking to their temporary midwife.

'Dr Reynolds.' Mrs Augusta's big voice boomed down the line, causing him to pull the phone away from his ear. 'I've been told I have to have a flu injection. I don't see why as I never get sick.'

Except for two hits with cancer that had nearly stolen her life. 'Mrs Augusta, it's your decision entirely but there are certain conditions whereby we recommend to a patient they have the vaccination. Your recent cancer puts you in the category for this. It's a preventative measure, that's all.'

'Why didn't Megan just tell me that?'

'Because she's our receptionist, not a qualified medical person. It's not her role to advise patients.'

'All right, can you put me back to her so I can book a time? Sorry to have been a nuisance.' Mrs Augusta suddenly sounded deflated, all the boom and bluster gone.

'Pat, is there something else that's bothering you?'

'No, I'm good as gold, Doctor. Don't you go worrying about me.'

'How about you make an appointment with me when you come for your jab?'

'I don't want to be a problem, Doctor.'

That exact attitude had almost cost her life. By the time the bowel cancer had been discovered it had nearly been too late and now she wore a bag permanently. 'I'll put you back to Megan and you make a time to see me.' When he got the receptionist on the line he told her, 'Book Mrs Augusta in with me at the first opening, and don't let her talk you out of it.'

A glance at his watch on his way out to the waiting room told him he was now behind the ball as far as keeping on time with appointments. 'Jane, come through.' As he led the woman down the hall, laughter came from the midwife's room. Sounded like Ally and Holly were getting along fine. A smile hovered on his mouth, gave him the warm fuzzies. Everyone got along with their temp midwife.

Jane limped into his room on her walking cane and sat down heavily. 'I'm up the duff again, Flynn.'

Not even ten o'clock and his second pregnant patient of the morning. What had the council put in the water? 'You're sure?' he asked with a smile. Nothing ever fazed this woman, certainly not her gammy leg, not a diabetic three-year-old, not a drunk for a husband.

'Yep, got all the usual signs. Thought I'd better let you know so I can get registered with Kat.'

Now, there was something that did tend to wind Jane up. Kat's attitude to her husband. Kat had tried to intervene one night at the pub when he'd been about to swing a fist at Jane. Something Flynn would've tried to prevent, too, if he'd been there. 'Kat's away at the moment so you'll get to meet Ally.' Of course, there were nine months to a pregnancy, and Kat was only away for one, but hopefully Ally could settle Jane into things so that she'd be happier with Kat this time round.

'Is she nice?' Jane's eyes lit up.

More than. 'You'll get along great guns. Now, I'm surmising that we need to discuss your arthritis meds for the duration of your pregnancy.'

The light in those eyes faded. She accepted her painful condition without a complaint, but she knew how hard the next few months were going to be. 'I've cut back already to what you've recommended before. There's no way I'm risking hurting junior in there.' Her hand did a circuit of her belly. 'Can't say I'm happy with the extra pain, but I want this wee one. Think I'll make it the last, though. Get my bits chopped out afterwards.'

As he made a note to that effect in her computer file, Flynn tried not to smile. Her bits. He got to hear all sorts of names for vaginas and Fallopian tubes in this job. 'How far along do you think you are?'

'I've missed two periods. Should've come to see you sooner, I know, but that family of mine keeps me busy.' Jane wasn't mentioning the lack of money, but he knew about it. 'Anyway, it's not like I don't know what to expect. They haven't changed the way it's done in the last three years, have they?'

'Not that anyone's told me.'

After writing out prescriptions, ordering blood tests, including an HCG for confirmation of the pregnancy, and taking Jane's blood pressure, he took her along to meet Ally.

It wasn't until he was returning to his room and he passed Faye, who rolled her eyes at him, that he realised he was walking with a bounce in his stride and a smile on his face. All due to a certain midwife.

What was it about her that had him sitting up and taking notice? It had happened instantly. Right from that moment when Sheba had knocked her down and he'd reached out a hand to haul the dog off, only to be sidetracked by the most startling pair of hazel eyes he'd ever seen.

Whatever it was, he'd better put a lid on the sizzle before anyone else in the clinic started noticing. That was the last thing he needed, and no doubt Ally felt the same.

CHAPTER THREE

'FLYNN,' MEGAN CALLED from her office as he was shrugging into his jacket. 'The path lab's on line one.'

'Put them through.' Damn, he'd just seen Ally head out the front door for home. He'd intended talking to her before she left, maybe even walk with her as far as Kat's flat, then backtrack to home. Which, given he lived on the opposite side of town, showed how fried his brain had become in the last twenty-four hours.

For an instant he resented being a GP. There were never any moments just for him. Like it had been any different working as an emergency specialist. Yeah, but he'd chosen that career pathway, not had it forced on him. So he'd give up trying to raise Adam properly, hand him over to spend even more hours with day carers? No, he wouldn't. The disgruntled feeling disappeared in a flash, replaced with love. His little guy meant everything to him.

'Flynn?' Megan yelled. 'Get that, will you?'

He kicked the door shut and grabbed the persistently ringing phone from his desk. 'Flynn Reynolds. How can I help?' *Could you hurry up? I'm on a mission.*

'Doctor, this is Andrew from the lab. I'm calling about some biochemistry results on William Foster.'

William Foster, fifty-six and heading down the overweight path through too much alcohol and fatty food since his wife had died twelve months back. He'd complained of shoulder pain and general malaise so he'd ordered urgent tests to check what his heart might be up to. 'I'm listening.'

'His troponin's raised. As are his glucose and cholesterol. But it's the troponin I'm ringing about.'

He took down details of the abnormal results, even though Andrew would email them through within the next five minutes. Finding William's phone number, he was about to dial but thought better of it. Instead, he phoned Marie on the run. 'I'm going to be late.'

'I'll feed Adam dinner, then.'

Flynn sighed. 'I owe you. Again.'

Marie chuckled. 'Get over yourself. I love having him.'

Yeah, she did, but that didn't make everything right. For Adam. Or for him.

William lived ten minutes away and halfway there Flynn decided he should've rung first to make sure the man was at home and not at the club, enjoying a beer. William didn't know it yet, but beer would be off the menu for a while.

William opened his front door on the third knock, and appeared taken aback to find Flynn on his doorstep after dark. 'Doc, what's up?'

'Can I come in for a minute?'

William's eyes shifted sideways. 'What you want to tell me?'

The man was ominously pale. He hadn't been like that earlier. 'Let me in and we'll discuss it.' From the state of William's breathing and speech, Flynn knew there'd be a bottle of whisky on the bench. That wouldn't be helping the situation. 'It's important.'

With a sigh the older man stepped back, hauling the

door wide at the same time. 'I haven't done the house-work this week, Doc, so mind where you step.'

This week? Flynn tried not to breathe too deeply, and didn't bother looking into the rooms they passed. It was all too obvious the man was living in squalor. He wasn't coping with Edna's passing, hadn't since day one, and nothing Flynn or William's daughter had done or said made the slightest bit of difference. The man had given up, hence Flynn's visit. A phone call would never have worked. Besides, he needed to be with William as he absorbed the news.

In the kitchen William's shaky hands fidgeted with an empty glass he'd lifted from the table. He didn't look directly at Flynn, not even for a moment, but every few seconds his eyes darted sideways across the kitchen. Sure enough, an almost full whisky bottle was on the bench, as were three empty ones. How long had it taken for him to drink his way through those?

It would be too easy to tell the man some cold hard facts about his living conditions and his drinking, but Flynn couldn't do it. He understood totally what it was like to lose the woman he loved more than life. He suspected if it hadn't been for Adam and having to put on a brave face every single day, he might've made as big a mess of his own life after Anna had been killed. He still struggled with the sense of living a life mapped out by fate, one that held none of his choices.

Pulling out a chair, he indicated William should sit down. Then he straddled another one, not looking at the condition of the once beautiful brocade on the seat. 'William, your test results have come back. They're not good, I'm afraid.'

'Figured that'd be why you're here.'

'The major concern is that you've had a cardiac incident. A heart attack, William.'

Rheumy eyes lifted to stare at him, but William said nothing, just shrugged.

'You need to go to hospital tonight. They'll run more tests and keep an eye on you until they find the cause of the attack.'

'What else?' William wheezed the question.

'They'll give you advice on diet and exercise.' Things he'd have no inclination to follow. The same as with any advice he had given him.

'I meant what other tests were bad?'

He was about to add to the man's gloomy outlook, but couldn't see a way around it. All he could hope for was that he shocked his patient into doing something about his lifestyle before it was too late. 'Your cholesterol's high, which probably explains your cardiac arrest. You've got diabetes and your liver's not in good nick.'

'I hit the jackpot, didn't I?' The sadness in William's voice told how much he didn't care any more. 'I don't suppose you went on a bender when you lost your wife, Doc.'

Yeah, he had. Just one huge bender, when he'd almost killed himself. Big enough and frightening enough to put him off ever doing it again. But he knew he still might've if it hadn't been for Adam. 'I couldn't afford to, William.'

'I get it. Your boy.'

'You've got family who care about you, too.' Flynn tried to think of something that might interest William in getting his act together, but nothing came to mind, apart from his daughter and grandkids. That had been tried before and William hadn't run with it. 'Now, don't get upset, but I've ordered the ambulance to transfer you to hospital. It should be here any minute.'

'I don't need that. I can drive myself there.'

'What if you have another heart attack and cause an accident that hurts someone?'

There was silence in the kitchen. Not a lot William could say to that. He was a decent man, unable to cope with a tragedy. He wasn't reckless with other people.

'I'll wait here until you're on your way. Want me to talk to your daughter?' Working in the ED, he'd have phoned the cardiologist and had William wheeled to the ward, no argument. Patients were in the ED because someone recognised the urgency of their situation. Urgent meant urgent—not talking and cajoling. He missed that fast pace at times, but if he got William under way to getting well then he'd feel deep satisfaction.

'After I've left. Don't want her telling me off tonight.' William stared around the kitchen, brought his gaze back to Flynn. 'Don't suppose I can have a whisky for the road.'

By the time Flynn finally made it home Adam was in his pyjamas and glued to the TV. 'Hiya, Dad.'

'Hello, my man.' Tonight he couldn't find it in him to make Adam stop watching—an Anna rule or not. Instead, he turned to Marie. 'I appreciate you bringing him home.'

Marie was already buttoning up her coat, the gaps between the buttons splayed wide over her baby bulge. 'Have you decided who's going to look after Adam when my little one arrives?' Marie was determined to look after Adam right up to the last minute. She'd also sorted through the numerous girls wanting to take her place until she was ready to take Adam back under her wing and had decided on two likely applicants.

'Caught. I'll get onto it.' He pushed his fingers through his hair. 'Tonight?'

'Whenever.' She laughed. 'It's not as though you'll be left high and dry. Half the island would love to look after Dr Reynolds's boy. Not just because he's such a cute little blighter either. There's a family likeness between father and son.'

'Haven't you got a husband waiting at home for his dinner?' He wasn't keen on dating any of the island's females. Too close to home and work. Anyway, no one had caught his interest in the last two years. Not until Ally had got knocked over by Sheba, that was.

Ally wasn't answering when he phoned after putting Adam to bed. She wasn't answering her phone when he called at nine, after giving in to the tiredness dragging at his bones and sitting down to watch a crime programme on TV. She might've answered if he'd rung as he was going to bed at ten thirty, but he didn't want her to think he was stalking her.

But she sure as hell stalked him right into bed. As he sprawled out under the covers he missed her not being there beside him, even though she'd never seen his bed, let alone lain in it. He stretched his legs wide to each side and got the same old empty spaces, only tonight they felt cold and lonely. Make that colder and lonelier. In his head, hot and sexy Ally with those brilliant hazel eyes was watching and laughing, teasing, playing with him. How was he supposed to remain aloof, for pity's sake? He was only human—last time he looked.

Was this what happened when he hadn't had sex for so long? Should he have been making an effort to find an obliging woman for a bit of relaxation and fun? He yawned.

Did Ally know she'd cranked up his libido? Yeah, it was quite possible she did, if the way the air crackled between them whenever they came within touching distance was any indication.

So follow up on it. Have some fun. Have sex. Have an affair with her. It would only be four weeks before Ally moved on. He wouldn't disrupt Adam's routine too much or for too long.

Flynn rolled over to punch his pillow and instead squashed his awakening reaction to the woman in his head. The air hissed out of his lungs as he grinned. That had to be a good sign for the future, didn't it?

'Morning, Ally,' Megan called as she stepped through the front door of the clinic on Tuesday. 'I see you've found the best coffee on the island already.'

'First thing I do on any job.' She sniffed the air appreciatively just to wind Megan up.

Scowling happily at her, Megan lifted her own container then asked, 'What did you think of the movie?'

'It was great. Nothing like a few vampires to fill in the evening.' She'd bumped into the receptionist and her boyfriend as they'd been walking into the theatre. 'Seeing you there made me feel I'd been living here for a while.'

Megan laughed. 'Small towns are like that. Believe me, people around here will know what you had for dinner last night.'

'Then they'll be giving me lectures on healthy eating. Fried chicken and chips from Mrs Chook's.' It had been delicious, even if she should've been looking for a salad bar. In winter? Hey, being good about food could sometimes be highly overrated. Anyway, she'd wanted comfort food because when she had gone back to the flat after work she'd felt unusually out of sorts. Arrival day in a new place, yes, that was normal; every other day thereafter, never.

This nomadic life had been one of her goals ever since she'd left school and become independent of the welfare system. Those goals had been simple—earn the money to put herself through a nursing degree then support herself entirely with a job that she could give everything to but which wouldn't tie her to one place. Along with that went to establish a life where she didn't depend on anyone for anything, including friendship or love.

So far it had worked out fine. Sure, there were the days when she wondered if she could risk getting close to someone. She had no experience of being loved, unconditionally or any other way, so the risks would be huge for everyone involved. She had enough painful memories of being moved on from one family to the next to prove how unworthy of being loved she was. At unsettled moments like this those memories underlined why she never intended taking a chance on finding someone to trust with her heart. Sometimes she wondered if her heart really was only there to pump blood.

In the midwife's room she dumped her bag and jacket, then wandered into the staffroom, surreptitiously on a mission to scope out Flynn, if he'd arrived. He must've, because suddenly her skin was warming up. Looking around the room, her eyes snagged with his where he sat on a chair balanced on two legs. She'd known he was there without seeing him. She'd felt an instant attraction before setting eyes on him. What was going on? Hadn't she just been remembering why she wasn't interested?

She took a gulp of coffee and spluttered as she burned her tongue. 'That's boiling.'

Concern replaced the heat in Flynn's gaze and the front legs of the chair banged onto the tiled floor as he came up onto his feet. 'You all right?' He snatched a paper towel off the roll on the wall. 'Here, spit it out.'

Taking the towel to wipe the dribble off her lips before he could, she muttered, 'Too late, I swallowed it instantly.' And could now feel it heating a track down her throat. 'I forget to take the lid off every time.' But usually she wasn't distracted enough to forget to sip first. 'Black coffee takes for ever to cool in these cardboard cups.'

'Slow learner, eh?' That smile should be banned. Or bottled. Or kissed.

It sent waves of heat expanding throughout her body, unfurling a need so great she felt a tug of fear. What if she did give in to this almost overwhelming attraction? Could she walk away from it unscathed? Like she always did? This thing with Flynn didn't feel the same as her usual trysts. There was something between them she couldn't explain. But they wouldn't be getting started. Staying remote would keep things on an even keel. *You're not lovable. Forget that and you're toast.*

'I called you last night to ask how you felt about your first day here.'

So much for remote. He wasn't supposed to play friendly after hours. 'That explains one of two missed calls. I went to a movie and switched it off for the duration.'

Flynn looked awkward. 'I rang twice.'

'Did I miss something?' Had one of her patients gone into labour? Or developed problems? Had Chrissie wanted to talk to her again? This wouldn't look good for her if she had.

'Relax. They were purely social calls.'

The way he drawled his words did everything but relax her. She managed through a dry mouth, 'That's all right, then.' Highly intelligent conversation going on here, but she was incapable of much more right now. He shouldn't be phoning her.

'Ally, I was wondering—'

'Morning, everyone.' Jerome strolled in. 'You came back for more, then, Ally?'

'Yes.' She shook her head to clear the heat haze. 'Missed the ferry back to the mainland so thought I'd fill in my day looking after your pregnant patients,' she joked pathetically.

Then Flynn asked, 'How was Chrissie when you talked to her after school?'

She wondered what he'd been going to ask before Jerome had interrupted. 'Resigned would best describe her attitude. But today might be a whole different story after a night thinking about it all.' Ally dropped onto a chair and stared her coffee. 'I hope she's going to be all right.' Chrissie still had to tell her mother. That'd be the toughest conversation of her young life.

'Like I said, Angela will be very supportive.' Flynn returned to his seat. 'Marie was happy with her new midwife, by the way.'

Marie was happy with her boss and his boy, with the impending birth of her baby, with her husband, with the whole world. 'I saw Adam for a few minutes when she came in. At least he'd stopped giggling.'

'Ah, you missed the standing in the dog's water bowl giggles, and the dollop of peanut butter on the floor right by Sheba's nose giggles.'

She could picture Adam now, bent over, howling with laughter. 'He's one very happy little boy, isn't he?'

Flynn's smile slipped. Oops. What had she gone and done? Sadness filtered into his eyes and she wanted to apologise with a hug for whatever she'd managed to stir up, but she didn't. Of course she didn't. Hugging a man she'd only met two days ago and who was one of her bosses wasn't the best idea she'd ever had. She sipped coffee instead—which perversely had turned lukewarm—and waited for the meeting to get under way.

'I see you had William admitted last night,' Faye said as she joined them.

Flynn looked relieved he'd been diverted from answering what she'd thought had been a harmless question. He hurried to explain. 'He'd had a cardiac event. Hardly surprising, given the way he's been living.'

'He'll be seen by a counsellor while in hospital. Maybe they can make him see reason,' Faye said. 'Not that we all haven't tried, I know.'

Flynn grimaced, his eyes still sad. 'I'm hoping this is the wake-up shock required to get him back on track.' He turned to Ally. 'William's wife succumbed to cancer last year.'

'That's terrible.' She shuddered. *See? Even if you got a good one, someone who never betrayed your trust, they still left you hurt and miserable.* No wonder Flynn looked sad. He seemed to hold all his patients dear.

Jerome spoke up. 'Ally, I believe you're doing house calls today. One of your patients is Matilda Livingstone. This is her first pregnancy. Be warned she's paranoid about something going wrong and will give you a million symptoms to sort through.'

Ally's interest perked up. 'Any particular reason for this behaviour?'

'She has a paranoid mother who suffered three miscarriages in her time and only carried one baby full term. She's fixated with making sure Matilda checks everything again and again. It's almost as though she doesn't want her daughter to have a stress-free pregnancy.' Jerome shook his head, looking very puzzled.

'Mothers, eh?' She smiled, knowing her real thoughts about some mothers weren't showing. Ironic, considering she spent her days working with mums—the loving kind. 'Thanks for the nod. I'll tread carefully.'

'You know you've got the use of the clinic's car for your rounds, don't you?' Flynn asked.

'Sure do. I'm hoping it's a V8 supercharged car with wide tyres and a triple exhaust.'

'Red, of course.' Flynn grinned.

Faye stood up. 'Time to get the day cranking up. There seems to be a kindergarten lot of small children creating havoc in the waiting room.'

'Toby's doing vaccinations. For some reason, the mothers thought it better if they had them all done at the same time,' Jerome explained. 'Seems a bit much, considering that if one cries, they'll all cry.'

Flynn stood up. 'Who's going to cry when they've got Toby? That man's magic when it comes to jabbing a child.' He turned to Ally. 'I heard that you're also no slug when it comes to drawing bloods. Chrissie was seriously impressed, even told Toby that he needs practice.'

'So Toby's magic doesn't extend to older children?' Chrissie was still a child in many ways, baby on the way or not. When they'd talked about her HCG result yesterday afternoon it had been difficult. One minute Chrissie had acted all grown up and the next Ally could picture her tucked up with her teddy and a thumb in her mouth as she watched cartoons on TV.

'Sure it does, just not Chrissie. Has she mentioned when she might apprise her mother of the situation?'

'I think never would be her preferred approach. But realistically she's preparing herself. She did ask if I'd be present.'

'How do you feel about that?' Flynn asked.

'Of course I'll do it if that's what she wants, but I'd

have thought you, as the family doctor, should be the one to talk to Angela with her.'

Flynn didn't look fazed. 'If she's relaxed with you then that's good. I'm not getting on my high horse because she's my patient. What works for her works for me. Or we can both be there.'

'Thanks.' Why was she thanking him? Shrugging, she added, 'Guess I'd better get on the road. My first appointment's at nine and I haven't looked at the map yet.'

Flynn gave her that devastating smile of his. 'You're not in Melbourne now. Come here and tell me who you're visiting.' He closed the door behind Jerome and Ally felt as though the air had been sucked out of the room.

What was he doing? Here? At work? Any minute someone could walk in for a coffee.

'Here's the clinic.' Flynn tapped his finger on the back of the door. 'Who's first on your list?'

Ally's face reddened as her gaze took in the map pinned to the door. 'Um.' Think, damn it, peanut brain. 'Erika Teale.'

She watched in fascination as Flynn's finger swept across the map and stopped to tap at some point that made no sense whatsoever. Running her tongue over her lips, she tried to sound sane and sensible. 'That's next to the golf ranch.' Too squeaky, but at least she'd got something out.

He turned to stare at her. 'Are you all right? Is map-reading not your forte?'

'I'm better with drawing bloods.' No one could read a map when Flynn was less than two feet away. Even a simple map like this one suddenly became too complex. Taking a step closer to the map—and Flynn—she leaned forwards to study the roads leading to Erika's house. Truth was, despite moving from town to town every few weeks she'd never got the hang of maps. 'So which side of the golf place is she on?' Why did he have to smell so yummy?

'What are you doing tonight?'

Gulp. Nothing. Why? 'Eating food and washing dirty clothes.' Like there was a lot of those, but she had to sound busy. Saying 'Nothing' was pathetic.

'Have dinner with me. We could go to the Italian café. It's simple but the food's delicious.'

She gasped. *Yes*, her head screamed. *I'd love to. Yes, yes, yes.* 'No, thanks,' came from her mouth. Sanity had prevailed. Just. 'You're married.'

Flynn's mouth flattened, and his thumb on his right hand flicked the tell-tale gold band round and round on his finger. The light went out in his eyes. 'I'm a widower. My wife died two years back.'

Her shoulders dropped their indignant stance as his words sank in. 'Oh.' She was getting good at these inane comments. 'I'm so sorry. That must be difficult for you and Adam. But he seems so happy, you must be a great father.'

Shut up, dribble mouth.

But he's free, available.

Yeah. I'm a cow.

Guilt followed and she reached a hand to his arm, touched him lightly. 'I don't know what else to say. How do you manage?' The way he looked at that moment, he'd be retracting his invitation any second.

'Adam keeps me sane and on the straight and narrow. If it wasn't for him, who knows what I might've done at the time?' Sadness flicked across his face and then he looked directly at her and banished it with a smile. 'For the record, you're the first woman I've asked on a date in the last two years. The only woman I've looked at twice and even considered taking out.' Then his smile faltered. 'I guess it's not much of an offer, going to the Italian café, considering what you must be used to in the city.'

'Flynn, it's not about where I go but who I go with. I'd love to try the local Italian with you.' She meant every word. A wave of excitement rolled through her. A date—with this man—who set her trembling just by looking at her. What more could she want? Bring it on.

'Then I'll pick you up after I've put Adam to bed and got the babysitter settled. Probably near eight, if that's all right?' There was relief and excitement mingling in his expression, in those cobalt eyes locked on her, in the way he stood tall.

She was struggling to keep up with all his emotions. 'Perfect.' She'd have time for a shower, to wash and blow-dry her hair, apply new make-up and generally tart herself up. Bring it on, she repeated silently.

CHAPTER FOUR

SOMEONE SHOULD'VE TOLD the pregnancy gods that Ally had a date and needed at the minimum an hour to get ready. Seems that memo had never gone out.

As she slammed through the front door of the flat at seven forty-five, Ally was cursing, fit to turn the air blue. 'Babies, love their wee souls, need to learn right from the get-go to hold off interrupting the well-laid plans of their midwife.'

Baby Hill thought cranking up his mum's blood pressure and making her ankles swell was a fun thing to do a couple of weeks out from his arrival. Pre-eclampsia ran through Vicky Hill's family but she'd been distressed about having to go to hospital for an evaluation, and it had taken a while to calm her down. Jerome had finally talked to his patient and managed to get her on her way with her thankfully calm husband.

Ally suspected some of Vicky's worry was because she was dealing with a new midwife right on the day she needed Kat to be there for her. Ally had no problem with that. Being a midwife had a lot to do with good relationships and they weren't formed easily with her, due to the come-and-go nature of her locum job.

The shower hadn't even fully warmed up when Ally leapt under the water. Goose bumps rose on her skin.

Washing her hair was off the list. A hard brush to remove the kinks from the tie that kept it back all day would suffice. If there was time. She'd make time. After slipping on a black G-string, she snatched up a pair of black, body-hugging jeans to wriggle her way into. The lace push-up bra did wonders for her breasts and gave a great line to the red merino top she tugged over her head.

The doorbell rang as she picked up the mascara wand. Flick, flick. Then a faster-than-planned brush of her hair and she was as ready as she was ever going to be.

She might not have had all the time she'd wanted, but by the look on Flynn's face she hadn't done too badly. His Adam's apple bobbed as his gaze cruised the length of her, making her feel happy with the hurried result.

'Let's go,' he croaked.

We could stay here and not bother with dinner. Or we can do both.

She slammed the front door shut behind her and stepped down the path. 'I'm starving.' For food. For man. For fun.

Flynn knew he should look away. Now. But how? His head had locked into place so that he stared at this amazing woman seated opposite him in the small cubicle they'd been shown to by the waiter. He hadn't seen her with her hair down before. Shining light brown hair gleaming in the light from wall sconces beside their table and setting his body on fire. He desperately wanted to run his hands through those silky layers, and over it, and underneath at the back of her neck.

'Excuse me, Dr Reynolds. Would you like to order wine with your meal?'

Caught. Staring at his lady friend. Reluctantly looking up, he saw one of his young patients holding out the wine menu. 'Hello, Jordan. How's the rugby going? Got a game this weekend?' He glanced down the blurred list of wines.

'It's high school reps this weekend. We're going up to Melbourne on Thursday.'

After checking with Ally about what she preferred, he ordered a bottle of Merlot, and told Jordan what meals they'd chosen. Then he leaned back and returned his attention to Ally, finding her watching him with a little smile curving that inviting mouth.

'How often do you get out like this?' she asked.

'Never. When I go out it's usually with people from work.' Comfortable but not exhilarating.

'Who's looking after Adam tonight? Not Marie?'

'No, she needs her baby sleep. Jerome's daughter came round, bringing her homework with her.' Better than having a boyfriend tag along, like the last girl he'd used when he'd had a meeting to attend. He'd sacked her because of that boyfriend distracting her so she hadn't heard Adam crying.

'So they know at work that you and I are out together?' Her eyes widened with caution.

'There's no point trying to be discreet on Phillip Island. Everyone knows everyone's business all too quickly, even if you try to hide it.'

The tip of her tongue licked the centre point of her top lip. In, out, in, out.

Flynn suppressed a groan and tried to ignore the flare of need unfurling low down. What was it about this woman compared to any of the other hundreds he'd crossed paths with over the last two years that had him wanting her so much? Admittedly, for a good part of those years he'd been wound up in grief and guilt so, of course, he hadn't been the slightest bit interested. His libido hadn't been tweaked once. Yet in walks Ally Parker and, slam-bang, he could no longer think straight.

The owner of the café brought their wine over and with a flourish poured a glass for Ally. '*Signorina*, welcome to the island. I am Giuseppe and this is my café. I am glad our favourite doctor has brought you here to enjoy our food.'

Ally raised her glass to Giuseppe. 'Thank you for your welcome. Is everyone on Phillip Island as kind as you and the medical centre staff?'

'*Si*, everyone. You've come at the right time of year when there are very few tourists. Summer is much busier and no time for the small chat.'

Finally Giuseppe got around to filling Flynn's glass, and gave him a surreptitious wink as he set the bottle on the table. 'Enjoy your evening, Doctor.'

Cheeky old man. Flynn grinned despite himself. 'I intend to.'

Ally watched him walk away, a smile lighting her pretty face. 'I could get to like this.' Then the smile slipped. 'But only for a month. Then I'll have somewhere else nice and friendly to visit while I relieve yet another midwife.'

He wanted to ask what compelled her to only take short-term contracts, but as he opened his mouth the thought of possibly spoiling what was potentially going to be a wonderful evening had him shutting up fast. Then their meals arrived and all questions evaporated in the hot scent of garlic and cream and tomatoes wafting between them.

Ally sighed as she gazed at her dish. 'Now, that looks like the perfect carbonara.' This time her tongue slid across first her bottom lip and then the top one. What else could she do with that tongue? Lifting her eyes, she studied his pizza. 'That looks delicious, too.'

'I know it will be.' The best pizzas he'd ever tasted had been made right here. 'One day I'll get to trying a pasta dish, but I can't get past the pizzas.'

Sipping her wine, Ally smiled directly at him. 'Thank you for bringing me here.'

'It's the best idea I've had in a long time.' Had he really just said that? Yes, and why not? It was only the truth. Picking up a wedge of pizza, he held it out to her. 'Try that.'

Her teeth were white and perfect. She bit into the wedge and sat back to savour the flavours of tomato and basil that would be exploding in her mouth. As he watched her enjoyment, he took a bite. Ally closed her eyes and smiled as she chewed. 'How do you do that?' he asked.

She swallowed and her eyelids lifted. 'Here, you must try this.' She twirled her fork in her pasta and leaned close to place it in his mouth.

The scent of hot food and Ally mingled, teasing him as he took her offering. The tastes of bacon and cream burst across his tongue. 'Divine.' Though he suspected cardboard would taste just as good right now.

They shared another wedge of pizza. Then Ally put her hands around her plate. 'Not sharing any more.'

Moments later she raised her glass to smile over the rim at him and let those sultry eyes study him.

Flynn sneaked his fork onto her plate and helped himself. 'You think you're keeping this to yourself?' Not that his stomach was in the mood for more food while she was looking at him like he was sexy. He felt alive and on top of his game, very different from his usual sad and exhausted state.

Her tongue ran around the edge of her glass, sending desire firing through his body heading straight for his manhood. *Pow.* 'You're flirting with me, Miss Ally.'

'Yes.' Her tongue lapped at her wine, sending his hormones into overdrive.

He placed the fork, still laden with carbonara, on his plate. 'Come here,' he growled. 'I've wanted to do this for two whole days.'

He placed his fingers on her cheeks to draw her closer. Pressing his mouth to her lips, all he was aware of was this amazing woman and the taste, the feel, the heat of her.

Finally, some time later—minutes or hours?—Flynn led Ally outside, only vaguely aware they'd eaten tiramisu for dessert, and hoped he'd had enough smarts to pay the bill before leaving. No worry, Giuseppe knew where to find him. In one hand he held the wine bottle, still half-full, while his other arm wrapped around Ally's waist as she leaned in close, her head on his shoulder, her arm around him with her hand in his pocket, stroking his hip, stroking, stroking.

Forget the car. He led her across the road and down to the beach. It was cold, but he was hot. They didn't talk, and the moment they were out of sight of the few people out on the road, Ally turned into him, pressing her body hard against his. Her hands linked at the back of his neck and she tugged his mouth down to hers.

The bottle dropped to the sand as he slid his hands under her top. Her skin was satin, hot satin. Splaying his fingers, he smoothed his hands back and forth, touching more of her, while his mouth tasted her, his tongue dancing around hers. He wanted her. Now.

'Ally?' he managed to groan out between kisses.

Between their crushed-together bodies she slipped

a hand to his trousers, tugged his zip down. The breath caught in his throat as her fingers wrapped around him.

'Ally.' This time there was no question in his mind.

She rubbed him, up, down. Up, down.

Reaching for her jeans, he pushed and pulled until he had access to her, trying—and nearly failing—to remain focused on giving her pleasure. She was wet to his touch, moaning as his fingers touched her, and she came almost instantly, crying out as she rocked against his hand. Her hand squeezed him, eased, squeezed again, and his release came quickly.

Too quickly. 'Can we do that again?' he murmured against that soft hair.

Ally had wrapped herself against him, her arms under his jacket, her breaths sharp against his chest. Her head moved up and down. 'Definitely.'

'Come on, we'll go home.'

Her head lifted. 'You've got a babysitter. We could go to the flat.'

His lips traced a kiss across her forehead and down her cheek. 'Are you always so sensible?' He'd fried any brain matter he had. 'Good thinking.'

'What are we waiting for?' Ally spun around and took his hand to drag him back up the beach to his car.

The flat was less than five minutes away. Thank goodness. He didn't know how he'd manage to keep two hands on the steering wheel for that long, let alone actually function well enough to drive.

The moment she shut the front door behind them Ally grabbed Flynn's hand and almost ran to the bedroom. That had been amazing on the beach, but it was only a taste of what she knew they could have. It had been nowhere near enough.

She laughed out loud. 'I want to wrap myself around you.' She began tearing clothes off. Flynn's and hers. 'I want to get naked and up close with you.'

'Stop.' It was a command.

And she obeyed. 'Yes?'

'Those knickers. Don't take them off. Not yet.'

So he was into G-strings. She turned and saucily moved her derrière, then slowly lifted her top up to her breasts, oh, so slowly over them, and finally above her head, tossing it into the corner.

Then turned around, reaching behind her to unclasp her bra. Flynn's eyes followed every move. When she shrugged out of the lace creation, his hands rose to her breasts, ever so lightly brushing across her nipples and sending swirls of need zipping through her. Once had definitely not been enough with this man.

Twice probably wouldn't be, either. This was already cranking up to be a fling of monumental proportions. Her time on Phillip Island had just got a whole lot more interesting and exciting. 'Flynn.' His name fell as a groan between them.

As he leaned over to take her nipple in his mouth he smiled. A smile full of wonder and longing. A smile that wound around her heart.

Back off. Now. Your heart never gets involved. Back off. Remember who, what you are. A nomad, soon to be on the road again. Remember. You take no passengers.

Flynn softly bit her breast, sending rationale out the window. Her hands gripped his head to keep his mouth exactly where it was. His hands cupped her backside. Tipping her head back so her hair fell down her back, Ally went with the overwhelming need crawling through her, filling every place, warming every muscle until she quivered with such desire she thought she'd explode.

Flynn's mouth traced kisses up her throat, then began a long, exploratory trip downward. Back to her breasts, then her stomach and beyond. It was impossible to keep up with him, to savour each and every stroke. They all melted into one, and when her legs trembled so much she could barely stand, Flynn gently guided her onto the bed, where he joined her, his erection throbbing when she placed her hand around him and brought him to where she throbbed for him.

Ally rolled over and groaned. *Is there any part of me that doesn't ache?* A delicious, morning-after-mind-blowing-sex ache that pulled the energy out of her and left her feeling relaxed and unwilling to get up to face the day.

She was expected at work by eight thirty. *Yeah, tell that to someone who cares.* But she dragged herself upright and stared around. The bed was a shambles, with the sheets twisted, the cover skew-whiff and the pillows on the floor.

What a night. Really only for an hour, but for once she doubted she could've gone all night. Not with Flynn. He took it out of her, he was so good.

The phone rang. It wasn't on her bedside table or on the floor next to the bed. But it did sound as though it was in this room. She tossed the cover aside, shivering as winter air hit her bare skin. Lifting the sheets and pillows, she found her jeans, but not what she was looking for. 'Don't hang up.' What if it was one of her mothers having contractions? 'Where is the blasted phone?'

Picking up her top from the corner where she'd thrown it last night, she pounced, pressed the phone's green button. 'Morning, Ally Parker speaking.'

'Morning, gorgeous,' Flynn's voice drawled in her ear. 'Thought I'd make sure you're wide-awake.'

'And if I hadn't been?' The concern backed off a notch at the sound of his warm tone. 'You'd have come around and hauled me out of bed?'

'My oath I would.'

'That does it. I'm sound asleep.' What was wrong with her? Encouraging Flynn was not the way to go.

His laugh filled her with happiness. 'Unfortunately I have a certain small individual with me this morning and I know he'd love nothing better than to try and pull you out of bed.'

'So not a good look, considering I'm naked.' She'd left her brain on the beach. Had to have.

Flynn growled. 'I certainly wouldn't be able to fault that.'

Then she saw the time. 'Is it really eight o'clock? It can't be. Got to go. I'm going to be late.' She hung up before he could say anything else and ran for the bathroom. The left side of her left brain argued with the right side about what she was doing with Flynn.

'Only five minutes late,' she gasped, as she charged into the staffroom. A large coffee in a takeout mug stood on the table at the spot where she usually sat. 'Black and strong,' Flynn muttered, as he joined her.

'You're wonderful.' She popped the lid off.

Jerome and Toby sauntered in. 'What did you think of our local Italian?' Jerome asked with a twinkle in his eye.

'I'm hooked. Definitely going back there again.' Her knee nudged Flynn's under the table.

He pushed back as he continued to stare across at the other men. 'She's got Giuseppe eating out of her hand.'

I thought that was your hand. 'He's a sweetheart.'

'Ally.' Megan popped her head around the door. 'You've got visitors. Chrissie and her mum.'

Back to earth with a thud. Reality kicked in. 'Showtime.' Ally stood up, sipped her coffee, found it cool enough to gulp some down. No way could she start her day without her fix, especially not this morning. Her stomach was complaining about the lack of breakfast, but it'd have to make do with caffeine. 'Is it okay if I go and see Chrissie? Or would you prefer I stay for the meeting?'

'Don't worry about the meeting. One of us can fill you in later if there's anything you need to know,' Toby told her.

Flynn spoke up. 'If you need me, just call. But I'm sure you'll be fine.'

'Chrissie's mum would have to be dense not to know why her daughter has requested an appointment with a midwife, wouldn't she?'

Flynn nodded. 'And dense is not a word I'd use to describe Angela. She's probably cottoned on but could be denying it.'

Angela didn't deny it for any longer than it took for the three of them to be seated in Ally's room with the door firmly shut. 'You're going to tell me Chrissie's pregnant, aren't you?'

'Actually, I was hoping Chrissie might've told you.' She looked at the girl and found nothing but despair blinking out at her. Dark shadows lined the skin beneath her sad eyes and her mouth was turned downwards, while her hands fidgeted on her thighs. 'Chrissie, did you get any sleep last night?'

She shook her head. 'I was thinking, you know? About everything.' Her shoulders dropped even lower. 'I'm sorry, Mum. I didn't mean it to happen.'

'Now, that I can understand.' Angela might have been expecting the news but she still looked shocked. 'All too well.' She breathed deeply, her chest rising. 'How far along are you, do you know?' Her gaze shifted from her daughter to Ally and then back to Chrissie.

'Nearly twelve weeks.' Chrissie's voice was little more than a whisper. 'You're disappointed in me, aren't you?'

Angela sat ramrod straight. Her hands were clenched together, but her eyes were soft and there was gentleness in her next words. 'No, sweetheart, I think you're the one who's going to be disappointed. You had so many plans for your future and none of them included a baby.'

'But you managed. You've got a good job. You're the best mum ever.'

'Chrissie, love.' Angela sniffed, and reached for one of her daughter's hands. 'A good job, yes, but not the career I'd planned on.'

Ally stood up and crossed to the window to give them some space. They didn't need her there. Yet. Flynn had been right. This woman was a good mum. *Why didn't I have one like her? Why didn't I have one at all? One who loved me from the day I was born?*

Behind her the conversation became erratic as Chrissie and Angela worked their way through the minefield they were facing. At least they were facing it together.

'Do you regret having me?' Chrissie squeaked.

'Never.' A chair scratched over the surface of the floor and when Ally took a quick peek she saw Angela holding her daughter in her arms. 'Never, ever. Not for one minute.'

'I'm keeping my baby, Mum.'

Ally held her breath. This was the moment when Angela might finally crack. She fully understood the pitfalls of single parenthood. And the joys. But she'd want more for Chrissie.

Angela was strong. 'I thought you'd say that. I hope your child will love its grandmother as much as you loved your grandfather, my girl, because we're in this together. Understand?'

As Chrissie burst into long-overdue tears, Ally sneaked out the door, closing it softly behind her. In the storeroom she wiped her own eyes. Did that girl understand how loved she was? How lucky?

'Hey, don't tell me it was that bad in there.' Flynn stood before her, holding the box of tissues she'd been groping for.

'It was beautiful.' Blow. 'What an amazing mother Angela is. Chrissie will be, too, if that's the example she's got to follow.'

'Told you.' Did he have to sound so pleased with himself? His finger tipped her chin up so she had to meet his kind gaze. 'Come and finish that coffee I bought you. We can zap it in the microwave.'

He'd be thinking she was a right idiot, hiding in the cupboard, crying, because her patient had just told her mother she was pregnant. 'I'll give them five minutes and then go and discuss pregnancy care and health.'

'Make it ten. You'll be feeling better and they'll have run out of things to say to each other for a while.' His hand on her elbow felt so right. And for the first time it wasn't about heat and desire but warmth and care.

More stupid tears spurted from her eyes. Her third day here and he was being gentle and kind to her. Right now she liked this new scenario. Thank goodness Flynn would think these fresh tears were more of the same—all about Chrissie and her mother, not about him. And her.

CHAPTER FIVE

THE MOMENT FLYNN saw the clinic's car turn into the parking lot on Friday night he couldn't hold back a smile. A smile for no other reason than he was glad to see Ally. Her image was pinned up in his skull like a photo on a noticeboard. More than one photo. There was the one of Ally in those leg-hugging, butt-defining jeans and the red jersey that accentuated her breasts. Then the other: a naked version showing those shapely legs, slim hips and delicious breasts.

There was a third: tearful Ally, hiding away and looking lost and lonely. What was that about?

The front door crashed against the wall as she elbowed it wide and carried her bag in. 'Hi, Flynn, you're working late. Had an emergency?'

Yep, two hours without laying eyes on you definitely constitutes an emergency. 'Do you want to join Adam and me for dinner? There's a chicken casserole cooking as we speak. Nothing flash, but it should be tasty.'

'A casserole's not flash?' Her smile warmed him right down to his toes. 'My mouth's watering already.'

'Is that a yes, then?' His lungs stopped functioning as he waited for her reply.

'Are you sure there'll be enough?' As he was about to answer in the affirmative, she asked, 'Shall I stop in at the supermarket and get some garlic bread to go with the meal? Some wine?'

'Good idea. I left the Merlot behind the other night. On the beach,' he added with a grin.

'You're too easily distracted, that's your problem.' Her mouth stretched into a return smile. 'Someone probably got lucky when they went for a walk that morning.'

A devilish look crossed his face and his eyes widened. 'I got lucky that night.'

'A dinner invitation will get me every time.' She swatted his arm. 'What's your address? Better give me precise directions if you really want me to join you.'

'The island's not too large and most people know where to find me.' Glancing at his watch, he added, 'I'll get home so Marie can leave.'

Flynn hummed all the way home, something he hadn't done in for ever. Even without Tuesday night's sexual encounters, the fact that Ally was coming to his place for a meal made him feel good. Mealtimes weren't lonely because Adam was there, but sometimes he wished for adult conversation while he enjoyed his dinner. He'd also like an occasional break from Adam's usual grizzles about what he was being made to eat. His boy was a picky eater. Just because his mother had wanted him to eat well, it didn't mean Adam agreed.

Flynn shook his head. Where did Adam come into this? This hyper mood had nothing to do with him. Try Ally. And himself. *Be honest, admit you want a repeat of Tuesday night's sex.*

Guilt hit hard and fast.

What was he thinking? How could he be having fun when Anna was gone? He didn't deserve to. It had been his fault she hadn't been happy with her life. He should've taken the time to listen to her when she'd tried to explain why it was so important to her to leave the city behind.

He'd loved his life in Melbourne, had thought he was well on the way to making a big name for himself in emergency medicine. Sure, he hadn't always been there for Anna and Adam, had missed meals and some firsts, like Adam saying 'Hello, Mummy', but they'd agreed before Adam had been conceived that he'd be working long hours, getting established, and that it would take a few years before he backed off so they could enjoy the lifestyle they both had wanted.

Anna had quickly forgotten their agreement once Adam had arrived, instead becoming more demanding for him to give up his aspirations and move to family-orientated Phillip Island. What he hadn't told Anna before she'd died was that he'd begun talks with the head of the ED to cut down his hours. It would've been a compromise. Too late. Anna had driven into an oncoming tram, and he and Adam had moved to her island full-time. Sometimes he had regrets about that—regrets that filled him with guilt. This was right for Adam. He should've done it for Anna while he could.

Turning into his drive, he automatically pressed the garage door opener and drove in, hauled on the handbrake and switched off the engine. He tipped his head back against the headrest. 'Anna, I miss you.'

A lone tear tracked down his cheek.

Is it wrong to want to have some fun? To want to move on and forge a new life for me and our boy? Adam misses his mummy so much I'm afraid I'm getting it all wrong. I try to do things as you'd want, but sometimes I feel I'm living your life, not mine.

The engine creaked as it began cooling down. Sheba nudged her wet nose against his window and Flynn dragged himself out of the car. He didn't have time to sit around feeling sorry for himself. Rightly or wrongly, Ally was coming to dinner.

After stopping off at the supermarket, Ally went back to the flat and had a quick shower, before changing into jeans and a clean shirt. She took a moment to brush her ponytail out, letting it fall onto her shoulders. If the way Flynn kept running his hands through it the other night was an indicator, he obviously liked her hair.

She checked her phone for texts. Nothing. Not even from Darcie. She quickly texted.

How's things?

The reply was instant.

The usual. What r u doing 2night?

Having dinner with hot man.

You're not wasting time.

Did I mention his 4-yr-old son?

Ally? That's different for you.

Ally slipped her phone into her pocket without answering. What could she say? In one short message Darcie had underlined her unease.

Swiping mascara over her lashes, she stared at her reflection in the mirror. Most of the day, even when busy with patients, a sense of restlessness had dogged her. Strange. Her first-day nerves weren't going away.

Get over it. Coming to a new job's nothing like starting over with a new family when you're scared and wondering if they'll love you enough to keep you past the end of the first week. Don't let the worry bugs tip you off track. You're in control these days.

She twisted the mascara stick into its holder so hard it snapped.

Thank goodness she had something to do tonight other than sit alone in that pokey lounge, eating takeaways and watching something boring on TV. She'd be with Flynn and his boy, and be able to have a conversation. What about didn't matter, as long as she had company for a few hours. It would be an added bonus if she and Flynn ended up in bed. But she wasn't sure if it would happen, with Adam being in the house, Flynn rightly being super-protective of him.

Then she laughed at herself. Since when did she put sex second to conversation? After one night with Flynn she hadn't stopped wondering where he'd been all her life. What was happening? Had her regular hormones packed their bags and taken a hike, only to be replaced with a needier version?

She froze, stared into the mirror, found only the same face she'd been covering with make-up for years. No drastic changes had occurred. The same old wariness mixed with a don't-mess-with-me glint blinked out of her eyes. And behind that the one emotion she hoped no one ever saw—her need to be loved.

Dropping her head, she planted her hands wide on the bathroom counter, stared into the basin and concentrated on forcing that old, childish yearning away.

Sex with Flynn and now this? Why now? Here? What was it about him that had the locks turning on her tightly sealed box of needs and longings?

She couldn't visit him. Throwing the mascara wand at the bin, she grimaced. She had to, then she'd see that he was just an everyday man working to raise his son and not someone to get in a stew over. If he was wise he'd never want a woman as mixed up as her in Adam's life.

A quick glance in the mirror and she dredged up a smile.

Attagirl. You're doing good. She kissed her finger-tips and waved them at her image. But right now she'd love a hug.

Ally got her hug within seconds of stepping inside Flynn's house.

'Hey, there.' His eyes were sombre and his mouth not smiling as he wrapped her in his arms. Her cheek automatically nestled against his chest. Her determination to be Ally the aloof midwife wobbled. *Should've stayed away. At least until this weird phase passes.*

Then Adam leapt at her, nearly knocking her off her feet and winding his arms around her waist.

'Is this a family thing?' she asked, as she staggered back against the wall. She dredged up a smile for Adam.

'Easy, Adam, not so hard. You're hurting Ally.'

'No, I'm not,' he answered. Then he was racing down the hall to where light spilled from a room. 'Now we can eat.'

'There's an honest welcome.' Kind of heart-warming. 'I'm sorry if I've kept you waiting.'

Flynn shook his head. 'You're not late. You could've got here by midday and Adam would've been waiting for dinner. He's a bottomless pit when it comes to his favourite food.'

'I bought him a wee treat at the supermarket. I hope that's all right.' The house was abnormally quiet. No blaring TV, she realised.

'The occasional one's fine, but I try not to spoil him with too much sugar and fatty foods. His mother held strong beliefs about giving children the right foods early on to establish a good lifestyle for growing up healthy. Healthy body, healthy mind was a saying close to her heart.'

He was trying to implement his late wife's beliefs. 'Fair enough.' Ally had no idea what it must be like to be suddenly left as a solo parent to a two-year-old, especially while juggling a demanding career. 'Have you always worked on Phillip Island?'

'Only since Anna died.' Flynn found matching glasses and poured the Chardonnay she'd brought. 'I was an emergency consultant in Melbourne. Being a GP is relatively new for me, and vastly different from my previous life.'

'So you had to re-specialise?' Why the drastic change?

'It was a formality really as my specialty leant itself to general practice.' He lifted his glass and tapped the rim to hers. 'Cheers. Thanks for this.'

The wine was delicious, and from the way Flynn's mouth finally tipped up into a smile after he'd tasted it, he thought so, too.

'Thanks for feeding me.' She pulled out a bar stool from under the bench and arranged herself on it to watch Flynn put the finishing touches to dinner. *Looking for the everyday man?*

As he chopped parsley he continued the conversation in a more relaxed tone. 'Anna grew up here and it had always been her intention to return once she had a family.' His finger slid along the flat of the knife to remove tiny pieces of the herb and add them to the small pile he'd created. 'I wasn't ready to give up my career in the city. I was doing well, making a name for myself, working every hour available and more. We lived in a big house in the right suburb, had Adam registered for the best schools before he was born. It was the life *I'd* dreamed of having.'

She sensed a deep well of sadness in Flynn as he sprinkled the parsley on the casserole and rinsed his hands under the tap. *Not quite the definition of an everyday man.* Hadn't he and Anna discussed where they wanted to live and work before they'd married? Before they'd started a family? 'Yet here you are, everyone's favourite GP, living in a quiet suburban neighbourhood, seemingly quite happy with it all. Apart from what happened to your wife, of course,' she added hurriedly.

She wanted to know more about him, his past, his plans for the future. She craved more than to share some nights in bed with him. *Leave. Now.* But her butt remained firmly on the seat and her feet tucked under the stool. She'd have to stay and work through whatever was ailing her.

Flynn's smile was wry. 'Odd how it turned out. It took Anna's death for me to wake up to what was important. Family is everything, and Adam is my family, so here we are.' He held cutlery out for her to take across to the table.

Did he add under his breath, 'Living the life Anna wanted for all of us?' If he did, then he'd pull the shutters down on any kind of relationship other than a fling. His late wife wouldn't be wanting him to have a woman flitting in and out of his life, and definitely not Adam's.

Relief was instant. She didn't have to fight this sense of wanting more from him. There wasn't going to be anything other than sex and a meal or two. *You're jumping the gun. He mightn't even want the sex part any more.* Except when she glanced across to where he was dishing up the meal, she knew he did. It was there in the way he watched her, not taking a blind bit of notice where he spooned chicken and gravy. When their gazes locked she was instantly transported back to the moment they'd come together on the beach. Oh, yes, there were going to be more bed games.

Games that didn't involve her heart and soul, just her hormones and body.

'What is there to do on the island during winter?' Apart from going to bed with sexy doctors. 'I read somewhere about a racetrack, but there's not going to be a race meeting this month.'

'Do you like watching cars going round and round for hours on end?' He looked bored just thinking about it.

'I've never been, but I'm always looking for new adventures.'

'So what do you do with your spare time?'

Not a lot. Her standard time-fillers were, 'Shopping, movies, sunbathing on the beach, swimming, listening to music.'

'That's it?' His eyebrows lifted. 'Seriously?'

'What's wrong with that? It's plenty.' *I don't have a child to look after. Or a house to clean and maintain. Or a partner who wants me to follow him around.*

Flynn shook his head. 'Don't tell me your life is all work and no play?'

She locked her eyes on him. 'No play? Care to rephrase that?' She'd done playing the other night—with him.

He grinned. 'How about we take you to see the penguins this weekend? It's something I can take Adam to with us.'

'Penguins?' Adam's head swivelled round so fast he should've got an instant headache.

'Big Ears always hears certain words.' Flynn shrugged.

'Can we really go, Dad? They're funny, Ally.' Adam leapt up from the table to do his best impersonation of a penguin, and Sheba got up to run circles around him. Next Adam was having a fit of giggles.

Ally chuckled. 'I love it when he does that. Okay, yes, let's go and see these creatures.' It would be something to look forward to. Going out with an everyday man and his child. Different from her usual pursuits. She bobbed her head at Adam and held her arms tightly by her sides as she shuffled across the floor.

Adam rewarded her with more giggles as they returned to the table.

'That's enough, you two.' Flynn looked so much better when he laughed. 'Sorry we're eating early, but Adam needs to have his bath and get to bed.' Flynn didn't look sorry at all.

'I understand you must have a routine. Don't ever think you have to change it for me. I'm more than happy being fed,' she said, before forking up a mouthful of chicken. 'This is better than anything I'd make, believe me.'

Adam pushed his plate aside. 'Are we having pudding, Dad?'

'I've chopped up some oranges and kiwi fruit. Just need to add the banana when we're ready.'

'Can I get the ice cream out of the freezer?'

'Yes, you can tonight since we've got a visitor.' Flynn winked at her. 'You'll get an invitation every day now.'

I wish. 'I'll clean up the kitchen after dinner.' A small price for a home-cooked meal.

While Flynn was putting Adam to bed, Ally cleared away the plates. Once she'd put the last pot into the dishwasher and wiped down the benches she approached the coffee machine and began preparing two cappuccinos.

'These things make decent frothy milk,' she commented as Flynn joined her. 'How's Adam?'

'Asleep, thank goodness.' He took the coffees over to the lounge.

Following, she asked, 'This your quiet time?'

'Definitely. Don't get me wrong, I love my boy, but to have a couple of hours to unwind from the day before I go to bed is bliss.'

Bed. There it was. The place she wanted to be with Flynn right now. But he'd sat down and was stretching his legs out in front of him. She remembered those legs with no clothing to hide the muscles or keep her hands off his skin. Skin that covered more muscle and hot body the farther up she trailed her gaze. *Stop it.* She sipped the coffee, gasped as it burned her tongue. 'I'm such a slow learner.'

He stood up to take the mug out of her hand and place it on a small table beside the chair. Then he reached for her hands and pulled her to her feet. His mouth was on hers in an instant; his kiss as hot, as sexy, as overwhelming as she remembered from the previous night. She hadn't been embellishing the details.

His arms held her close to his yummy body, his need as apparent to her as the need pulsing along her veins.

When he lifted his mouth away she put her hands up and brought his head back to hers. She liked him kissing her. More than any man before. *Scary. Don't think about what that means right now. Don't think at all. Enjoy the moment.* Her tongue slipped across his bottom lip, tasting him, sending enough heat to her legs to make them momentarily incapable of holding her upright without holding on to Flynn tighter.

'Ally, you're doing it to me again. Sending me over the

edge so quickly I can't keep up.' Thankfully he returned to kissing as soon as he stopped talking.

So not the moment for talking. This was when mouths had other, better, things to do. Since when had kissing got to be so wonderful anyway? Or was it just Flynn's kisses that turned her on so rapidly? Before Flynn she'd thought they were just a prelude to bedroom gymnastics, but now she could honestly spend the whole evening just kissing.

Then his hands slid under her top to touch her skin and she knew she'd been fooling herself. She had to have him, skin to skin, hips to hips. Hands touching, teasing, caressing. Now. Pulling her mouth free, she growled, 'The couch or your bedroom?'

His eyes widened, then he shook his head. 'Bedroom. There's a lock on the door.'

She hadn't had to think about children barging in before. But why did Flynn have a lock on his bedroom door? Did he do this often? No, he'd told her she was the first since Anna died. Somehow she knew he hadn't lied to her. Whatever the reason it was there, she was grateful or Flynn wouldn't have continued with this even with Adam sound asleep.

He said, 'I'm hoping you've got more of those condoms in your bag.'

'That's what the pharmacy's handy for. Called in at the one farthest from the clinic on my way back from visiting a patient.' No point in creating gossip if she didn't have to.

Flynn laughed. 'You don't honestly think they won't know who you are already?'

Her fingers caught his chin and pulled that talkative mouth down for another kiss. 'Let's get back to where we were.'

'Now who's talking too much?'

They both shut up from then on, too busy touching and

stroking, kissing, undressing one another as their desire coiled tighter and tighter. And tighter.

The phone woke Ally. It was a local number, though not one she knew. Seven o'clock on a Saturday morning. She might not know many people on this island, but it seemed someone always wanted to get her out of bed before she was ready. Or in bed, as with Flynn.

'Ally, is that you? It's Chrissie.'

'Hey, Chrissie, what's up?" Ally pushed up the bed to lean back against her pillow.

'I'm bleeding. I'm not losing the baby, am I?' Her voice rose.

'First of all, take a deep breath and try to calm down. I'll have to examine you to know the answer to that, but you're not necessarily having a miscarriage. Sometimes women do have some spotting and it's fine.'

'But what if I am miscarrying?' There were tears in Chrissie's voice. 'I don't want to lose it.'

Ally felt her heart squeeze for this brave young woman. 'How heavy is the bleeding?' Wrong question. To every pregnant mother it would be a flood.

'Not lots. Nothing like my period or anything.'

Got that wrong, then, didn't I? 'I'll come and see you this morning. Try to relax until I get there. This could just be due to hormonal changes or an irritation to your cervix after sex.' Had Chrissie been seeing the boy who'd had a part in this pregnancy? There'd still been no mention of the father and she was reluctant to ask. It wasn't any of her business, unless Chrissie was under undue pressure from him about the pregnancy and so far that didn't seem to be the case.

'Really?' Chrissie's indrawn breath was audible on the phone. Girls of this age didn't usually like talking about their sexual relations to the midwife. It was *embarrassing*. 'But that didn't happen before when I wasn't pregnant.'

'Your body is changing all the time now, and especially your cervix.' It sounded like they might have the cause of the spotting, but she needed to make absolutely sure. Ally got up and stretched, her body aware of last night's lovemaking with Flynn. Easing the kinks out of her neck and back, she used one hand to pull on a thick jersey and trackpants before making her way to the kettle for a revitalising coffee. 'Have you told your mum what's happening?'

'Yes. She said to ring you or Dr Reynolds.'

And I got the vote. Warmth surged through her. 'If I'm at all worried after the exam, you'll still need to see Dr Reynolds. He might want you to have an ultrasound. But first things first. I'll be at your house soon. Is that all right?' She wouldn't mention the blood tests she'd need samples for. Chrissie might've sailed through the last lot without a flinch, but she didn't need to be stressed over today's until the last minute.

'Thank you, Ally. That's cool. I'm sorry to spoil your day off.'

'Hey, you haven't. This is what being a midwife's about. You wait until junior is ready to come out. He or she won't care what day of the week it is, or even if it's day or night.'

'I'm going to find out if it's a boy or girl. I want time to think of a name and to get some nice things for it. I feel weird, calling the baby "it". Like I don't care or something.'

Talking about the scan was more positive than worrying she might be losing the baby. Ally sighed with relief. 'Catch you shortly.'

* * *

Four hours later Ally parked outside Flynn's house and rubbed her eyes. She was unusually tired. Her head felt weighed down—with what, she had no idea. Maybe the slower pace of the island did this to people. She'd noticed not everyone hurried from place to place, or with whatever they were doing. Certainly not the checkout operator at the supermarket, where she'd just been to stock up on a few essentials. The girl had been too busy talking to her pal she'd previously served to get on with the next load of groceries stacked on her conveyor belt.

Tap-tap on her window. Flynn opened her door. 'Hey, you coming in or going to sit out here for the rest of the day? Adam could run errands for you, bring you a coffee or a sandwich.'

'That sounds tempting.' The heaviness lifted a little and she swung out of the car. 'How's things in your house this morning?'

He ignored her question. 'You look exhausted. All that sexercise catching up with you?' He suddenly appeared genuinely concerned. 'You're not coming down with anything, are you?'

'Relax, I'm good. Just tired. I've spent most of this morning with Matilda Livingstone, trying to calm her down and make her understand that her pregnancy is going well, that she doesn't need to worry about eclampsia at this early stage, if at all.'

'Her mother's been bleating in her ear again, I take it?'

'Unfortunately, yes. Such a different outlook from Angela and Chrissie. I had an hour with Chrissie, as well. She had some mild spotting this morning, but hopefully I've allayed her concerns. We talked a lot about the trimesters and what's ahead for her and the baby. I'm amazed at how much detail she wanted to know.'

'Could be her way of keeping on top of the overwhelming fact that she's pregnant and still at school and hoping to go to university.'

Ally nodded. 'Yes, well, that plan of becoming a lawyer is on hold for a little while, but I bet she will do her degree. Maybe not in the next couple of years, but some time. There's a fierce determination building up in her that she'll not let baby change her life completely, that she's going to embrace the situation and make the most of everything.'

'That's fine until her friends leave the island to study and she's at home with a crying infant. That's the day she'll need all the strength she can muster.'

Ally shook her head at him. 'She'll love her precious baby so much she'll be fine.'

'Spoken like someone who hasn't had a major disappointment in her life.'

Spoken like a woman who's had more than her fair share of those, and has learned to try and see only the best in life by not involving herself with people so they can't hurt her.

'That's me—Pollyanna's cousin.' It shouldn't hurt that Flynn didn't see more to her than her cheery facade, didn't see how forced that sometimes was, but it did. Even if she cut him some slack because it had barely been a week since they'd met and outside work they'd only had fun times, she felt a twinge of regret.

What would it be like to have someone in her life who truly knew her? Where she'd come from. Why she kept moving from one clinic to the next, one temporary house to another. She'd thought she'd won the lottery with the Bartletts. She had come so close to belonging, had been promised love and everything, even adoption, so when it hadn't eventuated, the pain of being rejected for a cute three-year-old had underscored what she'd always known. She was unlovable. Letting people into her heart was foolish, and to have risked it to the Bartletts because they'd made promises of something she'd only ever dreamed of having had been the biggest mistake of her young life. So big she'd never contemplated it again.

Oh, they'd explained as kindly as they could how their own two children, younger than her, hadn't wanted a big sister. Being mindful of their children's needs made Mr and Mrs Bartlett good parents, but they should never have promised her the earth. She'd loved them with such devotion it had taken months to fully understand what had happened. They'd said she was always welcome at their home. Of course, she hadn't visited.

As she locked the car she watched Flynn with her bags of goodies striding up the path to his front door. Why did she feel differently about Flynn? Whatever the answer, it was all the more reason to remain indifferent.

Did his confidence come from having loved and been loved so well that despite his loss he knew who he was and why he was here? He wasn't going to share his life with her or another woman. It was so obvious in the way he looked out for Adam, in the balancing act he already had with his career and his son. She'd been aware right from the get-go that there would be no future for her here.

That's how she liked it, remember?

As Flynn stopped to look back at her she knew an almost overwhelming desire to run up to him and throw herself into his arms. So strong was this feeling that she unlocked the car. She had to drive away, go walk the beach or take a visit to the mainland.

'Ally? You gone to sleep on your feet?' The concern was genuine. 'I think you should see a doctor.' Then he smiled that stomach-tightening smile straight at her. 'This doctor.'

How could she refuse that invitation? There was friendship in that smile. There was mischief, as in sex, in that smile. That was more than enough. That's all she ever wanted.

She locked the car again and headed inside.

Flynn watched Ally with Adam. She didn't appear to be overly tired, more distracted. By what? Was she about to tell him thanks, she'd had a blast, but it was over? Already?

He wasn't ready to hear that news. Not yet. They'd just got started. It had come as a surprise to find he wanted her so much, needed to get to know her intimately. He understood it had to be a short-term affair. Ally would leave at the end of her contract in three weeks—no doubt about that. For that he should be grateful. There wasn't room in his life for anyone else. Adam came first, second, and took anything left over from the demands of the clinic.

Anyway, he doubted whether Ally had room for him or any man in her life. She was so intent on moving on, only touching down briefly in places chosen for her by her bosses and circumstances, doing her job with absolute dedication and then taking flight again.

'Hey, Adam, what've you been doing this morning?' The woman dominating his thoughts was talking to his boy and scratching Sheba's ears.

'We went to the beach to throw sticks for Sheba. I chucked them in the water. That's why she's all wet.' Mischief lightened that deep shade of blue radiating out of Adam's eyes. *Here we go, another round of giggles coming up.*

'The water must've been freezing.' Ally smiled softly

and ruffled his hair, which Adam seemed to like. And that simple show of affection put the kibosh on the giggles as he stepped close to Ally and patted the top of Sheba's head, too.

'Sheba likes swimming.' Adam looked up at Ally, hope in his eyes. 'Are you still coming to see the penguins with us?'

'That's why I'm here. You and I can do the funny walk on the beach, see if they want to be our friends.' She was good with him, no doubt about that.

Which set Flynn to more worrying. That look Adam had given her showed how much his boy already felt comfortable with Ally. Though, to be fair, he was comfortable with just about everybody. But was this a good idea, having Ally drop by for lunch and a drive around the island? His boy didn't need to lose anyone else in his life. It was only recently that he'd got past that debilitating grief after Anna's death. *He must not get close to Ally. He could not.*

'Flynn, you've caught the sleeping-on-your-feet bug.' Ally had crossed to his side and was nudging him none too gently in the ribs with her elbow. 'You with us?'

He relaxed. Let the sudden fire in his belly rule his head. 'You bet. Do you want to come back for dinner tonight?' *Afterwards we could have some more of that bedroom exercise.*

'Did you have anything else in mind for the evening? There's a wicked glint in your baby blues.'

'Dessert maybe.'

'With whipped cream?' Her tongue slid across her lips and sent heat to every corner of his body.

So this was what it was like to wake up after a long hibernation. Not slowly, but full-on wide-awake and ready to go. Making love with this woman had been like a promise come true. Exciting and beautiful. He wanted to do it again and again. *Making love as against having sex? Now, there's something to think about.*

'Can I have ice cream, too?' Adam asked, bringing them back to earth with a thud.

'We can get cones when we're out this afternoon.' How many hours before Adam was tucked up in bed fast asleep? How long until he could kiss Ally until she melted against him?

'Flynn,' she mock growled. 'We have plans for this afternoon. Let's get them under way, starting with lunch. My shout at a café or wherever you recommend near this penguin colony. The busier we are, the quicker the day will go by.'

'Can't argue with that.' She was so right he had to drop a kiss on her cheek as a reward. It would've been too easy to move slightly and cover her mouth with his. Thank goodness common sense prevailed just in time and he stepped back to come up with, 'I'm thinking of getting our flippers out of the cupboard in the garage so that you two human penguins can flip-flop along the beach.'

'Can we, Dad? Ally, want to?' Adam yelled, as he ran in the direction of the garage internal door.

Flynn waved a hand after him. 'Go easy on that cupboard door. You know what happened last time you opened it.'

'I'll help him.' Ally was already moving in the same direction, her fingers tracing the spot on her cheek he'd just kissed.

'Good idea. Things tend to spill all over the place when he starts poking through the junk on the shelves.' He relaxed. Adam was excited, and Ally was just being a part of that, helping make his day more fun. It wasn't like she'd moved in or would see him every day of the week. She'd be gone soon enough, and Adam would still have all his playmates and the many adults on the island who enjoyed spoiling and looking out for him. He'd be safe. He wasn't in danger of getting hurt.

Flynn paused. Neither was he. Despite being equally excited as his boy. Ally hadn't said anything about calling their affair—if that's what it was—quits yet, so he'd carry on for three more weeks and make the most of her company. It wasn't as though he'd be broken-hearted when she went, mad, crazy attraction for her and all. He'd miss her for sure. She was the woman who'd woken him up, but that didn't mean he had to have her in his life permanently.

CHAPTER SIX

'WHERE'S DAD?' ADAM bounced into the bedroom and jumped up on the bed, effectively ending any pretence of Ally sleeping.

Groaning, she rolled over to stare up at this little guy. Something warm and damp nudged her arm. Turning her head, she came eye to eye with Sheba. Another groan escaped her. So this was what it was like to wake up in a family-orientated house. Kind of cosy, though it would've been better if Flynn were here.

'Why are you here?' Adam asked, looking around as though he might find his father in the wardrobe or on the floor beside the bed.

'Dad had to go to work so I stayed to look after you.'

'Did someone have a crash?' No four-year-old should look so knowledgeable about his father's work.

'Yes, during the night.' The call had come through requesting Flynn's presence as Ally had been about to walk out the door to return to the flat. They'd agreed she shouldn't be there in the morning with him when Adam woke up. But when the call came Flynn had been quick to accept her offer to stay, so apparently he could break his own rules.

Jerome had picked up Flynn ten minutes later. Teens had been racing on the bridge in the wee hours of the morning after too much alcohol. Two cars had hit side on and spun, slamming into the side of the bridge, injuring four lads. Carnage, Flynn had told her when he'd phoned to explain he wouldn't be back until early morning as he was accompanying one of the boys to the Royal Melbourne Hospital.

'He doesn't like going to crashes. They're yucky.' Adam patted the bed and the next thing Ally felt the bed dipping as Sheba heaved herself up to join them.

'Is she allowed on the bed?' Ally shuffled sideways to avoid being squashed by half a ton of Labrador.

'Sometimes.'

'Right, and today's one of those times. Why did I not see that coming?' She chucked him under the chin. About to sit up, she stopped. Under the covers she wore only underwear. Definitely not the kind that decently covered all the girl bits. 'Adam, do you think you could take Sheba out to the kitchen while I get up?' Her clothes were in a tangled heap on the floor where she'd dropped them before climbing back into bed after Flynn had left.

'Do you want Dad's dressing gown? It's in the wardrobe. He never uses it.' Adam leapt off the bed, obviously unperturbed that she was there. Maybe he could explain that to his father. 'He walks around with no clothes on when he gets up in the morning.'

Too much information. At least while Flynn wasn't there and this little guy was. But she could picture Flynn buck naked as he strolled out to put the kettle on. Seriously sexy. 'I'd love the dressing gown.'

Adam had just dumped the robe on the bed when they both heard the front door opening. 'Dad's back.' He raced through the house, Sheba lumbering along behind him.

Making the most of the opportunity Ally slipped out of bed and into the dressing gown, tying the belt tightly around her waist. A glance in the mirror told her that as a fashion statement, an awful lot was lacking. Her face could do with a scrub, too. All that mascara had worked its way off her lashes and smudged her upper cheeks.

In the kitchen she plugged in the coffee maker and leaned her hip against the bench, waiting for the males of this house to join her.

Flynn sloped into the kitchen, with Adam hanging off his back like a monkey. Sheba brought up the rear. 'Morning, Ally. Sleep well?'

Huh?

Then he winked and she grinned. 'Like a lizard.'

'Like your outfit,' he tossed her way.

'I'm not sure about the colour. Brown has never been my favourite shade of anything. Want a coffee?'

'I'd kill for one, but can you give me five? I want to leap under a very hot shower.' His face dropped and his eyes saddened. 'It was messy out there,' he said quietly.

She nodded, wanting to ask more but reluctant to do so in front of Adam. Instead, she reached a hand to his cheek, cupped his face. 'Go and scrub up. I'll have the coffee waiting.' *Cosy, cosy.*

'Ta. You're a treasure.' For a moment she thought he was going to kiss her. His eyes locked on hers and he leaned closer. Then he must've remembered Adam on his back because he pulled away. 'I won't take long.'

He returned in jeans and a polo-neck black jersey that showed off his physique to perfection. His feet were bare, his hair a damp mess. He couldn't have looked more sexy if he'd tried. It came naturally.

Passing over a mug of strong coffee, she picked up the container she'd found in the pantry. 'Feel like croissants for breakfast?'

'Croissants it is. I'll heat them while you have a shower

if you like.' He didn't like her lounging around in his dressing gown? Then his eyes widened and she realised he was staring at her cleavage. An exposed cleavage.

Grabbing the edges of the robe, she tugged them closed. 'As soon as I've finished my coffee I'll get cleaned up.' Then what? Did she head home after breakfast? It would be fun to hang out with these two for a while. Talk about getting used to this cosy stuff all too quickly. Today she was simply ignoring the lessons learned and taking a chance. At what?

'We always go for a walk on the beach after breakfast in the weekends. You coming?' Flynn asked.

'Love to. Were you having a late breakfast when Sheba bowled me over last Sunday?' she asked around a smile, suddenly feeling good about herself. A chance at some normal, everyday fun that families all over the country would be doing. She wouldn't think about how often she'd stared through the proverbial window, longing for exactly this. She wouldn't contemplate next Sunday or the one three weeks away when she was back in Melbourne. Instead, she'd enjoy the day and keep the brakes on her emotions.

'No, two walks in one day. Makes up for the weekdays when she gets short-changed. I don't like dragging Adam out of bed too early. Marie walks her occasionally, but I think she's worried about being knocked over in her pregnant state.'

'Have you known Marie long?'

He nodded. 'Anna and Marie were school friends. They went their separate ways but kept in touch and Anna always talked about when they'd both be living back here with their families.' That sadness was back, this time for himself and his family.

Great. It was hard to compete with a woman who held

all the aces and wasn't around any more to make mistakes. *You're competing now? What happened to your fixed-in-concrete motto—Have Fun and Move On?* That was exactly what she was doing. Having fun. And…in three weeks she'd be moving on. So none of this mattered. *Really?* Really. She tried for a neutral tone even when she felt completely mixed up. 'Marie must miss her, too.'

'She does, especially now her first baby's due.'

'What would Marie have to say if she knew about us?' Would she stick up for Anna or accept that Flynn was entitled to get on with his life? *Hello? What does any of that matter? You're out of here soon enough.*

'I have no idea.' Flynn looked taken aback. 'It's nothing to do with her.' But now that Ally had put the question out there he seemed busy trying to figure out the answer.

Am I trying to wreck this fling early? Because Flynn is sure to pull the plug now.

Placing her empty mug in the sink, she headed for the bathroom. The hot water could ease the kinks in her body, but it was unlikely to quieten the unease weaving through her enjoyment of being with Flynn. It was ingrained in her to protect her heart, but already she understood this wasn't a fling she'd walk away from as easily as any other. What worried her was not understanding why. She already knew she was going to miss Flynn.

But she would go. That was non-negotiable.

Sheba and Adam raced ahead of them, one barking and one shouting as they kicked up sand and left huge footprints. Flynn stifled a yawn and muttered, 'Where do they get their energy?'

'Perhaps you should try dry dog pellets for breakfast

instead of hot, butter-soaked croissants,' a certain cheeky midwife answered from beside him.

'You're telling me Adam didn't eat a croissant with a banana and half a bottle of maple syrup poured on top? That was all for show and he actually scoffed down dog food?' Breakfast hadn't stacked up against Anna's ideas of healthy eating, but sometimes his boy was allowed to break the rules. Or *he* broke the rules and Adam enjoyed the result.

Ally's shoulder bumped his upper arm as she slewed sideways to avoid stepping on a fish carcass that had washed up on the tide. 'Yuk. That stinks.'

His hand found hers, their fingers interlaced, and he swung their arms between them. For a moment everything bothering him simply disappeared in this simple gesture. How much more relaxed could life get? He and Ally walking along the beach, hand in hand, watching Adam and the dog playing. Right now this was all he needed from life.

Then his phone broke the magic. 'Hello? Flynn Reynolds speaking.'

'This is William Foster's sister, Maisey. He's having chest pains again and refusing to go in the ambulance I called. Can you talk some sense into that stubborn head of his?'

'On my way. Can you hold on a moment?' He didn't wait for her reply. 'Ally, I've got to see a patient urgently. Can you take Adam home for me when you've finished your walk?' Asking for help twice in less than twenty-four hours didn't look like he managed very well. She'd probably be running away fast.

'No problem. Key to the house?'

'I'll need it to get my car out so I'll leave it in the

letterbox.' He waved Adam over. 'I've got to see a patient. Ally's going to stay with you, okay?'

'Can we get an ice cream, Ally?' Hope lightened his face.

'No, you can't.' He wiped that expectancy away. 'Not after that enormous breakfast.' Bending down, he dropped a quick kiss on Adam's forehead. 'See you in a bit, mate.'

'You haven't said goodbye to Sheba.'

'I'm sure she won't mind.' Straightening up, Flynn looked at Ally, leaned in and kissed her cheek. 'Thanks, I owe you.'

Then he started to jog the way they'd come and got back to talking to Maisey. 'I didn't know William had been discharged.'

'He wasn't.'

So the old boy had taken it in his own hands to get out of hospital. 'He definitely needs that talking to, but I have to say I've already tried on more than one occasion and he's never been very receptive to anything I've said.'

'He's lost the will to live.'

That was it in a nutshell. 'I'll talk to his daughter again.' Not that he held out any hope. She'd had no more luck than anyone else.

Glancing over his shoulder, he saw Adam throwing a stick for Sheba, laughing and shouting like only four-year-olds could. *When he's older, will he fight for me if the need arose? I hope I am such a good parent that he will.* Ally drifted into his vision as she chased another stick Adam had thrown, and he felt a frisson of longing touch him. Longing that followed him up and across the road and all the way home.

Longing that wasn't only sexual; longing that reminded him of lazy days with Anna and Adam, of friendship and love. Longing he had no right to explore. He'd been married to the love of his life. No one got a second whack at that. Anyway, as Anna had told him on the day she'd died, he hadn't been the perfect husband. He'd worked too many hours, putting his career before his family apparently. It hadn't mattered that the career had given them the lifestyle they'd had. Yeah, the one Anna apparently hadn't wanted. Not in the middle of Melbourne anyway. *Damn it, Anna, I'm so sorry we were always arguing. I'm sorry about so many things.*

He needed to scrub that from his mind and concentrate. William needed him urgently. Hitting the gas accelerator, he drove as fast as the law allowed—actually, a little faster.

Sure enough, the ambulance was parked in William's driveway. Maisey led him inside, where the paramedics had the heart monitor attached to William's chest. The reading they passed him was abnormal. He inclined his head towards the door, indicating everyone should leave him with his patient for a few minutes.

'Don't even start, Doc,' William wheezed the moment they were alone.

'You think you have the right to decide when you should clock out, do you?'

William blinked. 'It's my life.'

'From the moment you're born, it's not just yours. You have family, friends, colleagues. They all have a part of you, whether you care or not. Whether you love them or not.'

'I've lost interest in everything since Edna died. You know how it is, Doc.'

Yes, he sure did, but, 'Don't play that card with me, William. Look me in the eye and tell me Edna would want you ignoring your daughter's love? What about your grandchildren, for goodness' sake? What sort of example are you setting them with this attitude? You think teaching them to give up when the going gets tough is good for them?' Flynn sat down and waited. He wouldn't belabour the points he'd made. There was such a thing as overdoing it.

Silence fell between them. The house creaked as the sun warmed it. Somewhere inside he heard Maisey and the paramedics talking. He continued to wait.

William crossed his legs, uncrossed them. His hands smoothed his trousers. He stared around the room, his gaze stopping on a photograph of his family taken when Edna had still been alive.

Flynn held his breath.

William's gaze shifted, focused on a painting of a farmhouse somewhere on the mainland, then moved on to another of a rural scene. Paintings Edna had done.

Flynn breathed long and slow, hoping like hell his patient didn't have another cardiac incident in the next few minutes. What if he'd done the wrong thing? But he'd tried the soft approach. It was time to be blunt. They had to get William aboard that ambulance and manhandling him when he refused to go wasn't the answer—or legal. He had every right to say no. But he'd better not arrest, at least not until he was in hospital.

William had returned to that family photo, his gaze softening, his shoulders dropping a little from their indignant stance. Then one tear slipped from his right eye and slowly rolled down his cheek. He nodded once. 'I'll go. For my Edna.'

Good for you. 'I'll tell the paramedics.' And Maisey, who'd no doubt be phoning her niece the moment William had been driven away.

After Flynn had filled in some paperwork to go with

his patient, he talked briefly to Maisey and then headed
for his car. He was going home to Adam and Ally. They'd
go for a jaunt round to San Remo. If only he didn't feel so
drained of energy. Already tired after last night's emergency call-out, talking with William had taken more out
of him than he'd have expected. He understood all too
well how the other man felt; he also knew William was
wrong. Hopefully, one day the old guy would acknowledge that, at least to himself if no one else.

The sunny winter's day had brought everyone out to San
Remo to stroll along the wharves and look at the fishing
boats tied up. The restaurants and bars were humming
as the locals made the most of fewer tourists.

'What's your preference for lunch?' Flynn asked Ally,
after they'd walked the length of the township's main
street and had bumped into almost the entire register of
his patients at the clinic.

'Fish and chips on the beach.' Then she smiled at him.

Her smiles had been slow in coming since he'd returned home, making him wonder if she felt he'd been
using her. Which, he supposed, he had, but not as a
planned thing. She'd been there when he'd got both calls
and he hadn't hesitated to ask her. She could've said no.
'Good answer. There's a rug in the boot of my car we
can spread on the sand.'

Had he used Ally by putting his work before what she
might've wanted? *Just like old times.* But asking Ally
to stay was putting Adam first, just not her. Turning, he
touched a finger to her lips. 'Thank you.'

'What for?'

'Being you. I'm going to get lunch.'

'Adam and I will be over on that monster slide.'

'He's conned you into going down that?' Flynn grinned. 'Don't get stuck in the tube section.'

Yep, this felt like a regular family outing. Dad ordering the food, Adam wanting to play with Mum. Except Ally wasn't Mum, and never would be.

Which part of having a short affair had he forgotten? As much as Ally turned him on with the briefest of looks or lightest of touches, no matter how often they fell into bed together, this was only an affair with a limited number of days to run. When was that going to sink in?

While he waited for his order he watched the woman causing him sleepless nights. She smiled sweetly at his son bouncing alongside her, said something that made him giggle. Then she rubbed her hand over his head, as she often did. How come Adam didn't duck out the way as he did with other people who went to touch him?

Flynn sighed. Should he be getting worried here? How would his boy react when Ally left them? Yes, he'd asked himself this already, and would probably keep doing so until he knew what to do about it. He'd have the answer on the day Ally left.

The real problem was that he didn't want to stop what he and Ally had going on. It was for such a short time, couldn't he make the most of it? Wasn't he entitled to some fun? If only that's all it was, and the fun didn't come with these conflicting emotions.

The fish and chips were the best he'd ever had, the batter crisp, the fish so fresh it could've still been flapping. The company was perfect.

Ally rolled her eyes as her teeth bit into a piece of fish. 'This is awesome. I'm going to have to starve all week to make up for it.'

As if she needed to watch her perfect figure. 'We'll eat salads every day till next Sunday.'

Surprise widened those beautiful eyes. 'Something you haven't talked to me about yet?'

It had only occurred to him at that moment. 'You might as well join us for dinner every night. I like cooking while you obviously have an aversion to it. Next Saturday we can visit the wildlife centre.' Once he got started, his plan just grew and grew. 'Fancy a return visit to Giuseppe's on Saturday night? It's band night.'

'Don't tell me. The old two-step brigade.' She grinned to take the sting out of her words.

'Way better than that. The college has a rock band that's soon going to compete in a talent show. Giuseppe's way of supporting them is to hire them on Saturday nights. He says the music is crazy.'

'We can crazy dance, then. Yes to all those invitations. Thank you. You've saved me having to stock up on instant meals.' She wrapped up the paper their meal had come in and stood to take it across to a rubbish bin.

'Can we go to the wildlife park now, Dad?'

'Not today, Adam. You've already had a busy weekend, going places that you don't usually visit.'

'But, Dad, why can't I go? Now?'

'Don't push it, son. We're going home. I've got things to do around the house.' Flynn could feel that tiredness settling over him again, stronger this time. He yawned just as Ally sat down on the sand again.

'Can't hack the pace, eh, old boy?'

'I don't know anyone who can run a marathon first up after no practice for years.' Not that making out with Ally felt as difficult as running a marathon. It all came too naturally.

'So that's why we do sprints.' Her grin turned wicked and the glint in her eyes arrowed him right in his solar plexus.

It also tightened his groin and reminded him of the intensity of her attraction. They'd be waiting hours before they could act on the heat firing up between them. Adam did put a dampener on the desire running amok in his veins.

'Dad, we're going to the school tomorrow.'

'What school? What are you talking about?' First he'd heard of it.

'Where the big kids go. Marie's taking me with the play group to see what it's like.'

He'd phone Marie when they got home. 'Are you sure?' This sounded like something he should be doing. 'That's my job, taking you there. I'm your parent, not Marie.'

Ally put a hand on his forearm. 'Wait till you've talked to her. Adam might've got it wrong.' The voice of reason was irritating.

'I doubt it. Marie should've mentioned it. She knows that when it comes to the major parenting roles I'll do them. Not her or anyone else.' Now he sounded peevish, but he *was* peeved. 'I'm doing what Anna would've wanted. What I want. I'm not a surface parent, supplying warmth and shelter and avoiding everything else going on in Adam's life. No, thank you.'

She pulled her hand away, shoved it under her thigh. 'Has anyone suggested otherwise?' An edge had crept into her tone.

Had he come across too sharply? Probably. 'Sorry, but you don't understand.' Had she just ground her teeth? 'When Anna was alive she did most things with Adam. We agreed she'd be a stay-at-home mother, and when she died I wanted nothing more than to stay at home with him, but of course that's impossible.'

'How can you say I don't understand? What do you know about me? I might have ten kids back in Melbourne.'

'Perhaps you should try telling me something.' He drew a calming breath. This was crazy, arguing because Adam might be going to school with Marie tomorrow. It wasn't Ally's fault he hadn't known or that he felt left out. 'Have you had a child?' he asked softly after a few minutes. Had she been a teenage mother who'd had her baby adopted?

'No,' she muttered, then again, a lot louder. 'No. Never.'

'Got younger brothers and sisters, then?'

Now her hands fisted on her thighs. 'No.'

He backed off a bit, changed direction with his quest for knowledge about her. 'Why did you choose midwifery as your specialty?' Was that neutral enough? Or was her reason for becoming a midwife something to do with her past? A baby she wasn't admitting to?

'I wanted to be a midwife after helping deliver my foster-mother's baby at home when I was fifteen. The whole birthing process touched something in me. I'd never seen a newborn before and I knew immediately I wanted to be a part of the process.'

Flynn wanted to know how Ally had found herself in that situation, but he didn't dare ask. Instead, he said, 'Birth is pretty awe-inspiring.'

'You're saying that from a parent's perspective.' She stared out beyond the beach at who knew what. 'My foster-mother let me hold the baby and when she asked for him back I struggled to let him go. He was beautiful and perfect and tiny. And vulnerable.'

Flynn sat quietly, afraid to say anything in case she closed down.

'For the first time in my life I'd experienced something so amazing that I wanted to do it again and again.' Her fingers trailed through the sand. 'I felt a connection—something I'd never known in my life.'

The eyes that finally locked onto his knocked the air out of his lungs. The pain and loneliness had him reaching for her, but she put a hand on his chest to stay him, saying, 'Until that moment I'd supposed birth and babies were things to be avoided at all cost. My own mother abandoned me when I was only days old.'

He swore. Short and sharp but full of anger for an unknown woman. How could anyone do that? How could Ally's mother not have wanted her? But, then again, as a doctor he'd seen plenty of people who just couldn't cope. Drug problems, mental illness, abusive partners—sometimes bringing up a baby was beyond people when they couldn't even take care of themselves.

She continued as though she hadn't uttered such a horrific thing. 'There was something so special about witnessing a new life. New beginnings and hope, that instant love from the mother to her baby.' Ally blinked but didn't cry. No doubt she'd used up more than her share of tears over the years. 'It doesn't matter how many births I've attended, each one rips me up while also giving me hope for the future.'

'Yet you don't stay around long enough to get involved with your mums and their babies.'

'No.'

So Ally didn't believe in a happy future for herself.

Her laugh was brittle as she shifted the direction of the conversation. 'I had one goal—to become a midwife. Shortly after my foster-mother's baby arrived, I went back into a group home, but I enrolled for night lessons at high school and worked my backside off during the day. Finally I made it to nursing school and then did the midwifery course and here I am.' The words spilled out as though she wanted this finished. But she couldn't hide her pride.

'It must've been darned hard work.' Lots of questions popped into his head, questions he doubted she'd answer. Ally looked exhausted after revealing that much about herself. It obviously wasn't something she did often— or at all.

The drive home was quiet. Flynn's forefingers drummed a rhythm on the steering wheel as his frustration grew. He'd learnt something very important about Ally that had briefly touched on who she was, and yet it wasn't enough. There had to be so much behind what he'd heard, things she obviously kept locked up, and he needed to hear them. How else could he help her?

'Dad, stop. You're going past our house.'

Flynn braked, looked around. 'Just checking to see if you were awake.'

Ally stared at him like he'd grown another nose. 'It's dangerous not to concentrate when you're driving.'

Because she was right and he didn't want to tell her what had distracted him, he ignored her and pressed the automatic garage door opener.

Inside the house, Flynn reached for the kettle. 'What would you like to do now, Ally?'

She tensed briefly then shook her head. 'You know what? I'm going to head back to the flat. I've got a few chores that need doing.'

His heart lurched. 'Thank you for sharing some of your story.'

Her deliberate shrug closed him off from her. 'I'm just your regular girl. And this regular girl needs to do some washing and answer some emails before work tomorrow.'

He wanted to insist she stay and share a light dinner, watch a movie on TV with him, but for once he knew when to shut up. 'Okay. I'll see you in the morning, then.'

CHAPTER SEVEN

ALLY DROPPED HER keys on the bench and stared around Kat's flat. Not grand on any scale, but a cosy and comfortable bolthole for Kat at the end of her day, a place to kick off her shoes and be herself. A place to face the world from.

What had possessed her to spill her guts to Flynn? At least he'd understand why she wasn't mother material. But it was Adam's laughing face cruising through her mind, teasing her with hope when in reality she wasn't ready for a child, would never be. Ally caressed her two ornamental dogs, her mouth twisted in sadness. Real-life pets required stability in their lives. The idea of owning a home hadn't made it onto her list of goals for the next ten years. She faced everything the world threw her way by digging deep and putting on a mask. She didn't need bricks and mortar to hide behind. Honestly, she had no idea about setting up a home that she could feel comfortable in.

Would I feel more content, less alone, if I had a place I could call home? A place—the same place—to live in between jobs, instead of bunking with whoever has a spare bed?

Sweat broke out on her upper lip. Her stomach rolled with a sickening sensation. Thirty-one and she'd never had a home, not even as a child. Those foster-homes she'd lived in had been about survival, not about getting settled. She'd always tried so hard to please her foster-parents in the desperate hope they'd fall in love with her and adopt her, but that had never happened. The only time she'd believed she might be there long term had ended in tears and her packing her few possessions to take to the next stop in her life. She'd finally wised up to the fact— starting with her own mother—that no one cared for her enough to give her what she craved.

Don't go there. You've been over and over and over trying to understand why she left you on a stranger's doorstep. There is no answer.

Poking around in her bag, she found her music player, put the earbuds in and turned the volume up loud. Music helped to blot out the memories. Sometimes.

Then her phone vibrated against her hip and broke through her unease. Removing the earbuds, she answered the phone. 'Hey, Lilia, glad you rang.' Curling up on the settee she sighed with relief. A bit of girl talk would send those other thoughts away. 'What have you been up to?'

Lilia had refused to be pushed away while she'd been on a job in Lilia's home town, and they'd become friends despite her wariness.

'Just the usual. What about you? Having a blast on the island?'

'Yep, it's great.'

'Try to sound like you mean that,' Lilia said. 'Not like you've been sent to the middle of nowhere with no man in sight.'

That might've been boring, but it would've been safer. Flynn was sneaking in under her radar. She drew a breath and found some enthusiasm. 'Oh, there are men here. Even downright drop-dead sexy ones.'

'Ones, as in many? Or one? As in you're having fun?'

'One. Dr Flynn Reynolds. Do you know him? He used to work at one of Melbourne's hospitals, left about two years ago.'

'The name doesn't ring any bells, and I can't picture him. Is he a GP?'

'A GP, a widower and father of one. Perfect for a short fling.'

'Why do I hear a note of uncertainty?' Lilia suddenly laughed. 'Oh, my God, don't tell me you've gone and fallen for him? You? Miss Staying Single For Absolutely Ever? I don't believe it.'

'That's good because it's not true.' Not true. Not true. Her heart thudded so loudly Lilia probably heard it. Her fingers gripped the phone. 'We've been doing the leg-over thing, even taken the dog and kid for a walk, but that's as far as it's going.'

'Taken the kid and dog for a walk?' Lilia shrieked. 'That's Domesticity 101. You are *so* toasted.'

Panic began clawing through Ally, chilling her, cranking her heart rate up. 'Seriously.' She breathed deeply. 'Seriously, it's all about the sex. Nothing else.'

Lilia was still laughing. 'Go on, tell me some more. Is this Flynn gorgeous?'

'Yes, damn it, he is.'

'Good. Is he a great dad?'

'What's that got to do with anything?' The panic elbowed her. Adam was happy, but even if he wasn't, that had nothing to do with her. Unless she was contemplating having babies with the man. The phone hit the floor with a crash.

Slowly bending to retrieve the phone, she couldn't think of what to say to Lilia. She didn't know what to think, full stop.

Fortunately, Lilia had no such difficulty. 'What happened? You okay? I'm sorry if I've upset you. You know I mean nothing when I say these things.'

Swallow. 'Sure. I dropped the phone, that's all.' Another swallow. 'Lilia, what if I did like Flynn? I can't do anything about it. I know nothing about families or looking after kids or playing house.'

'Hey, girlfriend, go easy on yourself. You're so much better than you think. You're capable of anything you set your mind to. I know you haven't told me everything, but how you handled putting yourself through school and getting a degree shows that in bucketloads. Do you really like him?'

Unfortunately, it could be shaping up that way. It would explain her unease and sudden need to re-evaluate her life. But it was early days. She'd soon be out of here and so would whatever feelings she was dealing with. She'd settle back to her normal, solo life and forget Flynn. Easy. 'He's okay. So how's it going in Turraburra? Any interesting men coming your way?'

'That's why I rang.' Lilia got a giant-sized hint without having to be bashed over the head. 'You know Noah Jackson, don't you?'

'Enough to say hello to and swap a sentence or two about our weekends whenever I bump into him, which isn't often as I rarely see the surgical teams. Seems an okay guy, though.' She turned the tables. 'You interested in him?'

'I've heard he's starting here in a month or so, apparently.'

'He can't be. You've got the wrong guy. Noah doesn't do general practice. He's a senior surgical registrar, not a GP. Great guy he may be, but he's very determined to get to the top of his career—and that does not include sitting and talking to mothers and their colicky babies in a small town.'

Lilia sniffed. 'Nothing wrong with general practice.'

'I know that. But I can't see Noah fitting into it. Nah, you've got the wrong guy. The Noah I know wouldn't be seen dead in a place like Turraburra.'

'Well, I heard he'll be with us for four weeks. Perhaps it's a mistake.'

'Well, if he does turn up, the good news is he's a seriously good-looking dude and definitely sexy.' Didn't set her hormones dancing but plenty of women drooled over him.

No, her hormones got a kick out of a certain doctor living here on the island. She had to get a grip, put any stupid concerns behind her and get the job done. Three weeks to go. Twenty-one days. Couldn't be too hard to have some fun and not get involved with the source of that fun. Face it, Flynn no more wanted or needed anything more connected than she did. He definitely wouldn't want Adam getting too attached to her, and she felt exactly the same. More than anything, she couldn't abide hurting that cute wee boy because she understood more than most what it was like to be left behind or shunted on. And she certainly would never be moving into their home and becoming super-mum.

'You still with me?' Lilia interrupted her musings.

'All ears. When are you coming down to Melbourne next?'

After Lilia hung up, Ally went to tug on her running shoes and shorts. A good hard pounding of the pavement would help what ailed her and put everything back into perspective.

'You've got a busy morning stacked up,' Flynn greeted her the moment she walked into the medical centre the next morning. 'Seems word's out that we've got a great new midwife and everyone who's pregnant wants to meet you.' His smile was friendly, but there was caution in his eyes. Did he think she might start considering staying on?

Returning his smile, she shrugged. 'I won't be delivering most of them. Kat will be back before long.'

His smile dipped. 'The islanders are friendly, that's all it's about. Bet you get an invitation or two for a meal before the morning's out.'

'Cool. But I'm all booked up—most nights anyway.' She locked eyes with Flynn. He hadn't changed his mind on her joining him and Adam for dinners, had he? Of course, she should be backing off a little, but how when right this moment her body was bending in his direction in anticipation of being woken up again? *Back off.* Easy to say, hard to do.

'So you'll come to dinner tonight. I'm glad.' At last the caution disappeared. His smile widened, brought a different kind of warmth to her.

A warmth that touched her deep inside in that place she went when alone. A warmth she hadn't realised she'd needed until she'd walked in and seen him. She'd missed him overnight. Had reached out to hug him and come up empty-handed—empty-hearted as well. 'Babies withstanding, I'll be there at six. Is that okay?'

He leaned close, whispered, 'Bring your toothbrush.'

That warmth turned to heat, firing colour into her chilled cheeks and tightening her stomach. 'Think I'll buy a spare,' she whispered back, before entering the office to collect the notes in her tray.

Megan winked at her. 'Have a good weekend?'

How much had she heard? Ally bit back a retort. She and Flynn would have to learn to be far more careful. 'I went to San Remo.'

Megan laughed. 'Was that you I saw out running late yesterday?'

'Running?' Flynn looked surprised.

'As in putting one foot in front of the other at a fast pace.'

'That explains…' He spluttered to a stop as Megan's eyes widened. 'A lot,' he added lamely. 'Come on, meeting time.'

As she led the way to the staffroom, she wanted to turn around and wrap her arms around him. She wanted to feel his body against hers, his chest against her cheek, his shoulder muscles under her palms. She kept walking, facing directly ahead. She wouldn't be distracted by Flynn at work. She wouldn't. It was all very well for the others to know they'd had a meal out together, might even be aware they'd spent hours doing things over the weekend, but she couldn't show how her body craved his.

'Meeting's cancelled.' Faye barrelled out of her office. 'Flynn, we're needed at the school. Two kids on bikes have been hit by a car. Where's Toby?'

'Do you need me to come along?' Ally asked.

'No, we're sorted.' Faye sped to the back door and the car park, her medical bag in one hand.

Flynn glanced around, quickly dropped a kiss on Ally's mouth. 'See you later.' And he was gone.

Leaving her with her finger pressing her lips, holding that kiss in place. Yeah, she really had missed him all night. But she'd be seeing him tonight. The knot in her tummy loosened as she headed to her room and prepared for her first mum of the day.

Her relaxed mood stayed in place all day, and when she knocked on Flynn's door that night, she didn't hold back on her smiles.

'Ally, you came,' Adam swung the door wide, inadvertently letting Sheba out.

'Sheba, no,' Ally made a grab for her collar. 'Inside, you big lump.'

Sheba replied with a tongue swipe on her hand.

'Now the woman insults my dog.' Flynn stood behind Adam, grinning at her.

Were they both as happy to see her as she was them? Stepping inside, she closed the door behind her, shutting off the world and entering the cosy cocoon that was the Reynolds home. 'Sheba knows I think she's awesome.' Then she had a brainwave. 'I could take her with me when I go running.'

Flynn's eyebrows rose. 'She'd probably have a heart attack. Walks are one thing, but a run?'

'I'm not very quick. More of a snail.' She followed Flynn and Adam into the kitchen, suddenly very aware that by making that suggestion she'd committed herself to this little family for the rest of her stay. As she had that morning when she'd said she would be here for dinners. Nothing wrong with that, as long as she kept everything in perspective. As long as Adam didn't get too close and miss her when she left.

Flynn said, 'See how you go. You might find you just want to get on the beat and not have to swing by to collect her.'

Was he having second thoughts, too?

'Can I run, too?' Adam asked hopefully.

'No,' Flynn said emphatically.

As his little face began to crumple, Ally explained. 'It's usually very early when I go.'

'It's not fair.'

'Adam, you can't do everything just because you want to. Ally's told you why you can't go with her so leave it at that.' Worry filtered into Flynn's eyes as he watched his son stomp away. When Adam turned on the TV, Flynn growled. 'Turn it off, please.'

Ally glanced from Flynn to his boy's sulky face. 'Has he been naughty?'

'He's not allowed to watch TV often. Anna was against it.'

Ah, Anna's rules. 'Surely a little time watching kids' programmes can't hurt?' *Mind your own business.* 'Other kids don't turn out as delinquents because of it.' *Shut up.*

Flynn stared at Adam, not her. 'It's hard to let go. You know?'

No, she didn't. 'Fair enough. But Adam needs to fit in with his peers at times.'

'You have a point, I guess.' Then he changed the subject. 'How was your day? Angela called me, full of praise for the way you've handled Chrissie's crisis. She doesn't want you leaving before the baby's born.'

Sliding onto a stool and propping her elbows on the bench, she shook her head. 'Chrissie will be fine with Kat.'

Flynn nodded. 'Sure she will. It's just that with Chrissie being so young and this not being a planned pregnancy, she's taken a shine to you and won't be keen to start over. But it'll work out.'

'It has to.'

'It does, doesn't it?'

Ally stared at him. What did that mean exactly? 'I was never going to be here any longer than the month Kat's away.'

He locked his eyes with hers. 'I know. But sometimes I find myself wishing you were.'

Pow. That hit right in the solar plexus, and knocked her heart. Never in a million years would she have thought he'd say something like that. 'A month's long enough for a fling. Any longer and we'd have to start wondering just what we were doing.'

'You ever had a long-term relationship?' He picked up a wooden spoon and stirred the gravy so hard a glob flicked out onto the stovetop.

'No.' She reached for a cloth to wipe up the gravy.

'Never?'

'Never. I go for short flings. Makes leaving the job easier.' *Don't ask me any more.*

'Surely you haven't always moved around as much as you currently seem to do?' He'd stopped stirring, instead studying her as though she was an alien.

Compared to him and his normal family life, she probably was different to the point of being weird. 'I spent two years in Sydney while I went to school, then moved to Melbourne for the years it took to get my degree.' Which had seemed like for ever at the time. She wouldn't mention how often she'd moved flats during those years.

Reaching across to put her hand on his, she pushed the spoon around the pot. 'You're burning the gravy.' His hand was warm under hers, and she squeezed it gently. This was so intimate—in a way she'd never known before—that tears threatened. Tugging her hand away, she stood up and went to set the table.

Flynn watched Ally banging down cutlery on the table. She was hiding something. The answer hit him hard. *More of her past.* What was so bad that she couldn't talk about it? He wouldn't judge her, but maybe he could help her. From what little she'd disclosed about being abandoned, he'd surmised that she'd grown up in the welfare system. Had she gone off the rails as a teen? Asking her outright wouldn't get him any answers, more likely her usual blunt response of no or yes. Those tight shoulders showed the chance of learning anything tonight was less than winning the lottery and he never bought tickets.

He'd told her about Anna. *You call all of about five sentences spilling your guts?* He hadn't said he and Anna had been in love from the first day they'd met at university or all the promises he'd made about Adam at her funeral.

'When's dinner? I'm hungry.'

'Now, there's a surprise.' He saw Ally wink at his son and then Adam started showing off to her.

Yeah, Adam definitely liked her a lot. So did he. Enough to want more than this affair she was adamant was going nowhere? He began dishing up, thinking how he'd never once considered he might feel something for another woman. Anna had been his everything. Hard to believe he might want a second chance at love.

The pot banged onto the stove top. Love? Get outta here. No way. Too soon, too involved, too impossible.

'You all right?' Ally stood in front of him, studying him carefully.

Swallowing hard, he nodded. 'Of course. Here…' He handed her a plate and was shocked to see his hand shaking.

'You sure?' Her gaze had dropped to his hand. 'Flynn?'

'It's nothing,' he growled. 'Adam, sit up.'

Ally did that irritating shrug of hers and picked up Adam's plate just as he reached for it. Rather than play tug of war, Flynn backed off and headed for his seat at the table. As he gulped his water he struggled to calm down. It wasn't Ally's fault he'd just had a brain melt. But love? Not likely. He needed some space to think about this. How soon could he ask her to go home for the night? Guess she'd want to eat dinner first, though the way she was pushing the food around with her fork she wasn't so keen any more. 'Chicken not your favourite food?'

'I eat more chicken than anything.' She finally took a mouthful, but instead of her eyes lighting up she was thoughtful as she chewed. Swallowing, she asked, 'Do we have a problem? Would you like me to leave?'

Yes. No. 'Not really.' Damn it. 'Sorry. Please stay. For a while at least. I'd like to get to know you better and I can't do that if you're back at Kat's flat.' He'd taken a risk, but he had to learn more about her. Had to.

Her smile was wobbly. 'You want to know more about me? You are hard up for entertainment.'

Another diverting answer, but he wasn't going to be fobbed off any more. He'd start with something innocuous. 'What sort of books do you read?'

'Suspense and thrillers. The darker the better. You?'

'I'm more into autobiographies, especially of people who battle the odds to achieve their goals. Solo round-the-world sailors, mountain climbers, those kinds of people.' Definitely not dark, but it was staggering what a person could achieve if he was determined enough.

Her mouth curved deliciously. 'You're not a suppressed endurance man who wants to battle the odds, are you?'

He shuddered. 'Definitely not. I've got too much respect for my limbs to go off doing something that crazy. Quite happy to read about others' exploits, but that's as far as I go.'

'That's a relief. For a moment there I got worried. Think of that guy who recently tried to kayak from Australia to New Zealand. It must've been incredibly hard for his wife to have to wait for him to make it safe and sound.'

But you're not my partner, so why would you be worried? 'That's why I won't be letting Adam do anything remotely dangerous until he's old and decrepit.'

He leaned back in his chair as the tension eased out

of him. They were back on safe ground and suddenly he didn't want to ask even about the weather in case he put her on edge again. He enjoyed her company too much to chance her leaving early.

'Good luck with that.' She chuckled.

Unfortunately, Ally was referring to Adam. Or so he thought until Ally came around to stand by him, putting a finger on his chin, pressuring him to look at her. She bent to kiss him, softly, sweetly, and still the passion came through fiery and urgent.

At last they'd moved past that earlier little conundrum. The last thing he wanted was to watch Ally walk out the front door tonight. The only place he wanted to be with her was in his bed, making love, tangling the sheets around their legs and holding her so close they'd be as one. He returned her kiss, hard and fierce, trying to convey his need for her.

When she stepped back her eyes were slumberous and that hazel colour had darkened. How soon could he insist Adam go to bed? Because they'd be heading down the hall the moment his son closed his eyes.

Tonight he'd make up for sleeping alone last night. He'd pleasure Ally so much she'd never contemplate a night without him again while she was on the island. Hopefully then this crazy, wonderful desire for her might calm down enough for him to make rational decisions about where they were going with their fling. Ally's word, not his.

Though maybe a fling was still all he needed, and the fact that sex had become alien to him over the last two years could be the answer to why he was reacting like a teenager who'd finally discovered sex.

Ally nudged him in his side. 'Can I read Adam's stories tonight?'

Adam shrieked, 'Yes.'

Flynn spanked her gently on the bottom. 'Anything to get out of doing the dishes.'

She wriggled her butt under his hand. 'Just speeding up the process.'

Of course, Adam had no intention of settling down and going to sleep after only one story. He must've caught the vibes playing between Flynn and Ally because he was wide-awake. 'He's hyper. Unusual for him,' Flynn muttered to Ally when he looked in to see what the delay was.

'It's all right. We're having fun.'

'I'll make coffee, then.' *Go to sleep, Adam. Please, please. Oh, damn it, just go to sleep. I'm going to explode with need any minute.*

He listened as Ally read on, and on, and on. And told himself off for wanting to deny Adam his time with her. Adam came first. First.

Finally, an hour later than he'd hoped, Flynn swung Ally up into his arms and carried her to his bedroom, locking the door behind them. He stood her on her feet and leaned in to kiss that mouth that had been teasing him all night. 'At last.'

Ally already had her shirt over her head, and was pushing those magnificent breasts into his hands. 'You talk too much.'

So he shut up and showed her how much he wanted her, and gave her everything he had.

CHAPTER EIGHT

THE DAYS FLEW by but the nights went even faster. Ally had never known a placement to be so engaging. Was that entirely down to Flynn? Yes, if she was being honest, Flynn owned it—made her dizzy with excitement, warmed her with everyday fun and laughter, distracted her to the point she caught herself wondering how hard it would be to stop in one place for ever.

These heady days hinted at what her childhood dreams had been made of—someone to love her unconditionally for the rest of her life, someone she could give her heart to and not have it returned when the gloss rubbed off. But reality had taught her differently. The only difference now was that she chose where she moved to, and not some overworked, underpaid bleeding heart sitting behind a desk in a dimly lit welfare office. She was no longer a charity case.

Unfortunately, a reality check didn't slow her enthusiasm for all things Flynn. Her body ached in every muscle, her lips were sore from smiling too much, her eyes were heavy from lack of sleep. But would she wish for quiet nights at Kat's flat with only her music and a book for company? No. Not even knowing that the day of reckoning was approaching made her want to change a thing.

The complete opposite, in fact. She found herself needing to grab at more and more time with Flynn.

'Hey,' Flynn called as he walked past the medical storeroom. Then he was in there with her, sucking up all the oxygen and leaving her light-headed. When he traced her chin with his forefinger she caught it and licked the tip, delighting in the sound of his quickly indrawn breath. 'This room's never been so exciting.'

'Are we all set for tonight?' she asked.

'The table's booked at the restaurant. The babysitter's organised. The warning's gone out that no one on Phillip Island is to have an accident.' He ticked the points off his fingers. 'I've put clean sheets on the bed and bought more condoms since we must've used up your supply.'

Her giggle was immature, but that's how she reacted these days. She was always laughing or coming out with mixed-up, stupid things. 'I go to the supermarket on a regular basis.'

'I was beginning to wonder why you had so many.' He grinned, looking as loony as she felt.

'Everyone on the island must be talking about us by now. In fact, the women are probably giving their men a hard time about how many condoms we're getting through.' She didn't care at all. Every night she raced home to change into something relaxed and less midwife-like, touch up her make-up and put the washing on, then drove around to Flynn's house. She wasn't tired of him at all.

Flynn grinned. 'I'm sure they've all got better things to do than talk about their GP and the midwife.'

'I hope so.' Her heart lurched. That grin always got her behind the knees, making her nearly pitch forward onto her face. For a casual fling Flynn was breaking all the rules and turning her to mush, making her heart skip when no one had done that to her before. 'Does Giuseppe know we're returning to his restaurant?'

'I spoke to him earlier. He's planning a special meal for us. Unless there's something you don't like to eat, we are to sit back and let the courses come.'

'Sounds wonderful.' She planned on wearing a dress tonight, a short black number that she'd found in one of the local shops during her lunch break yesterday. It looked fantastic with her knee-high boots and black patterned stockings. She wouldn't be wearing anything else, bras and knickers being expendable.

'Are you two going to spend the day in that room?' Faye muttered loudly as she stomped past the door. 'There are patients waiting for both of you.'

Guilt had Ally leaping back from Flynn. 'Onto it,' she called out. 'Seriously, Doctor, you should know better than to kiss the nurse at work.'

'I'll do it out in the open next time.' His finger flicked her chin lightly. 'I'll pick you up at seven thirty.'

'I can't wait.' It was true. She'd see him on and off all day and yet she felt desperate to be with him, just the two of them sharing a meal in a restaurant, no interruptions from Adam or the phone or Sheba.

Uh-oh. What was happening? This was starting to feel way wrong. Keep this up and she'd have difficulty leaving at the end of her contract.

'Ally,' Megan called urgently from the office. 'Ally, you're needed. Lisa Shaw's on the line, her waters have broken.'

Now, that was reality. 'Coming.' She picked up her medical bag and dashed to the office, Flynn sent to the back of her mind only to be brought back out when she wasn't helping a baby into the world. This was the real stuff her life was about. The grounded, helping-others kind of thing that gave her the warm fuzzies without asking anything of her heart.

'I'm going to be late.' Ally phoned Flynn at five o'clock when it became obvious Baby Shaw had no intention of hurrying up for anyone, least of all so his mother's midwife could go out to dinner with the local GP. 'I have no idea when Ashton will make his entry. Lisa's contractions slowed nearly two hours ago and so far don't look like speeding up.' Not very medically technical terminology, but he'd get the gist.

'You can't hurry babies.' Disappointment laced Flynn's words. 'Is it selfish to wish Lisa hadn't wanted a home birth?'

'Yes, it is. I'd better go. I'll call you when I know if we're still on for our date.'

An image of that black dress hanging on the wardrobe door flicked across her mind, and she had to suppress a groan.

Lisa was the only person allowed to groan around here, which she was doing with deep intensity right this moment. Scott held her as she draped her pain-ridden body against him and gritted her teeth.

Ally rubbed Lisa's back. 'You're doing great. Seriously.'

'I have no choice, do I?' Lisa snapped. 'Next time I have a dumb idea that having a baby would be wonderful, tell me to take a hike.' She glared at Scott. 'Or you have it.'

Scott kissed her forehead and wisely refrained from commenting.

Ally went for diversion. 'How long have you been married?'

'Two years,' Lisa ground out.

'We've been wanting a baby right from the beginning.' Scott grinned. 'Couldn't get it right.'

Ally chuckled. 'Babies are control freaks. They get conceived when it suits them, arrive when they choose, and they've hardly started. But you know what? They're wonderful.'

Under her hand Lisa's shoulders tensed as she yelled out in the pain of the next contraction.

'Lisa, breathe that gas in. You're doing brilliantly.'

The next hour passed slowly. Ally took observations regularly, noting them on Lisa's chart, occasionally going for a walk to the letterbox and back to give the couple a few moments alone, then returning to give Lisa more encouragement. Six o'clock clicked over on her watch. *There goes dinner with Flynn.* Even if Baby Ashton miraculously popped out right then, she'd be needed for a time. Guilt hovered in her head. Never before had she cared how long the birthing process took, she just loved being there with the mums, dads and their babies. But now she loved being with Flynn, too.

Her head jerked up. Loved being with him? Or loved Flynn, full stop?

'Ally, come quick. Lisa's pushing,' Scott called down the hall.

Good, focus on what's important. 'That's good, but we could be a while yet.' Though for Lisa's sake she hoped not. She was exhausted.

Examining her, Ally was happy to announce, 'Baby's crowning. When the urge to push comes, go with it. Don't try to hold back.'

'It's too damn painful to push,' Lisa yelled.

'Come on, Lisa. He's got to come out of there.' Scott reached for Lisa's hand and grimaced as she gripped him.

'Easy for you to say,' his wife snarled.

Ally had heard it all before. 'As soon as Ashton makes his appearance, you two will forget everything but your beautiful little boy.' This parenthood thing was awesome. Babies were amazing, so cute and vulnerable and yet bonding their parents in a way nothing else could.

Why hadn't her mother felt like that about her? Was her mother a freak? She was definitely the reason Ally would never have her own baby. What if the don't-love-your-own-baby gene was hereditary? There was no way on earth she'd chance having a child, only to dump her into the welfare system and disappear. And even if she did love her baby—which she was sure she would despite her past—she didn't know the first about raising one, about providing all the things a child needed, including loads of love. Her experience of babies stopped once she knew they were able to feed from mum's breast.

'Ally, I think he's coming,' Lisa broke into her thoughts, brought her back to the here and now, away from the daydreams of someone who should know better.

When Ashton slid into her hands, Ally felt tears prick her eyelids. 'Wow, look, Scott, he's lovely.' She lifted him to meet his parents. Her knees were shaky and her heartbeat erratic. 'He's the most beautiful baby I've seen.'

'Of course he is,' Scott whispered.

All babies were. She'd reacted the same way at that very first birth that had started her on the path to becoming a midwife. *Thank you, wee Lloyd, wherever you are now. Not so wee any more, I guess.* Mopping her eyes with her arm, she cleaned the mucus from Ashton and placed him on Lisa's breast.

Flynn picked her up a little after eight. She was tired and exultant. 'Another little baby safely delivered and in good hands.' She clicked her seat belt into place. 'Do you remember when you first held Adam?' That hadn't exactly changed the subject, had it? Darn.

'Everything about him—his scrunched-up face, his red skin, spiky black hair and ear-shattering cry. He hasn't changed much.' Flynn smiled with a far-away look in his eye.

'His face isn't red.' The love in Flynn's voice brought tears to her eyes and she had to look out the window at the houses they were passing until she got herself back under control. It was too easy to picture Flynn carefully cradling Adam wrapped in a blanket, like he was made of something so fragile he'd break at the slightest pressure. *I want that. No. I don't. I can't have it. It would be wrong for everyone.*

'Ally? Where've you gone?'

Suck it up, play the game. You know how to. 'I'm thinking pasta and garlic and tomatoes. It's been a long day and I forgot to buy my lunch on the way to work so missed out what with Baby Ashton stealing the show.'

'I'm sure Giuseppe will fix what's ailing you.' Flynn pulled up outside the restaurant.

'Good.' Pity there was no cure for what really troubled her. She could not, would not get too involved. Flynn had been hurt badly with Anna's death. So had Adam. She couldn't risk hurting them again. Forget involvement being a risk; hurting them would be a certainty. She was clueless in the happy-families stakes, and they so didn't deserve or need to be hurt by her. She shoved the door wide before Flynn had a chance to come round to open it for her. 'Let's go and have the night of our lives.'

'Ally.' Flynn's hand on her arm stayed her. 'You look absolutely beautiful tonight. More beautiful, I mean.'

'Thank you.' Her heart rolled. Talk about making everything harder. 'I went shopping yesterday.'

'I'm not talking about the dress, though you look stunning in it. It fits you like a second skin, accentuates all those curves I love touching.' He hesitated, breathed deep. 'But it's you that's beautiful—from the inside out.'

Nothing could've made her move at that moment if she'd tried. His words had stolen the breath out of her, liquefied her muscles, making them soft and useless. She was supposed to be having dinner with Flynn and then going back to his house and bed. He was not meant to be saying things that undermined her determination to stick to her rules—no deep, attaching involvement.

'Ally? Did I go too far?'

Yes, you did. Way too far. You're frightening me. Forcing a smile, she laid her hand over his. 'Thank you. That was a lovely compliment.'

'A heartfelt one. Now, let's enjoy ourselves and I'll stop the sentimental stuff since it seems to be upsetting you.' He hopped out of the car and strode around the front to her side.

She'd let him down. But what was a girl supposed to do? She couldn't take in what he'd said and start believing. That would be dangerous, but at the same time she couldn't walk away from Flynn tonight, or tomorrow, or any time during the next two weeks. No, she couldn't. Pushing out of the car, she laced her fingers through his and walked up the path to the welcoming door of the restaurant. 'I see the tide's farther in tonight. We won't be having our wicked way on the beach.'

Grinning, Flynn held the door wide and ushered her inside, whispering as she passed, 'You give up too easily.'

Did she? 'I'm not going to ask what's on your mind. I want to eat first.' She ran a hand over his delectable butt before turning to follow the same young waiter they'd had last week.

Giuseppe was there before they'd sat down. 'Welcome back, Ally. I'm glad you enjoyed our food enough to return.'

'Come on, Giuseppe, how could I not?' She kissed her fingertips. 'That carbonara was superb.'

'The carbonara or the company you were keeping?' the older man asked with a twinkle in his eye. 'By the way, you might be wanting this.' He held up the half-full bottle of Merlot they'd left on the beach.

Flynn laughed loudly. 'You old rascal. Who found that?'

'I go for a walk along the beach every night after I close the door for the last time.' Giuseppe kept the bottle in his hand.

Uh-oh. What time had he closed the restaurant last Friday? Ally glanced across at Flynn, saw the same question register in his eyes. Had Giuseppe seen them making out? She croaked out, 'Thank you. It seemed a waste not to have finished a good wine.'

Giuseppe nodded, his eyes still twinkling, leaving her still wondering what he'd seen, as he said, 'Tonight you will try something different. Something I recommend to match the meal I have arranged. This half-finished one you can take with you when you leave.'

Ally watched as he walked away, pausing at other tables to have a word with his guests. 'Do you think he knows?'

'That we made love on the beach? Yes, I suspect he does.' Flynn reached across and took her hand in both his. 'You know what? I couldn't care less.'

'Then neither do I.' And she wouldn't worry about anything else tonight either.

The meal was beyond superb and the wine excellent. The company even better. Flynn made her laugh with stories from his training days and she told him about going to school as an adult. It was a night she'd remember for a long time. It was intimate, almost as though they had a future, and she refused to let those bleak thoughts refuting that spoil anything.

'Here.' She twined her arm around Flynn's, their glasses in their hands. 'To a hot night under the stars. Tide in or out.'

Flynn smiled, a deep smile that turned her stomach to mush and her heart to squeezing. 'To a wonderful night under the bright stars with a special lady.'

But when they stepped outside there were no stars. A heavy drizzle had dampened everything and was getting heavier by the minute. 'You forgot to order the weather.' Ally nudged Flynn as they hurried to the car.

'Never said I was perfect.' He held the car door while she bundled inside.

No, but he wasn't far off. Leaning over, she opened his door to save him a moment in the rain. 'How long will it take you to drop off the babysitter?'

'Ten minutes.'

'That long?'

'You can warm the bed while I'm away.' Flynn laid a hand on her thigh. 'Believe me, I'll be going as fast as allowed.'

Heat raced up her thigh to swirl around the apex between her legs, melting her. 'Pull over.'

'What? Now? Here?' The car was already slowing.

'Right now and here.' She was tugging at his zip. Under her palm his reaction to her move was more than obvious.

'I haven't done it in a car since I was at high school.'

'Hope you can still move your bones, you old man.'

He growled as he nibbled the skin at her cleavage. 'Just wait and learn.' His hand covered her centre, his fingers did things that blanked out all the doubts and yearnings in her mind and made her cry with need, followed with release.

Flynn rolled onto his side, his arm under his head and his gaze fixed on the beautiful woman sleeping beside him. He was addicted to Ally Parker. There was no other word for what he felt. Addiction. He'd never known such craving before. The more he had of her, the more he wanted. His need was insatiable. If it wasn't so damned exciting it would be frightening. Frightening because it was filled with pitfalls.

He'd loved Anna beyond reason and had still failed her. If he hadn't been so damned determined to follow his career the way he'd wanted it she wouldn't have been in Melbourne that day and the accident wouldn't have happened. If he'd listened to her wishes, instead paying them lip service, his boy would still have his mother. That, more than anything, he could never forgive himself for. Every child deserved two parents, and especially their mother, to nurture them as they grew up.

And this had what to do with Ally? Ally already enjoyed being with Adam, didn't treat him as a pawn to get to his father but rather as an individual in his own right. She'd nurture and mother Adam if they got together.

A chill lifted goose bumps on his skin. He withdrew his arm and rolled onto his back to stare at the ceiling. They could not get together. Firstly, Ally didn't do settling down. That was so clear he'd be a fool not to acknowledge it.

He glanced across at her sleeping form. 'What happened that you can't stop in one place for more than a few weeks? Who hurt you so badly that you're prepared to miss out on what life's all about?' he whispered. 'Someone other than your mother?' That would be enough to knock anyone sideways for ever. But he had this niggling feeling he hadn't heard it all.

As the chill lifted and his skin warmed back to normal he ran a hand over her hair, rubbed a strand between his fingers. 'I would never hurt you, let you down.'

Huh? Hadn't he just reminded himself of how badly he'd let Anna down? Yep. And Adam. Adam. The crux of the matter. He'd do anything for his son. Anything. Which meant not getting too close to Ally, not seeking the answers to those questions in case they drove him on to making her happy, not sharing his life with her.

Ally rolled over, blinked open her eyes and smiled in a just woken up and still sleepy way. 'Hi,' she whispered.

'Hi, yourself.' He leaned in to place a light kiss on her brow, then her cheek, her chin, her lips. Two weeks. *Make the most of them. Stop analysing the situation and enjoy what's left.*

As he reached for her, the door flew open.

'Dad. Why was the door shut?' Adam shouted, loud enough for the whole island to hear as he pushed it wide.

'Good morning to you, too.' Flynn smiled and pulled the bedcovers up to Ally's chin. 'Hope you're okay with this,' he whispered to her. 'I forgot to relock the door after I went to the bathroom.'

'Not a problem, unless he wants to get in here with us,' she whispered back. 'Hello, Adam. How long have you been awake?'

'A long time. I've been watching cartoons.' Adam started to climb onto the bed.

Hell, Ally was buck naked. Adam was used to seeing him in the nude, but not a woman. 'Adam, can you pass Ally my robe? She's getting cold.'

'She should wear pyjamas to bed.'

How did Adam know she hadn't? Distraction needed. 'Let's have pancakes for breakfast.' That'd get his attention, pancakes being his all-time favourite breakfast food. *Unhealthy. Tough.*

'Ally, are you coming for a sleepover every night now?'

Flynn mentally threw his hands into the air. If pancakes didn't work, then he had to get serious. 'Adam, go out to the lounge while we get up.'

Ally shook her head as though trying to make sense of everything. 'Sometimes when it's late I don't go home, but not every night. I've got my own place to go to.'

Adam nodded. 'I thought so. But if you want to stay every night we don't mind, do we, Dad?'

Which part of 'Go out to the lounge' hadn't he got? 'I guess not. Adam, we want to get up.'

'Okay. Are we having maple syrup and bacon on the pancakes?' Adam didn't look like he had any intention of moving this side of Christmas.

'We won't be having pancakes at all if you don't leave us.'

Under the covers Ally touched his thigh and squeezed it. 'Bacon, syrup *and* bananas. But I want to shower first and the longer we lie around, talking, the longer we're going to wait for our yummy breakfast.'

Adam nodded again. Where had this new habit come from? 'I'll get everything ready.'

'Great. See you out there soon.' Ally nodded back

with a smile. 'But promise me you won't start cooking anything.'

'I don't know how to mix the flour and stuff.'

As Adam ran out of the room Flynn stared after him. 'He listens to you.'

'I'm a novelty. You're Dad.' Her hand stroked where a moment ago it had been squeezing.

'Keep that up and breakfast will be postponed for hours.'

She instantly removed her hand. Damn it. 'Hours? Talk about bragging.' She grinned at him. Then slid out of bed and wrapped herself in the too-large robe. 'I'm going to look so good sitting down to breakfast in my little black dress. Why didn't I think to bring a change of clothes?'

'You should leave a set here for the morning after.'

'If I did that, I wouldn't have many clothes left at the flat.'

She travelled light. Very light. 'Go shopping. Get some gear to keep here. In the meantime...' he swung his legs over the side of the bed, dug into his drawers for a sweat-shirt and pair of trackpants '...try these for size.'

'I already know they'll be too long and loose around the waist, but my hips might hold them up.' She took the clothes and hugged them to her breasts. 'Who's first in the shower?'

'You go. I'll keep an eye on proceedings in the kitchen. Today could be the day Adam decides to try mixing the batter and that would be messy, not to mention uncook-able.'

'You're not fair. He's got to have a go at these things. How else is he going to learn to look out for himself?'

'But it's so much quicker to do everything myself.'

Her face tightened and her chin lifted. 'In the long run

you'll save heaps of time because Adam will be able to do these things for both of you.'

Ouch. She'd gone from Fun Ally to Serious Ally in an instant. She'd also had the nerve to tell him how his parenting sucked. 'Go and have that shower,' he ground out through clenched teeth.

He didn't want to start an argument by saying she should leave this to him, but it had nothing to do with her. Even if she might be right, Ally wasn't the one constantly working with a time deficit.

For a moment she stood there, staring at him. Was she holding back a retort, too? Or formulating a whole load more criticisms? Or, heaven forbid, was she about to explain why she felt so strongly about his son learning to cook?

Not likely. She'd never do that. Ally was a closed book when it came to herself. Except for that one time of sharing her past hurts, what drove her, and what held her back, her past was still blurred. He needed to remember that—all the time. But right this minute he had to get back onside with her. They were spoiling what had been a wonderful night and should be a great day ahead. 'Ally, please, go and get cleaned up. Let's not waste the morning arguing.'

Her eyes widened. Then her stance softened, her shoulders relaxed. 'You're right. We've got pancakes and a morning at the wildlife centre to enjoy. And we'll need to stop at the flat on the way so I can put on some proper clothes.'

He'd dodged a slam dunk. 'Proper clothes? Since when weren't trackies and a sweatshirt proper?'

'Since fashion became important. In other words,

since the first time a woman put on an animal hide.' She grinned and his world returned to normal.

His new normal. The one with Ally Parker in it. The normal that would expire in two weeks' time.

CHAPTER NINE

TUESDAY, AND ALLY parked outside the bakery just as her phone vibrated in her pocket. 'Hello?'

'It's Marie. I'm in labour.'

Her due date was in three weeks, but technically speaking Marie wasn't having her baby too early. Two weeks before due date was considered normal and nothing to be concerned about. 'I'm on my way. After I examine you we'll arrange to get you over to the mainland and hospital.'

'I doubt I'm going anywhere. The contractions are already coming fast.' Marie's voice rose with every word. 'Hurry, will you?'

'On my way. Try to relax. I know, easy for me to say, but concentrate on your breathing and time the contractions.' Great. The last thing Marie had said to her was that she never wanted to have a home birth. A friend of hers had had one last year and there'd been complications that had nearly cost the baby her life.

With a wistful glance at the bakery she jammed the gearshift in Reverse and backed out into the street.

Adam opened the door the moment she parked in Marie's driveway. 'Ally, Marie's got a tummyache. She's holding it tight.'

Adam was there. Of course he was. It was a weekday.

He wasn't going to be anywhere else in the afternoon. 'Does Flynn know you've gone into labour?' she asked Marie the moment she stepped inside.

'No. I needed a midwife, not a doctor.' Marie glanced in the direction Ally was looking. 'Oh, Adam. He'll be fine. Anyway, what can Flynn do? Take Adam to the surgery for the rest of the day?'

'Surely Flynn's got someone he can ask to look after him?'

Marie's face contorted as a contraction gripped her. She held on to the back of a chair and screwed her eyes shut.

'Breathe deep. That's it. You're doing good.' Ally stepped close to rub her back and mutter inane comments until the contraction passed. Then she got down to business. 'Let's go to your bedroom so I can examine you. Adam, sweetheart, Marie is having her baby so I want you to be very good for her. Okay?'

'She's having a baby? Really? Why does it hurt her?' His little eyes were wide.

'It's baby's way of letting everyone know it's coming.'

'Can I tell Dad?'

'Soon. I'm going with Marie to her bedroom.' His eyes filled with expectancy and she quickly stomped on those ideas. 'I want you to help me by getting things I need, like water or cushions or towels. But not until I ask you, all right?'

'Yes, I'll be good. Can I bring them into the bedroom?'

'No, leave them outside the door.' Hopefully Marie was wrong about her baby coming quickly and she'd soon be on her way to hospital. 'Why don't you watch TV until I call you?'

'I want to help.'

'I know, but first I have to check the baby, then I'll

know what you can do for us.' If Marie was heading to hospital she'd drop Adam off at the medical centre. Flynn would sort out childminding. He must have made alternative arrangements for this eventuality.

Adam's mouth did a downturn, but he trotted off to the lounge and flicked on the TV.

'Thank you, Adam,' she called, before hurrying to Marie's bedroom and closing the door behind her. 'Have you called your husband?'

Tears welled up in Marie's eyes. 'My call went straight to voice mail. He's at sea on the fishing boat. This wasn't supposed to happen. He's booked leave for when the baby's due. He can't get here for days,' she wailed.

Ally gave her a hug and a smile. 'Well, in the meantime it's you and me. Unless you've got a close friend you'd like here, or family?' Someone familiar would make things work more smoothly.

'My family all live on the mainland and my girlfriend would be hopeless. Faints if there's the hint of blood or anyone's in pain.' Marie sank onto the bed as another contraction gripped her. 'I don't think I'm going anywhere. These contractions are coming too fast. I seriously doubt I've got time to get to the hospital.' Her voice was strained.

Ally glanced at her watch. She'd already begun timing the contractions. 'Four minutes. You're right, they're close.' She held Marie's hand until the current contraction passed. 'If you lie down I'll see what's going on.'

Marie flopped back onto the bed. 'I feel this pushing sensation, but I don't want a home birth. What if something goes wrong?'

'We have doctors only five minutes away. But you're jumping the gun. Baby might just pop out.' Ally mentally crossed her fingers as she snapped on vinyl gloves and helped Marie out of her panties. She wasn't surprised at the measurement she obtained. 'You're ten centimetres, fully dilated, so, yes, baby's on its way.' She calmly told her patient, 'Sorry, Marie, but hospital's definitely out. There isn't time.'

Marie's face paled and her teeth dug deep into her bottom lip. The eyes she lifted to Ally were dark with worry.

'Hey.' Ally wrapped an arm around her shoulders. 'You're going to be fine. I'll phone the surgery to tell them what's going on.' One of the doctors would be on notice to drop everything and rush here if anything went wrong.

'Sorry, I'm not good at this.' A flood of tears wet her cheeks.

'Find me a mother who is. This is all new to you. Believe me, no one pops their baby out and carries on as though nothing has happened. It's an emotional time, for one. And tiring, for another.' She sat beside Marie. 'Take it one contraction at a time. You've done really well so far. I mean it.'

Marie gripped Ally's hands and crushed her fingers as another contraction ripped through her.

'Breathe, one, two, three.' Finally getting her hands back and able to flex her fingers to bring the circulation back, Ally said, 'I'll get the gas for you to suck on. It'll help with the pain.'

'That sounds good. But I do need to push.'

'Try to hold off until I'm back. Promise I'll hurry.' She dashed out of the room and nearly ran Adam down in the hallway. 'Oops, sorry, sweetheart, I didn't see you there.'

'Is the baby here yet?'

'No.' But it wasn't too far away. 'Can you fill two beakers with water and leave them outside the door?'

She had no idea if Marie wanted one, but giving Adam something to do was important.

His little shoulders pulled back as pride filtered through his eyes. 'I'll put them on a tray, like Dad does sometimes.'

'Good boy.' Out at the car she dug her phone out of her pocket and called the medical centre. 'Megan, it's Ally. Can you put me through to Flynn?'

'He's with a very distressed patient and said not to be interrupted unless it was an emergency.'

Define emergency. She guessed a baby arriving early didn't quite fit. 'When it's possible, will you let him know that I'm with Marie and she's having her baby at home? There isn't time to transfer her to hospital. Also mention it to Faye and Jerome in case I need help.'

'That's early. Tell her good luck from me. When Flynn's free I'll talk to him, but I suspect he's going to be a while. His patient is really on the edge.'

'Thanks, Megan, that'd be great.' She cut the receptionist off. Marie needed her. She gathered up the nitrous oxide tank, a bag of towels and another bag full of things she'd need.

'I'm still getting the water,' Adam called as she closed the front door.

'Good boy.' Back in the bedroom the temperature had dropped a degree or two. Sundown was hours away, but outside she'd noticed clouds gathering on the horizon. 'Marie, how are you doing?'

'Okay, I guess.'

'Here, suck on this whenever the pain gets bad.' Ally handed over the tube leading from the nitrous oxide tank. 'Have you got a heater we could use? I don't want baby arriving into a cold room, and I'd prefer to warm these towels as well.'

'There's an oil column one in the laundry. Adam knows where it is and can push it along on its wheels. It'll be perfect for what you're wanting.'

'Onto it.'

Outside the door Adam was placing the beakers ever so carefully on a tray he'd put on the floor earlier. 'Can you bring me the heater out of the laundry? Or do you want me to help?'

'I can do it. Do I have to leave it out here?'

'Yes, please.'

His little shoulders slumped. 'Why can't I see Marie?'

Ally knelt down and took his small hands in hers. 'When women have babies they don't like lots of people with them, watching what's happening. They get shy.'

'Why?'

'Because having a baby is private, and sometimes it hurts, and Marie wouldn't want you to see her upset.' *Sometimes it hurts?* Understatement of the century.

'No, she only likes me to see her laughing. I'll knock when I've got the heater.'

For a four-year-old, Adam was amazingly together about things. Nothing fazed him. But then he had lost his mother so he wasn't immune to distress, had probably learned a lot in his short life. He coped better than she did. He did have a great dad onside. 'Then you can play with all those toys I saw in a big box in the lounge.'

'But I like playing outside. Marie always lets me.'

'Today's different. I need you to play inside today, Adam.' She held up a finger. 'Promise me you won't go outside at all.'

'Promise, Ally.'

Her heartstrings tugged. What a guy. As she gave him a hug a groan sounded from inside the bedroom. 'You're a champ, you know that?' Now, please go away.

'What's a champ?' Adam didn't seem to have heard Marie.

'The best person there is.' The groan was going on and on. 'I've got to see Marie.' *Please, go away so you don't hear this.* Nothing was wrong but that deep, growling groan might frighten him, or at least upset him.

Thankfully Adam had his father's sensitivity and recognised a hint when it came. He raced down the hall towards the laundry and Ally let herself back into the bedroom.

'Hey, how's it going?' The pain on Marie's scrunched-up face was all the answer she needed. 'Feel like pushing some more, I take it.'

'How can you be so cheerful?'

So they were at the yell-at-anyone stage. 'Because you're having a baby and soon you'll forget all this as you hold him for the first time. Can you lie back so I can examine you again?'

'Examine, examine—that's all you do.' But Marie did as asked.

Kneeling on the floor, she gently lifted Marie's robe. 'The crown's further exposed. Baby's definitely on its way.' She stood up and dropped the gloves into a waste bag. 'Have you tried to get hold of your husband again?'

'His name's Mark and, no, I haven't. He's not going to answer if he's on deck, hauling in nets. They don't have time.' Tears tracked down her face. 'Anyway, I want him here, not on the end of a phone.'

Ally picked up Marie's phone. 'How do we get hold of him? Can we talk to his captain?'

Marie stared at her like she'd gone completely nuts. Then she muttered, 'Why didn't I think of that?'

'Because you're having a baby, that's why.' Ally handed her the phone. 'Go on. Try every contact you've got.'

Just then another contraction struck and Marie began pushing like her life depended on it, all thoughts of phone calls gone.

'That's it. You're doing well.' Ally again knelt at the end of the bed, watching the crown of the baby as it slipped a little farther out into the world.

Knock-knock. 'I got the heater,' Adam called.

'Thank you. Now you can play with those toys.' She gave him a minute to walk away before opening the door and bringing the heater in. Plugging it in, she switched it on and laid two towels on top of the columns to warm for baby.

'Hello?' Marie yelled at someone on her phone. 'It's Marie, Mark's wife. I can't get hold of him and I'm having our baby. I need to talk to him.'

Ally held her hand up, whispered, 'Slow down, give the guy a chance to say something.'

Marie glared at her but stopped shouting long enough to hear a reply. 'Thank you so much. Can you hurry? Tell Mark to phone back on the landline so I can put him on speaker.' A moment later she tossed the phone aside, grabbed the edges of the bed and pushed again.

The phone rang almost immediately. Ally answered, 'Hey, is that Mark? This is Ally, Marie's midwife.'

'Hello, yes, this is Mark. What's up? Is she all right? The baby's not due for weeks.'

'Marie's fine. You can be proud of how she's handling this. Baby has decided today's as good as any to arrive.'

Marie snatched the phone out of her hand and yelled, 'Why aren't you here with me? I need you right now.' Then she had to drop it and clutch her belly.

Ally pressed the speaker button and Mark's voice filled the room. 'Hey, babe, you know I'd be there if I'd thought this would happen. How're you doing? Come on, babe, talk to me, tell me what's going on.'

'I'm having a baby, and it hurts like hell. It's nearly here and I can't talk any more. I've got to push.'

'Babe, I'm listening. Imagine me holding you against my chest like I did when you dislocated your shoulder. Feel my hands on your back, rubbing soft circles, whispering how much I love you in your cute little ear. Can you feel me there with you?'

Ally tried to block out this very personal conversation, pretend she was deaf, but those words of love touched her, taunted her. These two had a beautiful relationship. If Mark was a deep-sea fisherman, he was no softy, would definitely be a tough guy, and yet here he was speaking his heart to his wife when she needed him so much.

Marie cried out with pain, and pushed and pushed.

'Hey, babe, you're doing great. I know you are. You're a star. I'm not going anywhere until you have our little nipper in your arms, okay?'

Ally blinked back a tear and slipped out the door for a moment to get herself sorted. It wouldn't do for the midwife to have a meltdown in the middle of a birth. Not that that had ever happened but Marie's birth was affecting her deeply, more so than any other she'd attended. Leaning back against the wall, she took deep breaths to get her heart and head under control. *What was it like to have a man love you that much?* She could take a chance with a man like that. Even if she screwed up he'd be there to help her back onto her feet.

I want what Marie's got. Shivers ran through her and her skin lifted in goose-bumps. *No. I can't, don't, won't.*

Straightening up, she slapped away the tears and returned to her patient. Marie was still talking to Mark and didn't seem to notice her return. Had she seen her leave?

Then Marie was pushing again and this time there was no relief. Baby was coming and Ally prepared for it. 'The head's out. Here come the shoulders. That's it. Nice and gentle now.' She spoke louder so Mark could hear everything. Her hands were under the baby's head, ready for any sudden rush as the baby slid out into its new world. And then, 'Here he is, a beautiful boy. Oh, he's a sweetheart.'

Her heart stuttered. She'd called Adam a sweetheart earlier. It was one thing to say that about a baby she wouldn't be seeing much of, but Adam? He was wriggling into her heart without trying and soon she'd have to say goodbye.

'Can I hold him?' Marie asked impatiently, reaching out.

'In a moment. The APGAR score's normal.' Ally gently wiped away vernix, mucus and blood spots from his sweet little face.

'Give him to me, give him to me. Mark, we've got a boy. He's gorgeous. Looks like his dad.'

Ally rolled her eyes as she placed the baby on Marie's swollen breasts. 'I need him back in a moment to weigh him.'

Mark was yelling out to his crewmates, 'It's a boy. I'm a dad.' And then he was crying. 'Wish I was with you, babe. Tell me everything, every last detail. Are we still going to name him Jacob?'

'Well, I can't name him after our midwife so I guess so. I think it suits him.' Marie was laughing and crying and drinking in the sight of her son lying over her breast.

'Here comes the placenta.' Ally clamped it and cut the cord. 'I need to examine you once more, then I'll cover you up and let you talk to Mark alone for a bit.' Adam would be getting lonely out in the lounge. She'd make him a bite to eat, poor kid.

Her examination showed a small tear. 'You need a couple of stitches. Nothing major,' she added when worry entered Marie's eyes. 'It often happens in fast deliveries.'

'Right.' Marie went back to talking to Mark, the worry gone already.

Ally quietly went about retaking Jacob's APGAR score. His appearance and complexion were good. Counting his pulse, she tried not to listen in to the conversation going on between Jacob's parents, concentrating on the sweet bundle of new life. Her heart swelled even as a snag of envy caught her again. She could have it all if only she found the right man. Flynn instantly popped up in her head. Losing count, she started taking Jacob's pulse again, this time totally concentrating and pushing a certain someone out of her skull.

'Pulse one hundred and ten. Good.' She flicked lightly on Jacob's fingers, watched as he immediately curled them tight. 'Reflex good, as is his activity.' His little legs were moving slowly against his mother's skin, and she couldn't resist running a finger down one leg. He hadn't done more than give a low gasp but his chest was rising and falling softly. So his respiratory effort was okay. Ally wrote down her obs and then dealt with the tear while Marie carried on talking.

She found Adam in the lounge, despondently pushing a wooden bulldozer around the floor. He leapt up the instant he saw her with the rubbish bag. 'Ally, has the baby come?'

'Yes, and it's a little boy.'

Adam stared up at her. 'Can I see him now?'

'I can't see why not.' She took his hand and walked

down to Marie's room, saying to the new mum, 'You've got your first visitor.' And then her heart squeezed.

Marie was cuddling her precious bundle and trying to put him on the breast. 'I hope Jacob takes to this easily.'

'Don't rush. It takes time to get the hang of it.' She went to help position Jacob.

Marie smiled down at her boy. Then looked up. 'Hello, Adam, want to see Jacob? Come round the bed so you can see his face. Isn't he beautiful?'

'Can I hold him?' Adam hopped from foot to foot and Ally saw the hesitancy in Marie's expression.

'Not today. He's all soft and needs careful holding. But tomorrow you can. He'll be stronger then.'

Adam stood close to Marie and stared at the baby. Slowly he placed one hand very carefully on his tiny arm and stroked it. His mouth widened into a smile. 'Hello, baby.'

Ally's eyes watered up. She'd never forget this moment. Adam's amazement, Marie's love, Jacob so tiny and cute. She'd seen it before, often, but today it was definitely different. Not because she'd begun to see herself in Marie's place, holding her own precious bundle of joy. Definitely not because of that.

She stood there, unable to take her gaze away from the scene, unable to move across to the towels that needed to be put into a bag for the laundry company. Just absorbing everything, as though it was her first delivery. The incredible sense of having been a part of a miracle swamped her. *Could I do this? Give birth myself?* Having a baby wasn't the issue. She'd be fine with that. But everything after the moment she held that baby in her arms—that was the problem. Did she have mothering instincts? Or had she inherited her mother's total lack of interest when it came to her own child, her own flesh and blood?

She couldn't afford to find out. It wouldn't be fair on her baby if she got it wrong.

'Marie, you certainly don't waste time when you decide you're ready to have your baby.' Flynn strode into the room and came to an abrupt halt. 'Adam, what are you doing in here?'

CHAPTER TEN

'DAD!' ADAM JUMPED up and down. 'Marie's got a new baby. I think it hurt her.'

'What?' Flynn spun around, his face horrified, and demanded, 'How does he know that?'

Ally stepped up to him. 'Adam did not see the birth, if that's what you're thinking.'

'Then explain his comment.'

Ally backed away from the anger glittering at her. 'He asked why he couldn't come in here and I said that having a baby is private and sometimes it hurts a little.' She had not done anything wrong.

Marie was staring at Flynn like she'd never met him before. 'For goodness' sake. Do you think either of us would've allowed him in here while I was giving birth? Seriously?'

Flynn shoved a hand through his hair, mussing it up, except this time that didn't turn Ally on one little bit. 'I guess not.'

'Dad, I helped Ally. I got water and the heater.'

Flynn's mouth tightened.

Ally told him, 'Adam left everything outside the door. The closed door.' Why can't he see the pride shining in his son's eyes? She ran a hand over Adam's head. 'My little helper.'

Flynn flinched. 'Sorry for jumping to conclusions, everyone.' He was starting to look a little guilty. 'I never did do anything about making alternative arrangements for this eventuality.' He gave Marie a rueful smile. 'Now can I meet Jacob?'

Reluctantly Marie handed the baby over. 'Only for a minute. I don't like letting him out of my arms.'

Ally watched Flynn's face soften as he peered into the soft blue blanket with its precious bundle, and felt her heart lurch so hard it hurt. There was so much love and wonder in his expression she knew he was seeing Adam the day he'd been born. It was a timely reminder that she didn't have a place in his life.

Spinning around, she shoved the baby's notes at Marie. 'I'll make that coffee I promised.' Like when?

Marie was quick, grabbing her hand to stop her tearing out of the room. Her eyes were full of understanding. 'White with two sugars.' She nodded and let Ally go.

Thank you for not outing me.

Flynn was oblivious anyway, so engrossed in Jacob that it was as though no one else was in the room.

When she returned with three coffees he was reading the notes and only grunted, 'Thanks,' at her. Guess he'd finally worked out where his loyalties truly lay, and they weren't with her.

Ally asked Marie, 'Is there anything you want me to do? Washing? Get some groceries in?'

Flynn answered before Marie could open her mouth. 'No need. Marie's mother will be here soon.'

Marie gaped at him. 'Tell me you didn't phone her.'

Colour crept into Flynn's cheeks and another dash of guilt lowered his eyebrows and darkened his eyes. He was having a bad afternoon. 'With Mark at sea for another week, you need someone here. Who better than your mother?'

'You know the answer to that,' Marie growled. 'Ring her back and tell her to turn around.'

'You don't think this is an opportune time to kiss and make up?' Flynn asked. 'Estelle sounded very excited about the new baby.'

Ally looked from Marie to Flynn. What was going on here? They knew each other well, but for Flynn to be telling Marie to sort her apparent problem with her mother could be stretching things too far. Time for a break from him. Taking Adam's hand, she said, 'Come on, let's get you some food. I bet your tummy's hungry.'

'It's always hungry.'

She glanced at Flynn as she reached the door and tripped. He was staring at her with disappointment in his eyes. 'What?' she demanded in a high-pitched voice.

He shook his head. 'Nothing.'

Hadn't she been telling herself what she and Flynn had going was only a short-term fling? If she needed proof, here it was.

In the kitchen Ally put together enough sandwiches for everyone. She got out plates and placed the food on them. Next she put the kettle on to make hot drinks all round. All the while she was trying to ignore that look she'd seen in Flynn's eyes.

Adam chomped through two sandwiches in record time.

'Slow down or you'll get a tummyache.'

'No, I won't. My tummy's strong.' He banged his glass on the table.

Ally smiled tiredly at the ring of milk around his mouth and ignored the tug at her heart. 'Wipe your face, you grub.'

Flynn strode into the kitchen and picked up one of the sandwiches, munched thoughtfully.

'Dad, can I see the baby again?'

'Of course you can. But be very careful if you touch him. He's only little.' Flynn watched his son run down the hall, a distant gleam in his eyes making Ally wonder what he was thinking. When Adam disappeared into Marie's room he closed the kitchen door and she found out. 'Marie's very happy with how you handled the birth. Said you were calm and reassuring all the time.'

'I'm a midwife, that's what we do. It's in the job description.'

'What I don't condone is my son's presence in the house at the time. He shouldn't have been with Marie from the moment she went into labour. Why couldn't you have gone next door to see if Mrs James could look after him?'

'One, there wasn't a lot of time. Two, as I don't know Mrs James, I'm hardly going to leave a small boy with her. Your small boy at that. You could've arranged for someone to come and collect him. You did get my message?' Two could play this game.

'Why didn't you get Megan to arrange someone?'

'It's not my place to make demands of your receptionist.'

Flynn didn't flinch. 'What was Adam doing while you were occupied with Marie? You weren't keeping a proper eye on him, were you?'

'You know what? Adam isn't my responsibility.' She was repeating herself, but somehow she had to get through that thick skull. Except she suspected she was wasting her time. Maybe shouting at him might make him listen. But as she opened her mouth her annoyance faded. She didn't want to fight with him.

'But you were here. You could've taken a few moments to find a solution. Marie's baby wasn't going to arrive that quickly.'

Maybe he had a point, and she had made a mistake. 'I'm sorry. I got here as soon as I could after Marie phoned to say she'd gone into labour. Everything was hectic and Adam was happy watching TV.' But she should've thought more about Adam. Just went to show how unmotherly her instincts were. 'I did my best in the situation. I explained to Adam what was happening and he was happy to bring towels and water to leave outside the bedroom door. Not once did he see anything he shouldn't.'

'He's a little boy.' Flynn wasn't accepting her explanation. 'He'd have heard her cries and groans. It's not a massive house.'

'He was safe. I didn't put him in a position where he'd be scared, and I honestly don't think he was.' Her guilt increased. She should've thought more about Adam's age, should've tried harder to find a solution. He might've heard things a young child was better off not hearing. What if he had nightmares about it? But he'd been excited to see Jacob, not frightened of the baby or Marie. But there was no denying she'd got it wrong. Apparently she should've seen to Adam before Marie.

Ally shivered. Forget thinking she might have her own baby. She wasn't mother material. Having never had the parental guidance that would've made her see how she should've cared for Adam had shown through this afternoon. One thing was for sure, she wouldn't be any better with her own.

At least she could be thankful that she'd had a reminder of that now and not after she'd given in to the yearning for her own baby that had begun growing in-

side her. She would not have her own children. That was
final. She squashed that hope back where it belonged—
in the dark, deep recesses of her mind, hopefully to stay
there until she was too old to conceive.

Flynn waited until Marie's mother arrived before he took
Adam home. *Talk about being a spare wheel.* Ally and
Marie talked and laughed a lot, getting on so well it re-
minded him of Anna with Marie. Ally had fussed over
the baby while his mum had taken a shower, but handed
Jacob back the moment Marie returned to her bedroom.
She hadn't been able to entirely hide the longing in her
eyes.

Flynn had tried to deny the distress he'd seen in Ally's
face earlier. The distress that had changed to bewilder-
ment and lastly guilt—brought on by him. The guilt had
still been there whenever she'd looked at him, which was
probably why she'd kept her head turned away as much
as possible. He'd become the outsider in that house. Marie
and Jacob and Adam had got all her attention. And he'd
hated that. So he'd taken Adam and left. *Like a spoilt child.*

Now at home he swore—silently so Adam didn't pick
up any words he'd then be told off for using. Then he deliberately focused on his son and not the woman who had
his gut in a knot and his head spinning. He really tried.
*Adam, my boy. I love you so much I'm being overprotec-
tive. But that's better than not caring.*

If ever there was a woman he could've expected to
look out for Adam it was Ally. Not to mention Marie.
He'd seen that stunned look on Marie's face when he'd
given Ally a hard time. Of course Marie would know
how unusual it was for him to lose his cool.

He cracked an egg and broke the yolk. 'Guess that
means scrambled eggs and not poached.' He found a glass

jug and put the pan away. Broke in some more eggs, whisked them into a froth and added a dash of milk. 'Adam, want to put the toast on?'

'Okay, Dad.' His boy stood on tiptoe at the pantry, reaching for the bread. 'Why isn't Ally sleeping over?'

Because your father's been a fool. 'She's tired after helping Jacob be born.'

'I like Jacob.'

Adam sounded perfectly happy, as if being around while a birth was going on was normal. And why wouldn't it be? Ally had made sure Adam wasn't affected by seeing anything untoward.

Flynn put the eggs into the microwave. *Ally, I'm so sorry for my rant. It was my responsibility to look out for my son, not yours, or anyone else's.* Ever since Anna's death he'd been determined to be the best dad he could to make up for Adam not having a mother. Hell, that's why they lived on the island and he did the job he did. Yet today he'd been quick to lay the blame right at Ally's feet for something that bothered him.

Sheba rubbed her nose against his thigh and he reached down to scratch behind her ears. 'Hey, girl, I've made a mess of things.' Picking up his phone, he punched in Ally's number. His call went straight to voice mail. 'Ally, it's Flynn. I'd like to talk to you tonight if you have a moment.'

But he knew that unless she was more forgiving than he deserved, she wouldn't call. Action was required.

'Adam, want to go and see Ally?'

The shout of 'Yes!' had him turning the microwave off and picking up his keys. 'Let's go.'

Despite the absence of the car in Kat's drive, Flynn still knocked on the front door and called out. 'Ally? Open up.'

Adam hopped out and added his entreaties but Ally wasn't answering.

Flynn doubted she'd be hiding behind the curtains. That wasn't her style. Ally wasn't at home.

Back on the road Flynn headed to town to cruise past the restaurants and cafés. 'There.' He pointed to a car parked outside the Chinese takeaway and diner.

'Yippee, we found her.' Adam was out of the car before Flynn had the handbrake on.

'Wait, Adam.' Though Ally was less likely to turn away from his son, he had to do this right or there'd be no more nights with her in his bed, or meals at Giuseppe's, or walks on the beach. *There aren't going to be many more anyway. She leaves at the end of next week.* He wouldn't think about that.

She sat in a corner, looking glum as she nodded her head to whatever music was playing through her earphones.

'Ally, we came to see you.'

Her head shot up when Adam tapped her hand. 'Hey.' She smiled directly at his son. 'Are you here for dinner?' Did she have to look as though she really hoped they weren't?

Flynn answered, 'Only if it's all right with you.'

Her eyes met his. No smile for him as she shrugged. 'I only need one table.'

'We'd like to share this one with you.' He held his breath.

Adam wasn't into finesse. He pulled out a chair and sat down. 'What can I have to eat, Dad?'

Flynn didn't take his gaze off Ally, saw her mouth soften as she glanced at his son. He said, 'I apologise for earlier. I was completely out of line.'

She didn't come close to smiling. 'Really?' Her gaze returned to him.

He took a chance and pulled out another chair. 'Really. I should've had something in place for today—for whatever day Marie had her baby. Adam is my responsibility, no one else's. It's been on my list to arrange another sitter but I never got around to it.' Much to his chagrin. He twisted the salt shaker back and forth between his fingers. 'I was angry for stuffing up, and I took it out on you. I apologise for everything I said.'

Ally pushed the menu across the table, a glimmer of a smile on her lips. 'I only ordered five minutes ago.'

That meant she accepted his apology, right? 'Adam, do you want fried rice with chicken?'

'Yes. Ally, are you coming for another sleepover tonight?'

Flynn's stomach tightened. *Too soon, my boy. Too soon. We need to have dinner and talk a bit before asking that.*

Ally shook her head. 'Not tonight. I need to do some washing and stuff.' She was looking at Adam, but Flynn knew she was talking to him.

Two steps forward, one back.

She hadn't finished. 'Besides, I'm always extra-tired after a delivery and need to spend time thinking about it all.' Her voice became melancholy, like she was unhappy about a bigger issue and not just about what he'd dumped on her earlier.

He gave the order to the woman hovering at his elbow and turned to lock eyes with Ally. 'What's up?' How could he have been so stupid as to rant at her? Now she wasn't staying the night, and who knew when she'd be back at his house, in his bed? Actually, he'd love nothing more than to sit down with a coffee or wine and try some plain old talking, getting to know each other better stuff. When she didn't answer he continued, 'What does a birth make you think about?'

'Everything and nothing. That whole wonderful process and a beautiful baby at the end of it. Like I told you the other day, I find it breathtakingly magical.' Her finger was picking at a spot on the tabletop. 'Yet I'm the observer, always wondering what's ahead for this new little person.'

'Do you want to have children someday?' Didn't most people?

The finger stopped. Ally lifted her head and looked around the diner, finally bringing her gaze back to him. 'No.'

'You'd be a great mother.'

Silence fell between them, broken only when Ally's meal arrived. But she didn't get stuck in, instead played with the rice, stirring and pushing it around the plate with her fork.

Adam asked, 'Where's my dinner?'

Flynn dragged his eyes away from Ally and answered. 'We ordered after Ally so it will be a few more minutes.'

Ally slid her plate across to Adam. 'Here, you have this one. It's the same as what you ordered.'

'You sound very certain—about no children of your own,' Flynn ventured.

'I am.'

'That's sad.'

'Believe me, it's not. If I'd had a child, that would be sad. Bad. Horrible.' The words fell off her trembling lips.

He couldn't help himself. He took her hand in his and was astonished to feel her skin so cold. 'Tell me.'

'I already did.' She'd found a point beyond his shoulder to focus on.

While he wished they were at home in the comfort and privacy of his lounge, he kept rubbing her hand with his thumb, urging her silently to enlighten him, let out what seemed to be chewing her up from the inside. 'Only that you were abandoned. Doesn't that make you determined to show yourself how good you'd be?'

Their meals arrived and they both ignored them.

'My mother didn't want me. I grew up in the welfare system. Moved from house to house, family to family, until I was old enough to go it alone.' Her flat monotone told him more than the words, though they were horrifying enough.

'Your father?'

'Probably never learned of my existence—if my mother even knew who he was.'

'You know,' Flynn said gently, 'your mother may have done what she did because she *did* love you. If she wasn't in a safe situation, or wasn't able to cope, it might have been that giving you up was her way of protecting you. Haven't you ever worked with women in that position?'

'Yes,' Ally admitted slowly. 'But if it was love, it didn't feel much like it to me.'

Flynn hated to think of Ally as a kid, adrift in the foster-care system without a steady and loving upbringing. It wasn't like that in all cases, he reminded himself. Anna's brother and sister-in-law had two foster-children that they loved as much as their own three. But look at Ally. Adorable, gorgeous, kind and caring. What's not to love about her? Was that his problem? Had he fallen for her? Nah, couldn't have. They'd only known each other a little more than two weeks. Hardly time to fall in love, especially when they knew nothing about each other. Except now he did know more about Ally than he would ever have guessed. And he wanted more. He could help her, bring her true potential to the fore.

Ally tugged her hand free, picked up her fork. 'See? You're speechless. It's shocking, but that's who I am, where I come from, what I'll always be. Now you know. You were right. I shouldn't have been in charge of Adam, even if by proxy. I know nothing about parenting.'

No. No way. Flynn grabbed both her hands, fork and all. 'Don't say that. I'd leave Adam with you any day or night. Today was me being precious. Since Marie and I are friends, I felt a little left out. Plain stupid, really.'

Ally tried to pull free, but he tightened his grip.

Finally she locked the saddest eyes he'd ever seen on him. 'Are we a messed-up pair, or what?' she whispered.

I'm not messed up. I get stuff wrong, but I think I've done well in moving on from Anna's death and raising our son.

'I am determined to do my absolute best for Adam, in everything.'

'You're doing that in spades.'

'So why do I feel guilty all the time?'

Her brow furrowed. 'About what?'

About Adam not having his mother in his life. 'I try to raise him as his mother wanted.' This was getting too deep. He aimed for a lighter tone. 'Eating raw vegetables every day and never having a sweet treat is too hard even for me, and I'm supposed to make Adam stick to that.' *But it isn't always what I want, or how I'd bring my boy up.*

Her fingers curled around his hands. 'That's not realistic. Even if you succeed at home, the world is full of people eating lollies and ice cream, roast vegetables and cheese sauces.' At last her eyes lightened and her mouth finally curved into a delicious smile that melted the cold inside him.

The smile he looked for every day at work, at night in his house. 'Like Danish pastries, you mean.'

'You've got it.' Her shoulders lifted as she straightened her back. Digging her fork into her rice, she hesitated. 'I haven't known you very long, but it's obvious how committed you are to your son, and how much you love him. Believe me, those are the most important things you can give him.'

Said someone who knew what it was like to grow up without either of those important things. He answered around a blockage in his throat, 'Thank you. Being a solo dad isn't always a level road. Scary at times.'

'It's probably like that when there are two parents. Come on, let's eat. I'm suddenly very hungry.'

'Something you and Adam have in common. You're always hungry.' The last hour being the exception.

She grinned around a mouthful of chicken and rice.

His stomach knotted. He loved that grin. It was warm and funny. But now he understood she used it to hide a lot of hurt. Hard to imagine her childhood when he'd grown up in what he'd always thought of as a normal family. Mum, Dad and his brothers. No one deliberately hurt anyone or was ungrateful for anything. Everyone backed each other in any endeavours. When Anna had died he'd been swamped with his family and their loving support to the point he'd finally had to ask them to get back to their own lives and let him try to work out his new one.

'Dad, can I have ice cream for pudding?'

Ally smirked around her mouthful.

'Gloating doesn't suit you.' He laughed. 'Yes, Adam,

you can. Ask that lady behind the counter for some while Ally and I finish our dinner.'

As Adam sped across the diner, probably afraid he'd be called back and told to forget that idea, Flynn watched him with a hitch in his chest and a sense that maybe he was getting this parenting stuff right after all.

'Good answer,' said Ally.

'Would you change your mind about a sleepover?' Might as well go for broke. After being so angry with Ally, then getting the guilts, all he wanted now was some cuddle time. Yeah, okay, and maybe something hotter later. But seriously? He wanted to be with Ally, sex or no sex.

Her smile stayed in place. 'I meant it when I said I get exhausted after a delivery. And I do like to think it all through, go over everything again.'

Huge disappointment clenched his gut but he wouldn't pressure her. 'Fair enough. But if you decide you need a shoulder to put your head on during the night, you know where to find me.' Huh? What happened to no pressure? 'If you want company without the perks, I mean.' He smiled to show he meant exactly what he'd said, and got a big one in return.

'You have no idea how much that means to me. But this is how I deal with my work. I'm not used to dumping my thoughts on anyone else.'

'You should try it. You might find it cathartic.' Next he'd be begging. 'Tell me to shut up if you like.'

She took his hands in hers, and this time her skin was warm. Comfort warm, friendly warm. 'I'm not used to being with a man every night of the week. I'm used to my own company and like my own space. Don't take it personally, it's just the way I am.'

Sounded awfully lonely to him. 'I'll cook you dinner tomorrow night.' When would he learn to zip his mouth shut? 'If you'd like that.'

'It's a date. I'll bring dessert. Something Adam will love.'

'You're corrupting my kid now?'

'You'd better believe it.'

CHAPTER ELEVEN

'You look worse than the chewed-up mess my cat dragged in this morning,' Megan greeted Ally the next morning when she walked into the surgery. 'Not a lot of sleep going on in your bed?'

'No. I tossed and turned for hours.'

'Haven't heard it called tossing and turning before, though I see the resemblance.' Megan laughed.

'Trust me, I was very much alone. Is everyone here yet?' Was Flynn here? He mightn't have kept her awake in the flesh, but she'd spent hours thinking about him. Hours and hours. Nothing like her usual night after a birth.

'I think they're all in the tearoom.'

Ally looked at the list of her appointments for the morning. 'At least there's no chance of falling asleep at my desk with all these women to visit.'

In the tearoom a large coffee from her favourite coffee shop was set at what had become her place. 'Thanks,' she muttered, as Flynn nodded to her. He was the only one in there.

'I was out early visiting Marie and Jacob so Adam and I had breakfast at the café.'

Ally chuckled. 'Now who's spoiling him?' Then wished

the words back as his smile dipped. 'Spoiling's good. Who's looking after Adam today?'

'A friend on the other side of the island. She's had him before when Marie needed to go somewhere little boys weren't welcome.' Flynn pulled her chair out.

Sinking onto it, she lifted the lid on her coffee and tentatively sipped the steaming liquid. 'That's so good. Caffeine's just what I need. If I hadn't been running late I'd have stopped for one myself.' So Flynn had lots of friends he could call on. Lucky man. But friends also meant staying in touch, being there when needed, opening up about things best left shut off. *Has he changed how he feels about me now that he knows the truth?* 'Is Adam happy to go to this lady?'

'Absolutely. He gets to take Sheba so they can go for walks in the park with Gina's two spaniels.'

Cosy. Did the woman have a husband? *Down, green monster, down. You have no right poking your head up.* So far her night-time lectures to herself about falling in love with a man who was out of reach didn't seem to have sunk in. Slow learner. *Flynn is totally committed to Adam and his job. There is no room for you in his life.* She repeated what she'd said over and over throughout the night. And again it didn't make a blind bit of difference. Try, *There's no room for Flynn and Adam in your life. They live in the same place every day of the year. You move somewhere new so often you're like a spinning top.*

'Morning, Ally.' Faye strolled into the room. 'I hear Marie's baby arrived in a bit of a hurry.'

'He sure did. And he's absolutely gorgeous.' She couldn't wait to visit this morning.

'Humph. Babies are all the same to me. Cry and poo in their nappies a lot. Very uninteresting at that age.'

Ally blinked. Had she heard right? 'You haven't had

your own children?' All babies were beautiful, even if some were more so than others.

'Got three of the blighters. Love each and every one, but that doesn't mean I thought they were cute when they arrived.'

What a strange lady. But at least she was there for her kids and probably did a lot with them. 'How was Marie this morning?' She looked at Flynn.

'Arguing with her mother about who was bathing Jacob.' He grinned like he'd been naughty. Which he had. If not for him Marie's mother wouldn't be there. 'But at least they're talking, which is a vast improvement.'

Jerome joined them and the meeting got under way. Thankfully it was short as Ally was itching to get on the road and go visiting patients, to get away from that distracting smile of Flynn's. As she headed to the door and her car, he called, 'You still on for tonight?'

'I'm buying the dessert after my house calls.' She shouldn't join him for the whole night, but she couldn't resist. This had been a fling like no other she'd ever had. This time she dreaded finishing it and heading away. Not that she wanted to stay put on Phillip Island for however long the fling took to run its course either. But there was this feeling of so much more to be done, to share with Flynn, to enjoy with his son.

For the first time in her adult life she didn't want to move on. For the first time ever a person had got under her skin, warmed her heart in a way it had never been warmed. It made her long for the impossible—a family she could truly call her own.

She should've said no, that she'd be staying home to wash her hair.

But there was no denying the liquid heat pouring through her body just at the thought of a night with Flynn.

So—how could she leave next week without shattering her heart?

It's too late. Might as well grab every moment going. It'd be silly to go through the rest of my time here staying in the flat, being miserable. Miserable would come—later, back on the mainland.

'Chocolate Bavarian pie.' Ally placed the box she'd bought in the supermarket on Flynn's bench. 'It's defrosted and ready to go.' She bent down to scratch Sheba's ears. 'Hey, girl, how're you doing? Recovered from that run yet?'

Lick, lick. Yes or no? Sheba had struggled a bit as they'd loped along the beach early yesterday morning.

Flynn slid a glass of red wine in her direction. 'Merlot tonight. Goes with the sausages I'm cooking.' He grinned that cheeky grin that got to her every time. 'They're beef.'

'Beef and red wine. A perfect combination,' she said with her tongue firmly in her cheek. That navy striped shirt he wore with the top button open to show a delectable V of chest was also perfect. Just enough visible chest to tantalise and heat her up in places that only Flynn seemed able to scorch. She winked. 'What time does Adam go to bed on Fridays?'

'Half past nine,' Flynn told her, straight-faced.

She spluttered into her glass. 'Half past nine? You've got to be kidding me.' Three hours before she could get her hands on the skin under that shirt? She'd combust with heat.

'Yep, I am.' Then he grinned again. 'You're so easy to wind up.'

'Phew. For a moment there I thought I'd have to lock him in the lounge with Sheba and race you down the hall for a quickie.'

Desire matching hers flicked into his eyes. 'Now, there's a thought.'

This banter she could do. It was easy and fun and how flings were run. 'Guess I'd better stick to wine for now.'

'We're invited to Jerome's tomorrow night for an indoor barbecue, along with the rest of the staff. But he specifically asked us as a couple.'

The air leaked out of her lungs. This might be something she couldn't do. It hinted at something more than a casual relationship, like a date involving his colleagues and friends. Colleagues and friends who'd read more into the situation than was there. Was Jerome playing matchmaker? 'That's nice.' Well, it would be under other circumstances.

'You're not happy?'

She shrugged. 'I'm sure it will be fun, but maybe I'll give it a miss.'

A furrow appeared between his eyes. 'I accepted for both of us.'

'Then you'll have to *un*accept.' What had happened to consulting her first?

'Why? You've been working with everyone for three weeks so what's the big deal?' Then that furrow softened. 'I get it. The *couple* word. That's what's got your knickers in a twist, isn't it?'

'So what if it has? We're not a couple. Not in the true sense. We're having an affair. Next weekend it will be over. How do you face your colleagues then, if they're thinking we've got something more serious going on?'

How do I look Megan in the eye next week and say of course we're only friends. Even friends with benefits doesn't cover it. I'm falling for you and I need to be pulling back, not stepping into a deeper mire.

'Ally, relax. Everyone's aware you're moving on and

I'm staying put. Jerome thought it would be more comfortable for you to go with me as there will be others there you haven't met. That's all there is to it.'

'You're ignoring that *couple* word.' Didn't it bother him? Because he was so comfortable in his life that he thought it ludicrous to even consider he was in a relationship?

Flynn set his glass carefully on the bench and ran his fingertip over her lips. 'Sure I am. It was the wrong word to use. We've spent a lot of time together since you turned up on the beach that first day. You've given me something special, and I'm going to miss you, but we've both known right from that first kiss that whatever we have between us would never be long-term. I don't care what anyone else thinks. It's no one's business.'

Where was the relief when she needed it? Flynn had saved her a lot of hassle by saying what they had going was a short-term thing. But the reality hurt. A lot. In her tummy, especially in her heart. Her head said the best thing for everyone was that she'd be leaving. Her heart said she should stay and see if she could make a go of a relationship with Flynn and his son.

'Ally? Would you please come to the barbecue with me as my partner for the night?' When she didn't answer he added, 'People know we've been seeing each other—going out for meals, taking Adam to the beach and other places. It's not as though this is going to be a shock for them or the source of any gossip.' He drew a breath and continued. 'I want this last week with you.' His smile was soft and yet determined. It arrowed right into her chest, stabbed her heart.

And made everything even more complicated.

How could she say no when she wanted it, too? In the end it was Flynn who'd be left to face any gossip. In the end it would be agony to leave him whether she went out with him again or not. She had to grab whatever she could and stack up the memories for later. 'I'd love to go with you,' she said quietly.

The days were flying by and Ally was withdrawing from him. Flynn hated it. Sure, she still came home with him for the night, but there seemed to be a barrier growing up between her and them as a twosome. She'd already begun moving on in her mind. There, he'd said it. He'd started denying the fact she would be leaving soon, even when it was there in black and white on the noticeboard in this office. Kat would return home on Friday—tomorrow. She'd take over the reins on Saturday and Ally would leave the island and head for her next job. He knew all that. He'd signed the contract with Ally's employers.

But knowing and facing up to what her leaving truly meant were entirely different. He refused to admit the other half of his bed would be cold and empty again. Wouldn't contemplate sitting down to an evening meal with only Adam for company. Daren't think how he'd fill in the weekends without her laughter and eagerness for fun pulling him along.

'That needs photocopying so the hospital in Melbourne have records.' Ally dropped a file beside Megan. 'Hey, Flynn, got a minute?'

'Of course.' *Always got hours for you.* Had he been hasty in thinking she was putting space between them? Did she have a plan for what they might do on her last nights?

'I'm concerned about Chrissie.'

So much for plans and hot farewells. 'Come into my office.' He nodded at the patients sitting in the waiting room.

Ally got the message. 'Sure.' The moment she stepped

inside his room she spun to face him. 'Chrissie's doing great physically. But she's got attached to me already and that's not good. She says she doesn't want to see Kat.'

'Strange. Kat gets on with everyone.' Like Ally. 'Did she give a reason?'

'Something about Kat's sister and Chrissie being rivals at school.' Ally shrugged those shoulders he'd spent a long time kissing last night. 'I was wondering if you could see her, maybe talk sense into her. I've explained that Kat would never tell her sister a single thing about the pregnancy, but Chrissie's not wearing it.'

'I'll talk to Chrissie, maybe with Angela there.' But he wondered how much of this had to do with Kat and how much was due to the way Chrissie had taken to Ally. 'You handled the situation very tactfully and sympathetically at a time when Chrissie was beside herself with worry. This could be about her not wanting you to leave.' He didn't want her going. Adam wouldn't, either.

A soft sigh crossed Ally's lips. 'There's not much I can do about that. I am going.'

'I know.' All too well. 'Do you ever get tired of moving on?'

Her eyes met his and she seemed to draw a breath before answering. 'No. It's how I live and there's a certain simplicity to not owning a house or a truckload of furniture or even a carful of clothes.' She looked away.

Flynn couldn't read her. He wanted to know if she felt sad about leaving him, or happy about another job done and their affair coming to an end. But as he started to ask his heart knocked so hard against his ribs he gasped. *I love her. I love Ally Parker. I'm not wondering any more. I know.* Asking her about her feelings just became impossible. She might ask some questions in return, questions he still wasn't ready to answer.

So he continued to study her while not being able to lock gazes with her, and he thought he saw no regret in her stance, her face or her big eyes. So Ally hadn't come to love him in the way he had her. Pain filled him, blurred his vision for a moment. Rocked him to the core. How could he have fallen in love with Ally? He'd never believed he'd love again, and yet it only taken a few short weeks. Had it happened that first day when Sheba had dumped her on the beach?

Ally's soft voice cut through his mind like a well-honed blade. 'I'd better get a move on. I'm going to weigh Jacob this morning.'

He watched her retreating back, his hands curled into fists to stop from reaching after her. So much for thinking she might reciprocate his feelings. It wasn't going to be at all difficult for her to walk away.

Ally stayed in the shower until she heard Flynn and Adam leave for their walk on the beach with Sheba. She'd cried off, saying she had a headache. That was no lie. Behind her eyes her skull pounded like a bongo drum. Her hands trembled as she towelled herself dry. Her knees knocked as she tried to haul her jeans up her legs. It was Saturday.

'Goodbye, Flynn.' She hiccupped around the solid lump of pain in her throat. 'Bye-bye, Adam. Be a good boy for your dad.' *I will not cry. I don't cry. Ever.*

Reaching out blindly, she snatched a handful of tissues and blew her nose hard, scrubbed at her eyes. One glance at her hands and she knew it'd be a waste of time trying to apply make-up. 'Go plain Jane today.' What did it matter anyway? It wasn't as though she'd be seeing Flynn.

Tears threatened and she took as deep a breath as possible. 'Suck it up, be tough, get through the day. Tomorrow will look a whole heap better.'

Now she'd taken to lying to herself. But if it got her

out of the house and on the road before Flynn and Adam returned, then it was the right thing to do.

Yesterday she'd packed up her few possessions and the bags sat in the boot of the medical centre's car. The key to Kat's flat was back under the flowerpot on the top step, her contact details written on a pad inside in case she'd left anything behind. Now all she had to do was drive to the surgery to dump the car and be on her way.

But she turned the car in the direction of Marie's house. 'One last cuddle with Jacob.' So much for leaving unobtrusively. But she couldn't bring herself to turn away yet.

Marie opened her front door before Ally had time to knock. 'Hey, you're out and about early.'

'Yeah, thought I'd see everything's okay with you.'

'Come in. Want a coffee?' Marie headed for the kitchen. 'Jacob's just gone down.'

'Then I probably should carry on.'

There was already a mug of steaming coffee on the bench and Marie poured another without waiting to see if Ally wanted it. 'We had a good night. Jacob only woke four times.' She grinned.

'How do you manage to look so good after that?' Ally paced back and forth.

'Mark's coming home today.' Marie slid the mug in Ally's direction. 'Excuse me for being blunt but *you* look terrible. What's up?'

'Nothing.' She tried to shrug, but her shoulders were too heavy.

'Ally, I don't know you well, but something's not right. Has Flynn done something wrong?'

'No. Not at all.' She'd gone and fallen in love with him, but that didn't make him a bad man. She was the fool.

'Good, I'd have been surprised. He thinks the world

of you and would do anything for you. Apart from that hiccup the day Jacob was born.'

Coming here had been a mistake. 'I'd better go. I've to be somewhere. Thanks for the coffee.' Which she hadn't even tried. 'I'll see myself out.'

'Don't go,' Marie called.

Ally shut the door behind herself and ran to the car.

A taxi dropped her off at the ferry terminal half an hour later. Once on board she found an empty seat out of the way of the happy hordes and pushed her earbuds in, turned up the music on her music player and pretended all was right with her world. Except it wasn't, as proved by the onset of deep sobs that began racking her body as the ferry pulled out. Her fingers dug into the palms of her hands and she squeezed her eyes tight against the cascade of tears.

Someone tapped her knee. 'Here. Have these.' An older woman sitting opposite handed her a pack of tissues.

'Th-thanks,' she managed, before the next wave of despair overtook her.

Flynn. I love you so much it's painful.

Flynn. What I wouldn't give to feel your arms around me one more time.

Flynn. I had to go. It wouldn't have worked.

For every wipe at her face more tears came, drenching the front of her jersey. 'I love you, Flynn Reynolds,' she whispered. Shudders racked her body from her shoulders all the way down to her feet.

This was terrible. The last time she'd cried when moving on had been the day she'd left her favourite foster-family—the Bartletts.

The woman opposite stirred. 'We're docking.'

Ally blew her nose and swiped her eyes once more, drew a breath and looked up. 'Thank you again.'

'You'll be all right?'

'Yes, of course.' Never again. With one last sniff she inched forward in the queue to disembark and headed for her real life; the one she'd worked hard to make happen and that now seemed lonely and cold.

Flynn felt a chill settle over him the moment he turned into his street. Ally's car was gone. Somehow he wasn't surprised but, damn it, he was hurt. How hard would it have been to say goodbye?

Spinning the steering wheel, he did an about-turn and headed for Kat's flat to say to Ally the goodbye she hadn't been willing to give him.

But it was Marie's car outside Kat's flat, not the one Ally had been using. As soon as Flynn pulled up Marie was at his window. 'Do you know where Ally's gone?'

'I hoped she'd be here.' He was too late.

'She came to my place about an hour ago. She was very upset. I tried to find out why, but she left again. In a hurry, at that. That's why I came around here.'

Flynn's mouth soured. Ally was upset? Why? *Did you want to stay on? With me? No, that was going too far.* 'I'd say she's on the ferry, heading home.' Except she didn't have a home to head to. Just a bed she borrowed on a daily basis.

'Flynn, what's going on? Why's Ally upset? As in looking like she was about to burst into tears?' Marie's voice rose.

Ally and tears didn't mix. He'd never seen her close to crying. *Duh.* There hadn't been any reason for it. His gut clenched. If Ally was crying, then he wanted to be with her, holding her, calming her down and helping sort whatever her problem was. 'She's finished her contract with us, but from what I've learned about her that wouldn't be the reason for her being unhappy.'

Marie clamped her hands on her hips. 'Unhappy? Broken-hearted more like. Downright miserable.' She stared at him. 'A little bit like how you're looking, only more so.'

'I look miserable? Broken-hearted?' Here he'd been thinking he could hide his feelings. But, then, most people didn't know him as well as Marie did.

Marie's stance softened. 'You love her, don't you?'

Ouch. This might not go well, Anna having been Marie's best friend and all. 'You don't pull any punches, do you?'

'Have you told Ally?'

He shook his head.

'What's held you back? Anna? Because if that's the case, you have to let her go. The last thing Anna would've wanted would be for you to be on your own for the rest of your life.'

Flynn growled, 'Since when did you become my therapist?'

She smiled. 'Just being a good friend. So? Spill. Why haven't you talked to Ally about this?'

'All of the above. And Adam. I'm totally focused on giving him everything he needs in life and I don't know if there's room for Ally. But, yes, I love her, so I guess I'll be making space.' Over the past weeks he'd begun to feel comfortable living here, enjoying his work more. Without Ally, life wouldn't be as much fun.

'I hope you come up with a more romantic approach when you tell Ally all this.' Marie leaned in and brushed a kiss over his chin. 'Adam adores Ally, and vice versa. What's more, he needs a mother figure in his life. You're not so hot on the soft, womanly touch.'

'Thank goodness for that.' Flynn felt something give way deep inside and a flood of love and tenderness swamped him. *Ally, love, where are you?* 'She's afraid she isn't mother material.' When astonishment appeared on Marie's face, he hurried to add, 'She's a welfare kid, lived in the system all her childhood.'

'Oh, my God. Now I get it. She was running from you. She doesn't want to make things any worse for you.'

'Yep, and I let her go.' Actually, no, he hadn't. He'd fully expected Ally to be waiting when he and Adam had got back. He should've known better. If he hadn't diverted to the vet's to pick up dog shampoo, would he have been in time to see her before she'd left? 'Marie, thanks, you're a treasure. Now, go home to that baby of yours and tell your mother to leave before Mark gets here.'

'On my way. What are you going to do?'

'Adam and I are taking a trip.'

CHAPTER TWELVE

'THE COFFEE'S ON,' Darcie said as she buzzed Ally into the apartment building.

'Hope it's stronger than tar,' Ally muttered, as she waited for the lift that would take her to the penthouse. She was wiped out. All those tears and that emotional stuff had left her exhausted. No wonder she tried so hard not to get upset.

The apartment door stood wide open as Ally tripped along the carpet to her latest abode, and she felt a temporary safety from the outside world descend.

'Hey, how's things?' Darcie appeared around the corner, took one look at her face and said, 'Not good. Forget coffee. I think this calls for wine.'

A true friend. 'Isn't it a bit early? It's not quite eleven yet.'

'It's got to be afternoon somewhere in the world.'

Good answer. 'I'll dump my bags.' And dip my face under a cold tap. But when Ally looked into the bathroom's gilt-edged mirror she was horrified at the blotchy face staring back at her. 'Who are you?' she whispered.

Cold water made her feel a little more alive but no less sad. She found her make-up and applied a thick layer in a misguided attempt to hide some of the red stains on her cheeks. Quickly brushing her hair and tying it up in a ponytail, she went out to Darcie. 'Sorry about that. I needed to freshen up a bit.'

Darcie immediately handed her a glass of Sauvignon Blanc. 'Let's go out on the deck. The sun's a treat for this time of year.'

She followed, blanking out everything to do with Phillip Island and Flynn, instead trying to focus on what might've been going on at the midwifery centre while she'd been away. 'Tell me all the gossip. Who's gone out with who, who's leaving, or starting.'

Sitting in a cane chair, Darcie sipped her wine and chuckled. 'You won't believe what's happening.'

Ally sprawled out on the cane two-seater, soaked up the sun coming through the plate-glass windows, and tried to relax. Darcie was very understanding. She'd wait to be told what was going on in Ally's life. And if Ally never told her she wouldn't get the hump. A rare quality, that. Exactly what Ally needed right now. 'Great wine.' She raised her glass towards Darcie. 'Cheers.'

At some point Darcie got up and made toasted sandwiches and they carried on talking about the mundane.

It was the perfect antidote to the tumultuous emotions that had been gripping Ally all morning. There was nothing left in her tanks. She'd given it all on Phillip Island, left her heart with Flynn and his boy. Thank goodness she had tomorrow to recover some energy and enthusiasm for work before turning up at the midwifery unit on Monday.

Then Darcie spoilt it all. 'Who's this Flynn you keep mentioning?'

Ally sat up straight. 'I don't.'

Darcie held her hand up, fingers splayed. 'Five times, but I'm not counting.'

I can't have. I would have noticed. 'He's one of the doctors I've been working with.'

'Yet I don't recall you mentioning any of the others. Guess this Flynn made an impact on you.'

You could say that. 'Okay, I'll fess up and admit to having a couple of meals with him and his wee boy.'

Darcie said nothing for so long Ally thought she'd got away with it and started to go back to her relaxed state.

Until, 'Ally, what else do you do when you're not being a midwife?'

That had her spine cracking as she straightened too fast. 'Isn't that enough? I'm dedicated to my career.' Apart from shopping for high-end clothes and getting in the minimum of groceries once in a while, what else was there to do?

'Your career shouldn't be everything. Don't you ever want a partner? A family? Your own home? Most of us do.'

'I'm not most of you.'

'What about this Flynn? Do you want to see him again?'

Yes. But she wasn't about to admit that. 'No,' she muttered, hating herself as she lied.

'You haven't fallen in love with him, have you?'

And if I have? Ally raised her eyes to Darcie and when she went to deny that suggestion she couldn't find the words. Not a single one.

'I see. That bad, huh?' Darcie leaned back in her seat. 'I don't know what's gone on in your life, Ally, and I'm not asking.' She paused, stared around her beautiful apartment before returning her gaze to Ally. 'Sometimes we have to take chances.'

Ally shook her head. 'Not on love,' she managed to croak.

'Loving someone can hurt as much as denying that

love. But there's always a chance of having something wonderful if you accept it.'

There really wasn't anything she could say to that so she kept quiet.

The buzzer sounded throughout the apartment, its screech jarring. Darcie stood up. 'That's probably Mary from the ward. We're heading out to St Kilda for a few hours. Want to join us?'

Ally shook her head. 'Thanks, but, no, thanks. I've got a couple of chores to do and then I'm going to blob out right here. But with coffee, not wine.'

She tipped her head back and closed her eyes, pulled off the band from her ponytail and shook her hair free. Her hand kneaded the knots in her neck. What was Flynn doing? Had he taken Adam around to see Jacob? Her heart squeezed. *I miss you guys already.*

'Hello, Ally.'

She jerked upright. 'Flynn?' Couldn't be. Her imagination had to be working overtime.

'Ally, we came to see you.' No mistaking that excited shriek. Or the arms that reached for her and held tight.

Not her imagination, then. Adam was here. *Flynn* was here. Meaning what? Lifting her head, she stared at the man who'd stolen her heart when it was supposed to be locked away. The man she'd walked away from only hours ago without a word of goodbye or a glance over her shoulder—because any of those actions would've nailed her to the floor of his home and she'd still be on Phillip Island.

Adam tightened his hold. 'I'm missing you, Ally. You didn't wait for us.' Out of the mouths of babes—came the truth.

Her head dropped so her chin rested on Adam's head. 'Adam, sweetheart.' Then her throat dried and she couldn't say a word. Finally, after a long moment of trying not to think what this was about, she raised her eyes to find Flynn gazing at her like a thirsty man would a glass of cold water on a hot day. The same emotions she'd been dealing with all day were glittering out from her favourite blue eyes. 'Flynn,' she managed.

'Hey.' He took a step closer. 'The house didn't feel the same when we got back from our walk. Kind of empty.' Flynn didn't sound angry with her, but he should. She had done a runner.

She owed him. 'I'm really sorry but I couldn't wait.' *If I did I'd never have left.* Her heart seemed to have increased its rate to such a level it hurt. 'It's an old habit. Get out quick. Don't look back.'

Bleakness filled his gaze, his tongue did a lap of his lips. 'I see.'

Adam wriggled free of her arms and sat on the floor beside her.

Flynn didn't move, just kept watching her.

Suddenly Ally became very aware that this was the defining moment in her life. Everything she'd faced, battled, conquered, yearned for—it all came down to now and how she handled the situation. She loved Flynn. Before— *Gulp.* Before she told him—if she found the courage—she had to explain. 'It's an ingrained habit because of all those shifts I made as a child. I learned not to stare out the back window of the car as my social worker took me away from my latest family to place me in the midst of more strangers.'

Flynn crossed to sit in the chair Darcie had been using earlier. He still didn't say a word, just let her take her time.

Her chest rose and fell as she spoke. 'I know it's not the same as what I did today, that you do care about me and never promised me anything that you haven't already delivered, but I come pre-conditioned. I'm sorry.'

'You were waiting for one of those families to adopt you.' Flynn looked so sad it nearly brought on her tears.

Adam, who shouldn't be taking the slightest notice of this conversation, stared up at her and asked, 'What's adopt mean?'

'Oh, sweetheart. It's when people give someone else a place in their family, share everything they've got, including, and most importantly of all, their hearts.'

'Don't you have a family?' He'd understood far too much.

'No, Adam, I don't.'

'We can adopt you. Can't we, Dad?'

Ally's mouth dropped open. Her stomach tightened in on itself. Her hands clenched on her thighs. What? No. Not possible. He didn't understand. It wasn't that simple.

She leapt up and charged across to the floor-to-ceiling window showcasing Melbourne city. Her heart was thudding hard, and the tears that should've run out hours ago started again.

'Ally.' A familiar hand gripped her shoulder.

She gasped. 'You've taken your ring off.' Could she start believing?

He tugged gently until she gave in and turned around. But she couldn't look up, couldn't face the denial of Adam's silly statement if it was staring at her out of Flynn's eyes. 'Ally, look at me. Please.'

Slowly she raised her head, her eyes downcast, noting the expanse of chest she'd come to know over the last month, the Adam's apple that moved as Flynn swallowed, that gorgeous mouth that had woken every part of her body and could kiss like no other man she'd known. Expelling all the air in her lungs, she finally met Flynn's gaze. There was no apology there, no *It's been nice knowing you but we don't want to know you any more.* All she found was love. Genuine love, deep love that spelled a bond and a future if she dared take it.

'Flynn,' she whispered. 'I have to tell you something.' The breath lodged painfully in her chest, but if she was going to gamble, then she had to start by being honest. 'Today was different. For the first time ever I didn't want to go. That's why I ran.' Tremors rippled through her. This was way too hard. But there was a lot to lose—or gain. A deep breath and she continued. 'I've fallen in love with you. Both of you.' And then she couldn't utter another word as tears clogged her throat.

His arms came around her, held her loosely so he could still watch her face. 'This is the last time you're walking away. You're not on your own any more. You have me, us. We are your family.' His mouth grazed hers.

'You want to adopt me?' she croaked against his lips, being flippant because she was afraid to acknowledge what he'd said for fear his words would vaporise in a flash.

'Try amalgamate. We want to bring you in with us, make us a threesome, a family.'

'Amalgamate? Sounds like a business deal.' But the warmth lacing his voice was beginning to nudge the chill out of her bones. 'I'll bring two bags of clothes and my music player and you'll supply a home.' She smiled to show she wasn't having a poke at him. Then she gasped and dashed to her bag to pull out the dogs. 'Plus these two. I take them everywhere. This time when I put them on the shelf they'll stay there so long they'll gather dust.'

Flynn looked ready to cry. 'That's the closest you've got to owning a pet?' His arms came around her again.

'Bonkers, eh?'

He stepped back, shoved his hand through his hair. 'You have no idea how much I mean every word. I love you so much it hurts sometimes.'

She gasped. Had Flynn said he loved her?

He hadn't finished. 'I could've told you that days ago, but I got cold feet. I put Adam before everything else. Which I have to do, but I used him as an excuse not to let you know where my feelings for you were headed. I didn't want you to leave, yet I didn't know how to tell you that. I think I was kind of hoping you'd just hang around and that would solve my dilemma.'

She stared at him as a smile began breaking out across her lips, banishing the sadness that had dominated all day. 'You said you love me.'

'Yes, Ally, I did. I mean it. I love you.'

'No one's ever told me that before.' Oh, my goodness. Flynn loved her. But it wouldn't feel so warm and thrilling and wonderful if she didn't love him back. '*I've* never loved anyone before.' There hadn't been anyone to bestow that gift on. 'This love is for real, I promise.'

'Hey, I can see it in your eyes. It's been there for days if only I'd known what to look for.'

'Adam, look away. I'm going to kiss your father.'

'Why?'

'Because I love him.'

'Do you love me?'

'Absolutely.' She bent down to press a kiss on his forehead. 'Yes.' When she straightened Flynn was waiting for her, his arms outstretched to bring her close. His head lowered and his mouth claimed hers.

This kiss was like no other they'd shared. This was full of promises and love and life.

'How long are you going to kiss Dad?' Adam tapped her waist.

'For ever,' she murmured against Flynn's mouth, before reluctantly pulling away. She was afraid to let him go. She needed to keep reassuring herself he'd always be there.

Flynn took her hand and laced their fingers together. 'Want to come home with us for the rest of the weekend?'

'I can't think of anything I'd rather do.'

'Thank goodness.' Until he'd relaxed she hadn't realised how tense he'd become.

'I have to be back here on Monday.'

He nodded. 'But now you have a home to go to when you're not on a job.'

Her heart turned over. 'You're not expecting me to give up working for the midwifery unit, then?'

'You'll do that when you're good and ready. We've got all the time in the world to learn to live together and for you to feel right at home on the island. I won't be rushing you, sweetheart.' Then he really stole her heart with, 'When I say I love you, I mean through the best times and the worst, through summer, winter and Christmas and birthdays. I'm here for you, with you, Ally, for ever.'

'But what if I fail? This will be new for me.'

'You won't fail, Ally. You'll make mistakes.'

'Fine. What happens when I make these mistakes?' she asked, her heart in her mouth.

'We sort them and we move on. Together.'

Her heart cracked completely open. Could she do this? 'Can I do this? Really?' She locked her eyes on the man who'd turned her world on its head.

'Your call, sweetheart. But I believe you can do anything you set your mind to.'

Was Flynn not as scared as she was? For all his understanding, maybe he didn't get it. But looking into those eyes she'd come to trust, she saw nothing but his confidence in her. He trusted her to look out for Adam to the best of her ability, even if that ability needed fine-tuning along the way. He trusted her to love him as much as she'd declared. Her mouth was dry. Finally she managed to croak, 'Let's go home.'

'Yes.' Adam jumped up and down, then ran circles around the lounge. 'Yes, Ally's coming back home with us.'

Flynn reached for her, his smile wobbly with relief. 'Home. Our home. The three of us.' Then his smile strengthened. 'And the dogs.'

Eighteen months later...

Ally laid baby Charlotte over her shoulder and rubbed her tiny back. 'Bring up the wind, sweetheart, and you'll feel so much better.'

Flynn grinned. 'Look at you. Anyone would think you'd been burping babies for ever. Charlotte is completely relaxed lying there.'

Ally's heart swelled with pride and happiness. 'Seems I got the mothering gene after all.'

Flynn's grin became a warm, loving smile. 'Ally, I was never in doubt about that. I've seen you with Jacob, with Chrissie's Xavier and half the other new babies on the island. You're a natural when it comes to making babies happy.'

She blinked back a threatening tear at his belief in her. That belief had helped her through the doubts that had reared up throughout her pregnancy, had meant he hadn't hovered as she'd learned to feed and bath and love her baby. And Adam. Well. 'Adam's been complaining this morning. Apparently I should've made a boy so he had a brother to play football with.'

'He'll have to wait a year or two.'

'We're having more?'

'Why not?'

She blinked. That told her how much he believed in her. In her chest her heart swelled even larger.

The bed tipped as Flynn sat down beside her and reached for his daughter. 'Hello, gorgeous.' He laid Charlotte over his shoulder and held her with one hand.

'Hello,' said Ally, her tongue in her cheek.

He leaned over and kissed her. 'Hello, gorgeous number one. Did you get any sleep last night?'

'An hour maybe.' Charlotte had had colic and nothing had settled her. But Ally had been happy, pacing up and down the house, cuddling her precious bundle, kissing and caressing. Just plain loving her baby. She'd known what to do, hadn't had any moments of doubt when Charlotte wouldn't settle. And this morning she was being rewarded with a contented baby.

Yep, she did have the right instincts. When Charlotte had been born three weeks ago she'd been stunned at the instant love and connection she'd felt for her baby. It had been blinding in its strength. For the first time ever, Ally realised how hard it must have been for her mother to give her up. She might have desperately wanted to keep her baby but had been too scared, troubled or unable to support herself. Now, as a mother, Ally knew it wasn't a decision any woman would make lightly. She'd never know the reason her mother had left her on that doorstep. But now at last, with Flynn by her side, she was moving on, making a loving life for her family and herself.

'Flynn.' She wrapped her hands around his free one. 'I love you so much. I'm so lucky.'

'You and me both, sweetheart.'

'Let's get married.' She hadn't thought about it. The

words had just popped out, but she certainly didn't want to retract them.

His eyes widened and that delicious mouth tipped up into a big smile. 'That's the best idea you've had since we decided to get pregnant.'

'I thought so.' Her lips kissed the palm of his hand, and then his fingers. Life couldn't get any better.

* * * * *

IT STARTED WITH
A PREGNANCY

SCARLET WILSON

For my own three personal heroes:
Kevin, Elliott & Rhys.
And to Nancy Holroyd, a valued critique partner,
with patience, insight and lots of good advice,
and to Rachael Johns for her support and
encouragement.

CHAPTER ONE

COOPER noticed her straight away. The music throbbed in his ears as the dozens of bodies around him pushed and jostled to gain a better position at the oak-topped bar. She was standing alone, looking calm and serene, if a little awkward. He knew instantly she wasn't used to being in a place like this. He watched as she sipped at her drink and glanced at her silver watch, her left forefinger twiddling with a strand of chestnut hair. He wished he could reach out and tuck it behind her ear.

'Why don't you go and speak to her?'

The voice made him start. He turned to face his friend Jake, who was pointing in her direction. 'Go on, then. You've been staring at her for the last ten minutes. Go talk to her.'

Cooper frowned. 'Don't be ridiculous. She might be waiting for someone. I can't go and speak to her.' He shook his head in a decided way before picking up his drink again.

Jake put his hand on Cooper's arm. Compassion showed in his dark blue eyes. 'Coop, it's been two years. It's time to get back on the wagon. You're in a new city, with a new job and nobody knows you. Nobody knows your history.'

He gestured in the direction of the beautiful woman.

'Over there is a gorgeous-looking woman, who looks as if some fool has stood her up. This is your chance. Go and take it.' He gave Cooper's arm a little squeeze. 'It's time to start living again.'

Cooper's stomach churned. He felt little beads of sweat breaking out on his forehead. Jake was right. When was the last time he had actually noticed a woman? When was the last time he'd asked a woman out? He couldn't even remember. Last time he could recall his stomach doing flip-flops like this had been at the Christmas dance at school when he'd gone to ask Clara to dance with him. That must have been fifteen years ago.

He glanced over at her again. She was beginning to look uncomfortable. He could take a chance and speak to her or he could go home and sit in his darkened, empty flat—just like he'd done for the last few months. What harm could it do? He took a quick drink from his glass and put it down on the bar. Jake was right. No one knew him here. No one would be looking at him with their sympathetic eyes. No one would describe him as that 'poor consultant who'd been widowed'. No one would talk about the family he'd lost. Here he was just Cooper. It was time for change.

He walked over towards her, but as he neared her his footsteps slowed and his courage started to falter. She turned towards him and their eyes met. Stunning really and they caught him by surprise. Startling bright green. He had expected her eyes to be blue, or brown even, to match her glossy chestnut hair. The emerald-green eyes under long, lustrous eyelashes were bright and clear and for a second he wondered if she was wearing coloured contacts, but then dismissed the idea as he neared her.

The noise in the pub was prohibitive. He would have to be standing close to her if he wanted to speak to her.

She hadn't moved. Her eyes were still fixed on his. He leaned over to whisper in her ear, his hand automatically resting on her hip. He felt her suck in a breath at his touch. She spoke first, turning her lips towards his ear. 'You've been watching me for the last ten minutes. I wondered when you were going to come and introduce yourself.'

She leaned backwards, a smile dancing across her lips as she noticed the rush of colour in his cheeks. He hesitated for a second, caught off guard as he saw the glint in her eyes. She was teasing him.

He remembered his last thought. It was time for change. He could be a whole new different person. Someone who was confident. Someone who was bold. Someone who believed himself to be attractive and who never went home alone. Tonight, he could be Jake. He cut to the chase. 'Hi, are you waiting for someone?'

She smiled and nodded. 'Yes, my friend appears to have got lost in the ladies.'

He felt a surge of relief—she was here with a friend. She wasn't waiting for a man. He frowned, his natural instinct taking over. 'Maybe you should go and check on her, she might be unwell.' This time the glint was in his eyes. 'Don't worry, I'll wait for you.'

Her face broke into a wide grin. She raised her eyebrow at him. 'Really?'

She was totally unaware of the captivating picture she made when she smiled. Cooper nodded, gesturing towards the ladies, while the hand that was resting on her hip decided to follow another story and unconsciously pull her closer to him. Her eyes dropped to where his hand was resting. 'Are you planning on letting go of me?'

He pulled his hand back reluctantly and gave a little shrug. 'Sorry'.

She shook her head. 'Actually, I don't think I need to go check on my friend.' She pointed towards the bar. 'She seems to have made her way to another engagement.'

He followed where her finger was pointing and saw a small blonde figure wrapped around a man standing next to the bar.

'Looks like you've been left in the lurch.' He smiled. He glanced at her empty wine glass. 'So, mysterious woman, can I buy you a drink?'

She glanced at her watch, as if she was weighing up her options. Cooper caught his breath. Don't let her decide to go home! It was only eleven o'clock. She hesitated for a second, before finally handing him her wine glass and fixing him again with her green eyes. 'I'll have a glass of rosé wine, please.'

Cooper took the glass, his fingers brushing hers. He felt the air around him sizzle. This was what it felt like. This was how other people lived. He had forgotten about this side of life. He had forgotten about the feeling in the pit of your stomach when you met someone you were attracted to. He shot her a quick smile and turned towards the bar.

Melissa breathed a huge sigh of relief, the breath hissing out slowly through her tensed lips. She hadn't even realised she'd been holding it. She hadn't believed it when she'd spotted him at the other side of the bar. He was gorgeous. What was he doing in here? Men who looked like that didn't live around here. And what was he doing, talking to her? She took another deep breath, trying to calm the clamouring heart in her chest. She had tried to be blasé when he spoke to her. She had tried to act as if men as handsome as him spoke to her every day. But now she could feel panic setting in. She glanced over at her friend at the bar. Lynn was still wrapped around her latest victim. She would be no help whatsoever.

Cooper turned back around and handed her the wine glass, his fingers brushing hers. She felt the electricity streak up her arm in a delicious buzz. She hadn't been mistaken first time round and she could sense he felt it too. He shot her a beaming smile. 'So, mystery woman, are you going to tell me your name?'

'Melissa,' she replied, before giving a little shake of her head, 'well, Missy.' Her breathing had finally slowed and her heart had stopped hammering on the wall of her chest. She gathered herself and her confidence grew. She could do this. She could talk to the most handsome man for miles. 'My friends call me Missy,' she explained, holding out her hand to shake his.

'Missy,' he repeated, nodding his head as if in approval. His strong hand caught her slim wrist, giving it a firm shake. And for a few seconds it stayed there, held in an automatic pause because neither party wanted to let go.

'What's yours?'

For a fraction of a second he seemed to hesitate. 'Cooper,' he answered, before regaining his composure and saying, 'Well, actually, my friends call me Coop.'

Her hand reluctantly pulled away from his, her fingers lightly dragging down the palm of his hand, sending delicious shockwaves down his spine. His breath caught in his chest. For a second there he had nearly told her a lie. Just for some wild second he had almost told her his name was Jake. Jake, his friend at the bar, who had no history, no past to haunt him. Jake, who never went home alone. The person he had wanted to be tonight. But he couldn't do it. Not when he was looking into those beautiful eyes. The eyes that were fixed on him right now.

'Pleased to meet you, then, Coop.' She had moved a little closer to him now, the noise in the bar making it difficult to be heard. He caught a waft of her perfume. Not what he'd expected. Something subtle, with a hint of orange. Most women that he knew wore floral scents, but this was something much more scintillating. He inhaled a little deeper, trying to catch her essence.

'What brings you here, Coop?' Her eyes flickered up and down the length of his body. 'I've definitely never seen you around before.'

No. Melissa was absolutely sure she'd never seen him here before. Because he wasn't someone that you'd forget in a hurry. Black shirt tucked into black jeans. Wide shoulders, tapering to a slim waist with long legs and a very watcher-friendly bottom. Then there was his hair. Light brown, slightly longer than normal, which sort of flopped over his right eye. His rich chocolate-coloured eyes. The kind that once you started looking at they drew you in, further and further, until you could almost feel yourself enveloped by the warm hues.

Melissa gave herself a shake. What was she doing? She never had thoughts like this! Even if the man in front of her looked like something from a jeans ad. This was the first time in months she'd felt even vaguely attracted to a man again. Had it really been that long? Had it really been six months since David had stalled once again on starting a family together? Something he knew Melissa desperately wanted. Had it really been six months since Melissa had finally had the courage to call off their engagement? Melissa gave herself another shake. The time span hadn't even registered with her. It was definitely time to move on. Time to move from the lost-in-space zone she'd inhabited for the last six months. And here, right in front of her, was the perfect opportunity.

Cooper gave her a lazy smile, showing off perfect straight white teeth and a little dimple in his right cheek. It made him look like a cheeky schoolboy.

'You're right, I'm not from here. I just moved up this week.'

She quickly glanced at his left hand, cursing herself for not doing it earlier. *Relief, no wedding band.* 'Did you move up yourself?'

Cooper nodded swiftly, taking another quick gulp of his drink. His right hand slipped into his pocket and subconsciously started to touch the cool metal band. He hadn't worn it on his finger for the last few months but he just couldn't bring himself to put it back in the box yet. So he kept it in his pocket, where every now and then he had the urge to reach in and touch it.

'Whereabouts are you staying?'

He nodded towards the right. 'In the new flats, next to the marina. They're only about five minutes from here.'

Melissa felt her stomach flip. She'd seen them. She'd walked through the show flat as if she'd been in a dream world. Or a nightmare, once she'd seen the price. It had been gorgeous, a silver bespoke kitchen with appliances to die for, the most luxurious red velvet sofa she'd ever seen, with cushions you could just sink into, matching curtains with a view over the spectacular marina where all the million-pound boats were moored. And the *pièce de résistance*, the huge white bedroom with mahogany four-poster bed. Every little girl's dream bedroom. The kind of carpet so white you were scared to step on it in case you left a mark. She remembered the blue plastic covers they had been forced to put on over their own shoes before they had been allowed in the show flat. Once she'd seen the white bedroom Melissa had completely understood. He must be a millionaire to own a flat like that.

'So what brings you to Kessington?' she asked curiously. One of the largest towns in the North of England, Kessington had a thriving marina and affluent business district. She wondered what he did for a living. Her interest was definitely piqued.

A frown flickered across his brow. It was the second time she'd seen that moment of hesitation from him. What was he hiding?

His eyes met hers again. Heat flared between them. 'This and that,' he answered dismissively. The noise in the bar swelled again as another crowd of revellers surged through the door. His hand automatically went to her waist again, pulling her closer so that his lips were brushing the top of her earlobe. The movement sent tiny electrical impulses down her spine, leaving the little hairs at the back of her neck standing deliciously on end. Melissa could hear imaginary voices in her head screaming, *He's gorgeous. Go for it, girl!* She could feel her knees start to tremble. When was the last time someone had tried to chat her up? She couldn't even remember. For the first time in her life she felt as if she was about to be swept off her feet, like some damsel in distress being rescued by a white knight on a beautiful stallion. A smile danced across her lips as she stared at the gorgeous man in front of her. If only he could see the picture inside her head right now, he would probably run screaming from the room! She pulled her mind from her fantasy and brought it back to the present. What did 'this and that' mean? Their eyes connected again, leaving her in no doubt that the feelings were entirely mutual.

Cooper gave her a wide smile. This was just what he needed. The last two years at work had been painful. The last year had been especially painful as his colleagues had seemed to decide that the official 'mourning period' should be over. That had resulted in a procession of female colleagues under his nose who had obviously decided he was an eligible bachelor again. It had become almost painful to have a conversation with a member of the female staff. It hadn't helped that hospitals seemed to have an unending supply of women. Heavy hints had been dropped all around him, telling him it was time to move on.

But this was different. This was his decision. To see a beautiful woman in a bar and have a conversation with her. To know that he felt attracted to her. There was freedom in this that he'd never experienced before and it felt like a huge weight had been lifted off his shoulders. He didn't even want to think about work right now. He gave a little sigh. His eyes swept downwards. The thin fabric of her green dress clung to her curves, showing just enough of her cleavage to give him a hint of what lay beneath. He found his voice again. 'What about you?'

Melissa was conscious of his fingers at her waist. Tingles swept along her skin where his hand lay, causing her to suck her breath in again deeply. There was something enticing about the mystery between them.

She liked the fact that someone, especially a tall, dark handsome someone, was interested in her. She decided to play him at his own game.

She threw back her head, tossing her chestnut curls over her shoulder. 'I'm a bit like yourself,' she teased, a twinkle in her eyes, 'a bit of this and a bit of that.'

Cooper almost laughed. He could see the flicker of panic that whizzed across her face. He knew she wasn't used to this. But then again, neither was he. He hadn't felt this good in a long time. It made him determined not to let this night end. He leaned forward, his breath on the skin at the side of her neck. 'So, mysterious Missy, let's have some fun.'

She delighted in the shivers that quivered down her spine and the thoughts that were immediately conjured up in her mind. His voice was rich and husky; it made him all the more attractive to her. *Boy, he was sexy.*

Her bright eyes fixed on his. 'What do you mean?' Was it time for her to start panicking? How had he interpreted what she'd just said? This was so unlike her. She wasn't used to meeting men in pubs and having flirtatious conversations. But there was just something about him that was irresistible. And she knew she didn't want this to end.

'Well, I don't know much about you—you don't know much about me. How about we remedy that?' His hand around her waist had tightened its grip, turning her around to face him. Her breasts were now skimming his chest. She could feel the response of her nipples underneath the confines of her clingy dress. On an ordinary day she would have been horrified and embarrassed, but tonight she didn't even look down—she didn't have to—she just moved a little closer.

His right hand came out from his pocket to rest on

her other hip. 'I've got a suggestion. Some questions—but only completely truthful answers.' His smile was a little crooked, so he wasn't quite so perfect after all.

She raised herself up on her tiptoes, her hands resting on his broad shoulders as she whispered in his ear, 'I think I'm up for that.'

He looked quickly round the crowded bar. 'It's too noisy in here. Let's take a walk,' he said, turning her towards the door. He lifted her thick black coat and held it open for her to slip her arms inside. Melissa glanced around the bar. She couldn't see her friend at the bar any more and didn't want to waste time looking for her. She'd probably already left without her. Her stomach fluttered a little. She didn't do this. She didn't meet strange men in pubs and leave with them. She was Melissa. Reliable. Dependable. Great in a crisis. Sister in the labour ward and the most sensible person that even she knew. No one would believe her if she told them about this. Part of that was the attraction. Missy instinctively felt safe with him and her instincts had always been good. She'd spent the last six months eating, sleeping and working. There was more to life and she knew it. It was time to throw caution to the wind and act on instinct. And it felt delicious.

His hand pressed gently on her back as he ushered her through the crowd and out the door. The biting cold wind hit her immediately and she fastened her coat up round her neck. He stood next to her, patiently waiting. 'Give me a second,' she said, pulling her mobile from her pocket. 'I'm just going to send my friend a text to let her know I've left.' She dabbed quickly on the keypad, her fingers rapidly going white with cold, before finally pressing 'Send'. She lifted her hands to her mouth, blowing on them to try and revive them. In an instant she felt his warm hand encircle hers and she stuck the other hand deep in her pocket, pushing her phone away safely. A smile danced across her face as she pictured her friend receiving the text

Left with the gorgeous man in black WOO HOO!

Lynn would be stunned. She hadn't met the new, reckless Melissa. She was used to the sensible friend who made sure she got home safely at the end of the night. Another little wave of excitement ran through Melissa. *This felt good.*

'Let's go this way,' Cooper said as he automatically turned towards the marina. She felt her heart quicken in her chest. The roads and pavements were glistening with frost that was starting to form on the cold winter's night. She grasped his hand a little tighter. Her beautiful black high-heeled shoes were a joy to look at, but not so much of a joy to walk in. She teetered along precariously next to him, shooting him a smile and pretending to walk with confidence.

'So, Missy,' he said, 'tell me a bit about yourself. Do you often leave pubs with strange men?'

'Oh.' She was caught off guard. She stopped walking abruptly. 'Of course I don't!' The words came out more harshly than she'd expected. Did he think she was easy?

'Calm down,' he said quietly, moving his arm around her waist. 'It's all right, Missy. I kind of guessed this was all new to you.'

'You did?' Her wide eyes met his steady gaze. His deep eyes pulling her in even closer.

'Yes, I did,' he said assuredly. 'Would it help if I told you I was new at all this too?'

'You are?' She could hardly believe it. Surely women were beating down his door with a stick?

He gave her a nod, pulling her a little closer. 'Now relax. You're safe with me. Tell me something unusual. What's the one thing most people don't know about you? Something that only your good friends would know.'

Her mind was spinning and her heart was beating frantically in her chest again. How did this man do this to her? How could one man cause her body to be all aquiver and turn her brain to mush? She'd expected him to ask her something mundane. Her befuddled brain blurted out the first answer that came into her head. 'I'm a sci-fi freak.'

'Wow!' He stopped walking and turned to look at her under the yellow streetlight. Nothing could change the glow coming from those beguiling green eyes. He couldn't hide the amusement on his face. 'Really? Well, you've certainly surprised me.'

'Why?' She tried to look offended, before adding defensively, 'I think they're the most exciting films in the cinema. Give me anything with a laser gun and spacesuit and I'm sold. Take me to see a chick flick and you've had it.'

'Mmm.' He looked her up and down.

'What?'

'I'm just imagining you in one of those *really* short space dresses.' He nodded approvingly. 'I'm liking what I see.'

'Get lost!' She thumped him through his thick grey jacket. 'Right, my turn. Are you the chick-flick type?'

She waited for his answer while silently scolding herself. She needed to get some more imagination if she wanted to win this game.

'Westerns,' he said decisively. 'All that testosterone, horses and guns blazing. Any boy's dream.'

A testosterone-loving man. She wondered how much she should read into that. 'My turn this time.' As they came to an icy puddle on the pavement, he wrapped his arm further around her waist and pulled her towards his hip.

She felt oddly comfortable tucked under his protective hold. She lifted her head as she heard some people pass by on the other side of the street. From over there they would look like a couple in love, wrapped around each other on a cold winter's night. A couple of young women walked around them on the pavement, both women's eyes automatically running up and down Cooper's body with unhidden admiration. Melissa smiled. *Look all you want, ladies, this man is with me.* From this position she raised her head, her nose brushing against his cold cheek, and looked straight into his magnetic eyes. The smallest of gestures. The most intimate of gestures. She wanted this night to last forever. Her brain pulled itself into focus. It was time for another question. 'What do you like to read?'

He nodded in recognition of the question, taking a few seconds to decide on his answer. He let out a big sigh. 'Is this the point I'm supposed to tell you I don't read much? Because I fear I'm about to reveal a childhood secret.'

Her face lit up with a bright smile. 'Then I think I will too, so go ahead.'

'I love to read. I always have done. So it's absolutely got to be any of the old-fashioned detective novels. But I mean really old, long before everything became so scientific and crimes were solved with DNA and microscopic evidence. I always loved them as a child. Even now as an adult I still sometimes pick them up. I love the characters.'

She gave him a curious smile. 'Okay, now I'm intrigued. What's so good about the characters?'

'Everything. Their intelligence. Their wit. Even their complications. Sometimes even their mistakes. I loved them all.' She was staring at him again with those luminescent eyes. Her chestnut curls were waving gently in the wind. It was all he could do not to reach up and run his fingers through her tresses. Then his hand would be at the back of her head and he could pull her towards him...

Her face was shining. 'For me it was the classics, particularly *Little Women*, which I still read on occasion. The copy I have is so tatty and dog-eared that some of the pages are about to fall out. I still cry every time I read it. It breaks my heart when Beth dies.'

He watched. She was so caught up in what she was saying her eyes were glistening with unshed tears. Something tugged at his heartstrings. Something almost primal. When was the last time he'd felt this protective towards a woman?

She caught the expression on his face and it stopped her as she was about to continue. She sensed the deep emotions that were smouldering inside him. But what were they? Was it a memory? Or was it something more primitive, like lust?

They'd reached the marina and were now standing next to the barrier, looking out over the array of million-pound boats, all costing more than Melissa would earn in a lifetime. His arm was still locked firmly around her waist.

His voice cut through the darkness. 'Let's go with the dream theme. What would be your dream job?'

Instantly her voice caught in her throat. Missy had her dream job. Being a midwife was the only job she had ever wanted to do, and would ever want to do. But for some reason she wasn't inclined to tell him that. He'd been coy about work earlier. He didn't want to talk about it. So she intended to be coy too.

It was easier to stick with the sci-fi theme. 'My dream job would be an astronaut.' She waved her arm above her head. 'To fly amongst the stars would be magical.'

'And the reason you didn't train at NASA?' he queried playfully.

She heaved a huge sigh and turned, releasing herself from his grasp and leaning backwards against the railings. 'What can I say? I failed physics at school and I think it was a basic requirement of astronaut training. So that put me out.'

'What a shame,' Coop said, standing directly in front of her and putting a hand on either side of her hips. He pulled her gently towards him. 'I could have met you there.' He lowered his face towards hers, his breath visible in the cold night air.

'You're telling me that was your dream job too?' she whispered. Her face was only inches from his.

'Absolutely. Just look at how much we have in common. We were obviously destined to meet.' He ran his hands around her hips, cradling her bottom. She caught her breath at the intimacy of the movement. A word sang in her head. Destiny. She knew it was crazy but it certainly felt like that. What if somewhere, in some lifetime, this gorgeous man was indeed her perfect match? What if she hadn't spoken to him? What if she'd gone home early? What if she'd been too scared to throw caution to the wind and leave with him—something she would never normally have done?

But everything about this felt perfect. She felt as if she was meant to be there, in his arms, at this moment. Everything about this just felt so right.

He gave her a slow smile. 'See,' he whispered, 'we're a match made in heaven.' She moved closer, her hips pressing against his, her hands resting on his shoulders. She shivered. 'It's really cold out here.' Her eyes met his.

'We could go inside.' His lips brushed against her ear. 'You might have failed physics at school but how did you do at biology?'

Melissa's heart stopped. 'I got first prize,' she said breathlessly.

The words hung in the darkness for a few seconds. Both knew where this was leading. Melissa could feel the heat between their bodies. She knew she should say no. She knew she should walk away. But she didn't want to. She hardly knew anything about Coop. She didn't even know his second name. But, then, he didn't know hers. Most of all, she didn't want to walk away. She wanted to have this one night of reckless passion with this mysterious stranger. She wanted to break free from the 'sensible' sign that followed her wherever she went. She wanted to follow her destiny. After all, who would ever know? She dropped her hand from his shoulder and placed her hand in his.

He led her wordlessly to the front door of the flats she had viewed earlier that year. They entered the lift and she stifled a gasp when he pressed the button for the top floor. Moments later he opened his front door into the flat of her dreams.

'You bought the show flat?' she asked in astonishment.

He nodded nonchalantly. 'It seemed easier just to

buy the one with the furniture included.' He spread his arms out around the wide space. 'I was never any good at that sort of thing anyway.'

He gestured towards her and she handed him her thick coat, which he hung in a nearby cupboard. Melissa walked in awe around the open-plan kitchen, running her finger along the black marble worktop, her heels clicking on the slate floor. Cooper turned and opened the blinds in the living area to show the view over the marina. If she'd thought it was stunning downstairs, up here it was breathtaking. The boats glistened, gleaming white against the black water. Her fingers automatically went up to touch the red curtains. They were thick and luxurious, just as she'd imagined. She pointed towards the sumptuous sofa that she'd admired from afar. 'Can I?'

Coop looked puzzled. 'Of course.'

She sank into the huge cushions, closed her eyes and let out a huge sigh. 'Oh, it's just as gorgeous as I imagined.' She snuggled her shoulders deeper into the soft fabric.

'What are you talking about?'

Her eyes flickered open. 'I came to see this flat when it was the show flat for the development and I *really, really* wanted to do this.'

'You wanted to sit on the sofa?' His right eyebrow rose in amusement.

'Well—yes, but the woman that was showing us around was a bear and I was too scared to touch anything. I think she could tell just by looking that I could never afford to stay anywhere like this.'

Cooper let out a laugh. It was deep, warm and rich. Not what she had expected.

Her train of thought hadn't shifted. 'So how can you afford this?'

He lowered his eyes slightly. 'I came into some money and I earn a relatively good salary.' He plumped down next to her on the oversized sofa.

Melissa nodded. She could tell when not to press him. She turned sideways to face him. 'Whose turn is it to ask a question?'

He ran his finger down her arm, causing her skin to come out in tiny goose-bumps. 'I've lost track,' he whispered, leaning forward and twisting a finger in her chestnut curls, pulling her face towards his.

She expected his kiss to be light, gentle, and it was anything but. It was hard and passionate, instantly setting her body alight with desire. She felt the heat spreading throughout her being. Heat she hadn't felt in months—no, heat like this she had never felt. His other hand came up and caught the other side of her head, cradling her face. He drew his head back from hers, looking her in the eye. 'I didn't have any plans like this tonight,' he said sincerely, 'but right now I'm going to ask you if you want to come through to the bedroom with me.'

Melissa went to speak but he placed one finger on her lips. 'Shh. Missy, if you want to leave I won't stand in your way. But I would really like it if you'd stay.' His breath was slightly ragged now, as if he was trying to fight the fire building inside him.

Her heart was pounding. This was sexual chemistry like she'd never felt before. She reached her hands around his neck and whispered in his ear.

His eyes lit up with wild excitement. 'What was that?' he asked in amazement.

'My next question,' Melissa said with quiet assurance. 'I just decided what I wanted to ask.'

Cooper looked at her with his steady brown eyes, a smile forming across his lips. 'In that case, this takes me back to show and tell from school, and this answer is definitely a show.' And he took her by the hand and led her to the white bedroom.

CHAPTER TWO

Eight weeks later

MELISSA had just finished zipping up her tunic when she heard the shouting at the top of the labour ward. Hurrying to pull her newly washed curls back into a ponytail, she straightened her tunic, and set off down the corridor at speed.

Melissa had been one of the sisters in the labour ward for nearly three years and when she was on duty she prided herself on the calm running of the ward. Today, though, the midwives station at the central point in the labour ward seemed to be in chaos. Melissa tried to make herself heard above the rabble surrounding her. Two junior doctors appeared to be having an argument, two midwives were trying to deal with telephone calls, one consultant was angrily trying to attract the attention of anyone at all, and in the midst of it all stood a man, holding an empty jug of water. He was holding it out gingerly, saying, 'Excuse me, excuse me?'

Melissa shook her head, lengthening her last few strides as she reached the station. 'Enough!' Her hand thudded on the desk and immediately silenced her bickering colleagues. 'You two…' she pointed at the junior doctors '…take your discussion elsewhere. My

midwives are trying to deal with telephone enquiries.'
She grabbed one of the passing nursing auxiliaries,
'Fran, can you assist this gentleman, please?' she asked,
gesturing in the direction of the bewildered man.

Finally she turned to the consultant standing at the
desk. 'Dr Mackay, can I help you with something?'

He nodded and pointed towards the nearby room. 'I
need a set of notes for the lady in Room 4, Katherine
Kelly. I'm not happy with her presentation.'

Melissa nodded and walked around to the other side
of the midwives' station and retrieved a set of case notes
from the trolley. It was the same place where notes had
been kept on the labour ward for the last twenty years.
She handed him the buff-coloured folder. He took them
with a sigh of relief, 'Thank God you're on duty today,'
he muttered as he turned and headed back down the
corridor.

Melissa watched his retreating back with a smile on
her face. Had that been a compliment? Dr Mackay was
not famed for his compliments. He was nearing retire-
ment and becoming increasingly grumpy with age. A
new consultant had been appointed but Melissa hadn't
met him yet.

She waited until one of the midwives at the desk had
hung up her phone. 'Carrie, what's going on in here
today?'

'Just what you'd expect. The new junior and senior
doctors have started today and the place is in chaos.
We seem to have more women in labour than usual and
we've had a few late presentations with complications.'
She pointed in the direction of the midwifery suite.
'Sister Baird is in charge of the midwifery side today—
she can update you on the admissions. Jen Connell was

in charge of the medical side—she's still in Room 4 with the patient Dr Mackay just collected the notes for.'

Melissa nodded and set off towards the midwifery unit to touch base with her colleague. The labour ward was divided into two sides: the midwifery side, where women with routine pregnancies and routine labours were looked after by a team of midwives from start to finish; and the medical side, where women with high-risk pregnancies were looked after by a team of doctors and midwives. Both sides of the labour ward had a midwifery sister or senior midwife on duty at all times, along with a team of more junior midwives to help support all women through the labour process. Melissa had always worked on the medical side. She had been diabetic since childhood and in this hospital all women with diabetes were automatically under the care of the medical staff. Knowing how single-minded the medical staff could be made Melissa all the more determined that women like her had the best possible birth experience. The only way that would happen was if experienced midwives like her worked hand in hand with their medical associates.

She heard her colleague's voice and pushed open the nearest door. 'Hi, Andrea.' Her colleague looked up from the foetal monitor she was watching. 'Just letting you know that I'll be taking over in the medical side. Let me know if there are any patients you need to discuss.'

Andrea tucked a stray piece of short blonde hair behind her ear and shot her a quick smile as she pressed a button on the monitor for a printout of the foetal heart. 'Any word on our lady with the breech presentation yet?'

Melissa shook her head. 'I haven't had a report yet

from Jen—I'm just going to see her. It was bedlam at the midwifery station when I arrived.'

Andrea gave her a big smile. 'So you haven't seen the new consultant yet? I believe he's in with that patient. She arrived less than an hour ago, already in labour with a breech presentation. We had to transfer her over to the medical side.'

She crossed the room away from the patient she was dealing with and whispered under her breath, 'He's spent the last month covering all the outlying areas, but he's here permanently now. Hunk, total hunk.'

'What?'

'You'll see. Let me know how the patient does, will you?'

Melissa gave her a quick nod and ducked back out of the door. The three midwives she would be working with were waiting at the midwives' station and she assigned them each to an area of the ward before going to take over from Jen.

'Hi, Jen,' she said breezily as she entered the room, crossing behind the curtains to join Jen and the patient. 'I'm here to take over from you—can you give me a report?'

Jen looked up from the notes she had just finished writing and put her pen down. 'Hi, Missy, that's great. Thanks.'

The woman lying on the bed was pale and sweating. Her dark hair lay limp in a cloud around her white face. She was breathing shallowly, small rapid gasps, leaning forward at first and then sagging back against the pillows whenever another contraction took hold. As an experienced midwife Melissa could tell from the shape of the woman's abdomen that the baby was in the wrong position.

Jen continued quickly, 'This is Katherine Kelly. She's twenty-two and this is her first pregnancy. She missed her last two antenatal appointments and presented in labour just under an hour ago. Her contractions were only four minutes apart when she arrived and it was noticed on admission that baby was in the frank breech position. Her blood pressure had also spiked so she was transferred through to the medical side.' She handed the observation chart she was holding over to Melissa, who cast her eyes over it rapidly.

'She's 40 weeks' gestation. We've just done an ultrasound to confirm the position and size of the baby. Everything looks normal. Her contractions are now two minutes apart. We are too late to turn the baby, and Dr Mackay had been considering Caesarean section, but thankfully our new consultant...' she gestured into the corner of the room '...has plenty of experience of this type of delivery and is happy to take the lead.'

Melissa nodded, assimilating all the information she'd just been given. If Katherine had attended her last two antenatal appointments it was likely that the breech presentation would have been picked up beforehand and dealt with. Now it meant that the baby was going to come out bottom first instead of head first. Some congenital malformations could result in a breech presentation but the ultrasound must have ruled that out. This meant that all that was really left to do now was to assist the new consultant in the delivery of this baby.

She sat on the bed next to Katherine and took her hand. 'Hi,' she said, 'I'm Melissa and very soon I'm going to help you have this baby.' She turned to face Jen again. 'Is the paediatrician on his way?'

Jen nodded. 'He said he'd be here in the next five minutes.'

Melissa fastened the blood-pressure cuff around Katherine's arm and set the machine to record every five minutes. She turned to face the new consultant in the corner of the room and stretched out her hand towards him. 'Pleased to meet you. I'm Melissa Bell, one of the midwifery sisters.'

He looked up from the notes he had been checking over and her heart froze. Time stopped. Cooper. *Cooper was the new consultant obstetrician?*

Cooper—the man who'd said he did a bit of 'this and that'. Cooper, the man who lived in the show flat overlooking the marina. Cooper, the man who had taken her through to the glistening white bedroom with the mahogany four-poster bed and...

Cooper ran one of his hands through his floppy brown hair and reached his other hand out to meet hers. 'Pleased to meet you, Melissa. I'm Cooper Roberts.' Not a flicker of recognition. His actions were as smooth as silk, the consummate professional.

He stood up from his chair and pushed the bed table he had been leaning on away from him. Melissa hadn't moved. She stood rooted to the spot. The last time she'd seen this man they'd both been naked and he'd been trailing his tongue around every part of her body, awakening sensations she'd never felt before. Her brain was spinning so fast that she thought she might fall over. She wrenched her hand free of his, conscious of the electricity that had just shot up her arm, and grasped the bottom of the bed. Cooper moved effortlessly past her and sat down on the side of the bed to talk to Katherine.

'Is there anyone with you?'

Katherine shook her pale head. 'No, it's just me. My mum lives miles away. I phoned her early this morning but I don't think she'll be here in time.'

'Is there anyone else I can phone for you?'

Melissa was still in shock. She knew what he was doing and why he was doing it. A breech delivery could be traumatic and it would be better if Katherine had someone to support her. He spoke soft, reassuring words to Katherine, whilst resting his hand on her abdomen and explaining how the delivery would proceed.

'If my baby is the wrong position, shouldn't I have a Caesarean section?'

Cooper glanced at her chart. 'From your history you've been in labour for more than twenty-four hours. Your waters have broken and we've already examined you and established that you're fully dilated.' He held her hand reassuringly. 'If we'd known about the baby's position in advance we may well have considered a Caesarean section. But you're pretty far along now and the baby is ready to come out. There's no reason to think there will be any problems.' He gave her hand a little squeeze as another contraction clearly gripped her. 'Do you feel the sensation to push yet?'

Katherine's face crumpled and she nodded. She was clearly growing tired. 'I just want this to be over.' She started to sob.

The blood-pressure cuff round her arm automatically started to inflate again and Cooper's eyes followed the reading carefully. The door opened and the paediatrician appeared, pushing a special cot to allow assessment of the newborn. He gave Cooper a quick nod. 'Nice to see you again, Dr Roberts.' Then shot a smile over towards her. 'And you, Melissa.'

Melissa started. What was she doing? She had to get hold of herself. Cooper had managed to keep his composure without any problems. But it was claustrophobic being in a room with a man she'd seen naked. Naked.

There was that word again. She couldn't get it out of her head. But if she closed her eyes for a second she could see his broad torso and muscular arms, all with a little smattering of dark hair that curled downwards towards…

'Sister Bell… Missy?'

She spun abruptly, caught by the informal use of her name. That was what she'd told him to call her that night. His dark chocolate eyes were watching her carefully. He was cool and composed. His gaze never faltered. The ultimate professional. He expected her to be the same.

'Are you ready to assist me?'

Melissa gave a quick nod, tearing her eyes away from his. She moved swiftly over the bed to help assist Katherine into the most appropriate position for delivery at the end of the bed. The semi-recumbent position would allow space at the end of the bed for the baby to hang. Cooper washed his hands and pulled on some gloves before positioning himself at the end of the bed, while Melissa remained at Katherine's side, monitoring the recordings from the foetal monitor and blood-pressure gauge. Cooper swiftly examined Katherine again.

'Okay, Katherine. The baby's bottom is right at the cervix. On your next contraction you can start to push. We'll let you know if you need to stop. Just let us know how you're feeling.'

Katherine nodded tensely as the next contraction took hold of her body. Cooper continued to talk to her quietly but firmly over the next few minutes. 'Good, Katherine, keep pushing. That's the posterior buttock, now the anterior buttock.' The baby's legs were spontaneously delivered. He nodded swiftly at Melissa and the paediatrician to let them know that things were proceeding smoothly. 'Take a deep breath again, Katherine. Things are going well.'

Melissa watched carefully as Cooper delivered the baby's shoulders then checked the position of the arms and umbilicus. If the baby's arms were extended, that could cause problems with the delivery.

'Get ready, people, the baby's arms are flexed so they'll be delivered on the next push.' He shot Katherine a big smile. He had managed to put the patient at ease and was clearly confident in his clinical abilities. 'We're nearly there now, Katherine, just another few big pushes.'

Katherine grimaced and gathered herself for the next push, gripping Melissa's hand so tightly that she thought her bones might break. Melissa sat down on the bed, wrapping her arm around Katherine's shoulders. 'Do you know what you're having?' she asked, trying to distract her into letting go of her other hand.

Katherine shook her head fiercely. 'I didn't want to know. I wanted a surprise.'

Melissa nodded in understanding. Her view of the earlier ultrasound had revealed the baby's sex but she wasn't about to let Katherine know. She felt Katherine's abdominal muscles begin to tense again. 'Another big push now.'

Cooper positioned his hand to check the position of the baby's head. 'Okay, it's going to be the Burns-Marshall manoeuvre,' he said, clarifying the position to the waiting team. 'This might be a little uncomfortable, Katherine, as we need to turn the baby one hundred and eighty degrees and we have to do it slowly to prevent sudden changes in pressure.'

With his focus entirely on the job in hand, Cooper

grasped the baby's ankles, waited for the hairline to appear and then slowly pivoted the baby until the nose and mouth were free. There was silence in the room for the two minutes while he carried out the procedure and the staff silently held their breath. When it was done Cooper handed the baby over to the waiting arms of the paediatrician, who made a quick assessment and used some suction to clear the baby's airways. A quick whiff of oxygen later and the room was filled with the angry roar of a baby who was well and truly awake. The paediatrician gave Melissa a little nod and she picked up a nearby blanket to wrap round the screaming bundle, who was rapidly turning a nice shade of pink.

Just for a second she stopped. This was one of the moments that she loved. Those first few minutes where the baby adjusted to its new surroundings. Some hated the transition and screamed, others were mesmerised and looked around wildly with unfocused eyes. Those first few seconds were precious and it was one of the reasons Melissa loved her job so much. Her stomach gave a little squeeze as she stared at the little one in her arms. When would it be her turn? Would she ever be the person whose heart filled with joy at the first sight of her baby? Her biological clock was ticking and with no potential partner on the horizon, a baby was a long way off.

She glanced down once more at the perfect little pink face in her arms and pulled her mind back into the present.

'Here we go, Katherine,' she said, handing over the precious gift. 'Meet your son.'

Katherine seemed oblivious to the noise in the room and took him with trembling arms. 'Isn't he gorgeous?' she breathed heavily.

Melissa sat down next to her on the bed. 'Have you got a name picked out for him yet?'

Katherine nodded. 'I'm going to name him James, after my dad.'

'That's lovely. I'm sure he'll be delighted.'

She looked up as one of the junior midwives stuck her head around the door. 'Just to let you know that Katherine's mum has arrived.' She caught sight of the little bundle lying Katherine's arms. 'Oh, great, the baby is here. Do you want me to send her in?'

Melissa turned to Katherine. 'We're not quite finished yet, but do you want her to come in and see the baby?'

Katherine nodded silently. Her eyes hadn't left her baby's. She was still in the newborn glow of motherhood.

Melissa looked at Cooper carefully. It had been her first experience of the new consultant and it was one of the smoothest breech deliveries she had ever seen. He clearly knew his stuff. Melissa went to leave the room and find Katherine's mother. She brushed past Cooper, who was standing talking quietly to the paediatrician. It was a tight squeeze and her breasts brushed against the back of Cooper's white coat. 'Sorry,' she muttered on the way past, and breathed a sigh of relief as she ducked out of the door.

Cooper finished his conversation with the paediatrician and had a few final words with Katherine before picking up her notes and carrying them out the room.

His registrar was waiting outside the room for him. 'Anything I can do, Cooper?'

He nodded quickly. 'Yes. Katherine still has to deliver her placenta. Can you go and supervise for me?'

Cooper didn't normally like to leave a patient

immediately after delivery but he was still getting over the shock of seeing Melissa in the room. He walked into the nearest consulting room and closed the door behind him. Sitting at the desk, his hand automatically went to his trouser pocket where he turned his wedding ring over and over in his pocket.

What on earth was she doing here? He'd been dumbfounded when she'd walked into the room. She hadn't even noticed him to begin with, she'd been too focused on the patient. But when she had seen him she'd looked as if she'd been hit with a ton of bricks. It was obvious she hadn't wanted to see him again. He'd realised that as soon as he'd woken up the next morning and she'd gone. No note. No nothing. Wham! Bam! Thank you, Ma'am!

She hadn't seemed like that type of girl. He'd almost believed she'd never had a one-night stand before. But six weeks later and with no sign of her, his opinion had changed. The last place he'd expected to see her was on the first day of his new job. Why hadn't she told him she was a midwife? He groaned and put his head in his hands. But he hadn't told her he was a doctor either. She had been stunned to see him.

He'd come here to be a new person. He'd wanted to be in a new place where no one knew his history. He wanted to be in a place where he had no ties. Where he could just focus on the job. This was a nightmare. Once word got out he'd slept with the ward sister he would be at the mercy of the hospital grapevine. It had been bad enough at his old post, where everyone had seemed to have a 'wonderful single female friend who would be just perfect for him.' He didn't want to mix business with pleasure. He hadn't even really decided if he was ready for the pleasure side. Cooper sighed and leaned back in his chair. This was the last thing that he wanted. He'd had experience of the hospital grapevine. The whispered words *'That's the consultant whose wife died'* had haunted him for months. That was why he was here. In a new place where there would be no discussion about his personal life, no interference. And now this.

He couldn't bear it. This was the job he loved. This was the one constant in his life. This was the thing that still gave him a reason to get up in the morning, because even after everything that had happened to him, this was the job he was good at. There were patients who needed him, patients that he *could* save. Other doctors might have hidden away, retrained and entered a different branch of medicine, but that had never even entered his mind. His own hospital had held too many painful memories to stay, but here it was different— here a whole new set of memories was waiting to be made and he couldn't allow anything to spoil that for him. He had to be the ultimate professional. This was work and he could manage to maintain a professional relationship with Sister Bell. Couldn't he?

Sister Bell—that was exactly how he would think of her. Not Melissa and certainly not Missy. No. He stood up and straightened his white coat. He could do this.

Cooper's eyes scanned over the sports arena. He'd been too late to catch Melissa at work but one of the other midwives—Andrea, after wrinkling her nose at him—had told him that she usually came for a run after work. He spotted the figure at the other side of the running track. He'd recognise that body anywhere and that thought triggered a little twist in his gut.

Just as she'd caught his eye in the pub, so she caught his eye here too. She was wearing a bright red tracksuit with a grey running vest and white trainers. Her chestnut hair was pulled up in a ponytail and he watched as she finished her lap and checked the time on her watch. He started to jog slowly around the track towards her. He didn't even know what he was going to say. That he was sorry? That this was awkward? That every time he saw her he had flashbacks to their night together?

He watched as she sat down on the arena steps and pulled her rucksack towards her, pulling a mini chocolate bar from it and eating it in two bites. Then she leaned forward and rested her head on her arms, obviously trying to catch her breath. He slowed as he approached her; there was no time like the present.

Melissa's heart was pounding. She checked her pulse then wondered if her heart was pounding due to her exercise or the day she'd just had at work. The events of the day played over and over in her mind like some bad Groundhog day.

She felt her cheeks flush as she remembered when she'd had to brush past him. Just as well she'd been wearing a hideous sports bra under her uniform. She would have died if he'd noticed her nipples' automatic response. She wasn't used to being haunted by erotic thoughts at work. Which seemed strange since she used to work with her ex, David. But David hadn't conjured up the wild responses that she'd experienced with Cooper. If this was what happened to her mind after one day, how on earth was she going to work with him?

Then there was the fact he hadn't told her he was a doctor—worse, an obstetrician. She'd just come out of a relationship with a doctor and she certainly wasn't looking for another! Why on earth did he have to be working here?

She groaned and stuck her head in her hands. Oh, wake up, Missy! She'd met him in a pub that was five minutes away from the hospital—a known haunt of hospital personnel. He'd picked a flat that was less than a ten-minute walk from the hospital. Most of the new staff tended to look for properties close by, until they had a chance to get to know the local area. And he'd been a new face, someone she'd never seen before. She should have known he was a doctor.

Junior doctors changed jobs every six months, some seniors did too, registrars usually every couple of years, but always around the same time of year. But he was a consultant. Come to think of it, he was pretty young to be a consultant obstetrician. But then again, what age was he?

She couldn't remember if she'd asked him that—she was sure she hadn't. And there weren't many details about that night she'd forgotten. No, she'd spent the last six weeks reliving that night over and over in her head.

How could she work with this man? The thought of seeing him every day sent delicious tingles along her spine. He was one of the most handsome men she'd ever seen. She'd seen him under cover of darkness before and through a haze of wine, and sometimes that hid a multitude of sins. But not for Cooper. No, he was just as much a Greek god in the cold, harsh light of day as he'd been on that crisp winter's night. She knew that already he'd be the talk of the hospital. There weren't that many handsome, unattached doctors in their midst. She could probably write a list of the names of colleagues who would attempt to ensnare him. That gave her a little flare of, what—jealousy? About someone she hardly knew?

She remembered the delicious excitement that night

of leaving with the mysterious stranger. She remembered her thoughts about destiny. She remembered her thought, *Who would ever know?* Melissa groaned. Once. Just once in her life she'd thrown caution to the wind and acted on her instincts. Everything about that night had been magical. So much so that when she'd woken in the morning she'd picked up her clothes and crept out, reluctant to do anything to break the spell from the night before. But at work she was sensible Melissa. Reliable, dependable and good at her job, not the bumbling, distracted idiot she'd felt like today. She wanted to keep her personal and professional lives separate. She was going to have to speak to him. There really wasn't any way around this.

She lifted her head at the slowing footsteps approaching her. Missy was startled. He was the absolute *last* person she expected to see right now.

He slowed his jog and walked the last couple of steps towards her in his navy jogging shorts and T-shirt. No other clothes could showcase his muscled legs so perfectly. A wicked thought filled her mind and instantly a smile danced across her lips as he thumped down next to her.

She leaned back against the steps. 'So, *Dr* Roberts, what can I do for you?' The mixed scent of his sweat and cologne instantly invaded her senses, making her head swim with memories of their night together.

That was it. That was what he'd loved about her. That had been the attraction—the fact she wasn't afraid to say whatever was on her sassy mind. He leaned back against the steps next to her, 'Well, *Sister* Bell, I'm not quite sure,' he said. 'We seem to have got ourselves into a bit of a predicament.'

He turned towards her, his face only inches from

hers. And then she saw them, those chocolate eyes again. Those deep eyes. The type that drew you in and made you forget who you were and where you were. The same eyes that had mesmerised her on that long, hot night together.

'You're a distraction,' she said.

'What?'

He flinched backwards and drew his gaze away from hers and she blinked twice. Apparently she was the only person caught in the memory.

'You distracted me at work today, Cooper. It's really difficult to be in a confined space with someone you last saw naked.'

He raised an eyebrow at her candour. 'Get straight to the point, why don't you?'

'It needs to be said.' Her fingers twiddled with a lock of her hair. She was trying to appear cool and casual. 'I felt as if I couldn't concentrate at work today and that's not me. I'm *very* good at my job.'

He nodded thoughtfully. 'I'm sure you are.' He ran his hand through his hair, catching the big brown strand that fell over his eyes. He looked sideways at her and gave a grin. 'I'd hate to be responsible for your mind not being on your work.'

There it was again, that sexual tension that seemed to spring up whenever they were near each other. There was silence between them for a second as his words hung in the air. Did he really need a distraction at work? No, he didn't. What he needed was to take some time to settle into his new position and find his feet again. His eyes darted around the empty jogging track. If he didn't look at her then he couldn't think illicit thoughts. He struggled to find the words he felt he had to say. 'This is probably a bit awkward for us both.'

Melissa groaned. She raised her hand in disgust. 'Please don't give me the speech.'

This time his eyes did meet hers, and his brow furrowed in confusion.

'What do you mean—the speech?'

She shook her head. 'I'm too old for all this. It's more than a little awkward. I asked you what you did for a living. You deliberately skirted the question. Do you think I would have gone home with you if I'd known I was going to spend the next year working with you?' She was getting annoyed now. Her pent-up frustration from spending the last few hours in the labour suite with him was finally bubbling to the surface.

'Well, I don't know, do I?' he answered calmly. 'Would it have made a difference?'

Melissa gritted her teeth. What was that supposed to mean? That she would have gone home with him anyway? Did he think she was some kind of tramp?

'Yes!' she spat out. 'I've learned from experience that work and pleasure shouldn't mix.'

Did she really mean that? What she'd learnt from experience was that she, David and work shouldn't have mixed. Or maybe she just shouldn't have mixed with David, full stop. But Cooper was someone entirely new. Did she really just want to be his one-night stand? Or did she want something more? Her mind was in such a turmoil of emotions right now she didn't know what she wanted. But the last thing she needed right now was another work-related romance. Last time around it had been a disaster, with everyone knowing every detail of her life. A private life should be just that—private. She took a deep breath, trying to regain her composure, and lowered her voice. 'Please tell me you haven't told all your new colleagues about the woman you picked up in the pub?'

Cooper sat wordlessly. She thought he would do that? He'd come here to tell her that what they'd had had been a mistake. He wanted to concentrate on his new job. A beautiful stranger had seemed like a great way to move back into the land of the living. But a beautiful colleague whom he'd see on a daily basis and would imagine in all sorts of ways would only confuse things for him. His gut twisted with the inevitable realisation that he wasn't ready for this yet.

His stomach clenched into a tight knot. He lifted up his finger and brushed it momentarily against her cheek. He thought this was what he had wanted too. No complications. To forget all about it. But all of a sudden, as the woman he'd shared the most passionate night of his life with sat beside him, he wasn't so sure.

'Of course I haven't said anything to anyone,' he said softly. 'I'm not that kind of guy.'

He heard her let out a huge sigh of relief. 'Thank you, Cooper,' she whispered. She saw the hurt expression on his face and gave her shoulders a little shrug. 'I don't know you, Cooper, I mean *really* know you. I had to ask.' She leaned forward, picking up some of the red asphalt from the running track and letting it run through her fingers. 'So what happens now?'

He turned to face her. Confusion spread across his face. 'What do you mean?'

'Cooper, you came halfway across town to come and speak to me.' She put her red-tinged fingers on his arm. 'What is it you want to say?'

Her heart was thumping in her chest. She knew what she wanted him to say, but from the expression on his face she knew he would never say it.

He bit his lip. He hated this. He wasn't even sure how to say it. Maybe if he'd been here a few months and had met her at work, maybe if he'd been six months down the line and had met her in the pub, it would be different, but right now it just didn't feel right and he had to tell her. 'I'm not looking for a relationship right now.'

The words came out rapidly and for some horrible reason it had an effect on her that she hadn't expected. It hurt. She'd been taught a valuable lesson years ago when her father had left her mother for another woman, and she'd spent months watching her mother break down. With that and David, she'd learnt never to depend on a man, only on herself. And she shouldn't forget it. 'I didn't ask you for a relationship, Cooper.'

'I know that but we've got to work together and—'

Melissa stood up, she didn't need to hear any more. She patted him on the shoulder. 'Don't worry, Coop, we can work together.'

She picked up her rucksack and shrugged her shoulders into it, before glancing at her watch and starting to jog back along the track. She had to move quickly, before the tears that were filling her eyes threatened to spill down her cheeks. Some nights were best just forgotten.

CHAPTER THREE

COOPER glanced at his watch. It was after five o'clock and his antenatal clinic had just finished. One of his overdue patients had already been in labour when she'd come to her appointment. She hadn't even realised it and had been shocked when Cooper had sent her along to the labour ward. It had been four hours and he wanted to go and check how she was doing. But going to the labour ward meant there was a good chance that he would run into Missy.

He'd spent the best part of the last ten days avoiding the labour ward as much as possible. It wasn't as difficult as it sounded as he had patients to see in the antenatal clinics in the hospital and the community, and he had patients to see in the wards after they had delivered. He really only got called to the labour suite if there was an immediate problem and his registrar wasn't available to deal with it. The joys of being a consultant.

On the few occasions he'd attended an emergency in the labour suite, he'd managed to avoid Missy altogether. She wasn't always on duty, or was sometimes attending to another patient. But today was different. His patient would be in the medical side of the labour suite, where Missy worked. And he had already seen her in one of the corridors a few hours ago when she'd come along to the clinic to pick up some notes for a patient. He was bound to meet her today.

This was ridiculous. He couldn't let a one-night stand affect his working practice, he was far too professional for that. He stood up from his chair and strode across the room, collecting his white coat from behind the door.

His heart stopped. Just for a second. A woman, sitting in a chair, was bent over, pulling something from her bag. Her blonde hair had fallen across her face and as she sat up, she put her hands to her back and arched backwards. She was obviously pregnant, six or seven months, but that wasn't the problem.

Just for a second, just for the tiniest second, he'd thought it was Clara. The same hairstyle, the same build, even the same stage of pregnancy. He felt as if someone had stabbed him in his side. Clara, his Clara. Of course it wasn't.

He moved backwards for a minute, leaning against the door. The woman glanced at her watch then stood up as a car pulled up outside. She gathered her coat and bag and headed outside. Cooper concentrated on breathing. This wasn't the first time this had happened. When Clara had first died, he'd thought he'd seen her everywhere—crossing a road, in a supermarket, even standing at a cash dispenser. But today was different. Today felt entirely different.

A sinking realisation filled his stomach. Guilt. Today, he felt guilt. Not because he hadn't been able to save his wife, no, that guilt was firmly tucked inside and would always burrow away at him. This was an entirely new kind of guilt.

It jolted him back to reality. He'd spent the last few weeks thinking about another woman. Missy. Not his wife. Not the woman he had planned to spend the rest of his life with and who used to occupy his every waking thought. No, his thoughts had been occupied by a woman with glorious chestnut hair, stunning green eyes and a fabulous cleavage, a woman he'd spent the hottest night of his life with.

He felt sick. Sick with guilt. Was this what moving on felt like? Why had he forgotten about Clara? No, he hadn't forgotten about her, but she'd been pushed gently to the side. And he felt horrible. Horribly confused.

He dragged his mind back to the present. Patients, he had patients to see. He took a deep breath. He had a job to do and it was time to do it.

The labour suite was in full flow when he arrived. Sister Jenkins replaced the phone at the desk as he arrived. A small, rotund woman with years of experience, he'd learned that within the labour suite she was probably worth her weight in gold.

'Hi, Flora.' He smiled, leaning over the desk towards her. 'I'm looking for Maisie Kerr. I sent her along from the antenatal clinic.'

'Yes, she's in room four, progressing nicely.' She shuffled some papers on the desk. Cooper went to start along the corridor when she spoke again. 'What about Claire Ferguson—aren't you going to see her?'

'Claire Ferguson? She's here?'

Flora nodded as she saw the surprised expression on his face. 'You didn't know?'

He shook his head. 'Where is she?'

Flora pointed down the corridor. 'Room seven in the medical suite. Melissa is looking after her.'

Cooper's face turned to stone. He had written in the patient's notes that he wanted to be informed if she was admitted for any reason. Claire Ferguson was a patient with high-risk complications of pregnancy; she was already scheduled for a Caesarean section in a few weeks' time. Claire also had some mental-health problems, which, due to her pregnancy, had caused complications as they had tried to adjust her medications. He wanted this patient treated with the most delicate of hands and was more than a little annoyed he hadn't been notified of her admission.

As he entered the room he noticed the curtains were drawn around the bed, the lights were dimmed and tranquil music was playing. When he walked in he found Melissa talking in a very low voice and gently massaging Claire's shoulders. Claire's eyes were closed and she looked calm and relaxed as Melissa continued slowly. She raised her fingers to her lips, 'Shh,' she mouthed to Cooper, and gestured for him to wait outside.

'Claire, I'm just going to leave you for a couple of minutes. Don't worry, I'll be right outside the door. Just continue with your breathing exercises and I'll be back soon.'

She adjusted the pillows on the bed, picked up the notes and followed Cooper outside.

'Didn't you see what was written on her case notes?' His voice hit her like an icy blast.

'Of course I did.'

'Then why didn't you contact me the minute Claire Ferguson was admitted?'

Melissa shook her head silently. She would never ignore something in a patient's notes. 'I asked your registrar to contact you, Dr Roberts, so I suggest you take it up with him. For your information, Claire has been admitted because her membranes have ruptured early. She was also in such an acute state of panic that I had to take the time to calm her properly before I could do an assessment of her condition.' She handed him the notes. 'I had just completed them for you. She's thirty-seven weeks' gestation. Her membrane rupture has been confirmed. She hasn't started to labour yet and will be ready to go to Theatre for her Caesarean section in the next ten minutes. The anaesthetist has been notified—I know, because I did that myself. I was just about to come and phone you to see where you were.'

Cooper lowered his eyes and attempted to open the notes but Melissa was still tightly grasping the other side. Her voice was low and steady. 'I've just spent a lot of time calming your patient to prepare her for Theatre so *don't* go in there and upset her.'

Cooper could tell by the expression on her face that she was entirely serious. What did she take him for? 'I'm not going to do that,' he said quickly, then added, 'And I will take it up with my registrar. Thank you for bringing it to my attention.'

She nodded and headed over to the midwives' station. 'Hi, Andrea, I'm just going to get my patient ready for Theatre and then I'll go for my break—is that okay?'

Andrea glanced at the disappearing coat tails of Cooper as he headed into Claire's room. 'What's up with you and Dr Hunk?'

Melissa immediately became defensive and folded her arms across her chest. 'What on earth do you mean?'

Andrea's top lip curled in indignation. 'I don't know who you think you're kidding. The pair of you prowl around each other like a pair of rival lions stalking their prey. Have you two had a tiff?'

No matter how hard she tried, Melissa could feel the colour starting to creep up her cheeks. 'No, we haven't, and I hardly know him.'

'Yeah, yeah, whatever.' Andrea's throw-away remark was coupled with a wave of her hand. She leaned forward. 'More importantly, I want to know how you're feeling. You've been looking a bit peaky lately.'

'Have I? I'm fine.' But inside she suddenly realised her colleague was right. She hadn't felt herself in quite some time. She gave a little shake of her head. 'Anyway, I'd better go and finish with Claire. I'll see you after lunch.'

Melissa headed back in to Claire, her mind spinning. Andrea was really perceptive. Had she guessed something had happened between Cooper and herself? Surely not. She had hardly seen Cooper lately. She was sure he was avoiding her. More importantly, she was furious with the way he'd just spoken to her. How dare he question her competence at work? She finished with Claire and sent the happy and calm mum-to-be off to Theatre before heading for lunch.

Lunch, however, was a spartan affair for Melissa. She sat down to the sandwiches she had brought with her, took two bites and spent the next ten minutes pushing them around the table. Was this what the mere sight of Cooper was doing to her? Putting her off her food? He could turn out to be the best diet control *ever*.

Melissa gave up and flung the sandwiches in the bin. She was never going to get her appetite back now. She normally did her injections before she ate, but because she hadn't been feeling too hungry she had waited a little longer, which was just as well as this meant she could adjust her insulin to suit her appetite.

One of the other midwives stuck her head around the door. 'Melissa, sorry to interrupt you but Dr Roberts is looking for you.'

She looked up from where she had been injecting her insulin into her stomach to see Cooper walking through the door towards her.

She quickly finished her injection and put it back in her bag. Cooper was standing next to her, looking a bit uncomfortable. 'Sorry, Melissa, I didn't mean to disturb you.'

She shook her head. 'It's all right, Cooper. Working somewhere like this, you get used to interruptions.'

He fixed her with his steady brown-eyed gaze. 'I didn't realise you were diabetic. Have you been injecting for long?'

'Since I was eight. It's like second nature to me now.' Great. She was stuck in an enclosed space yet again with Dr Hunk. Oh, my—and now she'd started using that stupid nickname. The last time her stomach had done flip-flops like this had been when she'd been a teenager and had gone to see her favourite boy band. If she could bottle and sell what she was currently feeling, she could be a millionaire.

He sat down in the chair next to her, the sleeve of his white coat brushing against her bare arm. Zing. She could practically see the sparks of electricity fly. 'Are you well controlled?'

She gave a mock look of indignation. 'That's a bit personal. Are you asking me as a professional colleague or as a friend? No, sorry that's right—we're not friends.'

'What do you mean, we're not friends?' He shifted awkwardly in his chair. Melissa was definitely taking a bit of getting used to. How could a woman who made him feel so hot under the collar put him in his place so much? She certainly never minced her words.

'Well, I hardly think we got off to the best start, did we? You purposely avoid me at work and, when we do have to work together, you can be downright rude. My "friends" don't normally behave like that around me.'

She was annoyed. He could tell because of the way

her eyes were shooting sparks at him. *Lord, she was sexy.* 'Actually, I thought we got off to a great start.' His voice was very quiet, almost a whisper in the empty staffroom.

Melissa felt the hairs instantly stand up on the back of her neck in response to the implication of his words. Silence hung between them. She wasn't quite sure how to respond to that. Had she missed something?

She ignored what he'd just said and answered his original question. 'If you're asking as a *colleague* if my diabetes is well controlled then the response is, yes, it is and you don't have to worry about me being unwell while we work together. If you're asking as a *friend* then the truth is I'm a complete control freak. I check my blood sugar and adjust my insulin all the time. I want to have the best control that I possibly can.'

Cooper looked at her through thick eyelashes. 'Okay, so I feel a bit sheepish now.'

'Why?'

He cringed. 'Because I came in here to complain that you hadn't taken Claire Ferguson along to Theatre yourself. Now I realise you probably needed to get something to eat.'

She shook her head silently. 'Cooper, as a rule we never take the patients along to Theatre ourselves— unless it's an emergency. The theatre staff always come along and pick the patient up. And this...' she pulled a wrapped chocolate biscuit, which looked a little worse for wear, from her pocket for effect '...is proof that I *always* have something on standby to make sure I would never leave a patient in the lurch.' She let out a big sigh and flopped backwards in the chair. 'I was finished with Claire. I had done everything she needed and will be here waiting to receive her when she comes back from Theatre. Why are you trying to pick fault with everything I do?'

He ran his hand through his hair in frustration. 'I guess I'm just not too good at this. I've never had a relationship with someone at work before and I find the whole thing really strange. And you're right—I have been avoiding you.' He shrugged his shoulders like a scolded schoolboy.

Melissa felt her voice start to tremble. 'We don't have a relationship, Cooper. We had a one-night stand. Something that I'm not proud to admit, or that I've ever done before. It really wasn't the way I wanted to meet my new colleague. This is not something I want to do at work. And I know exactly how you feel, because I've been avoiding you too.'

'You have?' His eyes ran up and down the length of her body. This woman really didn't understand how attractive she was, did she? 'You've never had a relationship at work?' He almost couldn't believe that. If she'd worked at the last hospital he'd been a consultant at, they would practically have been jousting in the car park over her.

'That's not what I said. My ex-fiancé used to be one of the registrars here but when we split up he left, so I haven't really had to deal with any awkwardness at work before. It makes me really uncomfortable.'

So she had had a relationship at work. Why did that bother him so much? 'Why did you split up?'

Melissa shifted uncomfortably in the chair. 'David and I were together for almost three years. I wanted to start a family and he wasn't ready.'

Cooper suppressed the snort he wanted to let out. The man was obviously a fool. 'Why didn't you just wait?' It seemed like a simple enough question and it was one she'd asked herself a million times, both before and after she'd spilt up with David.

She stayed silent for a second, thinking before she answered. Only her closest friends really knew how she felt about all this. Why would she tell Cooper? Then again, Cooper had seen more of her than even her closest friends had and, truth be told, she was tired of pussyfooting round about him, watching what she said. She was exhausted. Literally exhausted. Maybe she should just tell the truth? Maybe if she did, he would run a mile. She shrugged. 'I'm twenty-nine now. I've been diabetic for twenty-one years. You know the risks for both the baby and me. Having a long-term condition like diabetes means I'm at higher risk of complications. I don't want to wait forever. I want to be healthy and I want my family to be healthy. The way that David behaved, I don't know that he would ever have been ready for a family and I didn't want to lose the opportunity by waiting to find out. I've learned in life not to depend on a man for anything.'

Wow! Why had she told him all that? From a male perspective it could look quite cold and Missy knew that. It looked as if she was just waiting for a sperm donor, rather than a loving relationship.

Cooper gave a little smile. 'But there are certain things that you just can't do on your own.' The woman really did have fire in her belly. He quirked an eyebrow at her. 'It can't really have helped, working in a maternity unit.'

She met his gaze with surprise. 'What do you mean?'

He lifted his hand and pointed to the ward outside. 'Being in here every day and seeing lots of babies being brought into the world.' He gave a guarded little smile.

'It sounds as though your biological clock is ticking so loudly it's practically thudding in your ears!'

She was stunned. Was it at his perceptiveness? Or was it his candour? Either way, what he'd just said had made her look and feel like the maddest person in the room. Why had she said anything?

Cooper was still watching her carefully. He could almost see the thoughts tearing through her brain like a washing machine on a spin cycle. For the second time he saw a sheen come over Missy's eyes. Almost automatically a fire lit up in his belly. He'd felt this way the night he'd met her. Fiercely protective. No rhyme or reason to it. He'd hit a nerve and been too forward.

'Missy, I'm sorry. Please don't be upset with me. I shouldn't have said that.'

He reached out and grasped her hand. She flinched, as if she was about to pull away, then changed her mind and stopped. It was too hard to talk. Her mind was spinning and she couldn't make sense of any of her thoughts. She'd spent a wonderful night with a gorgeous man, a man she'd never expected to see again. Now he was haunting her everyday life. Every thought she had was about him. Every time she came to work all she could think about was him. Her stomach was constantly in a knot, wondering if when she turned the next corner he would be there. And the thoughts she was having in her bed at night....

'Missy, let me fix this.' He grasped both her hands now and turned to face her. He knew what he needed to do now, the guilt he'd felt earlier when he'd thought he'd seen Clara giving him new clarity. This was all part of moving on. Missy was the first woman he'd been attracted to in two years, and he wasn't about to let her slip from his grasp because he was behaving like an ass. 'Let's start from the beginning again. Let's have a clean slate. I like you, Missy, and I know you like me, but the reality is I hardly know you. So why don't we start from scratch?'

He stood up and put out his hand. 'Hi, pleased to meet you. I'm Cooper Roberts and I work at St Jude's as a consultant obstetrician. I think you're wildly attractive. Could I take you out for coffee some time?'

Missy's bottom lip was definitely trembling now. The unshed tears in her eyes were ready to spill down her cheeks at a moment's notice. She stretched her hand out to meet his, willing her arm to stop shaking and pushing herself up from her chair.

'Hi, I'm Melissa Bell, I'm a midwife in the labour suite at St Jude's. It's nice to meet you.' She stopped for a second, fighting to stop herself breaking into tears.

Her eyes met his. Her heart was pounding in her chest. Everything she'd noticed about him that night was still there. His muscular build, floppy brown hair and the deep chocolate eyes that looked good enough to eat. Most of all there was just him, the man that caused continual butterflies in her chest. No man had ever had that effect on her before and she couldn't walk away from it.

'I would love to go for coffee with you, Coop.'

So why was he nervous? He'd asked her to go for coffee to try and find a way to be friends. He had to make their relationship at work easier and he was struggling with it as much as she was. Cooper had just finished fastening his deep blue shirt when his mobile rang. He glanced at the caller display, and saw it was Jake. He remembered how he'd almost told Missy his name was Jake—how embarrassing would that have made things now?

He picked up the phone. 'What's up?'

'Hi, Coop, what you up to?'

'I'm just heading out. Is something up?'

'Just wondered if you wanted to meet me for a few drinks.'

Cooper hesitated just a second too long.

'What's up, Coop? Spit it out.'

'Well, sorry, I can't. I'm meeting someone.'

'What—you've got a date?' Jake let out a wolf whistle, which reverberated down the phone and just about ruptured his eardrum.

'Calm down, Jake. It's not a date. I'm just meeting a friend for coffee.'

'Is it a female friend?'

'Yes.'

'The mystery woman you met a couple of months ago?'

'Well…yes.'

'Hate to break it to you, buddy, but that's called a date.' There was a pause for a second. 'And, Cooper?'

'Yes?'

'Good luck, it's about time.'

Cooper hung up the phone and felt himself break out into a sweat. It *was* a date, wasn't it? He hadn't really thought of it like that. The last person he'd been out on a date with had been his wife. Somehow he didn't think his one night with Missy really counted. He stared out his window at the panoramic view of the marina. Clara had been dead for two years. They'd been married for four years, had dated for four before then, so that made…ten, ten years since he'd been out on a date. Would he even remember what he was supposed to do?

He panicked and picked up his phone. He could phone and make an excuse, say he had to go into work for something. Then it struck him. No, he couldn't. He didn't even have her mobile number.

He walked over to the window. It was a beautiful winter's day. He could see various people down at the marina among the boats. Some of them were beauties. Some of the boats must have cost more than he could earn in a lifetime. He watched one family loading up their boat with supplies. They must be going out for the day. Mum, dad and two children, both boys. They were smiling and laughing. The kids were jumping up and down, both carrying fishing rods. The mum was holding a large brown hamper—probably packed with food for the day. The dad came over and slung his arm around her shoulders, giving her a kiss on the side of the head. Cooper felt as if an arrow had pierced his heart. That should have been him. Him and Clara, with their children.

But even as he had those thoughts something shifted in his mind. That might not be his life, but why shouldn't he still have it? He'd moved to a new city, got a new job, taken his wedding ring off and decided to move on. Okay, he might have made a bit of a mess of it so far but that didn't mean that he couldn't improve things.

He tore his eyes away from the marina and marched over to the mirror. He checked his reflection quickly. Hair maybe a little too long, eyes and skin clear. He turned sideways and pulled his stomach in. Why? He didn't need to do that, he had a good physique. It was time to get back out there. He'd met a beautiful woman he was wildly attracted to. What could go wrong? With renewed vigour he picked up his jacket, glanced at his watch and headed for the door.

* * *

Melissa was almost ready. At the last count she'd
changed her top four times and wiped her lipstick three
times before finally settling on a cherry-red top and
some lip gloss. She glanced at her watch. She'd only
ten minutes to get there and her head was pounding.
Was it stress? Or was the thought of meeting Cooper
giving her a headache?

She picked up her brown leather bag and threw the
lip gloss and a bottle of water inside. She could take
some painkillers on the way. Missy opened the bathroom cabinet and started searching through what was
inside. She could almost swear that these mini-bottles
of lotions and potions reproduced as soon as she closed
the door. Her hand hit a cardboard box and stopped her
in her tracks. Tampons. When was the last time she'd
used those?

The hairs on her arms stood on end. She fumbled in
her bag for her diary and flicked through it. She'd had
a few irregular periods and some mild symptoms so
her GP had started some investigations for polycystic
ovarian syndrome. So this wasn't such a big deal, was
it? Her breath caught in her throat. Eight weeks. It had
been eight weeks since she'd had a period. She flicked
back a little further, confirming her already mounting
suspicions. Even though her periods had been irregular
before, there had never been a gap this long.

She felt sick. She felt physically sick. This couldn't
be happening. She glanced at her watch again. There
was no time. She was going to be late. She grabbed her
bag and took a deep breath. This was all in her head.
There was nothing to worry about. She couldn't possibly be pregnant. She'd taken every precaution. The
delayed period must just be the PCOS. She glanced at
her reflection in the mirror. A deathly pale face stared

back. Her brain flicked into furious overtime. Did her breasts feel tender? Was this nausea something more than shock? Was she pale because she was anaemic? Missy gave herself a shake. She would pick up a pregnancy test on the way home and put her mind at rest. All this worry would be for nothing. She was sure of it.

Missy crossed the street and pushed open the door of the café. There he was, wearing blue jeans, a dark blue shirt and a black leather jacket. He looked up at her from the table where he was sitting, running his fingers through his hair. He looked nervous. Good. So was she.

'Hi, Cooper. I'm sorry I'm late. Have you been waiting long?'

She gave him an uneasy smile, fingering the gold necklace around her slim throat. She was nervous. He was relieved.

'It's fine.' He folded his newspaper and put it down on one of the chairs. 'I thought I would just come in and have a seat.'

She pulled out the chair next to her and sat down.

'What can I get you?' The voice came from a bored, slim, blonde waitress who'd already been over the table twice while Cooper had been sitting himself.

'I'll have a cappuccino and… What will you have, Missy?'

'I'll have the same.'

The waitress nodded and slopped off in the direction of the kitchen.

'So what did you do today?' he asked, leaning across the table. She looked even more beautiful today. Her chestnut curls were pulled up on either side of her face with an ornate studded clasp. She was wearing a cherry-red top, which clung to her curves and showed a hint of her delicious cleavage. She had a little mascara on, which highlighted her green eyes, and a little lip gloss. Very natural. A passer-by might call her pretty but to Cooper she was more beautiful than any catwalk model. There was something immensely attractive about being in the company of a woman who was comfortable in her own skin.

She reached her hand up and started twiddling with one of her curls. Just like she'd been doing the first time he had seen her. 'I haven't done much this morning. I just got a little caught up at home.' That was an understatement. Her brain had been in hyperdrive all the way over here. She was beginning to imagine herself having all these pregnancy-related symptoms. Things she would never have thought about in a million years if she hadn't seen that box of tampons.

The waitress appeared again and thumped the cups on the table, coffee sloshing onto the white saucers.

Cooper watched her retreating back. 'Service with a smile, eh?'

Melissa smiled and shrugged her shoulders sympathetically. 'She's probably in a job she hates with another hundred things on her mind. I can forgive her a little spilt coffee.'

'So why do you work on the medical side of the labour suite? I would have thought most midwives would have preferred to be on the midwifery side where they have control of the labour.'

His question caught her unawares. He couldn't possibly know what was spilling around in her mind. She took a deep breath and focused. 'I'm not "most midwives".'

He looked at her with amusement, a smile creeping across his face. 'Well, I've guessed that.'

'I usually specialise in the diabetic maternity clinic. I want to make sure women with high-risk conditions have the same rights to experience a natural birth and have control over their labour. Most of the women I see in the clinic are termed as requiring "medical care" so I try to provide some continuity for them.'

Cooper nodded thoughtfully then noticed she was pushing her coffee cup around the table. 'What's wrong—don't you like it?'

Missy gave a little grimace. 'I don't know what's wrong. I just don't have the stomach for it this morning.'

He glanced at his watch. 'Well, it's just after eleven, so why don't we make this an early lunch? You might feel better if you eat something.' He signalled to the waitress. 'I'll shout Happy Harry over to take our order.'

Food. Now she really did think she was going to throw up all over the table. 'No, don't—please.'

His head tilted to the side and his brow furrowed. 'Is everything okay, Missy?'

Missy. He'd called her Missy again and even the way he said her name made her legs turn to mush. She looked over the table at the Greek god she'd had the one-night stand with. Only he wasn't a Greek god to her any more. He was a man, with thoughts and feelings that she had to consider. He wasn't part of the fantasy dreams she'd had every night. He was a real, live person and this was supposed to be what? Their 'first proper date'? And she was about to ruin it.

'Missy, what's wrong?'

She glanced downwards. Her throat was bone dry and that coffee would be the last thing she would be swallowing. She played nervously with her fingers, refusing to lift her head and meet his gaze. It was easier this way. 'Cooper, I don't want you to panic but I'm a bit worried about something.'

'What?' He leaned forward and put his elbows on the table so he was closer to her. She looked awful and why wasn't she looking at him? What was she going to say?

'I think…I mean, I'm not sure…well, I think there could be a possibility that I might be pregnant.'

There, she'd said it. She watched as the colour drained from his face and he sat back in his chair.

'Oh.'

'That's all you've got to say? Oh?'

'You took me by surprise. I mean, I know there was an issue with the condom, but I thought you were going to go and get—'

'I did.'

'You did?' His voice rose, almost hopefully, it seemed.

'Yes, I did, but we both know it's not foolproof.'

He sighed and put his hand across the table and took her hand. 'But it's been weeks. Surely you would have missed a few periods by now?

She nodded. 'Normally I probably would have. But I've been having investigations for PCOS as my periods have been really irregular. And because I'd taken the morning-after pill I just assumed everything was fine. It wasn't until today that I realised how long it had been since I'd had a normal period.'

He nodded slowly, taking in everything she's just said. 'How are you feeling?'

'Right now, awful.' Her eyes met his and he could see the worry and confusion in her face. 'I don't know if I'm imagining symptoms for myself. On the way over here

I seem to have given myself every pregnancy symptom in the world.'

Somewhere deep inside her head a voice was screaming. *Baby! Baby!* Pregnancy was measured from the date of the last proper period so, if she was expecting, that would make her between ten and eleven weeks pregnant. The realisation made the hairs on her arms stand on end.

Cooper pushed his cup away. 'Why don't we find out?'

Melissa felt sick. 'What do you mean?'

'Let's go and get a test. You could do it now.'

Everything about this seemed wrong. 'This isn't a spectator sport.' If she was going to do a pregnancy test, she wanted to do it in private. More than that, she needed some time alone to think. What on earth was she going to do? This was supposed to have been a 'starting again, getting to know you' date, not a 'guess who might be pregnant' date. She couldn't believe this was happening.

'I've got as much right to know as you have.' His voice was low and firm. He was watching her with those brooding brown eyes. The ones that still made her heart leap. The ones that got her into this situation in the first place.

'I know that,' she whispered. Lunch was forgotten. The nice, quiet meeting for coffee was forgotten. Their first official date was forgotten. Everything paled into insignificance next to this. Why this? Why now?

Cooper signalled to the waitress for their bill. He thrust his hand deep into the pocket of his jeans to pull out some money and sent coins scattering across the floor. Melissa bent down to help him retrieve them and froze. Something glistened at her from the dark-tiled floor. There was no mistaking it. A gold wedding band.

Cooper hadn't noticed as he was picking up coins from under his chair. 'I'm such a klutz,' he muttered, gathering up the coins and sitting back down in the seat opposite. The waitress thumped the bill down on the table and walked away. Cooper watched her retreating back. 'Well, I guess we won't be leaving a tip for the service.'

Melissa hadn't moved. She couldn't believe it. Every hair on her body stood on end, the nerve endings instantly intensified. She could feel bile rise in the back of her throat. Any moment now she was going to be physically sick. She reached out her hand and dropped the gold wedding band onto the table.

Silence. Silence was golden, that's what they said. On this occasion, silence was a gold wedding band.

She could see the pain. It was written all over his face. 'I can explain.'

'You'd better.' Please, no. Please, don't let me have bedded a married man. Please, don't let me find out that I'm pregnant by a man who has a wife and 2.4 children stashed away somewhere.

'I'm a widower.'

Wow! She hadn't been expecting that.

He turned the ring over and over in his hand. 'My wife died two years ago.' His voice was trembling now. That hadn't been there before. This was still raw. 'I've only recently taken my wedding ring off, but I still keep it in my pocket. That was part of the reason why I came here.' He lifted his heavy eyelids and looked at her through thick dark lashes. 'To start anew. None of the people I work with here know I'm a widower. It saves too many difficult questions.'

Melissa nodded. She still hadn't spoken. A widower, well, it was better than a married man. Her heart reached out to him. He was obviously still grieving. But her head screamed at her. She could be pregnant by a man who was still grieving for his dead wife. A man who still carried his wedding ring in his pocket. A man who obviously wasn't ready to move on.

'Say something.'

Melissa stood up and picked up her bag. 'I've got a lot to think about. I'll let you know what happens.'

'Are you going to do a test?'

'Obviously.'

'Can I be there?'

'No.'

He stood up. 'I'm sorry, Missy. This is my fault. I've put you in this position. Let me be there for you. Don't do the test alone.'

The words echoed around her head. How could he be there for her? He still carried his wedding ring in his pocket.

'Cooper, I just don't know. I think I should do this on my own. This might all be a panic over nothing.'

'Then let's find out.' His voice was calm and steady and he reached over and took her hand. She hesitated for a second. He did have the right to know. He wasn't married, he wasn't cheating on anyone, he just wasn't *hers*, and this was not how she'd imagined having a family. But it was time to be an adult. And it was time to find out.

It took ten minutes to find a pharmacy, buy a test and get home.

Missy was desperate to pee and didn't want to waste the opportunity. She might be a midwife but she'd no idea there were so many different kinds of pregnancy tests. She was so used to the one that they used routinely in the hospital that the array of boxes had bewildered her. In the end Cooper had grabbed the first two that he'd seen and paid for them, while she'd still stood there, dithering.

A quick glance at the instructions and she headed for the toilet. She looked at her watch. Who knew two minutes could be so long?

She'd wanted a child for so long. But she'd wanted the loving relationship that went with having a child. At least in her mind it did. She was twenty-nine. She'd been diabetic for twenty-one years. She didn't want to wait any longer. She wasn't going to.

She glanced at her watch. One minute up.

Cooper was standing, glancing out of her window, with his hands deep in his pockets. He didn't seem to be looking at his watch. He seemed lost in another world. She couldn't really have picked a worse candidate for a father. Would an anonymous one-night stand have been better? She was going to have to see Cooper at work every day. Would he interfere in her life? Would he want to have contact with her baby? *Her baby.* She was already starting to think that way.

Her eyes glanced across the counter as Cooper came and sat next to her. They didn't have to wait a whole two minutes. He'd bought the most expensive test on the market. This one didn't have pink or blue lines. This one told it like it was.

One word. *Pregnant.*

CHAPTER FOUR

COOPER looked at the test. He felt as if he were in a bad dream. What was she thinking about? A chill came over his body. Melissa had told him that she wanted a baby, but what if she didn't want *his* baby?

Melissa was a wonderful woman, almost a tonic for the two previous years. She was beautiful, and dedicated to her job. She was independent, not clingy. She understood the pressures of work and the problems they could cause for someone like him. Who knows where this could have led? Maybe she would have been a stepping stone for him. A nice way to ease back into the land of dating. Maybe he would have grown to love her and their relationship would have deepened. Maybe she would only ever have been a one-night stand. But now...

He had to ask the question. 'What do you want to do?'

She looked stunned. 'What do you mean?'

'Do you want to have the baby?'

His words came out colder, harsher than he had meant them to. The timing was a disaster. An unexpected pregnancy. They hadn't had a chance to get to know each other, to develop any potential relationship, and now a pregnancy? Cooper felt ill. Then, to top it all off, there had been the wedding-ring incident. Her face had been unreadable. He'd no idea what she thought about that. Was she angry with him? Upset?

He'd told her about Clara. But he hadn't told her about Lily, his daughter. Even her name brought pain to his heart. His perfect baby who should have been pink and screaming had been blue and quiet. He couldn't even bear to think about it. He wasn't ready to talk about her yet. Melissa was pregnant, how could he tell her his wife had died due to pregnancy complications? How could he tell her his baby had died too? It would frighten her, terrify her even. He couldn't do that. Their relationship wasn't stable enough for that.

'Why on earth would you think I wouldn't want this baby?' Her hands flew automatically to her stomach in a protective gesture. Her eyes seemed wide and afraid. She was protecting her baby, *their baby*. And another range of wild thoughts flew through his head.

Melissa was diabetic. Making her more at risk of complications than others. Could he really support her through a pregnancy? Could he watch her body change shape and see the little life grow under her skin, while the whole time he would be terrified something would happen again?

He hesitated. 'I'm just not sure, Melissa. Truth be told, I don't know what you want.'

And he didn't know what he wanted either. Pregnancy had brought the whole world into perspective for him. A tight fist clenched around his heart as he thought about his daughter. He couldn't go through that again. *Get a grip, Cooper!*

This was his second chance. He couldn't possibly walk away—he wasn't that kind of man. He would support her, he would help her. He would do anything possible to make sure this time his child made it into the world alive. It was his job, his duty and his responsibility. His heart? Well, it would just have to be put to the side right now. Facts he could deal with, emotions would just have to wait.

Melissa was in shock. She was still sitting in the same position with her hand on her stomach. She still couldn't believe this was happening. She'd always wanted to be a mother. But her dreams of being a mother had always gone alongside dreams of a happy family, a family that involved a father, something she'd been deprived of. This wasn't how she had imagined finding out she was pregnant—in her house with a man she'd had a one-night stand with.

And how on earth could Cooper think that she might not want this baby? She could never ever not want this baby. But maybe this wasn't about her, maybe this was about him?

She took a deep breath, 'Do *you* want to have this baby?'

Her voice brought him into check. 'Of course I do, Melissa.'

She nodded in relief at his words. He'd said what she needed to hear.

But her head was spinning. Where would Cooper fit into this equation? When her father had left, she'd vowed never to rely on a man for anything. Her mother had been left financially and emotionally bereft. Even in her relationship with David, she'd kept her own flat, her own finances, which in the end, had turned out to be just as well. Because he had left too.

But now that she knew they both wanted this baby, her mind flew off at a tangent. She knew that her long-term diabetes control was good. And she knew that was one of the key factors influencing her baby's health.

But she hadn't been planning a pregnancy so she hadn't taken any folic-acid supplements or watched what she had been eating. Could these things affect her baby? What if she'd done something that could have damaged her developing baby?

'I need to know if this baby's okay.' Tears pricked her eyes and her voice was so quiet it was barely a whisper.

'What?' Cooper was a little stunned by her words.

'I need to know, Cooper.' She lifted her heavy lids to meet his gaze. 'I didn't plan this pregnancy, I haven't been taking folic acid. You know that I'm at higher risk of just about everything. What if something is wrong with this baby because I didn't know I was pregnant?'

He could hear the panic in her voice as it rose in pitch. He was an obstetrician. He could understand her feelings, her panic. She was only vocalising what he'd thought about a few moments before. He walked around the counter and put his arm around her shoulders. 'Calm down, Missy. You have no reason to worry like that, do you?' His voice was calm. 'You told me yourself that you're a control freak.' His hand rubbed her arm in reassurance. 'So I'm imagining that your blood-glucose levels will have been good and your baby won't have been put at any greater risk.'

She looked lost in thought but nodded almost absent-mindedly.

'Do you want me to arrange a scan appointment for you? Will that make you feel a little better? I could do it in the next few days.'

'Could you?' Her head turned anxiously towards his.

'Of course I could.' He gave her a little smile and planted a kiss on her forehead. 'It's one of the perks of the job.'

'As soon as I visit the scan room everyone will know

that I'm pregnant—there's no secrets in that place.' She could almost hear the jungle drums in her head.

He nodded his head. 'I know that,' he said. 'I'm not worried.'

She hesitated. 'It's just that…I understand why you might not have wanted people at work to know you were widowed. I can appreciate you wanting to keep parts of your life private. But now, with this…' Her hands pointed towards her belly.

Cooper nodded. 'Let me worry about that, Melissa.'

He wrapped his arms around her and they stood, locked together. He'd spent the last two years staying away from personal issues that he couldn't have control over—it had been the only thing that had kept him sane. But for the second time in his life Cooper felt that certain elements were spiralling out of his grasp. Could he survive again?

Melissa tapped her foot impatiently on the waiting-room floor. Cooper was sitting next to her in jeans and a jumper, his white coat left in the confines of his office. She wasn't going to let him play the 'I work here' card today. Today she wanted them to be normal parents-to-be. Everything else had to be left at the door.

She sipped at the plastic cup of water in her hand. Her bladder was about to burst. It was all very well, telling mums-to-be they had to have a full bladder to get the best possible view on their scan, it was quite another to try and consume four cups of chilled water.

'Melissa Bell?' The sonographer stood at the entrance to the waiting room, her eyes peering into the gloomy room. 'Oh, it is you; I thought I recognised the name. Come on in.'

She came over, gave Melissa's hand a little squeeze

and led the way to the darkened scan room. Melissa had known Fiona for over seven years. She was always completely professional and there wasn't a flicker of surprise on her face as Cooper followed them into the small space.

'You know the drill, Melissa. Get yourself up on the couch and we'll see if I can show you this baby.'

Melissa lay up on the paper-covered couch and loosened her jeans. Her heart started beating frantically in her chest. She took a deep breath. She'd accompanied many women to their scans before, but this was different. She wasn't here as a midwife, she was here as a patient. Everything suddenly had a new perspective for her. Cooper pulled out the chair next to her and sat down. His eyes were fixed entirely on the blank screen.

Fiona checked the card she'd been given. She gave Melissa a little smile. 'Well, I don't need to check your name with you. Are you still at the same address?' Melissa nodded silently. 'And with the same GP? Good. Okay, I'm going to put a little gel on your stomach. I did try to warm it up, so it shouldn't be too cold.'

Melissa inhaled sharply as the gel squirted onto her stomach. *Please, let everything be all right.* Fiona positioned the transducer and started moving it across Melissa's abdomen. She moved down a little lower and pressed firmly.

Melissa heard the noise before she recognised the shape on the screen. A small, rapid heartbeat. As clear as could be. Melissa felt a grin spread across her face and a sense of relief stretch through her body. Fiona started to point at the screen. 'Look, here we are. There is baby's heart—look at the flicker on the screen.'

Melissa nodded enthusiastically. She couldn't speak. She couldn't wipe the smile off her face.

Fiona adjusted the transducer and started to take some measurements. 'Look, there's the baby's head, femur, and the baby's arm. And, oh, it looks as if baby is trying to wave at us!' She shot Melissa a huge smile. 'How far along did you think you were?' She looked down and glanced at the white card again, answering her own question. 'About eleven weeks?'

Melissa felt her breath catch in her throat. *Was something wrong? Did the dates not match?*

Fiona's voice was loud and clear, banishing any bad thoughts. 'Well, you're almost spot on. Eleven weeks and four days, according to this scan. And everything looks great.' She took down a few notes before trying to get a good image of the baby.

Melissa squirmed uncomfortably as the pressure on her abdomen mounted. She didn't want to move but she desperately needed to go to the toilet. Fiona shot her a knowing smile. 'I'll just be second. There, now, baby's in just the right position. I take it you want the nuchal translucency scan done?'

Melissa glanced over at Cooper and gave a nod. The nuchal translucency test was a simple scan that, used with the age of the baby and the age of the mother, gave an estimated risk of the baby having Down's syndrome. It was yet another thing she was at higher risk of.

Fiona spent a few seconds measuring the fluid at the back of the baby's neck and recording her results. 'This scan picture, along with your details and your blood test, will go up to the central lab. Your test results will take about two weeks. Okay?'

Melissa nodded gratefully, thankful her baby had been lying in the correct position for the scan. She didn't know how much longer her bladder was going to last.

Fiona swept the transducer across her abdomen. 'I want to get a good picture for you.'

A few seconds later she pressed a button on the screen and a little black and white image printed out for Melissa.

'And one for Dad?'

Silence. Melissa turned. In the darkened room she had to screw her eyes up to see Cooper's face. It hadn't moved. He was still staring at the screen.

Cooper felt as if the black walls were closing in around him. The only light in the room came from the monitor in front of him. There was his baby. Alive, on the screen. He'd been here before. He'd attended three scans with Clara and watched his daughter grow before his eyes. Until, one day, she was gone. Nothing. He focused on the flickering heartbeat on the screen, which gave him reassurance that this baby was alive and developing just as it should. He knew the problems diabetes could cause for a developing foetus—hell, he could write a book on them. But everything looked good. They wouldn't really know for sure until the detailed scan around twenty weeks but right now his child was alive and growing. He should feel comforted, relieved. Instead, he just felt sick with worry. What if something went wrong again?

'Cooper?' Missy reached out and touched his hand. He started.

'What? Oh, yes….yes, sorry, Fiona. Yes, can I have a picture please?'

He watched as the little picture printed out and Fiona tore it off and handed it to him. Fiona wiped the remaining gel from Missy's abdomen. She leapt up and ducked into the strategically placed toilet leading off the scanning room.

Instant. Relief. Her eyes fell to the image of her baby, enclosed in a little plastic envelope, which she'd placed up next to the sink. Magic. After all these years, she really was going to have a baby. Her hands began to tremble. This was real. She didn't care what anyone else thought, or how Cooper fitted into this equation. She could do this. She could do this on her own. She washed her hands and went back to meet Cooper.

He was still outside, talking to Fiona. 'So the expected date of delivery will be the 4th of October?'

Fiona nodded. 'Finished, Melissa? Good. Come over here and I'll set up appointment times for the rest of your scans. I take it you'll be attending the diabetic antenatal clinic?'

Melissa nodded in response.

'In that case, Dr McPherson likes all his ladies to have a scan every month to check for growth and development, but you know that, don't you? I'll also give you a time for your detailed scan at twenty-one weeks. We've got a new state-of-the-art scanner. It gives 3D images of the baby's face. You'll love it.'

Melissa nodded enthusiastically as Fiona wrote down the appointment times on a card for her.

Cooper was standing in the corner of the room. His eyes were fixed on the little photograph in front of him. She watched him. He was breathing in slowly through his nose and blowing the air back out in a steady stream through his lips. It was a control exercise. Some women used it when they were in labour. Others used it to stop panic attacks or control temper.

Chills ran down Melissa's spine. How well did she really know this man? Why on earth would a consultant obstetrician, a man who looked at baby scans all day, need to practise a control technique when looking at a scan of their baby?

She took the card being proffered by Fiona. 'That was great, Fiona, thanks very much.' She went to walk out of the scanning room but Fiona placed a hand on her arm, her eyes glancing over to where Cooper stood. 'You know if you're ever concerned at all, about anything, scan appointment or not, just come and see me. I'll always fit you in if you have any worries.'

Melissa nodded appreciatively, refusing to even look back towards Cooper. 'I know, Fiona, and thank you.'

She lifted her bag from the floor and took off down the corridor at a brisk pace. She should be on top of the world right now. Maybe it wasn't an ideal situation, but it certainly wasn't the worst. She pushed her scan picture into her handbag. She would look at it again later, when she didn't feel as if the weight of the world was pressing down on her shoulders. Her eyes began to fill up. *No! Dash these hormones!*

Cooper appeared at her elbow. 'Melissa, slow down.' He grabbed her arm, halting her steps and turning her around to face him. 'What's wrong?'

She couldn't help it. All her frustrations were jumbled up in her brain, she couldn't translate them into words, and before she knew it, tears were streaming down her face.

Cooper's face fell. He knew this was his fault and he enveloped her in a bear hug in the middle of the hospital corridor. 'Everything was fine, Missy.' He stroked the hair at the back of her neck. 'You know the baby is healthy. Don't be upset.'

'Don't be upset!' She landed both hands on his chest and pushed him away fiercely. 'What was wrong with you in there?' She spat the words out through gritted teeth. 'You've just ruined what should have been one of the happiest moments of my life. You sat in there as if you were waiting for an executioner—not seeing your baby for the first time. What on earth was wrong with you? I wish I'd never asked you to come!'

All her frustration came bubbling to the surface. She'd seen her baby now and everything about this seemed so *real*. She'd had a one-night stand, with someone she didn't know that well and apparently didn't understand, and now she was paying the price. It didn't matter to her if she and Cooper didn't have a relationship—she wasn't going to get the happy husband and the house with the white picket fence. But she wanted her baby to have a relationship with its father. She didn't just want him to be a name on a birth certificate. She wanted her baby to be loved. *To be wanted.*

After her father had left, Melissa had never seen him again. She'd only received a few letters and birthday cards. The feeling of desertion in her had been enormous. And she *never* wanted her child to feel like that.

Cooper struggled to find words. It was so easy to be a doctor and look at other people's baby scans. Even when they were filled with bad news, he was there as the professional, the person to guide and advise. This was *so* different. This was his child. A child he wanted to protect from all harm and keep safe. He wanted to be in control. But he wasn't and he didn't know how to tell her—without telling her why he was so scared and probably terrifying her to death and giving her sleepless nights.

He shook his head. 'Don't say that, Missy. Look, I can't explain right now, but I found it quite hard, okay?' He looked about him. They were standing in the middle of a hospital corridor, hardly the time or the place for the thoughts that were circulating in his mind.

'But it shouldn't be hard, Cooper. It should be happy. This should be a happy time for you and for me. We get to see our baby's heartbeat for the first time, we should be shouting from the rooftops!'

'I know that and I am happy, I am.'

'No, Cooper, you're not, and I don't understand. You're an obstetrician—you see hundreds of scans—why on earth couldn't you conjure up a bit of happiness at seeing your baby for the first time?' She was clearly getting agitated and this was the last thing he wanted. 'You told me you wanted this baby. But it didn't seem like that in there. I know this wasn't planned. I know this probably shouldn't have happened. But do you know what? I'm glad. I'm glad this happened. Even if you're not.'

It was the first time Cooper had ever heard her shout. And from the concerned looks from the some of the staff members passing in the corridor, it was obviously the first time they had heard her shout too. Her face was scarlet with anger, hot tears dropping in large splotches onto the corridor floor.

Cooper had that horrible feeling of everything being out of his control again. If this was a nice tale he would take her by the hand and tell her how he'd felt in that scan room, because this wasn't the first time he'd seen his child's heartbeat, it was the second. But that would involve a long, convoluted story about how he'd lost his wife and child through a pregnancy complication. And what kind of man would that make him? This wasn't a nice story, this was real life, for him and for Missy and their baby. If Missy was stressed now, that could only make her ten times worse.

How the hell had he got himself into this mess? He pulled a handkerchief from his pocket and handed it to her. 'I think you're overreacting. Calm down.' He knew that he was being condescending and he knew he shouldn't do it. But right now he couldn't handle the demons in his head. And he wasn't going to try and pretend to be perfect. 'Go and get something to eat and I'll see you later.'

As if conjured up by magic, Andrea appeared. She shot Cooper a look that should have flayed him. Her voice was quiet and steady. 'Missy, are you all right?' She took Melissa gently by the arm and led her down the corridor towards the staffroom. A single shake of her head told Cooper not to follow.

And for the first time ever he didn't want to.

CHAPTER FIVE

'CONGRATULATIONS, Sister Bell.'

'Sorry?' Melissa was startled by the voice behind her at the conference. Had someone guessed she was pregnant? She glanced down at her stomach—definitely nothing obvious there. She was due her results from her combined nuchal scan and blood test in the next day or so, but didn't think she'd started to show yet. She had just presented a paper on midwifery management of high-risk pregnancies. Cooper was with her today and had headed off in the direction of the refreshments to get her something to eat. She turned to face the woman behind her. A short, blonde, rotund woman with a friendly expression. 'I'm sorry,' said Melissa again as she turned in her chair. 'Have we met?'

The woman wedged herself in the chair next to Melissa. Melissa gave a little smile as she recognised the designer linen suit being rumpled beyond all recognition.

The woman followed her eyes and smiled. 'I hate this suit,' she sighed, pulling at the cream material. 'Linen crushes at the slightest touch but it was the only thing I could fit into this morning.' She put out her hand towards Melissa. 'I must look like a bag lady but I'm Karen Connelly, one of the obstetricians at St

Benjamin's in Leeds. I wanted to congratulate you on your paper.'

'Oh, thanks very much.' Missy felt a wave of relief as she realised the woman had no idea she was pregnant and was only a fellow professional here to discuss the paper.

Karen Connelly glanced over her shoulder, her messy blonde hair almost catching Melissa in the face. She gave a little smile as she saw Cooper approaching, precariously balancing two steaming cups and two plates loaded with food. 'I see you're here with Cooper.'

A strange sensation shot straight to the front of Missy's mind as she caught the expression on Karen Connelly's face. Was this woman interested in Cooper? Something twisted in her gut. Was that jealousy? You bet it was.

Watching him cross the room, she could see women's heads turning in appreciation of his lithe frame. He was dressed in a dark grey suit, crisp white shirt and red silk tie, and looked hot. The mere thought of him made her skin prickle. It had been a strange week. She was almost beginning to believe that he was right, that maybe she had overreacted outside the scan room. But something still niggled away at her, something she just couldn't put her finger on.

Cooper reached the table, his head still down and deep in concentration as he placed the cups and plates on the table. He gave a triumphant smile as he lifted his eyes to Melissa. A smile that spread even further when he saw who was sitting next to her.

'Coop, hi, it's lovely to see you again.' Karen pushed herself up and wrapped her arms around Cooper's neck, kissing him on both cheeks. 'It's been far too long.'

Cooper returned the kisses and sat down next to

Missy, pushing one of the plates in her direction. 'It's great to see you too. What are you doing here?'

She waved her arm towards Missy. 'Oh, I just came over to congratulate your Sister Bell on her presentation.'

Cooper nodded and took a drink of his coffee. 'That was nice of you, Karen.' He turned towards Missy. 'See, Missy, I told you your presentation was fine.' He turned back to Karen. 'She was up half the night, worrying about it.'

Karen raised her eyebrow at Cooper and gave him a wide smile, 'And how would you know that, Cooper?'

Cooper, who was in mid-sip of his coffee, coughed and spluttered. 'Well, what I meant was…that she told me,' he finished quickly as colour flooded into his cheeks.

Missy smiled. She'd never seen Coop blush before, and it was quite endearing. He was quite right—she had told him. But there was something kind of nice about Karen thinking it meant something else entirely.

Karen patted his arm and smiled at Missy. 'Cooper, don't get yourself in a state, I was only teasing. But…' she glanced between him and Missy '…I'm really glad that I hit the nail on the head, whether by accident or not.' She stood up and turned around. putting her hand out towards Missy. 'It's a pleasure to meet you, Missy, and I hope things work out well between you.'

Missy gave her a little smile as she shook the out-stretched hand.

Karen bent over and kissed Cooper on the cheek again as she gave his shoulder a squeeze. 'I'm so happy that you finally got back on the wagon, Cooper. After Clara and Lily, it's so nice to see you've met someone new.' She gave them a little wave. 'I'll leave you both

to eat your lunch and hopefully will see you both later.'
She walked off across the conference hall, leaving de-
struction in her wake.

Missy hadn't moved. She hadn't even blinked.
Cooper had just been about to take a bite from a sausage roll and his mouth remained open as the sausage
roll hovered at his lips.

Neither of them said anything. Melissa felt as if she'd
been punched. The air in the room felt heavy, claustrophobic. Melissa felt a wave of nausea sweep over her
and pushed the plate of food away untouched. She could
feel him staring at her, waiting for her to react, to say
something. But they were in the middle of a conference
room with hundreds of other delegates—was this really
the place for this discussion?

She could feel fury building in her chest. She hadn't
imagined anything last week. She hadn't overreacted
outside the scan room.

Her eyes met his. The shutters were still there. She
couldn't live like this. Her hands were automatically
positioned on her stomach in a protective manner. It
was bad enough finding out that Cooper was widowed
and still carried his wedding ring in his pocket. What
else was she about to find out? She couldn't bring this
baby into the world without having all the facts.

Melissa felt the tremble in her voice as she said the
words, 'What do you have to tell me, Cooper?'

Her voice got stronger, steadier as her determination
grew. 'You owe me, Cooper. You owe me and our baby.
We have a right to know.'

The silence was suffocating. But Melissa was determined not to break it. She needed answers.

The strain was visible on his face. He looked as
if his heart had been broken in two. The sausage roll

finally managed to make its way back down to the table and onto a plate. She could see him taking a few deep breaths. Karen's words started to settle in her brain where tiny little connections began to be made.

'Who is Lily, Cooper? And what happened to Clara?'

His worry lines had never looked so deep. The circles under his eyes had never been so dark.

'Clara…' He sucked in a deep breath, his eyes meeting hers in a steady gaze. 'She was pregnant when she died. Thirty-nine weeks. Our daughter Lily was stillborn.'

Melissa felt as if she had just run headlong into a brick wall. Oxygen left her body but didn't seem to come back in. Almost instantly every hair on her body stood on end, hypersensitive to their surroundings. The blood was pounding in her veins, she could feel her heart thudding in her chest. She struggled to speak. 'Wh…? What? What happened? Was it an accident?'

Cooper shook his head and reached out his hand to her. 'Clara had a PE.'

'A PE?' Her words were whispered, almost inaudible. A pulmonary embolism, or a clot in the lungs, was an unusual complication of pregnancy. 'Was she unwell? Did she have an underlying condition that caused it?' A thousand questions spun around in her mind.

He pulled his hand back from hers. His face was so pale it almost looked translucent. 'No, Missy. Clara had no underlying conditions. She had no major accidents beforehand, she hadn't even been off her feet for a few days. She became unwell really quickly, had shortness of breath and phoned for an ambulance herself. She'd tried to call me but I was in Theatre and she left me a message. By the time I got to the emergency department she was almost unconscious.' The words were staccato, coming out in short, sharp bursts. He ran his hand through his hair and stared over Missy's shoulder at a fixed point on the wall. 'My wife and daughter died because I missed something that cost them their lives.'

'Cooper, you can't possibly think—'

He cut her off with an ice-cold, almost blank stare. 'It turned out Clara had banged her leg a few days before. It seemed so unimportant that she hadn't even told me about it. Even when it *must* have been hurting her the next day and the day after, when the clot was forming in her leg.' The frustration he felt was evident.

She tried to suck in air. Her brain was racing. How could he not tell her something like this? In her mind, tiny pieces of the jigsaw puzzle started to fall into place. His flat had no family pictures on display. The wedding ring he still carried in his pocket. The way he'd acted in the scan room. Cooper wasn't ready to move on. It wasn't just that he wasn't ready for a relationship, it almost seemed as if he wasn't ready to have a life again. And now she understood why.

It felt like a betrayal. He'd misled her. He'd let her think that this was his first child, his first experience of having a partner who was pregnant.

'You should have told me.' Melissa shook her head. She was having trouble taking all of this in. Her head was swimming with a million questions that really couldn't be shouted across a busy conference room. She went to stand up and felt herself sway.

Cooper was at her side in an instant, his arm around her waist, supporting her weight on her unsteady legs. 'Missy, are you okay? God, I'm so sorry.' He looked frantically around the room until he spotted the nearest exit. 'Let's get out of here and get some fresh air. Can you manage?'

She nodded and walked with him, hating the fact her legs had turned to jelly and her head felt as if a thousand butterflies were flapping their wings inside it.

A welcome blast of cool air hit her as soon as they stepped outside the main doors into the reception area. Cooper's arm was still around her and he guided her over to some nearby comfortable sofas next to the bar. 'Can I get you something to drink?'

'Just some soda water, please.'

She took a few moments to gather her thoughts while he stood at the bar. He came back with a tray with two glasses, a bowl of soup and some crusty bread.

'Sorry,' he said apologetically, 'it was all they had. You never got a chance to eat in there—do you think your blood sugar could be low?'

She pulled her glucose meter from her bag and took a few seconds to prick to her finger and test her blood. 'I don't much feel like eating, Cooper.'

The machine buzzed and he sat down next to her, rather than at the other side of the table, looking over her shoulder at the result.

'Eat, Missy. This can wait until you feel a bit better.'

She knew he was right and it annoyed her. She didn't like anyone telling her what to do. She liked to control her diabetes and make her own decisions regarding her care. But she didn't just have herself to think about any more. She lifted the spoon to her mouth and reluctantly began to eat.

Cooper waited a few minutes until she'd finished, his hands turning over and over in his lap. 'Melissa, I couldn't tell you.' He gestured towards her stomach. 'How could I?'

'How could you not?' Her voice was low and steady but did nothing to disguise the anger she was feeling.

Cooper's face contorted. 'How could I tell you? You were worried enough about being pregnant, being diabetic and the possible effects on the baby. I couldn't tell you my wife had died due to a complication of pregnancy and that our daughter was stillborn. How insensitive would that have been?'

'You should have told me.' Her voice was firmer now as the jumbled thoughts became firmer in her mind. 'That's why you were strange in the scan room, wasn't it? I thought you were seeing your baby for the first time, but now I realise that you weren't. You'd done all this before.' How dare he not tell her something as important as this? She didn't think how her words might hurt him, she was too upset to give his feelings a second thought. Then another notion jumped into her head as realisation took hold.

'I must be your worst nightmare.'

Cooper looked stunned. 'What? What are you talking about?' He ran his hands through his hair in frustration.

'When I told you I was pregnant. It must have been your worst nightmare.' Her mind went into overdrive. She pointed a finger at him accusingly. 'You already had one wife who'd died with pregnancy complications and then you get me!' She gestured towards her barely extended abdomen. 'A diabetic who is at higher risk of just about everything!'

Cooper was silent, as if he didn't know how to respond. And in her mind that was enough. He agreed with her, but couldn't put those thoughts into words.

The thoughts continued to form in her mind. Cooper fumbled. He tried to speak but Melissa cut him off.

'This is impossible. This is never going to work. I can't get my head around any of this.' A single tear slid down her cheek and she hurriedly brushed it away. She looked at the man who made her blood race through her veins and her heart pound furiously. She was wildly attracted to him and easily in danger of falling in love with him. She'd never felt anything like this before.

But he couldn't possibly love her. They could never be a family while he was still mourning the loss of his wife and child. And the cold, harsh reality was that Missy wanted everything. She wanted what she'd never had. She wanted the beautiful baby and the beautiful husband to go with it.

Her hands ran over her stomach. Did he even want this baby?

Cooper watched the turmoil of emotions flash across Missy's face. She was in pain and this was his fault. Only he could fix this.

He placed one hand over hers on her stomach and used the other to lift her chin towards him.

'Missy, I'm glad that you know. This wasn't the best way for you to find out but now it means all my cards are on the table and there are no secrets between us.'

'Do you even want this baby, Cooper?' she whispered.

'Yes, absolutely.' His voice was resolute with no hesitation. 'Missy, I've already lost one child, this baby means everything to me.'

Her heart sank. He hadn't mentioned her. He'd only mentioned the baby.

'But what about me?' Her eyes searched his face. She had to ask the question. She had to prepare herself for the worst. 'Do you want me too?'

His eyes dropped from her face. 'Missy, I'm not going to tell you any lies. I'm only ever going to tell you the truth. And the truth is I don't know. I'm not ready to make that decision yet.' His hands were trembling and she could see he was struggling with this but that didn't make his answer any easier to take.

'What I can promise you is that I'm going to be with you every step of the way in this pregnancy. I guarantee it.'

Missy nodded numbly. Her child may be secure and loved, but what about her?

CHAPTER SIX

MISSY stuffed her bag into her locker and took a quick glance in the mirror to check her appearance. She had a glow. She'd put a little fake tan on her face and arms last night to take away her deathly pale complexion, but there was something else. She gave herself a little smile before turning and heading out the door.

The labour suite had a whole new meaning for her now. In around twenty-five weeks she would be a patient, not a member of staff. She was sure about what she wanted to do now. Her work colleagues had been great, all very supportive, and they were currently fighting over who got to deliver her baby. She could take up to a year off and when she wanted to return to work she knew the hospital had good crèche facilities. The only thing she hadn't worked out was where Cooper fitted into this equation. Word got round quickly in maternity units and everyone already knew that Cooper had attended the scan with her.

Melissa headed down to the midwives' station and took a quick glance at the whiteboard, which showed how many patients were in the unit and which midwife they were allocated to. Today she was in the medical unit, taking charge of the pre- and post-op mums. The theatre list was hanging at the side of the desk. Only two women were due for Caesarean sections today, both of whom weren't due to go to Theatre until after lunch-time. It could be a quiet day for her.

Melissa went along to the pre- and post-op room for a handover from the midwife due to go off duty.

'Hi, Sally, what have you got for me?'

'Hey, Melissa. Both ladies are ready for Theatre. Julie Bates is forty-one and a primipara. She's thirty-seven weeks' gestation and is being sectioned due to placenta praevia. Wendy Kerr is twenty-two and is a para plus one, currently thirty-nine weeks' gestation. Her pre-vious delivery had shoulder dystocia and scans have shown this baby is above ten pounds so Dr Cunningham has decided to deliver this baby by Caesarean. All ob-servations are normal and both women have been fast-ing since an early breakfast at six this morning.'

'That's great, thanks, Sally. I'll have a quick read of their notes and then I'll see if I can help out anywhere else until they're due to go Theatre.'

'No probs. Right, that's me off, then. See you to-morrow.' Sally picked up her bag and headed for the changing room.

It only took Melissa a few minutes to check the notes and then re-check both ladies' observations. She re-corded them in their charts and had a quick tidy up.

Julie and Wendy had their blue theatre gowns on and paper hats in place. They were both relaxed with no con-cerns about going to Theatre. 'Hurry up, Melissa,' urged Julie. '*Diagnosis Murder* is about to start and we want to watch it before we go to Theatre.' Melissa laughed and finished double-checking their name bands. She knew she was safe to leave the women for the moment and could help out elsewhere.

Cooper was sitting at the midwives' station when

she walked along from the post-op room. He finished writing up some notes and put them back in the trolley.

'How are you doing?'

'Since you spoke to me last night? I'm feeling fine.'

'Were you sick this morning?'

'After you phoned me at six or after you phoned me at seven?'

He gave a rueful smile. 'I take it you're trying to make a point. Am I coming on too strong?'

'You're maybe just a *little* over-protective, Coop. I'm a big girl. I've looked after myself for a long time.' She wasn't quite sure that she meant it. She had always loved having her own space and certainly her flat was tiny and couldn't accommodate two. But these last few days had been hard. She couldn't face going into the kitchen to prepare food and it would be nice if someone was there to help her. Even though she had a baby inside her, for the first time her independent streak was waning and she felt very alone.

He looked at her thoughtfully. Silence. Melissa shifted uncomfortably on her feet. The most handsome doctor in the place. She was having his baby. And she couldn't think of a word to say to him. Great. She glanced back up at the board. One of the senior students was handling her first delivery. She would go and see if she needed any support. She headed towards the room.

'Hi, Phoebe. I'm just in to see if you need anything.'

The red-haired senior student looked up from the notes she was recording and gave her a big smile. 'Hi, Melissa, that's great, thanks. This is Louise Hendry. She's twenty-four and this is her first baby. She's thirty-nine weeks' gestation. We've confirmed rupture of her membranes. Her contractions are still quite far apart, nearly seven minutes, so she's here a little earlier than normal. Louise's husband serves with the armed forces and is away on duty at the moment and she had to drive herself in. So she didn't want to wait.'

'He's due back tomorrow. I can't believe I've gone into labour today.' Melissa could hear the anxiety in the woman's voice.

Melissa gave her a smile. 'Don't worry, this is your first baby and things could take a while. Who knows? He might just make it in time.'

Melissa bent her head to check the notes. 'Everything looks fine, Phoebe.' Phoebe was a very conscientious student who would be a great midwife in the future. This was her second placement in the labour suite and Melissa was sure she would be more than capable of dealing with this delivery.

She looked at Louise, who was sitting comfortably on the bed. She'd changed into a hospital gown and had brought an array of magazines with her. Melissa noticed her crossed ankles and had a little prod at the flesh surrounding them. Her fingerprint seemed to leave the smallest imprint in the skin, which gradually disappeared in a few seconds. Slight oedema. Not unusual in pregnant women and definitely not unusual in a third trimester. She flicked the chart over to check the blood-pressure reading that Phoebe had recorded. Normal. Everything seemed fine. But Melissa just had the strangest feeling in the pit of her stomach.

Melissa fixed a bright smile on her face. 'How are you feeling, Louise?'

Louise gave a nervous smile. 'Okay, I guess. But I'd be better if I could get rid of this nagging headache.' She pressed her fingers to her temples. 'I was too worried to take anything but it's been there since last night.'

She frowned as Melissa came around the bed to her side. 'But it's not too bad, honestly.'

'Can you put out your hand for me and clench it into a fist?'

'What?' Louise was confused.

'Really, just try for me please.'

Within just a few seconds Louise completed the test. It took her just a little longer than normal to relax her fist again. Melissa could feel her senses buzzing. Hyperactive reflexes, oedema, headache. All signs of eclampsia. Her senses were never wrong. Eclampsia was a serious condition and relatively rare. Pre-eclampsia was more common in pregnancy but was usually picked up at antenatal checks and well controlled to allow the mother to have a healthy baby and normal delivery.

'Phoebe, would you mind collecting a specimen of urine and testing it, please?'

Phoebe looked over at her, slightly confused as everything appeared fine. 'Sure, Melissa, no problem.' She hurried out the door to collect a sterile specimen container.

Melissa turned back to Louise. 'Have you had any problems with your vision in the last few days?'

'It's been a bit strange today. It was a little fuzzy when I got up this morning, but it seemed okay when I drove to the hospital. Melissa…' Louise's face had started to twitch around her mouth. Melissa knew instantly what was about to happen. She moved quickly to Louise's side. The buzzer was at the other side of the bed. 'Cooper!' she shouted at the top of her voice. Louise took a sharp intake of breath and her whole body went rigid.

The doors within the labour suite where thick and heavy, primarily to keep out noise, but this could also prevent Melissa summoning help. Melissa knew that Cooper had just been sitting at the midwives' station opposite this room. He flung open the door just as Louise started to go into a full-blown convulsion, her legs and arms thrashing around the bed.

'Pull the alarm,' she shouted, 'and help me get her on her side.'

Cooper moved effortlessly, pulling the large red button on the wall above the bed before sliding his arms underneath Louise's convulsing body and turning her on her left side to help protect the baby by allowing good uterine blood flow. Melissa reached up, grabbed an oxygen mask from the wall and turned on the supply. Cooper helped lift Louise's head as Melissa slipped the mask over her nose and mouth to administer oxygen. It wasn't unusual for breathing to be interrupted during a seizure and it was important to try and keep the oxygen levels in the blood as high as possible, for both mother and baby.

The wail of the alarm brought the sound of thudding feet along the corridor. Phoebe appeared at the door, clutching the sterile container for the urine specimen, her face frozen with terror. 'But everything was fine...' she started to say.

'I need some help, Phoebe,' said Melissa abruptly. Her voice and tone brought Phoebe out of her stupor and she moved rapidly to Melissa's side.

'What do you want me to do?'

Louise's whole body was jerking and twitching as Melissa and Cooper attempted to hold her safely in place. Cooper's voice was clear and steady. 'Get me some magnesium sulphate, a cannula and a one-hundred-ml infusion bag.' As chaos erupted around him Cooper was the epitome of calm. Another midwife, pulling the crash cart behind her, entered the room, closely followed by the anaesthetist, whose page was still sounding. Phoebe moved swiftly, collected the supplies that Cooper needed, and placed them in his hands. 'Set up the CTG monitor,' he murmured in her ear. 'I need to see how this baby is doing.'

Melissa pulled the suction tube from the wall. 'I think we're coming to end of the seizure,' she said as Louise's limbs started to relax and cease twitching. She glanced at her watch. She had been bent low, with her ear next to Louise's mouth, to monitor her breathing while she'd been on her side. Quickly she suctioned away the oral secretions as the anaesthetist claimed his place at the head of the bed. 'All yours, Tim,' she said quietly, as she moved out of the way to allow him to take up position.

She released the brake from the bottom of the bed and pulled the bed sharply out from its place at the wall. Tim would need room to do his assessment. She turned on the cardiac monitor and set up the leads, blood-pressure cuff and slid the pulse oximeter onto one of Louise's fingers. As Phoebe started the CTG trace Melissa quickly checked the leads and monitored the reading as it came out. 'Oxygen saturation is ninety-two per cent and blood pressure has just spiked,' she called to Tim, who gave her a swift nod.

Melissa worked her way around to the other side of the bed. 'Seizure lasted forty-five seconds,' she said to Cooper, who had drawn up the drug to prevent subsequent seizures and had started to slowly administer it.

Melissa looked at the IV bag sitting on the locker top. 'Do you want me to set up the continuous infusion for once you're finished with the loading dose?'

Cooper nodded, watching the clock on the nearby

wall as he continued with the medicine. The loading dose had to be delivered slowly, over fifteen to twenty minutes. Melissa grabbed an IV giving set and pump. 'One gram an hour?' she double-checked with Cooper, before priming the pump and setting it to run. 'It's ready whenever you're finished.'

She made to turn and head back to other side of the room but Cooper grabbed her hand. 'Are you okay? Did you get kicked?'

'No, Cooper, I'm fine.'

'It was a good call, Melissa. I'm impressed.'

She was bewildered. She'd only shouted for him when the facial twitching had started. 'What do you mean?'

'You knew something was wrong, didn't you?'

She gave a little nod.

'Phoebe had stopped to speak to me outside. She told me you'd asked her to collect a urine specimen. And that you'd checked for oedema, hyperactive reflexes and a headache.' He glanced over to where Phoebe was recording Louise's latest readings. 'She wondered what made you suspect something was wrong.'

Melissa shrugged her shoulders. 'Initially it was just a hunch.' She smiled at his furrowed brow. 'I noticed the smallest amount of oedema in her legs. Her blood-pressure recording was entirely normal but I just got the strangest feeling. Once I'd established she had some other symptoms I just knew. But I didn't expect her to start seizing so quickly.'

He gave a thoughtful little nod. 'I was supposed to be heading to the clinic but when Phoebe started to speak to me I decided to hang around a little longer.' He shot her a glance. 'I was waiting to see if the urine specimen was positive for protein. I knew you would call me for a consult.' He stopped for a second, giving her a little smile. 'You've got good instincts, Missy.'

The words sent a warm feeling spreading through her. It was nice to know that he respected her professionally—even if she didn't really know how he felt about her.

He glanced over at Tim, who had signalled that Louise had started to come round. It was unlikely she would remember anything that had just happened. 'I'm going to consult with Tim about what we do next. We need to get this baby out soon.'

Melissa gave a nod of her head and moved away, grabbing the midwifery notes and taking another look at the CTG monitor. 'Baby's heart rate is a little slow, just as we'd expect after a seizure.'

She looked over at Phoebe. The student midwife was monitoring the baby's heart rate meticulously but her hands were trembling. Jen, one of the other midwives, had entered the room and followed Melissa's gaze. She put her hand on Melissa's shoulder and gave her an almost imperceptible nod. It wasn't uncommon for staff members to need some time out after a traumatic event, particularly if they were students. 'I'm just going to take Phoebe away for ten minutes for a debrief,' Melissa said as she stood up and placed her hand over Phoebe's. 'Jen will take over while we go and get a quick cup of tea.'

Phoebe nodded gratefully as Jen stepped up behind her to take her place.

Melissa headed over to the door then took a deep breath as she felt a pair of hands behind her, grasping her waist.

Cooper spoke in a low, husky voice. 'Are you sure you're okay?'

Melissa nodded wordlessly, aware of their close proximity in the tightly packed room.

'Good,' he said swiftly as he leaned over and his lips brushed the side of her cheek with a casualness as if he did it every day, in full view of everyone in the room.

Melissa's fingers flew to the spot on her cheek where he'd just kissed her. She was stunned. She knew she should be angry but as she left the room she could feel a warm glow spreading through her. Cooper was worried about her. He was worried about her and the baby. Maybe she wasn't as alone as she'd thought she was.

'Melissa!'

Cooper banged on the door for the third time and waited—still no response.

He glanced at his watch. It was nearly eight o'clock and Melissa should have reported for duty an hour ago. Andrea, one of the ward sisters, had phoned him to say Melissa hadn't appeared and wasn't answering her mobile or her home phone, something she would never do. Cooper had raced over to Missy's flat and had been able to duck inside the main doorway as another resident was leaving. But now he was left in the hallway with no sign of Melissa.

He glanced over his shoulders at the two facing doors. No one was at home in either of those flats, he'd already tried their doors. Biting his lip, he knelt down and prised open Melissa's letter box. Thankfully she hadn't opted for one of those 'bolt outside' mailboxes. It was dark in the hallway of Melissa's flat with a little light gleaming at the end of the hall coming from Melissa's living room. He inched over on his knees to try and get a better view. He thought he could see something…

Yes, there it was. A pair of feet. But not lying on the floor. Was she sitting on the sofa? Cooper pulled back from the letterbox. Why on earth would she be sitting on the sofa while he was bellowing at the door?

His heart sank when he realised something else. She still had her slippers on her feet—bright red fluffy slippers—not the flat, white work shoes she normally wore. And he knew immediately why she hadn't got that far.

He pulled his phone from his pocket to call the emergency services then shook his head. He glanced around him once more to make sure no one had sneaked up on him while he'd been peering through her door, but there was no one else there. No one else to help him.

And he wasn't going to wait. Who knew how long it would take an ambulance to get there? Then they would need the police to break down her door. No, this was the mother of his child and something was very wrong. Time was of the essence and there was no way Cooper could stand here, waiting for the police and ambulance to arrive, while Melissa was in there unwell.

He stepped back, lifted his foot and with all his strength...

The noise was phenomenal. Like a car ramming into a brick wall. Splintered wood flew all around as the door lay in pieces before him. For a second he hesitated, expecting people to appear shouting all around him. But there was nothing.

Cooper stepped over the fractured pieces of wood and in three long strides was in her living room. His breath caught in his throat.

He'd never seen Melissa look like this before. She was sitting on the sofa in a tiny red satin nightdress with her huge slippers on her feet. Her skin was pale and washed out with tiny beads of sweat glistening on her brow. She had a glazed expression on her face, as if she was contemplating something really complicated, but her eyes remained blank. As if she was vacant, as if she was not really there. She hadn't even noticed him come into the room. More worryingly, she hadn't even reacted to the noise.

He'd never seen Melissa have a hypoglycaemic attack before. Every diabetic was an individual and had different signs and symptoms of an oncoming attack. But he had absolutely no doubt what was wrong with her. He had to get some kind of sugar into her, and fast.

He knelt down in front of her and grabbed her shoulders, flinching at how cold they were. 'Missy, Melissa, it's Cooper. Melissa, can you speak?'

Melissa's head was spinning. She knew something wasn't right, but she wasn't quite sure what it was. She felt as if she were in a dream. She was aware of lights flickering around her and of some noise in the background, but she didn't know what it was. And she was cold, so cold. She knew she should get up and put her housecoat on but her legs just felt so heavy. She would do it in a minute. Yes, that's what she'd do.

Cooper looked frantically around the flat. She didn't look in any fit state to eat, she looked as if she was barely conscious. He took a deep breath. Melissa was the most organised woman he knew. Glucagon. She would have glucagon somewhere. It was the glucose injection that doctors and paramedics gave to diabetic patients who had lost consciousness. It gave a sharp boost of glucose to the system, which generally brought the patient round.

He went into the kitchen and pulled open the fridge. There it was, the tell-tale orange box, in the shelf on the door next to her insulin. He yanked out one of the ready-made syringes and injected the water into the glucose powder solution, gave it a quick shake and withdrew the mixture again.

He stood at the doorway, contemplating for a second the best place to inject her, before lifting her slip and pushing the needle into her thigh. It would take too long to find a viable vein, she was too cold and too shut down. Intramuscular injection would take a few extra minutes to work but that was fine, he had all the time in the world.

He walked into her bedroom, barely even taking in the surroundings before grabbing her duvet from the bed, bringing it through to the living room and wrapping it around her. He took a few seconds to switch on the kettle and rummaged through the cupboards to find some teabags and sugar, obviously hardly ever used, in the cupboard. As soon as she was conscious he had to get some sugar into her.

Cooper sat back down on the sofa next to Melissa. He wrapped one arm around her shoulder and pulled her closer, his other arm on her leg, rubbing the injection site in the hope it would hasten the effects of the jag.

This was going to be the longest five minutes of his life.

Ouch! Melissa's head hurt and so did her leg. What had happened? She tried to make sense of her surroundings. Where was she? Her mouth felt dry and she was desperate for something to drink. Her eyes gradually focused. Cooper was sitting next to her on the sofa and she had her red duvet wrapped around her, but she was so cold. What on earth had happened? And what on earth was Cooper doing there? This didn't look good.

Her hand flew to her stomach. Was the baby okay?

Cooper's hand was on her leg. He was watching her closely. 'You had a hypo,' he said.

'What?' Her brain was slowly starting to work again. 'But my blood-sugar level was fine.'

'No, it wasn't,' Cooper said quietly. 'I checked it while you were passed out, it was way below normal.'

'Oh.' She caught sight of the tell-tale orange box that lay opened on the nearby table. That must be why her leg was hurting and why Cooper's hand was rubbing her thigh. He had injected her.

'I'm supposed to be at work.' She groaned and leaned back on the sofa. 'How did you get in here, Cooper? How did you even know I wasn't well?'

Cooper gave an apologetic smile. 'Andrea phoned me when you didn't report for duty. As for how I got in here....' His eyes glanced down the corridor towards the shattered door. 'We're going to have to discuss that. You really need to improve your security in this flat.'

Melissa gave half a smile. She still felt a little fuzzy.

Cooper stood up. 'Give me a second. I'm going to make you some toast and tea.'

He returned a few minutes later with two steaming cups of tea and pile of buttered toast, which he placed on the table in front of them.

Melissa lifted a cup and took a sip. 'Yuck! That tastes awful!'

He smiled. 'That's the taste of real sugar. Now, drink it, lady, whether you like it or not. Doctor's orders.' He winked at her. She was finally coming back to normal. He'd never felt so relieved. He watched for a few minutes as she ate her toast and drank her tea. He'd finally managed to take his hand from her thigh but, truth be told, his hand still tingled. In the heat of the moment he hadn't had time to admire Melissa in her short red satin nightdress. But, now as they sat companionably on the sofa, he could. Her breasts were definitely fuller than he remembered, more rounded in appearance and barely hidden behind the thin material and spaghetti straps. And then there had been the other discovery as he'd pushed the nightdress aside to administer the injection— Melissa didn't wear any panties under that nightie.

He'd averted his eyes from the tiny dark triangle of curls, because it had been the last thing on his mind, but now...

Melissa moved in his arms, turning around to face him and bringing his mind first and foremost to the present situation.

'What time is it, Cooper? You said that Andrea had phoned you. Am I late?'

He shook his head. 'Forget about work, Missy. Right now that's not important.'

'I'm really sorry about this, and I'm so embarrassed.' She gestured to her nightdress and slippers. 'I've no idea what state you found me in this morning. I'd obviously got up to get ready for work and I've no idea what happened after that. This just isn't like me.'

Cooper took in her serious expression with sympathy—she was definitely back to normal now. 'You know this can happen in pregnancy, Melissa. It doesn't matter how well controlled your diabetes has been in the past. This is a whole different ball game. Being pregnant can make your blood-sugar levels drop a lot quicker than normal. You've helped out at the diabetic antenatal clinic. You know that this happens to some of the women.'

Melissa gave a big sigh. 'But I didn't expect it to happen to me. I didn't get the warning signs that I normally get—the ones that give me enough time to go and eat something.' She threw her hands in the air in exasperation. 'I'm always in complete control. How am I supposed to figure this out?'

Alarm bells started going off in Cooper's head. There was something not right about her reaction to this. 'This has happened before, hasn't it?'

Her face as white as snow, she mumbled a response. 'What?'

He felt worried, irritated even, but now was not the time for that kind of response. He took her hand in his, noticing her skin was finally beginning to warm up again. 'Now, tell me, has this happened before?'

She sighed and ran her fingers through her unruly curls. 'A few times.'

'As bad as this?'

'No, no, of course not. I've always managed to eat something before it got too bad, well, almost always…'

'Melissa?' Cooper's brown eyes were filled with concern. 'What do you mean, "almost always"?'

'I've had a few near misses at night. I've been setting my alarm so I get up in the middle of the night and have something to eat.'

Cooper could feel his breath catch at the back of his throat. Why hadn't he seen any of this? Why hadn't she told him? He'd been speaking to her every day—sometimes three times a day—and she hadn't said a word. She needed help. Fast. And it was his job to give it. Her independent streak was putting her and their baby at risk. He looked at his surroundings, flinching as he remembered what he'd done to her door. 'You need to come and stay with me. It's not safe, for you or the baby.'

Melissa was horrified. 'No! I can't. I'll be fine—this is just a little blip. I've always managed my diabetes and I'll manage this too.'

Cooper shook his head. He was not taking no for an answer. He'd seen the state she'd been in that morning and he couldn't ever let that happen again. 'I would never forgive myself if something happened to you or the baby.'

Melissa felt as if the world was closing in on her. She tried to process the words he'd just said. *You or the baby.* Did that mean he felt something for her too? Or was this only just about the baby?

Her head was spinning. No matter how hard she tried to stop it, Cooper was getting well and truly under her skin. She'd started to find herself waiting for his texts and calls, and loving it when they finally came. But this was a man who was still grieving for his wife so she couldn't allow herself to become emotionally attached to him, not when he couldn't feel the same way about her. She'd seen what hurt like that did to a woman.

'Stop it. Leave me alone.' The tears were welling up in her eyes and before she knew it, they were spilling down her cheeks. 'I'm not giving up my independence for anyone. I love staying in my own flat. You can phone me, text me or come and visit, but I'm not going to stay with you.' She tried to sound determined.

Cooper put his arm around her. 'But I have been phoning you, Missy, and you haven't told me a thing. No one is asking you to give up your independence. You're right. This is only a blip. It might only last a few weeks but you still need some help. What if you had a really bad hypo during the night? Who could inject you to bring you round? If you were on duty the next day someone would notice when you didn't appear. But what if you weren't on duty? What if you were on days off? You could lie unconscious for three days before anyone came looking for you. I can't let that happen.'

The words cut through Melissa like a knife. The thought chilled her to the bone. She couldn't let that happen either. Her baby's safety was paramount. 'You could phone me every day, at the same time, and if I didn't answer—'

'Not good enough.' Cooper cut her off briskly. 'Like I said, I've been phoning you every day for the last three weeks but it obviously isn't enough. It would be better if we were under one roof. That way, I might realise when you were about to have a hypo and do something to stop it.'

Melissa shook her head. She knew he was right. She had always been able to tell when her blood-sugar levels were low. Sometimes she would break out in a sweat, other times she would tremble. Sometimes she just had the strangest feeling in the pit of her stomach. But now it was different. Her warning signs had changed, they were much more subtle, and she wasn't picking up on them.

Melissa stared blankly into space. This was turning into the worst day of her life. Could she separate her heart from her head? Could she stay with Cooper for a few weeks until her hypos were under control, without losing her heart completely?

Cooper gave her one of his winning smiles. The kind that was seen on an advertising billboard for toothpaste. 'Missy, I would offer to come and stay with you but we need to have a little chat about that. And about getting your door fixed.'

Her eyebrows lifted. She hadn't moved from this sofa since she'd had the hypo and she'd wondered how on earth Cooper had gotten into her flat. Now she knew.

Melissa took a deep breath. She felt as if this decision could cause her physical pain. Her heart was screaming

No but her head was screaming *Yes*! It went against all her principles. But she didn't just have herself to think about any more. She had to put the baby first and this was the most obvious solution. 'Okay, Cooper, I'll come and stay with you. But only on a temporary basis. Once this blip has passed I'll be moving back to my own flat, okay?'

Cooper nodded. Right now he would agree to anything. He needed to keep both her and the baby safe.

'And you're definitely getting me a new front door, right?'

He smiled and drew her into his arms, planting a kiss on her forehead. 'Everything's going to be okay, Missy.'

She sat for a few seconds, enjoying the waves of warmth that swept from his body to hers. She and Cooper alone together at last. Even the thought of it sent other types of waves running through her body causing her nipples to instantly prickle to attention. She shifted uncomfortably. She could try this. She had to try this, because she had to know. She had to know if she could be in a room with Cooper and stop thinking about him in ways that didn't involve him wearing no clothes. She had to know that she could become immune to those big brown eyes and killer smiles. She had to know that she could have a civilised relationship with the father of her child.

Melissa stood up. The side effects of the glucose injection were starting to kick in. On the few occasions she'd ever been given it she'd always been violently sick. The tell-tale waves of nausea began to sweep across her. She gave Cooper a weak smile. 'You might just live to regret this, Coop.'

CHAPTER SEVEN

COOPER stirred the pot for the nineteenth time and tried to stop the chicken sticking to the bottom of the pan. He wasn't too good at this but he was determined to try. The stainless-steel kitchen currently looked like a disaster zone. There were three pans in the kitchen sink, every worktop space was filled with ingredients and utensils, and the cookery book he'd propped against a wall kept sliding downwards and automatically closing. To top it all off, everything was covered in a thin coating of flour following an incident with a dropped bag. But no matter how much chaos ensued, above all Cooper was feeling happy.

After a week of sharing a home and cobbling meals together from the remnants of Cooper's freezer they'd finally gone shopping. That morning he'd learned that Melissa loved chicken, hated beef, was funny about fish and absolutely detested prawns. Just as well in her current condition. He knew she loved chocolate, but limited her supply to the occasional square and she seemed to drink gallons of a diet brand of drink from Scotland. And she had a penchant for beans on toast, late at night.

'Can I give you a hand in there?' called Melissa. She was currently lying across the red sofa, reading the latest bestseller. She could vaguely see the disarray surrounding Cooper, but she was having too much fun watching him trying to cook her dinner to go and help.

'No,' shouted Cooper. 'I've told you, just relax.' He stirred frantically as the chicken seemed to stick to the bottom of the pan for the twentieth time that evening. His rice boiled over with huge hissing sounds as the water hit the steel hob. He looked at the slightly over-done chicken and the definitely overdone rice, before heaving a sigh and turning off the gas hob. It would have to do.

He found a tray that he'd never known he owned and stuck the two plates on it to carry through to the living room. From a plastic bag hidden behind the microwave he found his secret purchase from that afternoon and put it next to her plate.

'Here we go.' Cooper plunked the tray down on the coffee table next to Melissa as she swung her legs off the sofa. He watched her as she gazed in amazement at the gift and a smile spread across her face. She leaned over and picked it up.

The little ultrasound picture had been placed in a red frame to match the décor in the room. 'You put it in a frame?' she asked, momentarily stunned.

'I thought it should have pride of place,' he said, leaning next to her to look at the picture. 'I also thought we could probably update it every four weeks when you get your new scans.'

The smile reached up to her ears. 'That's a nice thought,' she whispered quietly. She turned to face him and he automatically clasped his arms around her waist, pulling her close. 'Why did you do that?' she asked.

He ran his finger down her cheek. 'I knew that you'd been upset with me in the scan room. I also knew how big a deal it was for you to come and live here. I wanted you both to feel welcome.'

Melissa felt the warm feeling inside her begin to spread. Cooper had said *both. He wanted both of them to feel welcome.* Something about this just felt so right. Today had been a great day. She'd been relaxed and happy in his company. He'd been attentive without being overbearing. He'd massaged her shoulders when they'd come back from town and had made her tea.

She'd enjoyed going shopping with him, even though he was the most disorganised shopper she'd ever met. Now she understood why he piled food onto his plate in the hospital canteen as if it was going out of fashion. It was because he never ate at home. He didn't see the point in cooking for one. Her heart had almost melted when he'd said those words.

She'd reorganised his trolley with dinners for every night of the week for both of them and numerous snacks. She'd bought the biggest range of breakfast cereals, along with eggs, bacon and orange juice. 'Do not let me leave the house in the morning without breakfast,' she'd warned him, and he'd nodded dutifully and paid the huge grocery bill without a flicker of surprise.

Melissa had caught sight of them both in one of the large mirrors in the supermarket as they'd shopped. They had looked like any other couple, laughing and joking their way around the shop while he'd put things in the trolley and she'd taken them back out with a shake of her head. She'd felt a pang in her heart. This was only temporary. They hadn't had that discussion about the future yet. There was still so much she was unsure of. But the fact that he had put their baby's ultrasound picture in a frame was a good start.

She stared down at the congealing chicken on the

plate before her and stifled a laugh. 'Are all your dinners going to be as good as this one?'

He nodded enthusiastically at her. 'I've spent hours over that. I expect you to clean your plate.'

Melissa gulped and made to lift the fork in front of her.

'We need to talk about something.'

'Sure. What is it?' Anything that stopped her from eating this dinner.

'What do you want to do about work? After you have the baby, I mean.'

Melissa looked him, a little surprised at where the conversation had gone, but she knew it was time for them to talk about this. 'I think that I'd like to take my whole years' maternity leave and then go back to work.' She wondered if Cooper would object. Would he expect her to be a full-time mum?

But Cooper nodded thoughtfully. 'Do you still plan on working full time or will you reduce your hours?'

'I'd like to do fewer hours, it all depends on how things work out financially. In an ideal world I'd do two days and spend the rest of the time at home with the baby.'

His brown eyes were studying her carefully. 'You know that I'll support you, don't you? Financially and in real terms.' He went to continue but Melissa had already interrupted.

'I don't want your money, Cooper.'

He raised his hand. 'But the money isn't for *you*, Melissa, it's for our *baby*.' He raised his eyebrow at her defensive tone. 'You know this independent streak of yours runs a mile wide, but isn't always in your own best interests. Every man on the planet should support their child and that's what I intend to do. And if that helps you reduce the number of hours that you work, that's fine.'

She shifted uncomfortably. She hated talking about money. It was inevitable that they would have this conversation but it just didn't feel right. The reality was that child support from Cooper probably would allow her to reduce her working hours, but the thought of being dependent on someone else for something like that was alien to her.

'I just learned from an early age not to be dependent on a man.'

Cooper's eyes looked up at the quiet tone of her voice. 'How did you learn that, Missy?'

Her fingers went automatically to her hair, just as they always did when she was uncomfortable, and she started twisting a chestnut lock. 'My dad left when I was eleven. My mum had always thought the world revolved around him, she was devastated and fell apart. I was left to pick up the pieces.'

Cooper could feel the hair on his arms stand on end. This was the first time Missy had really shared something so important with him. 'That sounds tough. Do you still see him?'

'Not since the day he walked out. He left us for another woman. He sent me a few letters and cards, some money for birthdays, but it would have been too difficult on my mum if I'd tried to see him.'

Cooper felt annoyed. An eleven-year-old child shouldn't have to make a decision like that. 'Did he try to see you?'

She nodded. 'Yes, a few times. But it never worked out. On the days I had arranged to meet him, Mum always had one crisis or another.'

His hand reached out and encircled hers. 'But you were a child, you shouldn't have had to deal with that.'

'But I did. There was no one else. My mum was clinically depressed for a long time. We had to sell our house and move. She'd never had a job before and it took a long time before she was ready to go out and look for work.'

'And now?'

'She's doing well. She lives in her own flat and works in the local library. She just about manages her finances. I help her out occasionally. Her mental health is much better. But I never want to end up like her, end up in a state like that over a man.'

The words hung between them. Cooper was processing everything she'd just said. Now he understood her actions. Now he understood her independent streak. Missy took a deep breath. Cooper wasn't her father. And he wasn't David either. But she wasn't ready to agree to anything yet. There was still too much that could change between them.

'I'll wait until nearer the time,' she said quickly. 'I'll decide what I want to do then.' She bent her head over her dinner, to escape his watchful eyes.

'But what about Junior?'

'What about Junior?' The first mouthful of Cooper's chicken had just made it into her mouth. She wasn't altogether keen to try another.

'I'm not just talking about money here, Melissa. I want to be involved in our baby's life. All the time if I can.' He made a sweeping gesture with his arm. 'You know that I've got plenty of space here. If you were working at the weekend and I wasn't on call, I'd be happy to have Junior. During the day and overnight.'

Wow. Her baby staying somewhere else overnight. She hadn't even thought about that yet.

'And I could look at my shifts during the week too if that would help.'

Missy nodded, taking a deep breath. 'I had planned on using the hospital crèche if I had to. But if you could help out, that would be good too.' Her voice was hesitant. As if this was the first time she'd really given it any proper thought and the processes were just forming in her mind.

'I want to be here to help you and the baby.'

She turned to face him as he reached over and touched her arm. There it was again, that delicious zing that appeared out of nowhere whenever he touched her. She had just gone to lift a second mouthful of chicken to her lips but Cooper hadn't let her go yet. He was staring deeply into her eyes. 'I need to talk to you about something else.'

She sat the fork back down, noting the serious expression on his face. Her stomach clenched. *What was he going to say now?*

Cooper leaned forward, staring at her with those big chocolate eyes of his. 'I haven't slept a wink since you moved in here.'

She was confused. Why was he telling her this now? 'Why on earth can't you sleep?'

'I can't sleep because I'm constantly worrying that you could be having a hypo in the other room.'

'Oh.' She nodded her head slowly. 'And?'

A slow smile crept across his lips. 'I was thinking that it might make more sense if we slept in the same bed.'

'I see.' She breathed in slowly, her brain screaming one answer while her heart thudded another. She finally felt as if a weight had been lifted off her shoulders. Maybe Cooper would understand why she felt so strongly about things now? Maybe that could leave them free to concentrate on other things?

'If you were unwell during the night, I wouldn't realise until the next morning. If you were lying next to me, I would be much more likely to notice sooner.' Cooper gave her a lazy smile before moving closer and running a finger along the base of her neck. Missy felt her heartbeat quicken. Her breath caught in her lungs.

'So you want me to sleep in the white bedroom, then?'

Cooper raised his eyes from her neck and nodded slowly. 'What do you think?' He held his breath while he waited for her answer.

Missy looked at the plate of unappetising food on the table to her side. She could think of much better things to eat. This man was haunting her every waking thought. Part of her wondered if sleeping with Cooper again could get him finally out of her system. These pregnancy hormones were playing havoc with her senses, and it was all she could do not to pin him up against the wall. Other parts wondered if she was just trying to hold onto whatever little bit of him she could get. It was time to find out.

'Will there be any special treatment if I decide to sleep in the white room with you?'

Cooper's face relaxed. He knew where this was heading. 'I can think of some.'

Missy stood up and took his hand. 'Well, in that case I think I'll have a demonstration.'

She took him by the hand and led him across the living room, pushing open the door to his bedroom and stepping onto the thick white carpet. Her toes automatically curled in pleasure at the deep-piled carpet, reminding her of the last time she'd been in this room. Had that really been nearly five months ago?

She paused, turning to face him. It was dark outside, the lights from the flickering marina, reflecting on the black surface of the water like glistening stars, casting shadows into the dark bedroom. She shrugged off her thick cardigan, leaving it to puddle on the floor at her feet. She didn't want anything between them now. He lifted his hands and cupped her face, bending to kiss her. Missy's head started to spin. She'd just been about to say something, just been about to ask him if he was sure. But her words were lost as his lips touched hers, taking her back in time to a few months before.

Everything about this felt so right. They'd finally managed to have a conversation about 'their' child. To plan for the future. To look at practicalities. Maybe she could rely on Cooper?

Her body responded instantly to him, the fine hairs on her arms standing on end at the touch of his skin against hers. His hands dropped, and the slightest of stubble on his chin scraped against her face. His hands circled her waist and he walked her backwards, lowering her gently against the deep white duvet.

'Okay?' One word. It was all he said, his voice deep and husky with desire. She nodded. Nothing else mattered right now. The thousand words that needed to be said had vanished from her mind. He traced a finger from her shoulder, along the inside of her arm to the palm of her hand. She automatically closed her fingers around it, trapping it next to her, before raising her hand to her breast and releasing it there. This was what she wanted. She wanted him to touch her again, to make her feel the way he had that first magical night together. Could she ever recapture that?

His lips bent to her neck and she let out a moan. It was obvious he remembered the most sensitive part of her neck. The part that always distracted her and spun her into a new reality. A reality where she lived as a princess in a castle and this was her prince, the man who loved and adored her, and would stay with her forever. Where had that come from? Yup, she was definitely losing her mind.

She felt the tug of his hand at her jeans and automatically went to pull her stomach in, then realised that she couldn't. A remnant of their last night of passion. The last time she'd been in this bedroom.

He quickly removed her clothes, pulling her jeans from her legs and sliding her top from her shoulders. She sighed as he ran his hand slowly down the inside of her thigh, then back up again.

Missy tugged at his shirt, desperate to feel his skin against hers. The hairs on his chest brushed against her face as he pulled his shirt over his head.

She could practically feel the electricity sparking between them. She ran her fingers over his warm skin, pulling him even closer to her. .

She lifted her head, whispering in his ear, 'Why are we waiting, Coop?' A smile danced across her lips as she teased him. 'It's not like we need to worry about contraception.'

He was poised above her now, his arms on either side of her shoulders. There was a gleam in his deep brown eyes. 'I guess we don't,' he said huskily. His head bent downwards and she gasped as his tongue ran down her throat towards her nipple. He nudged her bra aside and teased her with his teeth.

'You're driving me crazy, Cooper,' she moaned, before catching his buttocks with the palms of her hands and driving him towards her. There, she could definitely feel him now. And she knew exactly what she wanted.

'No more teasing.' Her voice was low as she lifted her hips from the bed and moved herself against him. He lifted his head, his breathing hoarse. 'I hope you're sure, Missy.'

'I'm sure.'

His hand swept aside her silk panties, removing the final barrier between them. She heard a guttural moan in response before he thrust into her, filling her completely, then smiled and pulled backwards.

The sensations started seeping through Melissa. This was what she remembered. This was what she wanted. He was taunting her, teasing her. Her legs wrapped instinctively around him, keeping him close, her hands around his neck as his head dipped lower towards her sensitive nipples.

'Cooper,' she moaned. 'Don't stop.'

The pulses were growing stronger, her breath catching in her throat. She moved her hips in synch with his, lifting them off the bed to pull him deeper inside her.

'Missy,' he growled as his rhythm grew faster.

And she was lost. Nothing had felt this good. Nothing *could* feel this good. Only him.

Cooper woke just as the first rays of early morning sunshine streamed through the window. For a second he forgot where he was, encompassed by warmth, bare skin against bare skin, his arm wrapped around Missy's waist, the palm of his hand resting on her blossoming stomach. His eyes flickered open as her hair tickled his nose. Chestnut-brown hair.

He started, pulling back from Missy's warm body. His breath caught in his throat. He groaned, reality striking him like a hammer blow. Blonde. He had expected to see blonde hair.

Just for a second, when he'd been in that dream-like state between sleep and wakening, he'd been transported back in time. Back to a past where everything had been fine and he'd had hopes and expectations for the future. He gave an involuntary shudder. This had happened before. For the first few days after Clara and Lily had died, when he'd woken in the morning, for a second—just for a second—everything had been fine. Then, like an avalanche of tumbling rocks, it had hit him all again. The horror. The loss. The desperation.

He knew that this was normal. That anyone who had suffered a bereavement went through these feelings. But this wasn't Clara. He was lying in bed with another woman. Another woman who was carrying his child. Cooper pulled back. Last time he'd slept with Missy she'd disappeared before morning. He woken up to an empty bed, and he'd been disappointed. His eyes swept over her sleeping form. His hand still rested on her stomach. The first signs of gentle blooming were present and he felt numb. Everything was topsy-turvy between them and that said nothing about his feelings. Not because he wasn't happy about being a father, simply because he was numb with fear. But, just like last night, put him in an enclosed space with Melissa and all sense went out of the window and his raging hormones took over.

With every day that passed he was witnessing Missy's body bloom swell with his child. He would soon see the first little kicks and squirms of the life within. And no matter how hard he tried, he just couldn't feel joy. He'd seen the look on her face in the scan room; he'd seen the same wonder and awe on the faces of many parents at that first sight of their baby. But something had happened deep inside him. His heart felt as if it were wrapped in a layer of ice. He had to protect himself. He wanted to be a father. He wanted to have the happy life that he'd seen the family down at the marina having. He wanted to be excited and whip out the scan picture of his baby to show anyone who asked. But the fear wouldn't leave him. He'd done all these things the first time—the joy, the happiness, the plans.

In a couple of weeks they would be going for their detailed scan. The scan that would show their baby's development. *Please let everything be fine*. He sent a silent prayer upwards. Fear crept down his spine. The thought of packing up another nursery into boxes made him feel physically sick. Putting the tiny white and yellow vests and sleepsuits into a box had almost killed him. Phoning the shop to tell them he wouldn't be picking up the pram and hearing the sob at the back of the unknown woman's throat had been too much.

Packing away the cot had been the worst day of his life. It had finalised his grief. It had made him realise that it wasn't a bad dream and he wasn't going to wake up in the morning and find out that everything was all right. It had made him realise Clara and Lily were gone forever. It had almost been the undoing of him.

And now, two years on, he found himself in this position, an unplanned baby with a woman who had a long-term medical condition. A condition that meant she and the baby were at higher risk of everything, every complication his imagination could throw at him—and right now his mind was working overtime.

He couldn't deny the attraction he felt towards Missy.

She was magnetic. He'd caught sight of her numerous times at work when she'd been dealing with patients and seen the compassion in her eyes. He felt her presence as soon as she walked into the same room as him. He just couldn't stay away from her. But this?

His rational and methodical brain told him that after his previous experience he would never have chosen to start a family with Missy. She was just too high risk. Because of his medical background, everyone would expect him to be understanding of her condition, and he was. But everyone didn't know about his past experience. And that was with someone who had been apparently healthy. He just didn't know if his heart and brain could cope with the possibility of a loss again.

Which left him here, in this position, where he wanted to reach out and be happy but his heart wouldn't let him.

He wasn't even entirely sure how he felt about her. Did he love her? Did he even know what love was any more?

She had certainly gotten under his skin. But more than that, more than physical attraction, he liked her. He enjoyed being in her company, he loved how she was so passionate about her job. He had no doubt in the world that Missy would be a great mum. But if things went well for her and the baby, would she want to have a life with him? Would she even want to see him? Would she want him to be father to their child?

All these things were spinning around in Cooper's head and now, because he was worried about her and the baby, she was under his roof. He would see her every day. He would no longer have time to himself, to sit at night, stare out at the marina and sort out his thoughts from the day.

She looked so happy, so peaceful, even in her sleep. But his stomach was twisting. He shouldn't be here. Because, right or wrong, this felt like a betrayal. He needed some distance. He pulled back. Missy gave a sigh at his movement and turned towards him, seeking out the heat within the bed.

Cooper sat up abruptly, swinging his legs out of the bed. He took a few steps, pulling open a drawer and tugging on a pair of jogging bottoms before striding through to the kitchen. His fingers tugged at the handle on the door before he slowed his actions and quietly closed the door behind him. There was no point in making too much noise, he didn't want to wake Missy. He didn't want to have to face the consequences of what he'd done last night. He didn't want to have the inevitable conversation. What he needed right now was space.

Missy arched her back and gave a comfortable sigh. She stretched out like a cat, spreading her arms under the duvet. Space. Something wasn't right.

Her eyelids fluttered open, her hand lying in the wide open space next to her. And it was cold. There was no comfortable 'dip' in the mattress next to her. Cooper hadn't just got up to go to the toilet, he'd been gone some time.

Missy sat up, suddenly conscious of her nakedness, pulling the cover up to her chin. Where was he?

The sun was flooding through the exposed window, revealing the boats bobbing in the marina. She bit her lip. In their haste to reach the bed last night they hadn't even managed to pull the curtains. Colour flooded her cheeks as she saw her clothes scattered across the bedroom floor and she felt confusion build in her chest. Where was he? Why hadn't she woken up next to him?

The scattered clothes conjured up pictures in her mind of the heat between them last night. She didn't even want to shrug her way back into them. Her eyes caught sight of Cooper's navy fleece dressing gown hanging on a hook on the back of the bedroom door. That would do.

She opened the door and was hit by the strong aroma of coffee. As if it had been percolating for hours. Cooper cut a lonely figure, standing at the window, staring out over the marina. There was no steam rising from the mug of coffee in his hand. Probably long-cold. How long had he been standing there?

'Cooper?'

She started towards him, a tight feeling in her chest.

He flinched at her voice then turned towards her. 'Oh, you're awake.' His voice was flat, almost detached. He placed his coffee mug on the table. 'Are you hungry? Do you want me to make you breakfast?' He moved past her, almost as if she wasn't there, his eyes not making contact with hers.

Missy watched as he pulled some bread from a paper wrapper and slotted it into the toaster. He moved as if on autopilot, switching on the kettle, pulling plates from the cupboard and butter from the fridge. Never once looking at her. No friendly smile. No good-morning kiss.

A feeling of dread swept over her. She swallowed, her throat dry and parched, suddenly conscious of the ache between her legs from last night.

'Cooper.'

Nothing. Not even a flicker from him. It was as if she hadn't spoken.

She moved round behind the breakfast bar. 'Cooper.' Her voice was firmer, more definite and she laid her hand over his.

He flinched visibly. Then furiously started buttering toast.

'Cooper, what's wrong?'

'Nothing. Nothing's wrong.' He still hadn't looked at her.

'The hell it isn't!' She took the knife from his hand and put her hands on his shoulders, turning him to face her. 'Look at me, Cooper.'

She saw him bite his bottom lip, his eyes fixed firmly to the floor.

She gritted her teeth. 'I said look at me, Cooper.'

He shook his head and turned his attention to the kettle, pouring boiling water into two mugs.

She slammed her hand down on the counter next to him. 'Enough!'

That got his attention. He raised his eyebrow at her—as he had on so many other occasions—but the expression on his face wasn't amusement or annoyance. He looked exhausted. 'Leave it, Missy.'

'No, I won't leave it, Cooper. Is this it? I do this…' She swept her arms around the room. 'I agree to move in, just like you asked me to, we start to get to know each other a little better—maybe even start to have some kind of relationship—then we sleep together, and suddenly that's it? You shut me out?'

He hadn't moved. His eyes were fixed on hers. She saw him swallowing uncomfortably, as if her words were sticking in his throat.

She reached out and grabbed his arm. 'Why are you

making me feel as if we did something wrong? Because I don't think we did, Cooper. I thought we did something beautiful. I thought we were two single, consenting adults. So why are you making me feel like this?'

His words seemed to falter. 'It's just…' He stared back out over the marina. 'It's difficult. It's harder than I thought.'

Missy felt a wave of nausea sweep over her. This was about Clara.

She took a step backwards, her feet cold on the tiled floor. 'I can't do this,' she whispered. 'I can't stay with you—not when you treat me like this.'

There was no getting away from it. Missy felt used and abused. There was something so primitive about it. He didn't want her. They'd slept together again and he didn't want her. Not like she wanted him. And it hurt. It hurt so much.

She turned to leave but he grabbed her arm. 'You can't leave. You're still having hypos. You need someone to keep an eye on you.' It was the first time that morning his voice held any semblance of warmth.

Missy took a deep breath, raised her eyes to meet his. 'What I need, Cooper, is someone who can look out for my physical and *emotional* health. Someone who can be there for me.' Her hands rested on her stomach. 'And that's not you.'

'Yes, it is.' The words shot out. There was almost desperation in them. He ran his hands through his hair. They were trembling.

She could see he was struggling. She should feel sympathy for him, pity even, but she couldn't. Not now, not like this.

He took a deep breath. 'This is my fault,' he said, his

eyes still not quite meeting hers. 'I've confused things. I've made things complicated.'

'By sleeping together?'

He nodded.

'But we'd already done that, Cooper.'

'Not like this.' He spread his arms. 'Last time around, it was for fun. We didn't expect there to be any consequences. We didn't know each other.'

Missy was trying her best to keep her cool. 'And now?'

'This time it's different.' His words finally seemed to make sense to him and he raised his eyes to meet hers. 'I asked you to stay because I wanted to make sure that you and our baby would be healthy. Last night should never have happened. And that's my fault. I'm sorry. We have to go back. We have to sleep in separate rooms.'

Melissa could feel her heart pounding in her chest. She wasn't sorry. She didn't feel sorry at all. She only felt confused. She hadn't come here for a relationship. She hadn't wanted a relationship. But somewhere along the line her feelings had started to change. She wasn't sure what she wanted any more. He was right—last night had confused things. Her head started to spin and she felt herself sway.

'Melissa? Are you all right?' He caught her in his arms and sat her down at the kitchen table. He opened the fridge and pulled out some jam, grabbing the toast that he'd buttered and dumping a huge spoonful on top, before setting it in front of her. 'Eat.'

He dunked a teabag in a cup before adding a spoonful of sugar and placing it next to her, before sitting down opposite her.

Melissa had started mechanically lifting the toast to her mouth. She wasn't even sure if she was having a hypo or if she just felt light-headed because of the events.

'Missy, I'm sorry. I'm supposed to be looking after you.'

She lifted her eyes to meet his. Nothing made sense to her any more. Everything seemed too complicated.

Cooper reached over and took her hand. 'Don't move out. Not when things are like this. Please don't do anything that will put you and the baby at risk.'

He was pleading with her, she could see it in his eyes. This time he was speaking from the heart. She'd started to think he didn't have a heart.

She nodded numbly, her hand falling automatically to her stomach. He was right. She wasn't ready to be her own yet and no matter how much it hurt her, she couldn't do anything to hurt their baby.

CHAPTER EIGHT

'READY?'

Cooper pulled the car into the staff car park and turned off the engine.

Missy nodded nervously and pulled her bag from the floor of the car.

Today was their appointment for their detailed scan of the baby. The scan that would tell them if everything looked okay. If the brain, spine and organs were formed properly, if the bones were in proportion.

The first picture had already been replaced by another at fifteen weeks, and a second at nineteen weeks. In each picture the little image had grown in size and had become a little bit clearer. The red frame sat in pride of place in the middle of the coffee table, the first thing that anyone who entered the flat would see.

And Missy was still there. Still staying at the flat and still sleeping in a separate bedroom.

She and Cooper had fallen into an awkward routine. Her hypoglycaemic attacks were beginning to settle. Missy had managed to get herself back on an even keel and, as much as she didn't want to admit it, living with Cooper seemed to have helped. They did the shopping together and took turns making dinner. If they were working the same shifts they travelled to and from work together. Every night he ran her a warm bath to soothe her aching legs and feet. Companionable. That was how she would describe their relationship. But it made them sound like an elderly couple. The truth was the sexual tension continued to run between them like a gentle undercurrent. Every now and then, hands would brush together with the familiar zing of electricity sparking between them, only to be hastily retracted.

And Melissa would remind herself once more, *This is only temporary*. But something inside her was changing. And she didn't know how it had happened or when it had happened. Maybe it was the pregnancy, or the pregnancy hormones, but something was making her wonder about being on her own. Was it really what she wanted? Or was she beginning to want something more?

She stared at the figure walking ahead of her along the hospital corridor. Once again, Cooper was lost in his own thoughts. And once again Melissa felt as if she was excluded.

Fiona was on duty in the scan room again and she settled Melissa comfortably on the couch, before dimming the lights and readying the scanner.

'All set?'

Melissa gave her a little nod. Her body had gradually swollen over the last few weeks and nothing really fitted her any more. She was resisting the temptation to ask for maternity-style uniforms. They made anyone who wore them look like a giant walking white tent. Instead she'd traded tunic tops with a friend who was a size bigger than her and had recently lost some weight, although that didn't help her with the trousers, which would no longer fasten around her waist. Instead she'd had to content herself with leaving the top button unfastened.

Missy stared down at the little bump with pride, her

hand automatically resting on her swollen abdomen. A smile crept across her lips as she felt the little flutterings of movement underneath her fingertips. She gestured to Cooper.

In the darkness Cooper moved his warm hand over hers, laying his fingers in between hers as he tried to feel the light movements under her skin.

'Can you feel it yet?' she whispered. It had become a standing joke between them that Cooper couldn't feel the baby's movements yet. From the moment Missy had first felt the little quickenings around eighteen weeks she had encouraged him to press his hand on her stomach to try and feel the baby moving.

Cooper shook his head with a wry smile. 'No, not yet.' He moved his hand out of the way as Fiona squirted some gel on Missy's stomach and placed the scanner in position.

'Let's get a good look at this baby,' said Fiona decisively.

Missy held her breath. This was her fourth scan and she still held her breath every time the scanner was held in place. She knew she had no reason to worry—her blood-sugar levels had been good, never rising to levels that could put their baby's development at risk. All her other tests had shown she was at low risk of certain genetic conditions, so she knew there was no reason to worry, but it didn't stop her.

The picture appeared clearly on the screen. 'Okay, folks, you know the routine. I'm just going to check all of baby's organs and check the size and weight measurements again.' Fiona turned and faced them both. 'So the million-dollar question is—do you want to know the sex of your baby?'

Missy gulped. She knew this question had been

coming. Most midwives were quite traditional and didn't want to know what they were having—they wanted 'a surprise'. But Missy didn't want a surprise. She wanted to plan. She wanted to ask her mother to knit her little cardigans in pale pink or pale blue wool. She wanted to buy her baby a gorgeous outfit to come home from hospital in. Not the plain and boring white or lemon. She wanted colour to reflect the sex of her baby.

But fear flooded her. How would Cooper feel if it was a little girl? Missy bit her bottom lip. 'What do you think, Cooper?' she asked nervously. 'Should we find out?'

Cooper looked at her face and a knot turned in his stomach. He knew she wanted to know. He had dreaded this. He started saying silent prayers in his head. Prayers for a son. Another baby girl would just bring back the pain of losing Lily and he didn't want that. He couldn't tell Missy, though. She was becoming more and more twitchy as the pregnancy progressed. She was trying to pretend she was relaxed about the whole thing, but he could see the internet searches she'd done in his absence or when she'd had one of his well-thumbed obstetric books out, examining some hidden complaint in detail. He'd seen the pile of notes she'd made. She seemed to be obsessed by statistics. Diabetes and pregnancy complications statistics. How much more likely she was to have pre-eclampsia, premature labour, congenital malformations—the list was endless—because of her diabetes.

He reached over in the darkness and squeezed her hand. 'Whatever you want to do is fine with me, Missy.'

Missy glanced between his face and Fiona, who was patiently waiting for an answer.

'Well,' she started hesitantly, 'I think that—'

'We may as well find out,' cut in Cooper, trying to take the pressure off Missy. 'It makes sense as we'll probably be able to see during the scan anyway.' He gave Fiona a little nod of his head to acknowledge the fact she'd probably been dreading doing this scan, as it was likely that at some point the secret would have been revealed. It would be difficult for an experienced midwife like Missy and an obstetrician like Cooper to fail to notice.

Fiona continued to move the scanner across Missy's abdomen. 'There's the heart.' She pointed it out, monitoring the blood flow through the heart and giving them both a little smile. 'The head and brain all look normal. The spine looks good, well formed, everything intact. That little black circle is the baby's bladder.' She gave Missy a smile. 'Obviously full.'

A smile passed between Missy and Cooper, a smile of relief. Everything was good, their baby was healthy. Fiona took a few more notes. 'Growth and weight look normal for twenty-one weeks.' She swept the scanner lower down Missy's abdomen. 'Now, if baby will oblige we'll have a look to see if it's a he or a she. Yup, there we are, folks, say hello to Miss Roberts.'

A girl. The breath caught in her throat. She'd always wanted a little girl but had been afraid to say those words to Cooper. She could have a whole house filled with pink things. She could buy stripy tights. She could have a bobble-bag, a bag filled with hair bobbles to match every outfit. She could get her mum to knit one of those gorgeous baby hats, pale pink with the fluffy pink caribou around the rim. Or even better, one of the pom-pom hats, with a huge pom-pom practically the same size as the baby's head. All the things she'd said she'd never do. She'd almost missed the fact that Fiona had referred to her daughter as 'Miss Roberts'. They hadn't talked about surnames yet. But she was excited. She was having a girl. Wonderful.

But how would Cooper feel? Her eyes strained through the darkness of the scan room to try and catch the expression on his face.

A girl. Cooper felt a dagger of ice pierce his heart. The blade dug deeper and deeper, to be replaced by a tight cold hand, squeezing his heart so fiercely that the breath was struggling to leave his lungs. Lily. The small blue-tinged baby who should have been rosy and pink. The pale, perfect skin, dark hair and gorgeous features that had never been destined to draw breath in this world. And now two years later he was having another girl—once again, it felt like a betrayal.

'Cooper? Are you all right?' she whispered.

Conscious of his behaviour and her reaction previously, he squeezed Missy's hand and shot her a smile. 'Of course I am. We'll need to start thinking of names,' he said, trying to be enthusiastic.

'Yes,' she agreed, nodding her head while deep in thought.

'Missy?' Fiona started to wipe the gel from Missy's stomach. 'Would you like to come in next door and we'll get you a gorgeous picture of your daughter's face on the 3D scanner?'

'Oh, yes, please.' Missy edged herself off the examination couch and pulled her trousers up again. 'Coming, Coop?'

'Sure.'

They headed into the next door room and waited patiently while Fiona adjusted the scanner until they'd managed to capture a picture of their daughter's face.

She printed the scans off for them and handed them to Cooper, who quickly placed one inside the plastic folder that held Missy's midwifery notes, pushing the second one into his coat pocket.

'We'll put that in our frame,' he said giving her a quiet smile. 'I need to head along and do my clinic. I'll come along and see you later.'

She leaned forward and brushed against his hand, 'Cooper, are you okay?'

He gave her a tight smile, one that didn't reach his eyes and made him look as if a mask had been painted on his face.

Her heart squeezed. For once she didn't want to be at arm's length from him. He was hurting. She wanted to let him know she understood.

She wrapped her arms around his neck and whispered in his ear, 'I know this would have been easier on you if it was a boy. But this is different. This is our daughter, not Lily. And everything will be fine this time.'

She saw him shift uncomfortably as she spoke, but she had to say something. She couldn't for a second read what was going on inside his mind.

'It's fine, Missy. Honestly, it is. Now, I need to get to my clinic.'

Missy grasped the plastic folder in her hands and watched his figure retreating down the corridor. The scan room may have been dark but she'd seen the fleeting expression on his face. She also knew that he'd tried to hide his reaction from her. And she was trying to understand, truly she was. But she just wanted him to be as happy as she was and sing from the rooftops that they were having a baby girl. Was that so wrong?

But the truth of the matter was she didn't understand.

And no matter how uncomfortable their relationship was, Cooper had a right to be involved. Maybe she was just being hormonal? She could feel an ache in the pit of her stomach. He'd said all the right things but he hadn't been able to hide what had been in his eyes. Missy felt as if she was dangling on a cliff edge and the slightest push could send her tumbling into oblivion. She'd never felt so alone.

Cooper walked along the hallway, his mind in turmoil and his stomach churning. A hand reached out and grabbed him.

'Cooper?' Dave Hammond, an anaesthetist, was standing in front of him, his glance down the corridor on where Missy stood, staring out of one of the nearby windows. She looked lost and Dave's brow furrowed. 'Did everything go all right at the scan?'

Cooper nodded distractedly. 'Yes, yes, everything went fine.' He followed Dave's gaze down the corridor. 'Were you looking for me?'

Dave nodded. 'We need you in Theatre for an emergency section in around ten minutes.' He looked back towards Melissa. 'You do know you're an idiot, don't you Coop?'

Cooper's eyebrows shot upwards, taken aback by the normally placid Dave's words. 'What do you mean?'

Dave gestured down the corridor towards Melissa. 'Word travels fast, Coop. I know you lost your first wife and I'm sorry—truly I am. But you've got a second chance at happiness right in front of you and you're a fool not to take it.'

Cooper shook his head. 'You can't understand. It's complicated…'

'So's life.'

Cooper started at the blunt words.

Dave continued. 'My old dad was devastated when my mum died giving birth to me. He spent thirty years as a widower—he was never lucky enough to meet someone else—but he always told me if he'd ever met someone who gave him the same spark he'd had with Mum, he would grab her with both hands. You have the opportunity right in front of you, Cooper, but you're too big a fool to take it.' Dave shook his head. 'You're so lost in being miserable that you can't move on.' He gestured back to the forlorn figure of Melissa, who had picked up her bag and was slowly walking towards the exit door at the bottom of the corridor. 'Life's too short. It's for living, Coop—so go and live it.'

Dave turned and walked back towards the theatre doors, leaving a stunned Cooper in his wake.

Cooper's eyes followed Melissa as she pushed open the door. His eyes lingered on her rapidly expanding stomach. What had started as a gentle swell was now a well-defined bump. Twenty-one weeks. *His baby.* And the thought didn't fill him with panic, or dread.

He watched as she exited out into the brilliant sunshine, the opened door filling the corridor with a sharp stream of sunlight that disappeared as the door slammed closed behind her. It was almost symbolic. He wanted to run along the corridor and grab her. What was wrong with him? Why couldn't he just give himself a shake and move on?

He looked down at the piece of paper he'd pulled from his pocket. An updated scan image of his daughter. His finger traced the little outline in front of him. This was where he needed to concentrate his thoughts. This was his priority.

Melissa was a strong, independent woman. She

wouldn't wait for him forever. She might not wait for him at all.

It was time to get his house in order.

Last night's jeans lay in a crumpled heap on the floor and Cooper picked them up to toss them in the laundry basket. Something fell from his pocket, something glistening and gold. Cooper bent down and picked up his wedding ring.

He turned the ring over and over between his fingers. Taking it off had been a huge step but now it was time for something else. Now Melissa and their expected baby had moved in. It might only be on a temporary basis but if the truth be told, it was the push that he needed. It was time. He knew it was time. His heart twisted as he realised that it hadn't been Clara who'd been haunting his dreams for a while now. No, now his dreams were filled with a woman with beautiful emerald green eyes and chestnut hair. For a second he felt guilty. Was he forgetting Clara? Was he forgetting their time together? No, those memories would always be with him. But maybe, subconsciously, he was finally letting her go.

He had to make an effort. He had to stop holding Missy and the baby at arm's length. His eyes fell on a bunch of brochures sitting on the arm of the sofa. He knew exactly how to do it.

He held up the ring. For a second it caught a ray of sunlight streaming through the window, sending a warm reflection of gold onto the nearby wall. Cooper brought the ring to his lips and gave it a little kiss, then stood up, opened one of his nearby drawers and dropped it inside. Little by little, he was getting there.

* * *

They pulled up in front of the huge warehouse and Cooper turned to where Missy sat in the passenger seat, her hand held over her face. 'Okay, you can open your eyes now.'

She moved her hand and her eyes flickered open. She'd been squeezing them so tightly it took a second for the large, colourful sign to come into focus. A smile spread across her face. 'You brought me here?'

Cooper returned her smile. 'It seemed like the right time. Ready to go and take a look?'

Melissa nodded as he came around and helped her from the car. This was the last place she'd thought he would bring her. She'd wanted to visit the nursery warehouse for a while now, but hadn't wanted to tempt fate. Now she'd had her detailed scan and knew that everything was fine, it seemed like the ideal time.

They pushed open the doors and went inside. Her eyes swept over the wide expanse. For as far as the eye could see there were prams, cots, high chairs and every kind of baby paraphernalia that had ever been invented.

'Wow, where do we start?' asked Melissa as she looked around in wonder.

Cooper shrugged his shoulders. 'I guess wherever you want.'

She wandered among the nursery furniture, picking up brochures and stopping to look at various bedding sets and mobiles. Cooper followed her, dutifully nodding and smiling at everything she suggested.

'I suppose you want everything to be pink?' he asked as she picked up yet another pink border, before setting it down and moving on to the next.

'Well, not everything,' she said as she pointed in the direction of the prams. 'I've kind of got my heart set on a red pram.'

'Red?'

'I didn't think you'd want to push a pink pram.' She raised her eyebrow at him. 'You are going to be pushing a pram, aren't you, Cooper?'

'Of course. Of course I am.' He moved towards the sea of prams ahead of them. 'But you could be right, preferably not a pink one.'

Melissa walked over to one of red prams and ran her fingers over the hood. 'Yes, definitely red.' Her eyebrows lifted mischievously. 'And you do realise that the rules will apply.'

Cooper felt himself being sucked in. 'And what rules might that be?'

'New pram, new coat.'

He gave a little smile. 'If you wanted a new red coat, all you had to do was say so.' He walked around the brightly coloured pram. It was definitely a safer option than the pink version.

His eyes glanced over at the larger, more traditional prams. 'I thought you might have wanted something a little bigger. My mum had one of those.' He nodded in the direction of the carriage-built prams.

Melissa smiled. 'My mum had one of those too,' she said. 'But I hardly think it's practical for us—we both live in flats.' She looked over the large pram. 'I wouldn't be able to get that up my stairs.'

'You won't need to.' Cooper's voice was steady and determined.

Her eyes widened and she tucked a chestnut curl behind her ear. 'What do you mean?' Her voice was trembling, ever so slightly.

Cooper put his arm around her shoulder, tucking her under his. 'Why would you want to go back to your flat? Don't you like staying with me?'

She held her breath. What had brought this on? 'My diabetes is much more stable now. I haven't had a hypo in weeks.' She reached up and gently touched the side of his cheek. 'I think it's safe for me to go home now.'

'You are home,' he said instantly. His hand encircled the finger that was touching his cheek. 'I want you to stay, you and our baby.' He pointed across the array of baby goods. 'Pick what you like. I was thinking that we should use the other bedroom that overlooks the marina for our daughter. What do you think?'

Melissa felt herself torn in two. On one side she was elated. They'd never spoken about this. Moving in had been a temporary arrangement. On the other side she loved her independence, and she still wasn't sure what she meant to him. She wasn't ready to give up her flat, her security, for a man who was still unsure of his feelings. She'd already been burned once this year and wasn't sure she could deal with it again. More than that. She was terrified. 'I need to give it some thought,' she said quietly. 'This isn't really the kind of place we should be having a discussion like this.' She waved her arm around the nursery warehouse.

Cooper looked at her carefully. He raised his eyebrows. 'What's the point in having two of everything if we don't need it?'

Was that all this meant? A practical solution? Missy shook her head. 'Cooper, I'm not ready to think that far ahead.' She picked up a nearby brochure. 'I'm not sure what you want from me. While I'm happy to help you decorate the nursery at the flat, I'm still going to buy some things for the baby to keep at my flat.' She leaned backwards, resting her arms against a wooden cot. 'We're not exactly a couple, are we?' She folded her arms across her chest. 'You need to give me some time to think about this...' she ran her hands over her stomach '...but, in the meantime, we'll stay a few more weeks.'

'Good,' said Cooper, letting out the breath he'd been holding. He had no idea what she'd been about to say. He was trying to make an effort. He was trying in every way that he could to move this relationship along, in its most natural sense. He felt protective towards Missy. He wanted to make sure that she and the baby were fine. He glanced around him, looking for any kind of distraction to keep him from the thoughts currently running through his brain. His eyes caught sight of another bright red pram nearby. 'So what about this one?'

She gave a little smile at his quick change of subject. 'I fancy something a little more practical. One where the car seat can be attached onto the frame and has a separate carrycot part.'

He ran his eyes over the light-framed pram. 'Do you think it will be sturdy enough?'

'What do you mean?'

He folded his arms across his chest. 'Well, my mum used her pram for five of us. It lasted for years.' His eyes narrowed at the pram in front of him. 'I'm not sure this thing will be that robust.' He gave the pram a little shake, as if to emphasise his point.

She gave a little laugh. 'I'm not sure about you, Coop, but I'm only planning on using this pram for one baby.' She gave him a mischievous glance. 'Are you planning on selling it on? In an online auction maybe?'

He groaned. His late-night buying habits had been rumbled. 'How many parcels arrived today?'

She wagged her finger at him. 'Three, but then, while I was out, a card was put through the door for another.' She rummaged through her bag and pulled out the dog-eared card. 'Here, you can go for that one yourself.' She gave a little start. 'Quick!' She grabbed hold of his hand and placed it on her stomach. 'There! Do you feel it now?'

Even with his hand over her thin silver top Cooper could feel the delicate ripples of movement beneath the skin on her stomach. He couldn't wipe the smile from his face. Although he'd seen her on the scans it was the first time he'd felt their daughter move. He'd watched her little outline fill out and become more defined as the weeks progressed. But this was even more real. This was happening right now.

Melissa's eyes were shining brightly. 'Can you feel her?'

He nodded enthusiastically. 'I sure can.'

Melissa continued, the excitement evident on her face. 'I just feel so different now. Before I had the last scan, I was so worried.' She placed her hand over his. 'You know—that something might be wrong. But now we've had it and I know everything looks good, I feel as if I can finally plan for the future.' She waved her arm around the shop. 'I've been too terrified to come in anywhere like this. I didn't want to start ordering anything until I knew everything was all right. It's such a relief.'

Cooper took her in his arms and pulled her close.

Melissa took a deep breath and wrapped her arms around his waist. His hand was on her abdomen again, feeling their daughter dancing within. His deep brown eyes were shining with no hint of the shadow that sometimes crossed them. His mouth creased into a smile that showed his perfect white teeth. A genuine smile. Their baby was healthy, but what about their relationship? Right now they had an unbreakable bond. One that would keep them together forever. So why did it feel so fragile?

MELISSA was in a state of bliss. She was in the middle of the impossibly comfortable red sofa surrounded by baby catalogues. She'd spent the whole morning looking at cots, wardrobes, baby chairs, changing stations, curtains and bedding. She stared out the window across the marina. This place was really starting to feel like home. She was getting used to waking up to the spectacular view. But somewhere, deep inside her, there was still the distinct feeling of unease. She looked at the lists she'd made for baby items—one for her flat and one for Cooper's. She needed that. Needed that security. She needed to know that everything was in place for her and her baby, no matter where she was and what happened.

She stood up and walked through to the third bedroom, which had last night been designated the baby's room. Like the rest of the flat, it had plain white walls. She brushed her fingers along the wall as she walked over to the window. This bedroom was bigger than the living room in her one-bedroom flat. She'd barely visited her flat since moving in with Cooper, only checking in once a week to pick up her mail and ensure everything was secure. The tiniest knot formed in the bottom of her stomach. She imagined herself crammed into her tiny flat, surrounded by baby things. It would be a tight squeeze—the cot would have to be squashed into her bedroom. Now it seemed as if that might never happen. Could she really stay here with their daughter? Cooper had asked her again and she still hadn't given him an answer. The truth was that she really didn't need to stay any more. Her diabetes was under control. She hadn't had a hypoglycaemic attack in four weeks. It was safe for her to be on her own again. But did she want to be?

Melissa ran her hands over her bulging stomach. *Their daughter.* Even the thought brought a smile to her lips. She was twenty-six weeks now and she finally felt secure enough to start buying things for her arrival. The bottom drawer of her bedside cabinet was stuffed with pink socks, tiny white vests with little pink bows, a pink knitted cardigan her mother had given her, plus the gorgeous pink pom-pom hat she'd imagined. Every few days some other little treasure would be added to the pile, and Melissa would once again take everything out the drawer, one by one, smiling at the idea that one day soon her daughter would be wearing these clothes.

But for some strange reason Melissa hadn't felt able to share the excitement of her clothes buying with Cooper—and she wasn't quite sure why.

He was still being wonderful to her. Running her baths and helping make dinner most evenings. If he had to work late, he would phone her to make sure she was fine, often offering to pick up dinner on the way home. And his fan club seemed to be growing on a daily basis. He was an excellent doctor. He was conscientious and listened to both his colleagues and his patients. He seemed to have good instincts and had picked up on a number of unusual cases that could have had tricky outcomes if he had not intervened. Above all, people seemed to like him. To all intents and purposes, Cooper was the perfect partner.

But everything wasn't quite perfect. They still slept in separate rooms. In separate beds. At times it felt as if Cooper was scared to touch her. Sure, he would rub her back if it was sore, give her the occasional hug, even touch her stomach when the baby was kicking. But he didn't kiss her. He didn't touch her. Not in the way she wanted to be touched.

Melissa looked around the room again. She ran her hand along the pristine white wall once more. It would look nice in a shade of pale pink. Her eyes flickered to one of the brochures she'd left lying on the bed. Would she need one wardrobe or two? There was a built-in cupboard at one end of the room and she pulled the door open to get a feel for the space inside.

It was huge, with a rail for hanging clothes and a variety of shelves at the back. Her hand flicked on the switch just inside the door and the dark space was immediately filled with light. She stepped right inside. Wow! There was loads of storage space in here, none of it currently being used.

Then her eyes were caught by a cardboard box in the bottom right-hand corner of the cupboard. She knelt down beside it and pulled the box towards her. What was this doing in here? Maybe it was some kitchen equipment that Cooper had forgotten about? From the scarcity of items in the kitchen it seemed most likely. He had mentioned that he'd lost a box somewhere in the move.

She unfolded the four cardboard leaves of the box and stared at the contents. No, it definitely wasn't kitchen utensils. It was a strange array of items. She pulled out the first. A little porcelain ornament of a children's carousel. It was gorgeous. A red canopy with rows of different-coloured horses underneath, all mounted on red and white poles. She ran her fingers over the delicate ornament. Maybe it was a childhood memento? Or a family heirloom? It was difficult to judge the age of an item like this. She placed it carefully to one side and reached in for the next item. A small black velvet box.

Melissa's breath caught in her throat and her fingers trembled. All of a sudden she knew she shouldn't be doing this. She automatically glanced over her shoulder, as if she might be caught in the act. But there was no one there. Cooper was working at the hospital. She was alone.

Her eyes went back back to the box. No matter how much her head told her she shouldn't be looking at this, she opened the box. An engagement ring. A beautiful pink diamond glistened in the velvet lining. It must have been Clara's. Her fingers touched the thin gold band and stunning diamond.

Melissa snapped the box shut. This was private. Cooper had obviously put these things in here to try to forget. She should put them away and push the box back into the corner.

But she couldn't. She couldn't bear not to look in the box.

Her hands found the next item. It was heavy and she needed two hands to lift it out. It was a wedding album. Melissa gently unwrapped the delicate tissue paper surrounding the album. A photograph was inlaid into the black leather cover. A heart-shaped photograph of a happy couple, their arms wrapped around each other on a beautiful summer's day.

Melissa felt as if an arrow had pierced her heart. Cooper looked so young. She peered closely at the photograph before carefully opening the cover. On the first page was Clara, with an older man, probably her father, standing beside a silver Bentley. She had long blonde hair and beautiful blue eyes. Her dress was straight, with pearls encrusted around the pale bodice and a satin skirt. She had a sparkling tiara and short veil and carried a spray of pale pink roses in her hand. But more than all that, she glowed. The smile from her pretty lips reached all the way up into her eyes.

Melissa felt a sharp kick in her abdomen. Clara looked totally different from her. Small, blonde and blue eyed. Melissa's hand subconsciously reached up to touch her chestnut curls. They were totally different. Her brain started to scream in her ears. If he liked small blondes, what was he doing with her? Her hand went to her stomach. Again, the thought flew into her head: *Was he only with her because of the baby?*

She knew she should stop, but she couldn't. Melissa kept turning the pages, each one more heartbreaking than the one before. Cooper standing outside the church, waiting for his bride. Cooper and Jake, his best man, shaking hands outside the church. The bride and groom standing on the church steps, holding out their hands to show their wedding rings, the pink diamond clearly visible on Clara's finger. Cooper and Clara standing in the middle of a park, their arms around each other, throwing back their heads and laughing.

Melissa felt the hot tears spill down her cheeks. One splodged on the photograph she was looking at and she hurriedly wiped it away. Cooper looked so young and carefree. The little lines that were currently around his eyes and forehead were nowhere in sight in these pictures. The dark expression that could flit across his face at the most inopportune moments, before disappearing again in the blink of an eye, looked as if it had never been present when these pictures had been taken. Then there were the shadowed moments when he thought that no one was watching him and he looked as if he had the weight of the world on his shoulders.

None of those expressions were present in these photographs. Melissa continued to flick through the album. Cooper and Clara cutting their wedding cake, Cooper and Clara having their first dance, and finally the one that sliced her heart in two. Cooper and Clara caught in a private moment, staring deeply into one another's eyes. A couple clearly in love, with their whole future ahead of them.

And then there were others at the back of the album. Pictures from their honeymoon. A picture of Clara standing with her hand outstretched, pretending to hold up the Leaning Tower of Pisa. Melissa dropped the picture in shock. She was having flashbacks. A few weeks earlier she'd told Cooper she would love to visit Pisa and she'd seen something flit across his face. The pieces of the jigsaw puzzle were slowly fitting into place. The tears were flowing freely now. Melissa felt sick, not only from seeing how happy Cooper had been but also for the intrusion. She'd invaded his privacy. He'd put these pictures in this cupboard for a reason. They were too painful to look at. For him, and for her.

She pushed the album back into the box. There were other items still wrapped in tissue paper but she'd seen enough. She couldn't bear to look at anything else. Melissa shoved the box back into the corner of the cupboard and closed the door, resting back against it, as if to try and seal it from her thoughts. She pulled a handkerchief from her pocket to wipe her tears. All of a sudden she couldn't imagine the cool white room transformed into a warm pink nursery. Nothing about this seemed right.

Melissa slammed shut the catalogues on the bed. She couldn't bear to think about nursery furniture, or anything else for that matter.

As the hot angry tears continued to slip down her cheeks Melissa came to a startling conclusion. What had started out as a relationship of convenience had become something much more. The giant fist that was currently gripping and squeezing at her heart hadn't arrived overnight. Although their initial attraction had been instant and fleeting, their relationship had changed over the past few months. It had grown. So had her feelings.

She was in love. She was in love with Cooper, the father of her baby and the man who clearly still had to get over his wife. This was a love that had her on top of the world at one moment and at the bottom of a dark pit in the next. She'd never felt anything like this for David. She'd never felt a love that made her stomach ache like this. Melissa felt a little kick inside, as if her daughter was protesting at her mother's tears. She walked over to the window. As she stared out over at the bustling marina Melissa knew one thing. Baby or no baby, Clara's shadow was hanging over her like a black, looming cloud and until she was gone it felt as if she and Cooper could never move on to the next stage of their relationship.

The tears fell freely down her cheeks. She couldn't go on living her life in limbo. She didn't want to be his second choice. She didn't want to have Cooper because she was pregnant with his child. She wanted to have him because he was *hers*.

She walked through to the white bedroom and pulled

a bag from the cupboard—the same bag that she'd used weeks ago when she'd moved in. She started pulling clothes from the hangers in the cupboard and stuffing them into the bag. Shirts, dresses, trousers and all the new things that Cooper had purchased for her, all crushed into the bag. She didn't want to waste time. She should have done this weeks ago when he'd shut her out after they'd slept together. She didn't want to pack neatly and in an orderly fashion. She wanted to get out of here while she still had the courage to do it.

She pulled another bag from the cupboard and started throwing underwear and nightclothes from the bedside cabinet into it.

In ten minutes she was finished. The only trace left of her was the unmade bed and the red-framed ultrasound picture in the living room. She picked up her bags and walked through to the kitchen. She would write him a note.

Her mind shifted. She wasn't going to make any excuses. She was going to tell him exactly why she was leaving. She walked back through to the other bedroom, the bedroom that should be for their child, and picked up the box. She placed it on the kitchen counter, pulled out a pad and pen from one of the drawers and started to write.

Cooper bounded up the stairs, two at a time. He was home early and planned to take Missy out for dinner. He opened the heavy wooden door and stopped short.

Missy was at the kitchen counter, her face streaked with tears and two bags at her feet.

'What's going on?' He was breathless from running up the stairs. 'What are you doing, Missy?'

Her eyes met his. Something was different. It was

almost as if her vitality and spark had been drained out of her. 'I'm leaving.'

'You're *what*?' He crossed the kitchen in two steps. 'What on earth are you talking about?'

Missy put down the pen with a trembling hand and pushed the box in his direction. 'I can't live here, Cooper. You don't love me. You fell into this relationship, but you can't commit to it. I don't need you to explain, I know that you're still in love with your wife. But that's not enough for me. I want everything, and that includes your love.'

Cooper was dumbfounded. Then he saw it on the kitchen worktop. The box. She'd found the box. The one he'd hidden away in the back of cupboard somewhere. He hadn't thought about the box for months. He'd almost forgotten it was there. 'But, Missy—'

She raised her hand. 'Don't, Cooper. Don't make this harder than it already is. I need to get away from you.' She drew her hands across her stomach. 'I need to prepare myself for our baby coming. I need to sort all this out in my head.'

Cooper's words stuck in his mouth. This was it. This was the time that he was supposed to tell her that he loved her. That would stop her leaving. That would make her stay.

But the words choked him. He couldn't get them out. She'd taken him by surprise. He hadn't expected this and he wasn't prepared for it. All the thoughts and emotions that Missy evoked in him came bubbling to the surface. But what did they mean? He hesitated for too long, because she bent and picked up her bags.

'I want you to stay, Missy,' he said, as his voice broke and he reached for her arm.

She felt as if she were eleven years old again. She

felt the pain sear through her heart as it had when her father had walked out the door. The one thing she had vowed to protect herself from, the one thing she had never wanted to feel again.

'But we don't always get what we want, Cooper,' she said as she held her head high and walked out of the door.

CHAPTER TEN

THE phone rang at the midwives' station and Melissa picked it up quickly. 'Hello, Labour Ward, Sister Bell.' Andrea had just walked down the corridor and started to say something to her but Melissa held up her hand to silence her. She lifted a pen and paper and took some notes. 'Yes, how long? From where? We'll be on standby.'

She replaced the receiver. 'We're getting a transfer from the General Hospital A and E. Lydia Jones, twenty-four, thirty-seven weeks pregnant, with a suspected PE. She's apparently in a bad way; one of the surgical registrars is in the ambulance with her. We're going to need a team down here stat.'

Andrea gave a quick nod, moving instantly into professional mode. 'You page the anaesthetist and Cooper, I'll organise the room and the midwifery staff.'

She sped off down the corridor. Melissa picked up the phone, her hand trembling as she paged Cooper and Dave Hammond. Pulmonary embolism, or a clot in the lungs, was one of the leading causes of maternal death. It was very serious for both the mother and the baby. How would Cooper react—treating a woman with the same condition that had killed his wife and baby? Time would be of the essence here and it was essential the correct team of people was assembled to give Lydia and her baby the best possible chance of survival.

She sighed. Lydia was thirty-seven weeks, she herself had another ten weeks before she'd reach that stage. Her hand went automatically to her stomach. It was getting harder and harder to work in the labour ward. Physically, she was feeling fine, but mentally she was starting to struggle with some of the more intense deliveries she was dealing with. This last week had been the hardest yet, especially when every time she saw Cooper she thought her heart might break. At the last count there had been forty phone calls, over a hundred texts and three visits to her flat. But he still hadn't said the words. The three little words she need to hear.

And being at work wasn't helping. Her mind was working overtime. If the labours and deliveries she was attending went well, she would be overjoyed, or maybe it was relieved. If complications arose, with more serious outcomes for the mother or the baby, Melissa would instantly imagine herself being in that position. What if that was her? What if something happened to her baby?

She knew she shouldn't worry. Things were going well. Her last scan had showed the baby to be a little larger than normal, but that could be expected in diabetic pregnancies and the baby's growth was still within normal limits. And let's face it, she had a consultant obstetrician who constantly fussed around her. She was in good hands. Even if they weren't his hands…

The phone jolted her out of her wandering thoughts. 'Labour Ward… Hi, Cooper, we're going to need you down here. We're getting a transfer from the General's A and E department, a thirty-seven-weeker with a suspected PE. Cooper? Cooper? Did you hear me?'

All Melissa could hear at the end of the phone was a

deafening silence. Cooper was always on the ball and rarely ever distracted. But this was a PE. This was what had killed his wife and child. She glanced at her watch. He would be in the antenatal clinic right now, maybe one of the midwives was speaking to him. She gave it another few seconds. 'Cooper?' She lowered her voice. 'Are you okay? ETA is ten minutes. It must be serious as one of the surgical registrars is with her in the ambulance. Can you make your way down here, please?' She tried to make it sound like business as usual, even though she knew it wasn't.

Cooper mumbled something in reply. The other phone at the midwives' station started to ring. 'That'll be Dave. I'd better get it. See you in a few minutes.'

Cooper stared at the phone in his hand. Melissa had rung off and he could hear the hum of the dead tone. He knew he should replace the phone but he couldn't. He was numb.

As soon as she'd said 'PE' his heart had sunk like a stone. He'd always known that one day this would happen.

He replaced the receiver and sat for a few moments with his head in his hands. He was a professional. He could deal with this. Apart from Melissa, hardly anyone knew about his past. Some knew his wife had died but no one knew his wife had died in his arms of a PE. No one knew that for months he had relived the nightmare over and over in his dreams, waking drenched in sweat and calling out her name. Reaching out for his daughter that they'd been just too late to save.

But those dreams had changed a few months ago. Every night while Melissa lay sleeping, curled up in his arms, his mind would whirr with questions of what if?

What if the same thing happened to Melissa? What if he lost a second daughter? Should he have done something different? Why hadn't Clara had any of the normal signs of a PE?

Cooper shook his head. The feelings of self-doubt were surfacing in his mind. He knew he hadn't done anything wrong. He knew he hadn't missed anything with Clara. The post-mortem had confirmed it. It was just 'one of those things'.

The tears were hiding beneath his heavy lids. He was a good doctor. He was an excellent obstetrician. Everyone who worked with him told him that. He knew that in the last few months he'd saved the lives of a number of mothers and their babies. Only an hour ago he'd been called to assist in Theatre when one of the other consultants had run into some problems. All because of his knowledge and skills.

Cooper took a deep breath. He had to pull himself together. Right now, he was the best chance that this woman and her child would have. He had to be at the top of his game. It was time to work. It was time to focus.

He pulled down his white coat, which was hanging behind the door, and threw it over his theatre scrubs, an unreadable expression on his face as he headed down the corridor towards the labour suite.

The trolley came thundering down the corridor towards Melissa as she unlocked the double doors to the room. Pushed by two red-faced porters and one panting doctor, there was no time to delay. Andrea appeared at her side and together they helped pull the trolley next to the waiting bed.

Cooper walked straight past her and addressed the surgical registrar. 'Give me a report, please.'

The panting doctor took a deep breath. 'This is Lydia Jones, she's twenty-four. Presented with chest pain…' he glanced at his watch '…at the General around twenty minutes ago.' He gestured towards the patient. 'As you can see, she's thirty-seven weeks pregnant.' His eyes flicked to the notes in his hand. 'This is her second child. No underlying medical conditions that we know of, but her condition has deteriorated rapidly in the ambulance in the way over.' He gestured at Lydia's right arm. 'We've got IV access and a full set of bloods have already been sent to the lab as an emergency.' He closed the notes and left them at the foot of the bed. 'The only thing of note she told us was that she suffered from symphysis pubis dysfunction and has been on bed rest the last few weeks.' He pointed to the medical notes he'd left on the bed. 'She arrived without her hand-held midwifery record, so we were unsure of any other problems.'

Andrea gave a quick nod of the head at Cooper and then at Dave, who had just appeared through the door. 'I'll go and find her midwifery records to see if we can get a better picture.'

Melissa walked around to the other side of the bed and, with the rest of the team, helped move Lydia over from the trolley to the bed. She gave Lydia a little smile. 'I'm Melissa, one of the midwives who will be looking after you.' She gestured with her head to her right. 'This is Dave Hammond, the anaesthetist, and over there…' she pointed to the bottom of the bed '…is Cooper Roberts, one of the consultant obstetricians.' She gave Lydia's hand a squeeze. 'Don't worry Lydia, you're in good hands.'

Lydia was a small woman who appeared to be overweight. Her eyes were tightly screwed shut, as if she was trying to block out her surroundings. Her breathing was rapid and shallow. Melissa noted the peripheral oedema in her legs and silently gestured towards Dave, drawing his attention to her condition.

Melissa was struggling to place electrodes on Lydia's chest to monitor her heart rate. Dave instantly went to the side of the bed to give her a hand and to change over from the portable oxygen supply. Melissa's eyes went to Cooper. His face was a complete blank. It seemed impenetrable. Usually he would be the first person to give her a hand. She touched the side of his elbow. She understood that treating a patient with a PE would be difficult for Cooper, but he had a job to do.

'Cooper?'

Cooper was weighing up the options in his head. Most maternity units were attached to general hospitals, but not St Jude's. It had been a specialised maternity hospital for several decades and although the hospital had been updated, not all facilities were available. There was no ITU and no other specialities to assist with patients like this. The General was only five minutes away, but in some situations that five minutes could be the difference between life and death. He glanced at the surgical registrar. 'Who made the decision to transfer her here?'

The surgical registrar hesitated. 'Well, we weren't sure, but as we don't have facilities for neonates at the General, Mr Graves thought she would be better here.'

Cooper nodded. Mr Graves was a consultant surgeon and would probably have had a heart attack at the thought of Lydia delivering at the General. He was quite sure Mr Graves had arranged for an ambulance to transfer her in a flash. His mind seemed to shift into focus. His head lifted and turned towards Dave. 'Let's make an assessment of our patient.'

They moved quickly. Lydia was pale. Cooper turned to Melissa. 'We need an ECG right now.'

Melissa pulled the electrocardiograph machine from the corner of the room and started placing the leads on Lydia's chest. 'We're just going to do a little tracing of your heart Lydia, it will only take a minute.'

Dave was standing at the side of the bed, a stethoscope clutched in his hand as he listened to Lydia's chest sounds. 'I'm hearing crackles in the chest,' he said as he moved to the head of the bed. 'Her breathing is very shallow and laboured. I would definitely go with a PE.'

Cooper stood at the end of the bed, watching the printout of the ECG. 'Do we have a chest X-ray?'

The surgical registrar nodded and pulled the X-ray from its brown envelope. Cooper stuck it on one of the nearby light boxes and flicked the switch. Dave appeared at his elbow to peer at the film. Cooper raised his finger and pointed at a number of areas on the X-ray. 'It's certainly not a normal chest X-ray but we can't use this as a definitive diagnosis.' He leaned over and tore off the printout of the ECG. 'Abnormal ECG,' he muttered, before handing it over to Dave. 'Sinus tachycardia with ST wave abnormalities. There are also some changes showing right ventricular strain.' He turned his head towards the registrar. 'Did you manage to perform any other tests?'

The registrar shook his head. He gestured towards the bed. 'Her condition had deteriorated too much to perform a VQ scan. Our consultant tried to arrange an urgent echocardiogram but the on-call technician hadn't answered their page by the time I left.'

Cooper shook his head in disgust. He knew the latest

guidelines for managing PE in pregnancy off by heart. It was essential that an echocardiogram be carried out within the first hour. He pointed towards the door. 'Go and telephone your A and E department to see if the technician has answered their page yet. If they have, tell them to get here *now*. We need this test carried out.'

The registrar nodded quickly and shot out the door.

Dave had resumed his position and continued to listen to Lydia's chest. He'd removed the head of the bed to stand behind Lydia. His face clouded over. 'Coop, I'm hearing a third heart sound and there is a parasternal heave present.'

Melissa's head shot up from where she had just fastened the blood-pressure cuff around Lydia's right arm. Both of those symptoms were clinical signs of a pulmonary embolism. She pressed the button to measure Lydia's blood pressure. The cuff inflated in a matter of seconds. 'She's hypotensive,' she called to Cooper, who appeared lost in thought.

She knew what he was doing—blocking out all memories from the past. It was almost as if he was on autopilot. He walked over to Dave. 'I think we're going to have to thrombolyse her.'

Dave nodded. 'I know. Her respiratory effort is decreasing. I think I'm going to have to intubate her.' He glanced back at the patient. 'This is serious.'

Cooper turned his eyes to the cardiac monitor. 'She's tachycardic and there's a strong possibility we're going to have to take her to Theatre to deliver this baby.'

Andrea walked into the room and handed the midwifery notes over to Cooper. 'Absolutely nothing in them. She's only been on bed rest for the last three weeks. No medical history to predispose her to having a PE. She's been unlucky. It looks like it's just one of those things.'

Cooper felt his blood run cold. *One of those things.* Just like Clara. Before his very eyes the face on the bed morphed into Clara's. It wasn't Lydia Jones any more, it was Clara. Cooper tried to focus. He had to keep it together.

'Any relatives?'

Andrea checked the notes. 'There was no one with her in the General's A and E. She presented herself with the chest pain. She's given a contact number for her husband. I'll go and try and phone him.'

Cooper walked up to Dave Hammond, speaking in a low voice. 'I don't think the normal IV unfractionated heparin will be enough. It's not going to break up the clot quickly enough to stop there being long-term damage.'

Dave nodded his head. 'I'm in complete agreement with you, Coop, but it's your decision. If she doesn't respond and we have to take her to Theatre, there is real danger that she'll haemorrhage.'

'I know that, but I think the benefits outweigh the risks. Studies have shown that thrombolysis is more effective than heparin therapy in reducing the clot burden and rapidly improving the haemodynamics. The clot could dissolve and she could go on to have a normal delivery in three weeks.'

Cooper turned his head towards Melissa. 'Are you familiar with streptokinase?'

'I'm familiar with it, but I've never used it. I know they stock it in our pharmacy. Do you want me to get some?'

Cooper nodded, his head turning as the surgical registrar came back through the door. 'The technician will be here in five minutes,' said the registrar, who was pulling the echocardiogram machine behind him. 'I decided to go and get this for her to save time.'

Cooper walked back over to his patient. He touched her arm gently, trying to entice her to open her eyes. 'Lydia, I know that you're scared, but I need to explain what's going to happen. We think you might have a blood clot in your lungs.'

Her eyes flew open, terror registering on her face.

Cooper spoke slowly, trying to allay her fears. 'We've treated women with blood clots before. Things are a little trickier in your case as you're so near to your delivery date.'

Lydia opened her mouth, her breathing in short gasps. 'Why would I get a blood clot?'

'There could be a number of reasons. We know that you suffer from symphysis pubis dysfunction and that you've been unable to get about for the last few weeks. Pregnancy can increase your risk of developing a blood clot, and unfortunately limited mobility can also increase your risk.' Cooper felt his heart thudding in his chest. He knew what he had to do next. 'You've just been unlucky, Lydia.' The words almost caught in his throat.

He watched her struggling to breathe. Her short, gasping breaths. He felt as if someone had turned back the clock two years and he was looking directly at Clara's face as she desperately tried to speak. *Don't let anything happen to our baby, Cooper.'*

'You won't let anything happen to my baby, will you?'

'What?'

Lydia gasped again, clutching her oxygen mask to

her face. 'You won't let anything happen to my baby, will you, Doctor?'

Cooper put his hand around hers. 'I'm going to look after you and your baby, Lydia.' From the corner of his eye he saw Melissa come back into the room, clutching the vial with the drug. He had to remain focused. It was all he could do to hold it together.

'Melissa, can you find a syringe pump, please? The streptokinase infusion needs to be administered over one hour.'

Melissa could see how unwell Lydia was. Her skin was almost translucent, her lips a tinged with blue. She was starting to understand. She was starting to appreciate how Cooper must have felt seeing his wife like this and feeling powerless to do anything to help her. It was hard enough watching Lydia, another pregnant woman, in this state. But Lydia was a stranger to her. Lydia wasn't the person she loved with all her heart and soul and carrying their child. For the first time, through her skewed pregnancy hormones, she finally, truly started to understand how he must have felt.

Cooper turned back to Lydia as the cardiac technician appeared in the room. He left Dave to go and speak to her while he explained what would be happening to his patient. 'Lydia, this woman...' he gestured at the technician '...is going to do a test called an echocardiogram. It's similar to the scans you've had to look at the baby, only this time the scan is going to look at your heart. It will help us with the diagnosis.'

Cooper moved sideways as the technician approached with the machine to take up place at the side of the bed. She started the scan within a matter of seconds, with Cooper watching the monitor on the scanner closely.

The technician spoke quietly. 'Right ventricular

strain, which would agree with your diagnosis. It's probably a submassive PE.'

Cooper nodded, his head spinning. It was exactly as he had suspected. Lydia had a submassive PE, which was affecting the functioning of her heart. Patients who displayed these symptoms frequently had poorer outcomes.

His gut wrenched. This was exactly what had happened to Clara—only some of the testing equipment hadn't been available. They hadn't been able to make a definitive diagnosis and she'd been started on the preferred treatment for pregnant women—a heparin infusion. Only it had been too late and the treatment hadn't had time to work. That, and the delayed decision-making, had cost Clara her life.

Cooper took a deep breath. He could take the safe route and start Lydia on a heparin infusion. But he knew already that he wouldn't do that. Her symptoms were too severe. The clot was causing untold damage to her heart and lungs and soon it would compromise the oxygen supply to the baby. Thrombolysis was riskier. He knew that. He also knew it could break up the clot in Lydia's lungs in a matter of hours, giving her and her baby their best possible chance of survival.

He moved away from the scanner and sat down on the bed next to Lydia again. 'Lydia, the test confirms you have a blood clot in your lungs. It is affecting your breathing and how your heart is functioning. It's really important that we break the blood clot up.' He pointed at the syringe pump. 'We need to give you a medicine designed to break up the clot. We put it through a special pump…' he tapped the IV cannula in her arm '…and it goes directly into one of your veins.' He moved his hands and laid them gently on her distended abdomen.

'We will monitor your baby the whole time the infusion is going through.'

His eyes flicked over to Melissa, who was already connecting up the electrodes to monitor the baby. 'Start the infusion,' he said. 'She'll need her blood pressure measured every five minutes for the next hour while it goes through.'

Dave gave a little nod from the top of the bed. He looked at Melissa. 'I'm going to stay in the labour ward for the next hour, Melissa, so if you need me, I'll be right here.'

Cooper gave a quick nod. 'Good. I'm going to write up Lydia's notes. I'll be back in five minutes.' He swept out the room without a backward glance.

Melissa nodded and started the infusion. She took a seat next to Lydia and reset the button on the cardiac machine to measure her blood pressure every five minutes. Melissa could feel the tears forming at the backs of her eyes. Right now Lydia's life and her baby's were hanging in the balance. She knew exactly why Dave was hanging around. If something happened, if the clot moved and Lydia went into heart failure, it was unlikely she would survive. At that point the only hope left would be to get her to Theatre and get the baby out quickly. If they didn't, the baby would die too.

Andrea appeared at the door. 'I've just got hold of your husband, Lydia. He's apparently been phoning home for the last hour, looking for you. He's on his way in.' She turned to Melissa. 'Do you need any help?'

Melissa shook her head. 'I'm going to stay in here and monitor Lydia's blood pressure.' She pointed to the second monitor at her side. 'I'm going to keep an eye on the baby too. I'll shout to you if I need anything.'

Andrea nodded, then her brow furrowed. 'What's up with Cooper?'

The question caught Melissa unawares. Other people had noticed he was struggling. Melissa shook her head. Cooper hadn't told anyone else about Clara. 'I think he had a bad experience once with a patient with a PE,' she whispered.

Andrea shrugged her shoulders and ducked back out of the door. Melissa helped adjust Lydia's pillows to keep her in a more upright position to assist her breathing. Lydia closed her eyes and leaned back against the pillows. She was exhausted, her breathing still rapid and shallow, with no improvement yet in her colour.

Melissa sank back into her chair. The monitor sprung into life and the cuff tightened around Lydia's arm. Still hypotensive. Melissa recorded the result in the nearby chart. She wondered how soon she would see an improvement.

Her hands went automatically to her baby. Truth be told, she was glad to be sitting down. At twenty-seven weeks the shifts were getting harder and harder. But like most women due to go on maternity leave, Melissa was determined to work on as long as she could. She would hate to be sitting at home for weeks, waiting for her baby to arrive. For Melissa, it would seem like wasted time. She wanted to spend the extra time with her baby.

A few minutes later Lydia gripped her arm, her fingers digging into Melissa's wrist. She leaned forward. Melissa stood up quickly, 'What's wrong, Lydia?'

Underneath the oxygen mask Lydia's lips were tinged with blue. Melissa felt her heartbeat quicken. Lydia gasped, 'Tell Daisy that I love her.'

Melissa felt a chill descend over her body. According

to Lydia's chart, Daisy was Lydia's daughter. Patients with a PE often had feelings of impending doom. It was even listed as one of the clinical signs and symptoms. She opened her mouth to say some words of comfort to Lydia but was immediately stopped by the scream from the nearby cardiac monitor as Lydia's body flopped backwards.

Immediately she pulled the emergency buzzer and started pulling the pillows from Lydia's back to lay her flat on the bed.

Within seconds the room was full of people. Dave took up position at the head of the bed. Andrea appeared at his elbow, pulling the emergency trolley behind her. She automatically handed him the laryngoscope and an endotracheal tube, which he slid into place.

Cooper appeared in the room, his face stricken. His eyes swept over the scene and stopped at the cardiac monitor. 'PEA.' Pulseless electrical activity. The type of cardiac arrest most commonly associated with PE. It meant that the heart wasn't beating properly. It was producing electrical activity without producing a pulse.

Melissa put her knee up on the bed, ensuring her hands were positioned correctly and commenced cardiac massage. Dave connected the ET tube and began bagging the patient in conjunction with Melissa's massage. His face turned to Cooper's. 'We need to take her to the emergency theatre—we've got to get this baby out.' Andrea nodded her head at his words and headed out the door. 'I'll tell the theatre staff about the imminent arrival.'

Cooper stood frozen to the spot. His eyes watching the monitor helplessly. He stared at Lydia's lifeless form as Melissa and Dave tried to breathe life into her body. The worst part of his life was being relived in front of his eyes. He'd seen this scene before. Last time he'd been shouting in the corner of the room, being held back from Clara's body by one of the other doctors while he'd watched them perform their futile activities. This was his worst nightmare. Another woman was going to die in exactly the same way that Clara had.

'Cooper?'

The voice broke into his thoughts. Melissa had both knees up on the bed now, her face red from the exertion of performing cardiac massage. She was staring at him. 'Are we going to Theatre?' she panted. Melissa's heart was thudding in her chest. It had been years since she'd performed cardiac massage. She'd forgotten how even the smallest spell could make your arms and shoulders ache.

He took a deep breath. He looked downwards, suddenly conscious of his nails digging into the palms of his hands. He released his clenched fists. Time was of the essence. He may have lost his baby, but he could save this one.

'Let's go,' he said abruptly, his foot releasing the brake at the bottom of the bed. Dave jerked the bed suddenly towards the door, obviously forgetting Melissa was balanced on top of it. She lurched sideways with the sudden movement and let out a scream as she landed on the floor.

'Melissa!' Cooper looked stricken at the sight of Melissa lying in a crumpled heap on the floor.

'Oh, God, Cooper, I'm sorry, I didn't realise...' Dave stood frozen to the spot.

Andrea was stuck in the doorway, trying to open the door to allow the bed to leave the room. Her voice bellowed down the corridor, 'I need another midwife in here *now*!'

Two women appeared in seconds, Andrea pointed in the direction of the bed. 'One of you on there, doing massage, the other get me a wheelchair for Melissa now!'

Cooper turned to Dave, who hadn't moved from the spot. 'Get the patient to Theatre now, Dave. I'll be there as soon as I can.'

Dave nodded silently and pulled the bed, more gently this time, towards the open doors. Andrea and Cooper helped Melissa into the wheelchair that appeared silently behind them.

'How are you, Melissa? How do you feel?'

She groaned and clutched at her stomach.

'Are you pain?'

The tears glazed over her eyes as she caught her breath. 'Cooper, I think I'm having contractions.'

Cooper's eyes met Andrea's. This was the last thing they wanted to hear. He swept the wheelchair into the room next door and lifted Melissa onto the bed. Andrea started pulling out wires from monitors, switching them on and attaching them with ruthless efficiency.

Melissa clutched Cooper's arm. 'It's too soon, Coop. I'm only twenty-seven weeks. I can't have this baby now.' The tears were flowing freely down her face as the reality of the situation swept over her.

Andrea came round and touched Cooper's arm. 'You have to go, Cooper. They need you in Theatre.'

'I can't go,' he snapped. 'There's no way I'm leaving Melissa's side. She needs me here.'

Melissa shook her head. 'You have to go, Coop. You're the only consultant here right now. Lydia doesn't stand a chance without you. And what about her baby? The surgical resident won't have a clue how to deliver a premature baby.' Her words came out between sobs as another contraction gripped her.

Cooper shook his head frantically. 'I won't leave you, Melissa, not like this.'

Andrea tightened her grip on his arm. 'Cooper, I'll watch Melissa. I'll phone John Blair. He'll come in and oversee her care. You know you can trust him. Now, please, go.'

Cooper hesitated. John Blair was one of the most experienced obstetricians he'd ever worked with. And he did trust him.

Melissa nodded. 'Go, Cooper. Go and save Lydia and her baby.'

He looked into her green eyes. There were a hundred things he wanted to say to her right now. He didn't care that other people were in the room. Nothing mattered to him more right now than Melissa and their baby. He put his hand under her chin and bent forward. 'I'll go, Melissa, but know that there is nowhere I want to be right now other than by your side.' He leaned forward and kissed her on the mouth, wrapping his arms around her body and holding her for a few precious seconds.

'I know, Cooper,' she whispered in his ear.

And then he was gone, running down the corridor towards the theatre.

He burst through the doors and his eyes swept over the surgical registrar. 'Ever performed an embolectomy before?'

The registrar's eyes widened in shock. 'Yes, but not under these conditions.'

'Then scrub in.'

Cooper took up position at the nearby sink, pulled a sterile scrubbing brush from its container and started to scrub his hands in a frenzy. One of the theatre nurses appeared at his side, holding his gown ready. Cooper glanced at the clock. The theatre staff transferred Lydia onto the operating table and pulled the bed out of the way. One of the midwives resumed her position and continued with the massage while the theatre staff around her opened surgical packs and instruments. 'Time check?' he shouted at Dave, who was attaching Lydia to a ventilator.

Dave glanced at his watch. 'Four minutes.'

Cooper slid his arms into the green gown and held out his hands for his surgical gloves. Time was of the essence. He was usually meticulous about scrubbing for Theatre, taking at least ten minutes before putting on his surgical gloves. But this baby didn't have ten minutes.

His head was full of Melissa. Was she going to deliver? Would the contractions stop? What if he lost another baby? Another midwife appeared, pulling an incubator through the door, plugging the heat lamp above it into the nearby electrical supply. 'Paed is on his way,' she shouted. Cooper nodded. It was essential that a paediatrician was there to receive the baby after delivery. Who knew what state this baby would be in?

He took up position at the side of the bed. Beads of sweat were breaking out on his brow. 'Are you ready, Dave?'

Dave nodded. 'Cooper, I'm sorry, you know I didn't mean to...'

Cooper lifted his hand to silence him. It was trembling. His eyes fixed on his hand, willing it to stop shaking. Images of his daughter swam before his eyes. The small, blue, lifeless baby. The daughter who should have had her whole life before her. The daughter he should have taken to ballet lessons and horseriding classes. He could picture her now, a mini-version of her mother. Blonde hair in pigtails, dressed in the lilac checked dress that was the uniform of the school near where they had lived. He could see her sitting on a swing, leaning backwards, legs outstretched as the air streamed through her hair and she let out squeals of joy. He could see himself, kneeling at her bedside and reading her favourite bedtime story about caterpillars and ladybirds. All these things flitted through his mind. Then, in an instant, he was back, his hand outstretched over Lydia's prone body, the scalpel still wavering in his hand.

'Now, Cooper.' Dave's voice cut through the fog in his mind.

He took a deep breath, wiped her abdomen with Betadine and made the decisive cut. It was the quickest Caesarean section he'd ever done. One clean cut at Lydia's bikini line followed by another to free the baby from the womb. He placed both hands inside her and lifted the slippery bundle into the air. The silent baby was passed into the waiting hands of the paediatrician who had appeared at his side. He waited patiently while Cooper clipped the umbilical cord to allow him to carry the baby over to the incubator.

There was silence in the theatre. Everyone froze, afraid to move. Cooper held his breath, pain cutting through his chest. He said silent prayers over and over again. His head was thudding. He'd promised Lydia that her baby would be safe. The beads of sweat trickled freely down his brow. He shouldn't have made that promise—he'd had no right to do that.

The noise of suction pierced the theatre, followed by an angry scream from a baby. There was a collective gasp of relief. The paediatrician turned his head to the waiting spectators. 'We've got a little boy,' he said simply.

Beneath his mask, Cooper pursed his lips and let his breath out in a long, hard stream. His heart was beating frantically in his chest. He lifted his eyes from Lydia's abdomen.

Andrea appeared at the door, a mask held over her face. 'John Blair's here. He said to let you know that Melissa is still having contractions, but her waters haven't broken. The baby is showing some signs of distress but he's going to stay and monitor her. He'll let you know if you need to be there.'

Unspoken words from one professional to another. If there was going to be bad news, he would let Cooper know.

Cooper took a deep breath. More than anything in the world right now he wanted to be with Melissa. He wanted to be there, holding her hand and telling her everything would be all right. He wanted to be with the woman who made his heart sing every time he saw her. The woman who, without a doubt, was the most important thing in his life. He'd known that all along. From the second he'd seen those green eyes and they'd reminded him of his grandmother's engagement ring. His mind and body had been sending him the messages that it was time to move on. He *was* ready. But it had taken this to show him it.

He focused. He'd saved one life. It was time to try and save another. Cooper turned to the surgical registrar. 'I'm going to close now. It's up to you. Do your best, I'll assist in any way I can.'

* * *

His feet thudded down the corridor. He hadn't even changed out of his surgical scrubs or taken his mask or hat off.

He appeared at the door breathless and heart pounding. It was early evening and John Blair was sitting on the bed facing Melissa, talking to her in a low voice.

'What's wrong?' asked Cooper as he strode into the room and walked to the other side of the bed. 'What's happening?' He sat down and took Melissa's hand in his.

John pointed to the IV infusion that Melissa was connected to. 'We've had to start her on some magnesium sulphate to try and stop the contractions.' He lifted the edge of her gown. 'That was quite a blow she took when she fell, and the bruising is already beginning to show.'

Cooper drew in his breath at the livid purple bruising.

'We're lucky because her membranes haven't ruptured and after the initial jolt...' he pointed at the nearby monitor recording the foetal heart rate '...baby seems to be settling back down.'

Cooper nodded in relief. At least the baby wasn't in distress any more.

John Blair stood up and patted Melissa on the shoulder. 'I was just explaining to Melissa that she's probably worked her last shift here. If we can get these contractions stopped, I would recommend she rests easy for the rest of this pregnancy. She'll have to stay here for the next few days until we are sure everything's okay.'

Cooper nodded and stood up and reached over to shake John's hand. 'Thank you for looking after her, John. I appreciate it.'

John Blair shrugged his shoulders. 'Any time, folks.' He bent down and kissed Melissa on the cheek. 'It was my pleasure, Melissa. But just remember I'm in charge, not you.'

She nodded at him through tear-filled eyes as he left the room. Cooper resumed his position on the bed next to her and wrapped his arms around her.

'Missy, you're going to be okay.' He could see the tremor of her lips, her eyes brimming with tears.

'But it's too early, Cooper.' She was kneading her hands in her lap, over and over. 'This shouldn't be happening. What if something's wrong?' Her voice was barely a whisper.

He reached his hand towards her, curling a finger under her chin and turning her face back towards his. In the dim light of the room her green eyes seemed more electric than ever. Cooper bit his lip. It was one of the first things he'd noticed about her. It was one of the many things about her that entranced him. 'Missy—' his voice was warm and soothing '—I'm not going to let anything happen to you or the baby.' He leaned forward, wrapped both arms around her and pulled her towards him. He shifted uncomfortably as he tried to move nearer to her. 'Everything will be fine.' She was trembling and he ran his hands gently across her back and through her chestnut curls. After a few minutes the tension seemed to leave her muscles and she relaxed into him.

Her voice cut through the darkness. 'Do you promise?'

For Cooper, it took all the willpower in the world to stop his muscles stiffening in reaction to her question. He knew exactly what he had to do. No matter how difficult it was.

He drew back from their embrace and looked straight into her eyes. 'Absolutely. I promise.'

He heard her draw in a deep breath. 'How's Lydia?'

He pulled back. 'It's still touch and go. She's alive and she's been transferred to ICU at the General.' He gave a sigh as he pulled off the mask that still dangled around his neck and the theatre cap from his head. 'Her son is doing well. Apart from requiring a little oxygen and being transferred to Special Care for observation, he seems none the worse for his ordeal. At least we've got that to be thankful for.'

Melissa looked at him. For the first time since she'd known him Cooper finally looked as if he didn't have the weight of the world on his shoulders. His hair was sticking up in tufts after being trapped inside the theatre cap and his jaw and chin were shadowed with stubble. But although he looked tired, exhausted even, there was something different about him.

She shifted slightly on the bed, so he could lean back against the pillows next to her. 'Lydia's husband wants to call the baby Cooper.'

'What?'

'He wants to name the baby after me.'

Melissa bit her lip. 'How do you feel about that?'

He ran his hands through his hair, doing little to help the ragged appearance. 'I'm not sure. We don't know what will happen with Lydia. They think that the streptokinase and the prolonged cardiac massage might have helped break up the clot. The pulmonary angiogram managed to break up the rest of the clot but we don't know how much damage had already happened.' He paused for a moment, deep in thought. 'I'm not sure if Lydia will ever wake up and get to see her baby or not.'

'But if she does, Cooper, then it's because of your actions. Your actions saved her baby's life and might well have saved her life too.'

Cooper turned to face her. 'That's all very well, but I wasn't in the place I needed to be.' His hand encircled hers. 'I wasn't with you when you needed me most and for that I'm truly sorry.'

Melissa shook her head. 'You were exactly where you needed to be. And you did exactly what you needed to do.' She gave him a little smile. 'And you look different too.'

His brow wrinkled. 'I know I must look a complete mess. But how do I look different?'

'You just do. I think today has been cathartic for you. I think you finally got to face your demons.' She raised her hand as he started to speak. 'No, don't. I think it gave me a little perspective too. I honestly didn't realise how hard this must have been for you. I know you'd told me it was hard. But today, when I saw Lydia and the state she was in, I don't know how I would have coped if that had been the woman that I loved and everything was out of my control.' She lay back against her pillows. She wasn't afraid any more. She wasn't afraid about how she felt. She didn't feel the need to hide herself from the possibility of hurt. 'I guess what I'm saying is that if you still need time, I understand. And I'm willing to give it to you because I love you. I just don't want to be your second choice.'

There. She'd said it. The words were finally out there.

His hand slid around her back. 'I don't need time, Missy.'

The words didn't sink in properly because she was trying to stop herself from crying again. She was trying her best to hold it together. 'I understand, Cooper. I understand that you wanted to keep the box with the wedding pictures and Clara's engagement ring.'

Cooper shook his head. 'No, Missy, you don't

understand. I'm sorry you found that box, I meant to put it away in storage somewhere. I'll always have good and bad memories of Clara and Lily. But that's what they are now—memories. That part of my life is over.'

He pulled her close towards him, pulling a face at the IV line in her arm, which stopped him holding her just the way he wanted to.

'I haven't looked in that box in a long time. And the ring...' His eyes drifted off into the corner of the room. 'Clara knew she was going to die. She took off her engagement ring and asked me to give it to Lily. She expected me to save our baby. But I never got the chance.'

Melissa couldn't hold back tears at this point. She could see the expression on Lydia's face so clearly when she'd asked Melissa to tell her daughter that she loved her. She could only imagine that Clara had been swept by the same feeling when she'd asked Cooper to give her ring to her daughter. 'I'm so sorry, Cooper.'

'Don't be.' He pulled his arm from behind her back and knelt at the side of the bed, lifting his arms and capturing her face in his hands. 'Melissa, I realised something today that's been under my nose for months. I've already moved on. I don't need time.'

'But, Cooper—'

'Don't, Missy. You are the person that's in my dreams every night. You are the person that I think about every waking hour in every day. You are the person that makes my heart leap every time you come into a room. Today clarified everything for me. Nothing is more important to me than you and our baby.'

A single tear slid down her face again and Cooper brushed it away with his thumb. 'Don't cry, Missy. I can't stand it when you cry—it breaks my heart. I love you and I was a fool to not tell you before this, and for that I'm sorry.'

Missy's bottom lip trembled. She was struck by the sincerity in his deep brown eyes.

'Missy, you are not my second choice—you're my only choice. How could I ever want anyone else? I love you.'

'But you don't,' she sobbed. 'You still love Clara.'

Cooper lifted his hands to brush away her tears. 'No, Missy.' He spoke quietly into her ear. 'I've loved you for some time, I just wouldn't admit that to myself.' A smile appeared on his face. 'Every time I see you it makes my heart sing. Sometimes I haven't even seen you yet, but I know that you're there. My whole body reacts whenever you're near me, and being with you makes me the luckiest man alive.'

Missy's hands trembled as she touched her stomach. 'But we don't even know what's going to happen yet.'

He placed his hands over hers. 'But whatever happens, Missy, we'll be there together. Because we're family.'

EPILOGUE

'KEEP your eyes closed,' whispered Cooper as he held his daughter in one hand and guided Melissa with the other. He stopped her right outside the door of the room she had once slept in. 'Okay, you can open it.'

Cooper held their precious bundle. Born at thirty-seven weeks and as healthy as could be. Melissa stared at the door in front of her. 'GRACE'. Carved wooden letters spelling out their daughter's name were attached to the door. She lifted her hand to touch them. Painted in shades of pink, each with a little animal carved next to it. A butterfly, a duck, a bunny, a chick and a puppy. 'It's perfect,' breathed Melissa.

Cooper pressed his palm into her back. 'Well, go on, look inside.'

Melissa pushed the door open. The room had been transformed. The stark white walls and carpet had been replaced by pale pink walls with a border of jumping bunnies and an oatmeal carpet. In the centre of the room stood a carved wooden cot, complete with pink bedding and matching mobile. Melissa gazed around in wonder as she crossed the room to touch the matching wardrobe and baby changer.

She pulled open the cupboard door. Pink dresses, pink cardigans, lilac romper suits and striped tights.

And hanging up next to them was a beautiful adult-sized red wool coat. 'You remembered,' she gasped.

'Of course I remembered,' he said with a smile.

She turned her head to the window, where a leather nursing chair, complete with footrest, sat looking out over the glistening blue marina. Next to that was a white carved rocking horse with a bright red saddle.

'But when did you do this…?'

Cooper wrapped his arm around her shoulders. 'While you've been living in that luxury palace getting breakfast, lunch and dinner served to you.'

She laughed at his description of the hospital ward where she'd spent the last few days when she'd started having contractions again. Melissa walked over to the window and fingered the pale pink curtains. 'It's just exactly like I imagined it should be,' she murmured. Her eyes fell to the window ledge, where a small parcel lay wrapped up in green paper and ribbon. 'What's this?'

Cooper had put Grace on the baby changer and was leaning over her, kissing her nose. He looked up at what she was holding in her hand. 'Oh, that's something special—unwrap it.'

Melissa gave him a little smile and sat down in the leather nursing chair, easing herself backwards so it tilted slightly and putting her feet up on the rest. She untied the thick green ribbon and pulled the paper off. Inside was a leather-bound copy of *Little Women*. Her mouth dropped open. 'You remembered? From that first night?' Her smile reached from ear to ear.

Cooper picked up the sleeping bundle and walked across the room towards her. He lowered his head, dropping a feather-light kiss on her lips. 'I've remembered everything.' A glint came into his eyes as he pointed to the red coat. 'Especially new pram, new coat. Now, what colour do you want to go for next?'

She smiled then let out a gasp as something slipped from the pages of the book. A ring. A beautiful sparkling green emerald, so big it took her breath away. 'Oh, Cooper!'

He touched her hand. 'I have to warn you that it's second-hand.' He paused while she crooked her eyebrow at him in warning. 'But this was my grandmother's ring and from the first time I saw you I thought it would be a perfect match for your eyes.'

Melissa's face broke into a slow, thoughtful smile as she looked first at the ring and then at her daughter. 'It's perfect, Cooper,' she said, 'and it's just the kind of thing I would want to pass on to my daughter.' And with that she bent forward and sealed their family with a kiss.

* * * * *